# Praise for

# MY FUNNY DEMON VALENTINE

"A spicy supernatural good time. With endearing characters and humor baked into a fun and unique love story. I'm so excited for the next one!"

**—Hannah Nicole Maehrer, #1 *New York Times* bestselling author of *Assistant to the Villain***

"Holy hot grand piano keys! This one hooked me from the first chapter and didn't let go until the very end. Ash was so sweet and lovable but still had the vibe of a man who would bring you the head of your enemies! So perfect, basically. Eva was strong and held her own. Combined, these two make for a deliciously devilish romance."

**—Kimberly Lemming, *USA Today* bestselling author of *That Time I Got Drunk and Saved a Demon***

"A delightfully escapist paranormal romp that's utterly hilarious and steamy as hell. I had the time of my life reading about Ash's and Eva's path to each other and cannot wait for the rest of this series."

**—Jenna Levine, *USA Today* bestselling author of *My Roommate Is a Vampire***

# BY AURORA ASCHER

**The Hell Bent Series**

*My Demon Romance* (novella)
*My Funny Demon Valentine*
*My Demon Hunter*
*Demon with Benefits*
*Guardian Demon*
*Beauty and the Demon*
*Fallen Demon*

Hell Bent

# BEAUTY AND THE DEMON

Aurora Ascher

KENSINGTON PUBLISHING CORP.
kensingtonbooks.com

KENSINGTON BOOKS are published by:

Kensington Publishing Corp.
900 Third Avenue
New York, NY 10022

kensingtonbooks.com





All Kensington titles, imprints, and distributed lines are available at special quantity discounts for bulk purchases for sales promotions, premiums, fundraising, educational, or institutional use.

Special book excerpts or customized printings can also be created to fit specific needs. For details, write or phone the office of the Kensington sales manager: Kensington Publishing Corp., 900 Third Avenue, New York, NY 10022, attn: Sales Department; phone 1-800-221-2647.

The K with book logo Reg US Pat. & TM Off.

First Kensington Trade Paperback Printing: March 2026

ISBN 978-1-4967-5589-6 (trade paperback)

10 9 8 7 6 5 4 3 2 1

Printed in China

Electronic edition: ISBN 978-1-4967-5595-7 (ebook)

Interior art by the INKfluence

Content warnings: Graphic violence, blood/gore, explicit sex scenes with demon in his demon form, light bondage scenes with ghostly hands, FMC captured and imprisoned by MMC

The authorized representative in the EU for product safety and compliance
is eucomply OU, Parnu mnt 139b-14, Apt 123
Tallinn, Berlin 11317, hello@eucompliancepartner.com

M U R M U R

# 1

# The Secret Ingredient

SUYIN DROPPED THE CURTAIN AND STEPPED AWAY FROM the window, her pulse racing. The park across the street from her apartment was poorly lit, but there was still enough light to see the shadowy figure of a man lurking by the bushes.

She was pretty sure she had a stalker.

This wasn't the first time she'd seen him there. Her apartment was on the second floor of a street lined with three-story buildings. There had to be fifty different flats on her side of the block, yet every time she looked around that curtain, she felt eyes on her.

At home wasn't the only time she felt the skin-crawling sensation of being watched either. Whenever she left the house, she swore she was being followed, whether it was on busy sidewalks or empty side alleys.

It was making her paranoid as hell.

Still standing beside the window, she reached over and flicked the light off, plunging the room into darkness. Then, she crouched and lifted the bottom edge of the curtain, slowly peeking over the windowsill until she could see outside once more.

The figure was there, standing beside the tall lilac bushes. It was too dark to see anything except that the person was lean and broad shouldered. Probably male, but then, that was hardly a surprise. Most perpetrators of creepy activities were male.

She peered harder into the darkness, trying to discern any details of the man's face. Instead, her nape prickled, and her heart skipped a beat. She couldn't see his eyes, yet somehow, she was certain he was staring right at her.

She ducked behind the windowsill and slumped against the wall onto the floor, breathing hard. Then, she shook herself.

Fuck him. She wasn't scared of any man.

She was a powerful blood-born witch who'd trained her entire life to protect herself from things far more terrifying than some creep in the park. And she had more than a trick or two up her sleeve.

She climbed to her feet and flicked the light back on, standing in front of the window behind the closed curtain, knowing her silhouette would be visible from the street below. Then she raised both middle fingers and held them out so he'd see if he was watching.

Then she set about checking her wards.

She wasn't scared of some creep, but she'd had premonitions lately that were making her paranoia worse. And a few months ago, a real-life fucking *demon* had broken into her coven's gathering place, threatened one of her members, and stolen a grimoire from her.

She already knew she wouldn't be able to sleep if she wasn't hiding behind half a dozen of the most powerful wards she knew how to cast, and life was too short to spend in an exhausted haze.

She'd tried it before. Wasn't worth it.

Chalk in hand, she went over all the lines, making sure nothing had smudged. Then she lit the candles and spoke the appropriate incantations, the sacred syllables to match the symbols in the sigils.

When she finished, she stepped back and surveyed her work, equal parts proud and exasperated. The ridiculousness of needing six anti-demon wards just to fall asleep was not lost on her, but she didn't fucking care.

Not when she dreamed of Hell every night.

As for her stalker, he could be kept out with the deadbolt on the front door—or the baseball bat tucked between her mattress and headboard. If he actually tried to enter her house, she would kindly show him the error of his ways by bashing his skull in.

Feeling more relaxed, she went through her nightly routine and then tied her long black hair into a messy bun and threw on her pajamas—a vintage *Night of the Living Dead* T-shirt in XXL. She didn't wear shorts or underwear. It was healthy to let the lady parts breathe.

After checking her locks and wards one last time, she touched the baseball bat to make sure it was in its proper place and then turned the night-light off, plunging her apartment into darkness.

She jerked awake exactly five hours later.

Her eyes popped open, and she stared at the ceiling, chest moving with rapid breaths. Rolling over, she switched on the lamp and opened her nightstand drawer. She pulled out her notebook and flipped to her last entry.

*It was the same again. I'm chasing a feather down city alleys. The tip of the feather is writing something as it blows, like a quill, but I can't decipher it, and I can't remember any of the symbols once I'm awake.*

*Then I hit a wall—I think? That part isn't clear. But when I look up, I'm staring into eyes so bloodshot, the whites are fully red. And I keep getting the image of a scorpion. When the scorpion strikes, the dream changes.*

*I'm near the bottom of a huge pit, a wide circular chasm. I'm standing on a ledge, and below me is an enormous pit of fire. Above, the sky is red. There's a tunnel behind me with a glowing-red seal at the end. I walk toward it, and I see a stone door. I try to open it, but the stone is too heavy.*

The entry ended there. Suyin had been keeping this notebook since last winter, when she'd started having the nightmares. Today, there was nothing new to add—she'd dreamed the exact same thing for the last couple weeks—so she closed the notebook and stowed it back in the drawer. The clock on her nightstand told her it was quarter to five. The sun wouldn't rise for another hour, but there was no way she was falling asleep again.

She grabbed her phone, turned off her seven-o'clock alarm, and scrolled through her notifications. Yeah, she knew better than to check her phone first thing in the morning—alpha brain state and all that—but she wasn't in the mood for self-care today.

She'd been dreading this day for a while. Three hundred and sixty-five days, in fact.

There were several emails from yesterday that she'd put off answering. Coven members asking for help with whatever they were working on, mostly. She ignored them for now, planning to answer while at work.

As coven leader, she was not only a teacher to other members, but a mentor of sorts. Witchcraft relied heavily upon intuition, and it was often necessary to confront one's inner demons as part of the learning process. Many coven members came to Suyin with personal problems. It wasn't a responsibility she'd ever particularly wanted, but she valued the sense of purpose it brought her.

She had enough unanswered questions about her own life, and she'd spent most of it on her own, looking after herself, with a head full of secrets. It was nice to be able to provide answers to someone else and be a source of stability to her coven.

She climbed out of bed and went to the kitchen to make coffee. Decaf, because caffeine worked a little too well on her, and the last thing she needed today was a burst of manic activity followed by a crash into inescapable lethargy. Her phone buzzed just as she took the first sip, and she frowned when she saw it was a text from Iris.

*Happy birthday, witch bitch! Congrats on being old. I miss you. When are we hanging out?*

Six months ago, Suyin had thought of Iris as her closest friend. Maybe the closest friend she'd ever had. Now she wasn't sure what they were.

Things had shifted majorly, and Suyin wasn't entirely sure why. Iris's new boyfriend, Meph, had a lot to do with it, but she didn't think that was the only reason.

*There's a show this Friday at Les Katacombes that I want to catch*, Suyin replied. *Wanna come?*

She ignored the birthday part. She hadn't made it a secret that she hated birthdays—though she'd never explained why—and Iris was usually content to allow her to pretend not to have one. This time, however, she supposed it was an excuse for Iris to reach out when they hadn't spoken in almost two weeks.

Iris's response popped up seconds later. *I'm in. But it's 5 a.m. Why are you awake?*

*Just got up*, Suyin replied. *I like mornings. Can't say the same for you. What's your excuse?*

*I haven't gone to sleep yet.* Iris sent the awkward-smile-and-sweat-droplet emoji. *We threw a housewarming party for Meph's brother and tried to get him drunk enough to pass out. He outlasted all of us though. Jerk.*

*Didn't you throw him like, five housewarming parties already?*

*. . . No comment.*

Suyin rolled her eyes. *Go to sleep.*

*Text me the deets for the show*, Iris replied. *Looking forward to it.*

After finishing her coffee, Suyin went into the bathroom and splashed cold water on her face. Dabbing it dry, she leaned into the mirror and peered at her reflection.

She turned to each side, studying the skin of her face. She lifted her brows, causing her forehead to crease, and then relaxed them again, watching it smooth out. With two fingers, she stretched the corners of her mouth and then between her brows.

Nothing. Not a wrinkle to be found.

Of course there wasn't. And if she kept checking every day like this, she'd never notice them if they did appear.

But they weren't going to.

She was finally coming to terms with that, even if it scared the shit out of her. Even if staring at her face in the mirror, untouched by a single sign of aging, made her stomach feel like a hollow pit.

It was the opposite of every other person's experience, she knew. Most people grimaced at the sight of age spots and wrinkles. Suyin cringed at the lack of them.

But Suyin wasn't normal. And she had no idea why.

She was reaching a pivotal turning point in her life, and she didn't know what to do about it. In another ten years or so, her lack of aging would start drawing attention. Soon after, her IDs and passports wouldn't be any good anymore. Eventually, she'd have to go off-grid. Would she have to fake her death and find some sketchy black-market documents?

She could have told the coven, or Iris at the very least. She knew Iris and her twin, Lily, had a rare ability that allowed them to extend their lifespans. It wouldn't be unbelievable that Suyin had a similar gift. But talking about it would make it real and involve trust, and she and Iris were on shaky ground now. Suyin had always been guarded, and besides, she doubted anyone could fix whatever was happening to her anyway.

Her disinclination to share was partly why she'd left New York. The Montreal coven had put out a call for a blood-born witch to come help Iris and Lily maintain the cloaking spell that hid them from the demon hunting them, and Suyin had responded. But that had been a convenient excuse. In truth, she'd already been planning to go.

She stared at her reflection. The woman who stared back at her, with dark eyes, a downturned mouth, a small nose, and a squarish jaw, was youthful. Her thick hair was long and shiny with a short fringe cut above her brows, and not a single strand of gray stood out against the inky black.

But according to her birth certificate and IDs, today was her birthday, and she was fifty years old.

And she didn't have a clue why she wasn't aging.

The feeling of being watched crept up the back of Suyin's neck as soon as she stepped outside, though her stalker was nowhere to be seen. She'd checked out the front and back of the apartment before she left and had seen no sign of him.

But that didn't mean he wasn't there.

She scanned the alley carefully before descending the spiral staircase from her balcony to the downstairs neighbor's garden.

It was still spring, and the plants hadn't grown to their full lushness yet, but the trees were speckled with buds due to burst into foliage any day.

She opened the tall gate and peered around, seeing nothing except a couple neighborhood cats hissing at each other. Her skin still crawled. She swore she felt eyes on her.

She'd rented out the small garage behind her building, and she entered through the side door, careful to lock it again behind her. It smelled like engine oil. Her rusty piece-of-shit Civic was tucked as close to the wall as possible to make room for her brand-new baby: an all-black, 745cc Honda Shadow Phantom.

She'd traded in her beat-up old Harley a few months ago for the Phantom, going for something sturdier with a lower seat and room for a passenger on the back. The suspension and brakes had been upgraded, and the matte-black stealth paint job was too nice to pass up.

Still, the coven's meeting place and occult shop was only twenty minutes on foot, and normally, she would've walked. She didn't like leaving her bike outside for the long hours she was at work.

But now, all she could think about was how easy it would be to sneak up on her at a walking pace, and how quickly she could be ambushed around a corner.

She pulled her favorite helmet off the hook on the wall, zipped up her leather jacket, and lifted her satchel strap over her head. Rolling up the garage door, she pushed her bike out and then shut the door and locked it. She fired up the bike and shot down the alley, stray cats fleeing at the rumbling engine.

As she peeled around the corner onto the main road, she almost smiled. It felt good to ride, especially with all the doom and gloom she'd been carrying around lately.

She drove a few extra blocks to purge her heavy emotions, pulling up in the alley behind the shop half an hour later.

Engaging the disc locks on her tires, she covered the bike with the tarp she'd stashed behind the garbage bins. After one final scan of the alley, she opened the heavy back door and set about flicking on the lights.

Le Repaire des Sorcières—The Witches' Lair—was a cozy occult store full of casting supplies and other knickknacks witches found attractive. A lot of witches had mild hoarder tendencies when it came to their love of trinkets with potential use in their practice.

They loved crystals, charms, and figurines of goddesses from different cultures and mythologies. They loved herbs, incense, candles, and books. Le Repaire supplied those items to the witches in Montreal, and it also held appeal to non-witches who were curious or liked the aesthetic.

The spacious basement cellar where the coven met had a circle of chairs and a whiteboard for meetings, open floor space for sigil drawing, and several rows of bookshelves and worktables for study.

That was where Suyin's grimoire had been stolen from a few months ago. The demon had walked into the store and threatened to kill the witch on duty, Marie-Thérèse, if she didn't open the ward for him. Suyin didn't expect anyone to risk their life for grimoires, even priceless ones, and she was glad Marie hadn't been hurt.

She'd since upped the store's protections. Now, as long as her wards held, it would take a powerful demon a lot of effort to break in, giving them plenty of time to fight back or escape.

After completing the same ward-maintenance rituals she did at home, Suyin opened the store for business. An occult shop on a Monday morning wasn't the busiest place around, and she knew she'd have time to kill.

Settling onto the stool behind the front counter, she pulled her laptop out of her bag and fired it up. She didn't open her inbox to respond to her coven members' messages, though she probably should have. Instead, she pulled up the PDF she'd downloaded from the coven's database after the theft.

The demon had stolen one of Suyin's oldest possessions and left everything else untouched, and she wanted to know why. He may have taken her grimoire, but thankfully, Marie-Thérèse and a couple other coven members had faithfully scanned every book in their collection and saved the files on the computers downstairs.

Suyin had been poring over the scans of her grimoire for months now. As if it was going to make any more sense now than it had when she'd read it ten years ago, and ten years before that, and when her mother had first given it to her . . .

The grimoire was entitled *The Book of Gamigin*, and it was the last thing in their collection she would've guessed a demon would want. Supposedly written by a father she'd never met, the book had been her mother's most prized possession, though Suyin had never understood why. Even when she'd left it to Suyin before her death, on Suyin's eighteenth birthday, she'd been unable to provide a reasonable explanation of its importance.

*Keep it safe,* was all Fay had said. *This book contains knowledge beyond even what the angels perceive. Your father entrusted it to me, and now, I'm entrusting it to you.*

It was one of the few times Fay had spoken of Suyin's father, Samuel, and Suyin knew only the barest facts about him. According to Fay, Samuel had been an avid witch practitioner with a passion for demonology—hence the name of his grimoire—and he'd died of an illness only months after Suyin's birth.

Apparently, he'd tried to summon Gamigin, a demon known for wisdom and magical expertise, on several occasions throughout his life and failed each time. More surprising than the failure was that Samuel hadn't been killed in the process.

As a rule, demons did not respond well to humans trying to enslave them.

As for Fay, she'd never been a particularly nurturing or emotional person, but Suyin had always gotten the sense that she'd loved Samuel deeply and spent the rest of her life quietly grieving. She'd left China with baby Suyin immediately after his death, and for the most part, she'd never spoken of him again. Suyin had never even seen a photo of him.

After Fay's death, more than thirty years ago now, Suyin had cracked open the old grimoire, hoping it contained information about her father and why Fay had hidden it for so long. Unfortunately, it hadn't made a lick of sense.

After months of study, she'd concluded that either her father had suffered from a mental illness causing severe delusions—perhaps as a result of messing with black magic, one of the reasons Suyin had always steered clear herself—or he hadn't written the book at all. Maybe he'd gotten possession of it from a demon somehow. After all, it was written in Sheolic.

Now that it had been stolen, Suyin was motivated to read it again. She was desperate to understand why a demon might want it. Something had to make sense. Somehow, everything fit together. She was just missing the bigger picture.

After an hour or so of trying to decipher incoherent ramblings—cross-referencing everything with her Sheolic-English translation book—the little bells over the front door tinkled, offering a welcome distraction.

"Good morning," she called out, straightening from her computer. She blinked her eyes back into focus, realizing her nose had been only a couple inches from the screen.

Then she frowned.

The shop was empty. No one replied to her greeting because no one was there.

There was a clear view of the front door from behind the

counter, and none of the shelves were high enough for a person to hide behind. But she'd definitely heard the bell ring.

*If that fucking park creep found me at work, I swear to god I'll make him regret it.*

Nape prickling, she closed her laptop and slipped off the stool. She checked behind the shelves in the far corner. The shop was tiny; it wasn't like she would miss someone if they were here. She went to the front door and looked out onto the street. The wind blew bits of garbage and dead leaves. Nothing was out of the ordinary.

Fuck, was she losing her mind?

She gave one last look at the deserted street, shaking her head and—

"Hello."

Barely stifling a shout, she spun around and came face to face with another person.

*Bloodshot eyes. A scorpion's tail. A fiery pit. A glowing red seal—*

Suyin blinked. A woman stood in front of her. Middle-aged, graying hair. "I'm looking for a gift for my niece," she said with a wary smile. "Can you help me?"

"How'd you get in here?" Suyin demanded.

Tact had never been her strong suit. She was five-foot-two and weighed a hundred and thirty pounds. She'd learned a long time ago to be blunt or people would look right over her head.

The woman blinked. "I came in through the door, of course. I was just looking at the candles over there."

Suyin looked at the candle display. It was directly beside the front desk, but it was blocked from view by a tall rack of jewelry on the counter. She closed her eyes and cursed inwardly. She'd been so caught up in her paranoia that she thought she was in a horror movie jump-scare scene.

Was this her life now? Dreaming of Hell and impending

doom, dodging stalkers, and sinking farther into unsociability until she lost touch with reality?

There wasn't anything she could do about it now. She focused back on her customer. "Right. Your niece. What does she like?"

# 2

# Easy Prey

A heavy shoulder slammed into Suyin's, sending her flying until she crashed into another sweaty body. She shoved against the much larger man with two hands and launched back in another direction, only to be body-slammed right back the way she'd come. Another tall person crashed into her, their elbow cracking her on the side of the head.

Momentarily stunned, she stumbled and hit the ground.

With the mass of perspiring bodies undulating around her, one would expect her to be immediately trampled underfoot. Instead, a hand reached down. She grasped it, and with a tug, she was back on her feet.

The bearded metalhead raised his brows in question. She gave him a thumbs up, letting him know she was okay, and they both launched back into the melee. But her head was pounding now. The music was so loud her ears were numb.

She was fifty years old, damn it. Too old for mosh pits.

It didn't make her enjoy them any less, though. Nor did her diminutive stature or the fact that she was female. Men were dicks everywhere in life, but there was an etiquette to a good mosh pit. You fell—especially when you were her size—but someone always helped you up.

Still, Suyin could only take such a beating for so long, and she'd left her companion for the night over by the bar. At the end of the song, she slipped off by the side stage and pushed through the tight pack of bodies. Dragging her sweaty hair off her face, she searched the crowd for the familiar flash of blue and followed it like a beacon.

When she arrived, the owner of that bright hair took one look at Suyin's disheveled state and laughed. Not that it was audible over the start of the next song, as the blare of distorted guitar obliterated all else.

"You look like you got hit by a bus!" Iris shouted as Suyin hauled her weary body onto a barstool beside her. Iris handed over the beer she'd ordered while Suyin was gone.

It was Friday. Suyin had made it through the week without being killed by a stalker or taken to Hell, or whatever her constant sense of foreboding was trying to warn her about.

But her sense of dread hadn't lessened. If anything, it had gotten worse.

As promised, Iris had come out. Neither of them brought up Iris's sudden absence from the coven or why she was suddenly so cagey about her life. Just for tonight, Suyin wanted to pretend things were normal. That she had her best friend back. That her potentially endless future wasn't looming ahead of her like a yawning pit of infinitude.

Eternal youth had never seemed so unappealing.

Suyin forced a smile and took the condensation-slicked glass, clinking it against Iris's before taking a sip. Her blood-red lipstick left a print on the edge.

"Girl, your makeup is smudged down your face something fierce," Iris shouted in her ear. "You look like a goth zombie."

Suyin ran her fingers under her eyes and laughed when they

came away black. Then she shrugged. Goth zombie sounded like a good look to her.

Taking another sip, she shouted in her friend's ear, "Why don't you ever mosh with me anymore?"

Iris shook her head. "I'm too old for that shit."

Suyin arched a brow. If only she knew.

"Plus," Iris added, "if I came home covered in bruises, I think Meph would go on a murder spree."

She said it with a dreamy look in her eyes, but Suyin inwardly grimaced. Iris's new boyfriend was an awkward subject between them. It bothered her that Iris still refused to properly introduce them.

She'd seen "Meph" once at Iris and Lily's last birthday party—and she still wasn't sure what his weird name was an abbreviation for. He was in Lily's scary hot boyfriend's group of scary hot friends. Suyin remembered teasing Iris, telling her to go talk to the fuckboy she kept staring at. Iris had scoffed and told her he was toxic, and she wasn't going near him.

Next thing Suyin knew, they were madly in love. They'd even gotten a fucking dog together.

She rolled her eyes inwardly.

In the beginning, Iris's reluctance to properly introduce them had made sense. Iris normally went through a boyfriend every month or so, each more of an asshole than the last, and there was no need for Suyin to waste time meeting guys she hated the second she saw them.

But Iris had been dating the mysterious Meph for a while now, and she had yet to complain about him. At all. In fact, she seemed to get sappier as time passed. While that was vaguely nauseating, Suyin was happy for her friend. There was only so much male assholery a woman could endure before she became a total misandrist.

But Iris still wouldn't talk about him, and she avoided the subject of an introduction like the plague. Worse, because Iris's life was becoming more and more entwined with Meph's, it meant she and Suyin spent less and less time together. And the more Suyin felt like Iris was keeping secrets from her, the more she pulled away herself.

It felt like their friendship was ending, and Suyin didn't know how to stop it.

"Are you okay?" Iris's question snapped her out of her musings.

"Huh?"

"It's just, we haven't spoken a lot lately, and I can't help but notice you look a little stressed out."

Suyin waved her off instead of replying. Speaking meant shouting because of the volume of the music, and she didn't feel like shouting her secrets, let alone speaking them in a normal tone of voice.

Iris glanced around the club with a determined expression, and Suyin realized she'd come to the same conclusion. A moment later, Iris seized her arm in a vise grip and tugged her across the venue.

Suyin let herself be led. A part of her knew that if she really hadn't wanted to tell Iris anything, she could have made some excuse about not wanting to miss the show. But . . . she was so tired. Tired of feeling isolated. Tired of keeping secrets. Though she'd never admit it to Iris, she *wanted* to tell her.

They slipped through the door onto the bar's back patio, which was more of a narrow gap between two tall brick buildings. Cigarette butts littered the ground, and smoke filled the air from all the metalheads lighting up.

Iris dragged her to an empty picnic table that rocked dangerously when they sat. They chose opposite sides to balance it out and set their drinks down between them.

"I've been having dreams," Suyin blurted. She'd never been one for subtlety.

Iris blinked. "What kind of dreams?"

"They feel like nightmares while I'm having them, but afterward, they feel prophetic. Like they're trying to tell me something bad is coming."

"How often?"

"Almost every night."

"Damn." Iris took a sip of beer. "What happens?"

"It's usually the same, but it's changed recently." She proceeded to explain chasing the feather, trying to read the script, the bloodshot eyes and the scorpion, and then the bottomless pit and creepy door.

"In the beginning, I used to see a crow every time, but I don't see it anymore. And the pit and trying to open that stupid door—that's all new. I used to wake up once the scorpion stung me. And I swear, that pit is in Hell. There are flames, and the sky is—"

"Wait." Iris held up a hand. "What was that about the crow?"

"I used to see a crow at the beginning of the dream. It took flight, and when it spread its wings, it covered the face of the sun, and the day became night."

Iris made a strangled laugh and then covered it with a cough.

Suyin just stared at her. "What?"

"Oh, um—" She coughed again. "Nothing. A crow and the sun, huh? Weird."

Suyin frowned. She had the distinct impression that Iris was withholding something, which reminded her why she hadn't confided in her friend lately. "Does that mean anything to you?"

Iris hesitated. "Well, it's not hard to find meaning in that kind of symbology, is it?"

"That's not what I asked," Suyin said, a little sharper than intended. "I asked if it meant anything to *you*."

"Not really." Iris's voice wavered, and she became focused

on rotating her beer glass in circles inside the ring of condensation on the table.

She was lying.

Suyin couldn't fathom why Iris would choose to blatantly lie about her dreams, of all things. It was symbology. Why lie about it?

Whatever the reason, it pissed her off. Here she was opening up to her friend about something personal, and Iris couldn't even do her the courtesy of being honest.

"I'm ready to go back inside," Suyin said, planting her palms on the table and standing. This time her sharp tone was intentional.

"Wait." Iris's avoidant gaze snapped back to hers. "Su, I can't— I know you think I'm lying to you."

Suyin didn't sit. But she didn't leave either.

"I'll just say . . . The crow and the sun? I don't think it's a bad thing. Actually, I think it's a good thing."

Suyin frowned. "A bird of darkness covers the sun and snuffs out the light. How can you perceive that as a good omen?"

"Maybe . . ." Iris went back to staring at her beer glass. "Maybe the sun had been forced to shine for too long, and it needed to rest in the darkness. Take comfort in a secret space. Or let its own inner darkness out. Maybe the crow didn't snuff it out but gave it protection. Maybe it wanted to be dark for a long time, but it never could until the crow came along."

"That's a very unusual interpretation."

"I know. But it's worth considering."

Slowly, Suyin sat down again. "Maybe you're right, but it doesn't shake the foreboding I get from everything else. Right after the nightmares began, that demon showed up at the store. And now I think I'm being stalked. I'm checking over my shoulder everywhere I go. I have six different protection wards up at my place, and I'm on edge every time I'm outside of them."

"Su . . ." Iris's green eyes were full of concern. "I didn't realize— How long has this been going on?"

"A few weeks."

"Have you called the cops? If there's actually someone stalking you—"

"The police aren't going to do shit about some creep lurking in a public park. You know how seriously they take complaints like that. But that isn't what I'm worried about. It's these fucking dreams."

"But maybe that situation is amplifying your anxiety and making the dreams—"

"Why aren't you taking this seriously?" Suyin snapped. "Why are you so convinced that everything's okay?"

"I am taking this seriously, I swear. It's just . . . things are safe now. For the first time in my life, I genuinely feel safe, and I hate that you don't feel that way too."

Suyin took a breath, fighting back her rising temper. Unfortunately, it didn't work.

"Why on earth would you think that? Valefor is still out there. Or have you forgotten that there's a deranged Duke of Hell trying to kill you and your twin and steal your power for himself? Maybe you have, since you haven't been to the coven to help me maintain your cloaking spell in weeks."

Iris flinched visibly. "I'm sorry."

Further chastisement was on the tip of Suyin's tongue, but it died at that apology. Iris never apologized. Yet she just had. She really had changed.

"I should be there more, I know," Iris continued. "I know how much work it is keeping that spell going, and I know it's not fair of me to expect you and the coven to keep doing it when I'm not even around to help. But . . ." She took a breath and her gaze dropped to her hands, twisting together on the table's surface. "What if he's given up?"

"Who? Valefor?"

Iris nodded.

Suyin almost couldn't believe what she was hearing. "Your parents *died* because of him. Because he killed them trying to get to you. He's an immortal fucking demon. He doesn't give up."

"Maybe he's got other shit going on."

Suyin stared at her. It was a weak excuse and they both knew it.

"We're safe, Su. Me and Lily are safe. I can't say how, but I *know* we're safe."

Suyin's eyes narrowed, and she felt that distinct prickling at the back of her neck again.

Blood-born witch twins were extremely rare, and a prophecy had long ago been written that Iris and Lily would have great power. Valefor had found out and wanted to steal it for himself. The twins' mother had created a powerful cloaking spell to hide her daughters, and she and their father had died defending it.

After their deaths, when Iris and Lily first moved to Montreal, Iris was filled with rage, obsessed with protecting her sister and studying hard enough to one day get revenge. Suyin and Iris's entire friendship had been founded on Iris's hatred of demons and her desire to protect her twin. For Iris to be telling Suyin now that she felt safe and there was nothing to worry about anymore?

It was absurd. It made no sense.

"Regardless of your feelings," Suyin began coolly, "I know what I experienced, and I refuse to doubt myself."

There was a pause as the two of them stared at each other. Iris's eyes were sad again, and Suyin . . . Hers were probably flat. Like her mother, she wasn't one for emotional displays. She'd been told by ex-partners—men and women—that she was cold. That she had no heart.

It made it easy to disguise the hurt she felt now.

"Su . . ."

She stood once more. "I'm going back inside."

"I didn't mean to make you feel like I don't believe you." Iris didn't stand. "I'm just trying to explain how *I* feel."

"I understand." And she did. But she also knew Iris was keeping secrets, and until she understood why, there was no way to close the rift between them.

"I'm sorry you've been going through this lately. I should have reached out. I didn't realize—"

"It's not your fault." She meant that. "We've both been busy."

"I know, but—"

"Seriously. It's okay."

Suddenly, Suyin couldn't summon the will to be angry anymore. So they were drifting apart. It happened to a lot of friendships. She regretted it, but until either of them was willing to open up, nothing was going to change.

"I'm going inside," she said again, and then she picked up her drink and climbed off the picnic table.

Iris followed, but Suyin didn't wait for her. By the exit to the patio, the crowd was substantially thinner. The dance floor was set into the ground by two steps, giving people at the back a good view of the stage.

Suyin strode toward those steps, ready to get lost in the crowd, only to stop so suddenly that Iris bumped into her back.

"Whoa— You okay?"

Suyin didn't even hear her.

She was frozen in place, staring at an unmistakable tall figure standing all the way across the club. He was in the darkest corner, but she knew that silhouette well. Tall, slender, broad shouldered.

Staring right at her.

The fucking park creep was here. He'd followed her to the club.

Unlike the park, however, the club wasn't completely dark, even in the corner where he lurked, and for the first time, she could make out his features. Most startling of which was an incredible head of long, straight *white* hair. White, not blond. His skin was pale, and his bone structure was flawless, his face a picture of symmetry.

He was stupidly gorgeous. He looked like an angel. He was almost *too* pretty, and she squinted, trying to find at least one flaw.

It was his cheekbones, she decided. They were too sharp, and the hollow shadow cast beneath them gave his face a gaunt look.

She stared, frozen in place, and he stared back.

Why did it matter that he was attractive? He was still the creep who was stalking her. Was she really so shallow that knowing he was hot changed how she felt about that?

It didn't, she decided.

She was pissed off. She was tired of being afraid and angry at this douchebag for making her feel that way. Yeah, it was mostly the dreams, but this lurker wasn't helping. Who did he think he was, standing in a park at night, watching her? He didn't have anything better to do with his life? He didn't have a fucking job?

"Hold my beer," she said, and she shoved it into a confused Iris's hands.

"What—?"

She spun back around and . . . he was gone.

*Fuck.* Where had he gone? She searched the room—

*There.* He was pushing through the crowd, moving rapidly toward the front exit.

He'd pulled a hood over his bright white hair, but it couldn't hide the lengths falling down his torso over his black clothing, nor could it disguise the height that had him looming over everyone, despite the way he hunched forward as if trying to diminish his size.

The fact that he was suddenly in a hurry to escape made her instincts prickle. Images of her dreams flitted across her mind, putting all her senses on red alert.

But she'd never been one to back down from a challenge. Whatever kept her from aging also gave her more strength than a woman her size should have, even with training, and she healed from wounds faster than was normal.

There were witches, like Lily and Iris, with rare special abilities. But they were *abilities*, something they had to train and practice to use. For Suyin, it just happened naturally, and she didn't understand why.

But knowing she could lay out a grown man with one punch made her fearless, and she was sick of waiting. Day by day, the tension built as she waited for some unnamed darkness to overtake her or some catastrophic event to occur. She was sick of checking over her shoulder, putting up ward after ward and never feeling like it was enough. She wanted a confrontation. She *needed* it.

Without another word to Iris, Suyin went after him.

He was moving rapidly toward the exit, and though he hadn't looked over his shoulder to see her in pursuit, she was sure he was trying to escape before she caught up to him.

She pushed forward, weaving through the crowd. Her determination turned to foreboding as she watched his fluid movements ahead of her.

He moved with no care for who stood in his way. While she did the same to an extent, this was . . . too much. He walked straight forward without turning his shoulders to avoid hitting people or adjusting his steps to dodge others, even if their backs were turned and they didn't see him coming. He just cut right through them.

People stumbled into one another, and he paid them no mind. He didn't look back. He didn't break stride. It was like he was bushwhacking through a dense forest, swatting branches out of his face. Or mosquitoes.

He reached the exit, where someone was blocking the way, and he relocated that person by wrapping a palm all the way around their face and setting them aside. By the head. It wasn't aggressive or malicious. It was methodical. Cold. It was one of the most bizarrely disturbing things Suyin had ever seen.

He passed through the door and disappeared from view. Cursing, she increased her pace but was unable to summon the complete lack of fucks given to shove people aside as he had. And being as short as she was, that meant she had to do a lot of dodging and side-stepping.

She stepped outside only a moment later, but she already knew it was too late. She scanned the sidewalk in both directions for any sign of an unusually tall, hooded stranger with long white hair streaming behind him.

Nothing. Of course there was nothing.

"Motherfucker," she muttered. Her heart was still pounding.

With another murmured curse, she went back inside, weaving through the crowd until she was back at Iris's side. The music she normally enjoyed turned to white noise, fading into the background, drowned out by the tumult in her head. She tried to hide her unease, but apparently, she wasn't that successful.

Iris searched her face. "What just happened? Where did you go?"

Suyin shook her head, too lost in her thoughts to reply. She tried to remember what the stranger's eyes had looked like. Had they been bloodshot like the eyes in her dream? Surely the neighborhood creep in the park couldn't be related to her premonitions? But after seeing the way he moved, she wasn't so sure.

"Suyin? You okay?"

She blinked back to the present, finding Iris staring at her. "You wanna get out of here?"

Iris's frown deepened. "This is only the first band of the night. You want to leave already?"

She nodded. She wanted to get home where she was safe behind her wards. She wanted to succumb to her paranoia in privacy.

But she wasn't telling Iris any of that. "I'm just tired. Guess moshing took it out of me."

Iris looked dubious, which was fair. Suyin could mosh for hours on a good night. "All right," she said anyway. "Let's go."

They made their way out of the stuffy club. It was spring, but the humidity made it feel cooler. The dark street was full of people coming and going between venues. There was still no sign of the stranger.

But that didn't mean he wasn't out there somewhere, watching her.

Iris insisted on walking her home, and though Suyin would never admit it, she was glad. It took about half an hour to reach her neighborhood, and they took the path through the park across the street from her apartment.

As they approached the lilac bushes, Suyin almost hoped to find someone standing there. Now that she'd seen her stalker up close, she was determined to confront him. No more hiding behind the window curtain. The next time she saw him, she was going after him. If he tried to run every time she got close, maybe he'd give up and leave her alone for good. And if he tried to grab her, she'd stab him with her trusty boot knife.

But there was no one by the bushes. And she somehow wasn't surprised.

They stopped at the base of the outdoor staircase to Suyin's apartment.

"Are you sure everything's okay?" Iris asked.

"Everything's fine," Suyin lied straight to her face. Guess that was a thing for them now.

Iris pursed her lips like she was thinking the same. "All right, well . . . it was good to see you tonight. Maybe we can go out again soon?"

Suyin nodded noncommittally. She was far too distracted to worry about Iris right now.

They went their separate ways, and Suyin let herself into her flat. Inside, it felt too quiet. She was safe behind her wards. She could relax. Yet the music in the bar had left her ears ringing, and her head was still buzzing with the adrenaline of seeing her stalker.

She felt jittery and full of restless energy. Trying to sleep would be a form of torture. She wanted to act. She wanted to hit something. Or someone. Someone like that white-haired freak.

She locked the front door but didn't take off any of her outdoor clothes. Instead, she crossed the apartment and exited through the back.

She was going for a ride. Some fresh air and the feel of her bike's engine rumbling between her legs would help her calm down. And maybe she wanted to prowl the streets and hunt for her stalker a little too.

She descended the spiraling steps into the yard and slipped through the gate. Then, she rifled through her keys until she found the one for the garage. But when she stuck it into the door handle and turned, it didn't click open the way it usually did. Because it hadn't been locked.

She frowned. *Weird.* She always locked this door. Her bike was too precious to risk with carelessness.

Then again, she'd been way too stressed out and overtired lately. She was bound to make stupid mistakes. Shaking her head, she pushed open the door and stepped into the blackness. She reached out to feel the switch on the wall. She flipped it. Light flared on.

The next few seconds happened in slow motion.

She saw a huge, towering form. Bloodshot eyes stared down at her from a cruel, pale face. Tall black horns loomed high above.

A segmented tail with a sharp barb on the tip reared back.

It moved so fast, it was barely a blur. The barb struck her in the neck, and pain speared through her bloodstream.

*Scorpion*, she thought distantly.

It was the last thought she had before everything went black.

# 3

# Bells and Whistles

Belial, former King of Hell, hung the last shirt on the bar and then stepped back and surveyed the spacious closet.

After more than a month, he was officially moved into his new house.

The walk-in had hanger racks on three walls with shelves above and below. All of it was empty save for one small corner occupied by his existing wardrobe. It was hard to find clothes on Earth when one was seven feet tall.

There hadn't been much to move. In Hell, he'd had several castles full of shit, most of it loot Raum had stolen and hoarded away in Bel's spaces whether he liked it or not.

Now, he had next to nothing. A collection of top-of-the-line kitchen items (including his swanky espresso machine and grinder), a laptop, a couple bags of clothes, and that was it.

He had so little stuff that he'd only bought the house on the condition that all the staging furniture was included so he didn't have to buy it himself. Decorating wasn't exactly his strong suit. As long as a chair didn't collapse under his weight, he didn't give a damn what it looked like.

Backing out of the closet, he turned to survey the bedroom. On one side, a wall of tall windows overlooked the landscaped backyard. Beside it, a patio door went to a private balcony. Opposite the wall of windows was his brand-new bed.

He mentally amended his list of possessions to contain his "Alaskan" king. The biggest mattress on the market without going custom, at nine-by-nine feet, it was finally enough room for him to properly stretch out. He'd gotten sick of hanging off the end of his California king at the old place, and he'd been more than happy to get rid of it.

As for the rest of the house, it was big, expensive, and empty.

So very empty.

That was what he'd wanted. He was sick of listening to his brothers bitch at each other all hours of the day. He was sick of the messes they made in his kitchen and how they never fucking did the dishes. And ever since they'd all started dating, it had only gotten worse. He was sick of overhearing Meph and Iris bickering and then fucking at full volume five seconds later. He was sick of Asmodeus and Eva's music coming up through the floorboards from the apartment below. He was sick of Raum and Sunshine treating him like one of their rescue cases.

Every time something so much as momentarily irritated him, the rage reared its ugly head.

Putting away a cup someone else left out . . . his hands would shake while he did it. Telling someone to shut the fuck up . . . he would speak through gritted teeth. Listening to others argue . . . his fists would ball up so tightly, his knuckles turned white. Even being spoken to in a normal tone of voice caused his blood to boil slightly.

Being around other people, even his brothers, was a constant battle against the rage, and he was so goddamn tired of it.

He'd just wanted some peace and quiet. But now he was here, standing in his humongous empty house, wondering what the fuck he was doing with himself.

What was his goddamn purpose? Why had he even come to Earth anyway? With how he felt now, he'd have been better off staying in Hell. There at least, he had a reputation to live up to.

He'd had legions that feared and adored him. He'd had rivals and shady acquaintances. He was fucking *Belial*, King of Hell, one of the baddest motherfuckers in the underworld.

Here, he was just a human wannabe with a big fuck-off mansion.

Maybe he ought to buy a fuck-off car to go with it. The trick would be finding one he fit into.

Exiting the empty bedroom, he walked down the empty hallway and descended the empty staircase to the empty entranceway. From there, he passed under an arch he didn't have to duck under—another reason he'd chosen this house—into the kitchen.

The kitchen was the main reason he'd picked the house.

Eleven-foot ceilings meant he didn't feel like the roof was falling on his head, and if he did lose his temper, he had a bit of room to grow before he hit the ceiling.

The countertops were marble, the stainless, state-of-the-art appliances brand-new, including a second oven and a double-wide gas stove. There was lots of cupboard space and two double sinks with semi-professional faucets.

His espresso machine tucked nicely under the cupboards in the corner on one side, and his other appliances barely made a dent in the counter space on the other. Across the room, there was a dining table and French doors that led to the back patio by the pool. He liked to drink his morning coffee out there and watch the sunrise.

He busied himself by opening his laptop to the recipe he'd been reading the night before. Demons didn't need to eat to survive, so he never *felt* hungry, but he sure as hell liked food. He fucking loved food, in fact. Flavors and spices, the smell of cooking meat and vegetables . . . Sometimes he swore it was the only reason he was still sane.

It was late afternoon, and that seemed a reasonable enough time to cook a meal. Not that it mattered. He could eat at two in the morning for all the difference it would make.

The truth was, he didn't know what to do with himself now that he'd gotten what he wanted, and there was no one around to keep in line and no crises to solve. It didn't matter that things had finally calmed down. He was constantly on edge, and everyone around him knew it.

Worse, they'd all decided to make it their life's mission to fix him.

As if summoned by those very thoughts, a tidy little knock on the patio door interrupted his recipe reading. Sunshine stood outside, waving happily at him and smiling radiantly.

He groaned inwardly. It still weirded him out that a heavenly angel was not only dating but living with his brother Raum. And she wasn't just any angel. Sunshine was one of the Principalities, the highest ranking angels of the Third Sphere—the Sphere tasked with enforcing Heaven's rules on Earth.

With a sigh, Bel waved a hand, gesturing for her to come in. She made sure to close the door snugly and remove her shoes on the mat so not a speck of dirt got on his floor.

That was the thing about Sunshine. She was so careful and conscientious, it was impossible not to like her.

When Bel had first found out about her, he'd been fully on board with killing her. He'd attempted it too, but Raum had stopped him, the lovesick idiot.

But now that Sunshine had proven herself, he'd decided he didn't mind her after all. Chopping the archangel Raphael into tiny pieces and sending him to Hell for an eternity of torment at the Necromancer's hands was a great way to get into Bel's good books. And she'd done it all to protect Raum. He would always respect her for that.

Sunshine and Raum now lived together in the guest house on the other side of the backyard, and she always came up to Bel's house to help him with dishes, even when she didn't eat. She'd even snuck into his house when he wasn't around and cleaned a few times, just because she was so damn nice.

"Good evening, Belial," she said, sliding onto one of the bar stools at the center island. "How are you feeling tonight?"

He narrowed his eyes. "We already had our meeting last week. You don't get to psychoanalyze me."

She held up her palms. "I assure you, that's not my intention. I simply want to know how you're doing."

Sunshine's mentor, some high-up, big-cheese angel named Adriel, had done the impossible and managed to change the rules about demons living on Earth. Now, a demon could *apply* and be granted permission to live here if they submitted to counseling and followed certain rules. Adriel had put Sunshine in charge of the whole operation.

Bel and his brothers were the first demons to be part of the program, and Adriel had declared that they had to sit down for counseling with Sunshine if they wanted to be allowed to stay. It pissed Bel off being told what to do, but he did it for his brothers. And because Sunshine was aware of his anger issues and careful not to set him off.

"I'm fine," he told her, planting his palms on the counter on either side of his computer. "Finished moving in today."

"Oh. Congratulations." She smiled that angelic smile. She didn't ask why it had taken him a month to unpack all of six boxes.

"Where's Raum?"

"He stayed late at the shelter to help Caro with a new rescue. He'll be home in about an hour, I believe."

"You guys planning to eat tonight?" Bel asked, pretending

like he didn't give a shit and wasn't secretly hoping he'd have an excuse to cook for them.

Angels didn't need to eat to survive either. Demons liked food because they enjoyed indulgences of all kinds. Angels probably wept in shame if they so much as licked a chocolate, but Sunshine wasn't like the rest of them.

"I hadn't thought about it."

He grunted. "I'll make something."

"Oh, I wouldn't want to impose. Are you sure?"

He shot her a look. Again, he had to make it look like it was an imposition and not something he actually wanted to do. A demon had to keep up appearances.

"Well, then," she said, accurately interpreting his expression, "may I help you prepare?"

Deciding on a simple pasta dish, he set her up with a cutting board and showed her how he wanted the mushrooms and leek cut, and then he put a pot of water on to boil and grabbed a pan for the sauce.

She glanced up at him after a minute or so. "How have you been since our session?"

"Angry," he grunted, crushing some garlic cloves with the side of a knife.

"Hm. And have you given any thought to my idea?"

"I'm not opening a restaurant. I'd kill the first human to complain that it was too spicy or some shit. And if some incompetent fuck screwed up in the kitchen, I'd gut him with a serving spoon."

Sunshine winced. "Maybe you could find someone you trusted to help you with . . . personal relations."

"Who?" He cocked a brow. "I don't trust most people to fill up a glass of water from the tap."

"Well . . ." She grinned. "I did see Meph break a glass last time he tried that here, so I don't suppose I blame you."

"Exactly."

"But that doesn't mean everyone is like that." She chuckled. "There are lots of competent humans. Caro, the human Raum works with at the shelter, is very intelligent. I doubt she would break a glass."

"She would still shit her pants if I flew into a rage."

Sunshine pursed her lips. There was no denying that.

"Working with or even near humans isn't an option, Sunshine. You need to stop suggesting it. If I listened to you, people would end up dead when I inevitably lose it and burn down the building. Then you'd definitely have to send me back to Hell."

"I think you have more control than you believe, Belial."

"You willing to bet lives on that?"

She slid the chopped mushrooms across the cutting board with a sigh. "I agree you have a point. I just wish you could find something to sustain you the way your brothers have."

"I don't want to kill people. You should be glad. Isn't the whole purpose of your new job to make sure I'm not going on murder sprees?"

"I already know you're not." She smiled, chopping the leek next. Her pieces were a little uneven, and he was glad he'd sharpened his knives earlier; with the way she was cutting, she'd fillet herself if the blade slipped. But . . . she was all right.

He tossed the mushrooms in the pan to fry and then threw in the garlic. "Then why are we still talking about this?"

"Just doing my job," she replied evenly. "And part of that job is to make sure every demon under my care has a healthy outlet for their inevitable frustrations. It just so happens that your frustrations are more . . . explosive than others."

He snorted. Talk about an understatement.

Or maybe a very literal statement.

"Your brothers have all found somewhere they fit in. They have a purpose, goals they're working toward, and people around them who support that."

Yeah, they did, and he was fucking glad about it. When Asmodeus had convinced them all to escape Hell, Bel had never pictured they'd have ended up where they were now. All well-adjusted and balanced and shit.

Asmodeus had broken his curse. Mishetsu had escaped his slave bonds. Meph had made peace with his demon. Raum had finally solved the mystery of his lost memories, and Bel had even seen him laugh the other day, for fuck's sake.

Maybe Hell had turned into a frozen wasteland since they'd left.

"I want that for you," Sunshine said, abandoning her chopping efforts to look pointedly at him. He pretended not to notice, still tossing the veggies into the pan.

"I want you to find that kind of purpose and acceptance, Belial. I believe you can."

Problem was . . . he didn't share that belief. Not with his rage, and the fact that when he lost control, he turned into a flaming beast who obliterated everything in his path. While he was on Earth, his entire focus had to be on never letting that beast out of its cage. Otherwise people would die.

He hadn't left Hell for himself. Hell was the only place he was safe, really. The only place he was able to give into the rage without fear of hurting others. He didn't give a shit if he fried a bunch of demons. He didn't give much of a shit about humans either, but he didn't want to break the rules, and fried humans tended to stay dead, unlike regenerating demons.

He'd escaped Hell for his brothers. To give them a chance at a better life. He'd done it because they wouldn't have gone without him. Because for some stupid reason, they looked to him for some kind of leadership—something he'd never wanted to give.

And now . . .

From now until he fucked up and got himself banished back

to Hell, it was all about surviving. Holding in the rage. Keeping control of the anger. Never letting the flames take over.

*Just keep holding it in.*

One day, he'd probably snap, and the consequences would be disastrous. But he was going to put that day off for as long as possible. He'd keep trying. For his brothers.

# 4

# WITCH HUNT

MURMUR, AKA THE NECROMANCER, CAUGHT THE INGREDIENT as she slumped into his arms, unconscious.

*Finally.*

He'd been playing this game of cat and mouse long enough, slinking around street corners, lurking in the night like a wayward shadow. Despite coming to Earth to stalk her at every available opportunity, the acquisition had taken longer than he'd hoped. Efforts with his spell required constant attention, and he needed to keep a watchful eye on his territory. He couldn't simply disappear indefinitely.

While the hunt had actually been mildly entertaining, he detested taking human form, and he'd been forced to do it whenever he was here.

He despised humans in general. He hated their stumpy, fleshy fingertips, flat teeth, finite lifespans, and easily breakable bones.

He hated Earth too, and he hated that he'd had to spend time here, but it had taken weeks to find the perfect moment. He needed the witch—Suyin, she was called—to vanish without a hint as to where she'd gone. Because of her friendship with the blue-haired twin, if there was any trace of demonic involvement linked to her disappearance, Murmur risked Belial and his "brothers" coming after him.

In their latest bargain, Murmur had sworn to keep silent and leave Belial and those he cared about to live peacefully on Earth. In exchange, Belial owed him a second open-ended favor—Murmur still hadn't cashed in the first favor from a previous arrangement.

Belial hadn't specified Suyin as being under his protection, and therefore, Murmur's actions were not in violation of their terms. But he wasn't sure Belial would see it that way.

*Better he not know at all.*

That was why he hadn't grabbed her at the bar. Once he'd realized the other witch was with her, he'd decided against it. He'd hoped to retreat without drawing attention to himself, but Suyin had ruined that plan by coming after him.

He hadn't expected that. What kind of person ran *toward* someone they believed to be a dangerous stalker? It seemed she lacked basic survival instincts.

Despite his failure at the bar, he'd salvage the excursion by returning to her apartment building and breaking into her garage, forcing the door open with brute strength. He'd gotten an idea of her habits in the time he'd been watching her, and he'd hoped she would choose to go for a ride on her motorcycle.

Suyin had, obviously, come and gone many times from this garage in recent weeks, but Murmur hadn't been able to be here all the time. In his absence, he'd enlisted his souls to watch her so that he was always aware of her movements.

Their surveillance had informed him that she was almost as paranoid as he was, which was really saying something. If she wasn't at home, she was at her coven's lair. She rarely went anywhere else, and never anywhere away from other humans. Both the store and her apartment were heavily warded, and the quality of her castings was admittedly admirable. Sure, he could have broken them if he'd wanted, but it would have left remnants of his energy behind—something he couldn't allow, given his leave-no-trace abduction policy.

But here he was. Successful at last, the final missing piece of his years of experimentation limp in his grasp. Good things came to those who waited—wasn't that what the humans said?

He looked at the diminutive form in his arms. She weighed next to nothing. He'd shifted back to demon form to use his tail venom to incapacitate her, and their size difference was even greater now.

Her hair was a sleek black curtain with a sharp fringe cut straight across the middle of her forehead. Her skin was a light olive shade, her eyes painted with dark makeup, and her lips colored with blood-red lipstick. She wore clunky combat boots with a thick platform that did little to increase her paltry height, and her jeans and leather jacket were both black.

She had strong features, with a perpetually scowling mouth. But there was something . . . soft about her as well. Delicate. If he were to simply flex his grip, he could snap her bones like twigs.

Murmur concluded his appraisal with a frown. He finally had his most valuable ingredient, but her frailty made her a liability. He needed to get her back to his lair as soon as possible. He'd lock her up tighter than the archangel in his dungeon. There would be no escaping him until she had fulfilled her purpose. Until the end.

Either of him, or his plan.

He focused on the next step: *Return to the hellgate.*

*Focus.* A challenge for him lately. The constant screams of the enslaved souls at his command clouded his mind, and trying to decipher the many tangents of his own thoughts was like trying to peer into a murky pool. The bottom was somewhere, but there was far too much sediment in the way.

*Witch. In my arms. Still in demon form.*

Right. He should shift before he went outside. He did so, losing about a foot of height and all the features that made him appear formidable—horns, teeth, claws, and tail. Since he wore a wyrm-leather coat and pants, his clothing shrank with him.

He made a face. Really, he was lucky he'd remembered to wear clothes at all. It was yet another sign of his deteriorating mental faculties that he—

*Shut up. Focus. Witch. Hellgate.*

He secured the witch, cradling her carefully in his arms. Not because he was concerned for her wellbeing, but because he didn't want to damage his ingredient. And because anyone he encountered needed to assume he was carrying a willing participant and not abducting an unconscious woman.

Stepping out of the garage, he flipped off the light and closed the door. He stroked his ingredient's long hair, drawing the silky curtain over her face so that any passersby wouldn't notice her closed eyes and slackened features.

Then he strode down the alley toward the street.

The sidewalks were empty for the most part, and luckily, his destination wasn't far. *You chose it precisely for that reason, so there's really no luck about it.*

*Quiet*, he told his disorderly thoughts. Not that they ever listened.

Someone rounded the corner ahead. He approached them with his head high, daring them to question him. They didn't. They didn't even glance over. In fact, no one gave Murmur a second glance the entire way. The ease of his success both thrilled him and made him despise humanity all the more.

He was the villain here. He was the evil that was supposed to be stopped by the ultimate good of humankind. Instead, he was carrying an unconscious woman down the street toward a terrible fate, and not one person made a move to stop him.

Finally, he reached a shop-lined street, but instead of

turning down the sidewalk, he ducked down another side alley. With a quick glance around for nearby humans, he shifted back to demon form and unfurled his wings. He generally preferred to keep them hidden, finding their weight cumbersome when he was working in his library, but nothing beat the convenience of flight.

With several strong pumps of the leathery appendages, he flew up to the third-floor balcony of an empty apartment building at the end of the alley and climbed through one of the smashed-out windows. Once inside, he dragged the plywood that had once been nailed to the frame back into place.

He disappeared his wings again since the tiny human dwelling had not been fashioned for a being his size. Stooping so his horns wouldn't scrape the ceiling, he tightened his grip on the witch and stepped over the rubble in the stripped-bare kitchen. On the floor in the dusty living area was a series of chalk-drawn symbols enclosed in a circle—a hellgate. He'd been using this one to come and go, waiting for this moment.

A hellgate functioned by linking with another gate in one's desired destination. Murmur kept one in his study, which he had left open in anticipation of his return. Whenever he was back in his lair, he rendered the gate inert by smudging the outer line, preventing any unwelcome visitors.

He looked down at the witch in his arms. Still unconscious. *Inconvenient, but easily remedied.* Unconscious people could not travel by hellgate.

Dead people could. A dead body was like any other inanimate piece of luggage one might choose to travel with. But an unconscious person had a functioning brain, and it had to be emitting the proper electrical signals for the hellgate's magic to operate.

He used his free hand to lightly slap her cheek, careful not to gouge her eyes with his claws. Her face was so tiny, if he spread his fingers, he could cover it entirely with one hand.

In anticipation of this moment, he hadn't given her much venom, and he knew it wouldn't take her long to awaken.

Sure enough, after several moments, her eyes began to move beneath their lids, and she groaned softly.

"Wakey wakey," he said.

Her body tensed and her breathing changed, and then her eyes opened wide. She took one look at him and inhaled a sharp breath, possibly to scream, though from what he'd learned about her, she was more likely to hurl threats. But before she could—

He stepped into the hellgate.

The world spun violently, and he was briefly disoriented before arriving safely in his lair in Hell. Hellgate travel was far from pleasant, but one grew accustomed, and he barely noticed it now.

He looked around his familiar library and then at the bundle in his arms, who was momentarily stunned from the hellgate. He smiled. *Mine at last.* She was here, in his lair, where he controlled everything, and she would not escape. She would serve her purpose, exactly as he'd planned.

Everything was finally falling into place, and he allowed himself a moment to savor his victory.

That was until Suyin began to struggle violently in his grip. As predicted, she started shouting threats at him so loudly, it stung his ears. He fought to hold on to her, but the slippery witch actually wiggled out of his grasp, dropping unceremoniously to the floor.

He bent to grab her, but before he could get a proper grip, she reached to her boot, pulled out a switchblade, and fucking *stabbed* him with it. Right in the neck.

He snarled viciously and recoiled, ripping the knife out and tossing it out of reach. In the time that took, she immediately began crawling away on her forearms and knees like a crab-insect, scrambling toward the hellgate.

Cursing and covered in blood, he shot his tail out, wrapped it around her ankle, and yanked her back to his feet. He stabbed the tip into her neck, giving her a second dose of venom.

She slumped, unconscious once more.

He pressed a hand over his neck wound and eyed her with newfound wariness. *Perhaps not quite as fragile as you assumed.*

Suyin awoke to a dull ache in her left hip and shoulder. The surface she lay on was rock-hard—literally, it seemed she was lying on a slab of stone—and her body was stiff and sore because of it. How long had she been asleep?

Where had she fallen asleep anyway?

The lull of unconsciousness still held sway over her, so she shifted positions slightly, hoping to sink back into the abyss.

*Bloodshot eyes, tall horns, sharp claws—*

She snapped out of the haze in a second and sat up with a jerk. Blinking roughly, she squinted at the wall in front of her and waited for her eyes to focus.

The memories rushed in. The image of a long tail whipping toward her had her sucking in a breath.

*The scorpion.* Just like in her dreams. But it hadn't been an arachnid. The barbed and segmented tail belonged to the eyes and the horns of a . . .

*Demon.*

A fucking demon had taken her.

But of course it was a demon. This was what her dreams had been warning her about. This was the cause of the dread she'd been carrying around for weeks. She'd chastised herself endlessly for her paranoia, but it seemed she'd been well justified.

Not that being paranoid had helped. The owner of those

bloodshot eyes had found her nonetheless, and now, here she was—

*Where* was she?

She patted her pockets, not surprised to find her phone and keys gone. And she'd lost her knife earlier when she'd stabbed the demon—which hadn't made any difference, unfortunately. She touched the sore spot on her neck, feeling the two puncture wounds.

The room around her was square, all made of the same black rock, rough and unpolished. The only interruption in the stone was in the left corner—a small doorway was cut into the wall, covered by thick steel bars.

Opposite the door was a bucket with a lid. Was that supposed to be a crude toilet? The air had a stale, sour smell, with hints of sulfur, and she sensed she was underground. The only source of light came from a torch mounted on the wall outside the cell.

She was in some sort of archaic dungeon. A demon had taken her through a hellgate, and based on her surroundings, she could only conclude . . .

She was in Hell.

Heart suddenly slamming against her ribs, she lurched unsteadily to her feet, pressing her spine against the wall and staring at her cramped surroundings.

She was in fucking *Hell*. She was a living, breathing human in Hell. She was so fucking screwed.

But what use did she have to a demon? She was a bloodborn witch, which meant he could kill her without consequence from Heaven. So if he'd just wanted to mess with her, why not do that? And if he'd been out for witches in particular, why focus on her specifically?

He'd been stalking her for over two weeks—there was no doubt in her mind that the demon who'd taken her was her neighborhood park creep—so he'd obviously been after *her*.

This hadn't been a random snatching. This was a carefully planned operation. What did she have that a demon wanted? What warranted that kind of forethought?

Whatever the case, she had to find a way out of here. She had to gather her wits and make a plan. She pushed off the wall and approached the bars, the only way in or out of her cell. They were too close together for her to stick her head through, and she was only able to see a few feet down the passage outside.

"Hey!" Suyin hollered. Her voice didn't echo. It deadened immediately, like she'd shouted into a pile of blankets. It was eerie.

"Let me out of here!" As if that was going to work. "What do you want with me?"

Nothing but that muffled silence greeted her.

She fought her rising panic. She couldn't afford to go there. If she was going to have any hope of escaping, she needed to keep her head.

She'd been brought here by hellgate. That meant, all she needed to do was draw one on the floor of her cell, and she could leave the same way.

She hadn't drawn a hellgate in a long time, and her memory was shaky, but with some trial and error, she was sure she could get it. It would be a challenge, but she could hopefully link it to the gate the demon had used to get here by visualizing the dark room she'd seen for a split second before he'd stepped through.

Another challenge would be finding casting material. She had nothing to draw the sigil with.

But there was a solution for that too. A sigil could be drawn in blood. In fact, blood was more powerful than chalk or salt. She wasn't keen on bleeding herself out while she tried to remember the details of the hellgate sigil, but she would do whatever—

Footsteps snapped her out of her thoughts.

She retreated to the safer depths of the cell as a looming shadow stepped in front of the torch, blocking out the light.

The demon cut an impressive silhouette. He was easily seven feet tall, with impala-like horns crowning his head. He held his chin high and his spine erect like he fancied himself royalty.

But his intimidating presence wasn't what caught her attention.

At his feet, thick smoke swirled like he was walking on liquid nitrogen. Stray wisps rose and formed into hazy shapes, backlit by the torches. As the shapes coiled in and out of existence, Suyin swore she saw the outlines of faces and hands clawing at the air.

Chills raced up her spine, and she pressed herself harder against the stone wall.

"You're awake." His voice was gravelly and deep and somehow not what she'd expected. With that proud posture, she would've imagined it to be smooth and articulate.

"Who are you?" she demanded. "What do you want with me?"

"I think you can guess."

She shook her head. "I really can't."

His head tilted, those tall horns tilting with it. His face was too shadowed to see, and it made it even more disconcerting to speak to him.

"Who are you?" she asked again.

"You really don't know? I'm almost offended."

She said nothing. She wasn't going to apologize for not recognizing a creepy stalker demon on sight.

Her face must have betrayed her confusion because he said, "The souls are usually a dead giveaway." He gestured to the smoky mass swirling about his feet. His fingers were long and slender, tipped with sharp claws.

Her eyes widened. Those were . . . *souls*?

He sighed like he was disappointed in her for not figuring it out and playing his stupid game. "My name is Murmur, or the Necromancer. Either works. And yes, the rumors are true."

She sucked in a breath.

"That's more like it," he said, as if pleased by her reaction.

If she'd been any less shocked, she would have rolled her eyes. Instead, she could only stare at that towering silhouette and wonder how she'd fallen into such deep shit. Oh, she'd heard of him, all right, and what she knew didn't bode well for her.

She wasn't as obsessed with demonology as some other witches she knew. Many were drawn to witchcraft because of a certain fascination with the dark forces in creation, and they enjoyed studying the hierarchy of Hell, called the Order of Thrones.

Suyin had spent most of her life trying to make peace with the fact that she would never know her father because of his own obsession with Sheolic magic. It was for her own good that she stayed away from it.

But she still knew who the Necromancer was.

Every witch of any significance knew who he was. He was like the witch boogeyman, a cautionary tale to warn against dabbling in black magic. *Don't mess with demons or the Necromancer will steal your soul.*

The Necromancer's army of enslaved human souls was well known, and truthfully, she should have recognized him just from that, as he'd said. She also knew he couldn't actually *steal* souls—everyone in his army had agreed to be bound to his service to escape the torturous suffering of the Nine Rings.

It was a shitty trade, but some people would do anything to avoid the consequences of their actions.

"What do you want with me?" Suyin asked again in a hoarse whisper.

"Let's not play dumb," he replied in that gravelly, dark voice. "Attempting to manipulate me won't work. Really, it's insulting you'd even try."

Her mouth opened and then closed again. She didn't have a clue what he was talking about, but he apparently thought she did. She wasn't sure if it was better to play along or make him understand.

He wrapped a hand around one of the bars, leaning in. His face was still shrouded in darkness, but she could make out those slender fingers and sharp claws just fine.

"Listen closely because I will not repeat myself," he said. "I took you because I require your blood for a spell. This spell is possibly the greatest feat of magic ever undertaken, and the very fate of the underworld rests upon its success. You are the missing ingredient to that spell, and now that I have you, I will keep you here until I complete it."

He released the bar and moved back into the shadows, the torch behind his head creating the illusion that he glowed with an eerie orange halo.

"Luckily for you, since you're so useful, I will not waste a single drop of your blood. So long as you cooperate, you will not be harmed. But if you try to cross me, I have ways of making you suffer that do not involve spilling your blood."

Her mind was reeling. Why did he want her blood specifically? If he was after blood-born witches, she was definitely outclassed in raw power by Lily and Iris, even if she had more practical knowledge. Why hadn't he gone after them instead?

"And before you attempt to use a hellgate to escape," he added, "you should know that I put a seal on you that prevents you from accessing your magic. While it's active, you will be unable to cast."

She immediately did a body scan, running her hands down her torso. The kind of seal he was talking about had to involve carving a sigil into the skin, but she didn't feel any fresh wounds—

"I spelled it into a potion and made you drink it while you were unconscious. It's in your bloodstream. I already said I wouldn't waste your blood or risk weakening you prematurely."

Her eyes narrowed. He was lying—

"If you want to test it for yourself, go ahead." He reached into the pocket of his long coat and tossed something into the cell. It rolled across the stone to her feet, and when she glanced down, she saw it was a piece of chalk.

Her heart sank.

He had to be telling the truth. No way he would have given her this if there was any way to use it to escape.

She looked back at that looming shadow, the souls of the damned swirling at his feet.

"You will remain in this cell indefinitely. I will take the blood I need when I need it. I will keep returning for more until the spell is successful. You'd best pray that happens sooner rather than later. There's not much to look at down here."

And with that, he disappeared into the darkness.

She stood, frozen in place, her heart pounding in her chest for several seconds before she suddenly sprang into action.

"Wait!" she shouted, racing forward to grab the bars. "Wait!"

The muffled sound of retreating footsteps stopped. The demon—Murmur—didn't return, but she sensed he was there in the darkness, waiting for her to speak.

"I need food," she called down the tunnel. "And water. And fresh air. And somewhere to sleep and water to bathe. I can't survive down here with nothing but a fucking shit bucket!"

There was a long pause. She couldn't see into the dark; she didn't know for sure that he was even there. But judging by the way her skin prickled and the hairs on her neck still stood on end, he was.

And then he spoke.

"I already warned you not to try to manipulate me. When I give you a warning, it would be wise to heed it. I never make idle threats."

And with that, she heard the footsteps again. She listened as they grew fainter until they were gone completely.

Leaving her alone in the dark.

# 5

# Rock Bottom

After Murmur left, Suyin lay back down on the hard stone floor. Overwhelmed by everything, trying to fight feelings of despair, she eventually drifted into an uneasy sleep.

When she awoke, she wasn't sure how long she'd slept. Long enough that her back hurt like a bitch. Groaning, she pushed herself upright, wincing when she realized she needed to pee.

She eyed the bucket in the corner distastefully. At least it had a lid.

Afterward, she slumped back against the wall and slid down to the ground, feeling lightheaded. Whatever venom was in the demon's tail had left her woozy and disoriented, but she was feeling much better now. Her mind was sharper, but so was her hunger. And worse, her thirst.

Hunger, she could manage for a while, but the thirst was going to be a real killer.

Murmur had said he wouldn't harm her because he needed her blood for his spell. But he'd also seemed to think she was trying to trick him when she'd asked for food and water.

She knew demons didn't need to eat, but humans did. Surely the legendary Necromancer was intelligent enough to know that basic fact about human physiology? She couldn't be sure, and that made her nervous. He might claim to want her alive, but all the good intentions in the world didn't mean shit if he accidentally neglected her to death.

To give herself something else to focus on, she made a mental list of all possible escape routes. Which were really just two.

One: through the door.

Two: through a hellgate, once the potion binding her magic wore off.

Climbing to her feet, she stretched her stiff body until her spine cracked and then approached the door. She gripped the bars and shook them roughly. There wasn't any give.

Next, she studied the mechanics of the door. The bars were roughly three inches thick. Reaching through, she felt the hinges, finding no weaknesses. The door was secured with a sliding bar that went into a hole drilled into the stone on the opposite side.

She touched the padlock that secured the bar. It was so big it barely fit in her hand. She felt around as carefully as she could, but there didn't seem to be a keyhole anywhere. How did it open then? With magic, perhaps?

Either way, there wasn't an easy way out through the door. That left her with option two.

Even if Murmur's potion worked and she couldn't use magic, it would still be smart to refresh her memory on drawing a hellgate now. With any luck, there would be a window between when the spell wore off and when he refreshed it, and she could activate the gate and escape.

So passed the next few hours.

She drew small versions of the gate on the wall, careful not to waste her chalk unnecessarily. She made minor adjustments with each redraw until she was certain she had the correct design.

There was no point drawing the actual gate yet, in case Murmur returned and decided to thwart her efforts. Using the sleeve of her leather jacket, she rubbed away all her rough sketches on the wall, leaving only the final one to copy later. Then she put the chalk piece—about half its original size now—carefully into her pocket.

She sat back down against the wall and stared at the door, watching the flickering flames of the torch outside.

She was hungry and thirsty and her back hurt. Before long, her tailbone ached too from sitting on the stone, but it wasn't like there was anywhere comfier to be. She told herself it was wise to conserve her strength for when the potion wore off and it was time to escape.

She closed her eyes and forced herself back to sleep.

Muted footsteps pulled Suyin out of her uneasy slumber. Once again, she had no idea how much time had passed. A full day, or more? Her hunger had become uncomfortable, and her mouth was so dry it was glued shut.

She didn't bother trying to open it. Exposing it to air would just make it drier.

Moving at all felt like too much effort, and she reminded herself again that she needed to conserve her strength. A cynical voice in her mind scoffed, pointing out that she wasn't going to have much strength left to conserve if she didn't find a way out of here soon.

The dull footfalls awakened her hope and gave her a boost of energy, as stupid as it may have been. She couldn't help it. The human survival instinct was the strongest of them all.

A familiar looming shadow stepped in front of the torch. As before, he blocked the light, and all she could make out was his outline. It was just enough for her to see him prick his finger on one hand with the sharp claw of the other. He swiped the bloodied fingertip over the lock, and it sprang open. A magical seal, as she'd suspected.

The sound of metal shifting filled the deadened silence as he slid the lock free and pushed the cage door open. As he stepped inside, Suyin imagined leaping to her feet, ducking around him, and escaping into the passage behind him.

But he was huge. If he stretched out his arms, he could almost reach fully across her cell. If he stuck his leg out, he could trip her easily. And she'd seen how fast his tail could strike. The memory of that sharp barb piercing her neck and the sight of it swinging on the end of his tail now was enough to convince her to stay put.

He stopped in front of where she remained sitting against the wall. As he turned, the torch flame illuminated one side of his body, and she finally got a proper look at his face.

She recognized the features of the beautiful man she'd seen at the bar. The curve of full lips, the proud line of his nose, the arch of his cheekbones—that angelic perfection was still there. But unlike his human form, in which she'd struggled to find a single flaw, his demon form's beauty was marred by his apparent . . . deadness.

It was the only way to describe it.

His skin was a pale, grayish white that she'd only seen on corpses on TV. The coloring around his eyes darkened dramatically, with shadows so deep they almost looked like makeup. His lips were bloodless and pallid, and his horns and claws were obsidian black.

But his eyes were the worst.

The whites were so bloodshot, they weren't white at all but a sickly pinkish red. His irises were a light blue so pale it was almost colorless, and his pupils looked like tiny voids in the center of that circle of death. They were the exact eyes she'd seen in her dreams.

His hair was pure white, the same ethereal shade that had

caught her eye in the club. Looking back, she was a fool for not realizing what he was the second she saw him. No human had hair like that, and no dye or wig was capable of achieving that remarkable snow-white shade. It was too unearthly.

All of him looked a bit like a zombie. The undead. A beautiful corpse.

He was lean, perhaps too thin for his height, but he carried an unmistakable aura of power. And with those ghastly souls swirling at his feet, haunted faces occasionally forming in the smoke, it was easy to believe it.

He stared down his nose at her. His expression was as cold as his cadaverous complexion. She stayed on the floor, looking up at him while chills raced over her neck and the backs of her arms.

"What's wrong with you?" he asked suddenly.

She blinked. His gravelly voice still came as a surprise. As he spoke, she caught glimpses of sharp, pointed teeth.

Damn, he was freaky.

Still, "fake it till you make it" was the best advice she'd ever heard, and she lived by it. So she forced her face into a look of defiance, mustered as much attitude as she could, and said, "I'm dehydrated and starving."

He blinked. Like he was actually fucking surprised.

It was such an unexpected reaction that it took her a couple of seconds to gather her wits again. The dehydration and starvation didn't help either.

"That's what happens when you leave a human in a dungeon for days with no food or water," she added.

To her further surprise, his lips curved into a cruel smile.

He was hideous and beautiful at the same time. He looked cold and dead. He looked ethereal and elfin. His tall horns were majestic. His hair was stunning. His eyes were disturbing.

He was fucking terrifying.

"So you truly don't know," he said. "I suspected, but I wasn't sure."

"Know what?" The delirium of sensory deprivation made it hard to care about anything. This entire scenario was starting to feel like a fever dream.

Instead of responding, he knelt in front of her. In their close proximity, the misty souls at his feet brushed against her with an icy chill, and she shuddered in revulsion. He tilted his head and leaned closer, studying her like she was fuzzy bacteria growing in a petri dish and he was the lab tech trying to decipher the results.

She tilted her head at the same angle as his, trying to get a read on him, to figure out what went on in the mind of a being like him. His complexion implied decay, but up close, his skin looked smooth and supple.

"If you want me alive," she said, "you're going to have to feed me."

But apparently, he was done talking.

His hand shot out faster than her tired eyes could track, and cold fingers wrapped around her throat. *Ice*-cold. The sensation of touch was there, but there was none of the warmth that came from touching a living person.

Still holding her neck, he shoved her sharply, and she hit the ground on her side. "Stay," he growled.

He released her throat and whipped out a short blade from a holster beneath his black coat. Then, grasping her arm, he unsnapped the cuff of her jacket and shoved her sleeve up.

Suddenly, the knife was cutting across her forearm, and a hoarse cry escaped her at the sharp burn. She followed that by unleashing a stream of curses and trying to yank her arm out of his grip. Even tugging with all her strength, he held her easily, the flexing tendons in his hand the only sign he was expending any effort.

With his other hand, he pulled a long, cylindrical jar from

inside of his coat, dropped the knife, and gripped her arm, holding it over the receptacle.

She stopped struggling, though she probably shouldn't have. But her gaze was riveted to the sight of her blood spilling into the jar, the glass filling steadily.

After a couple minutes, the red flow eased into drips as her blood clotted and the wound started to close, but he continued to hold her there as if refusing to miss a single drop.

And then it was done. He dropped her arm, put a cork in the jar, and tucked it back in his coat. Then he pulled a strip of cloth from his pocket and tied it over her wound so tight she was pretty sure her hand would fall off. She gasped at the pain, but he ignored her, retrieving his bloody blade and wiping it on another piece of cloth. He stood and sheathed the knife in a smooth motion.

"Should be enough," he muttered, apparently speaking to himself. "The sacrifice will be strong."

"How do you keep it from clotting in the jar?" she found herself asking. Why she cared about that right now, she couldn't say. Probably shock.

He glanced sharply at her like he was surprised by the question. "The glass is coated with a potion prepared beforehand. The blood stays fresh as long as it's in there."

Before she had a chance to respond, he turned and swept out of the room.

The cage door slammed, the bar slid across, and the padlock clicked shut. His shadow moved out of the torch light as he began to walk away.

"Wait!" she cried again.

That dark shadow appeared once more.

"I need food. And water." She closed her eyes and then forced herself to add through gritted teeth, "Please."

"You don't," he replied, and then he was gone, the muffled sounds of his footsteps fading too quickly.

*Alone again.*

"You fucking dead-faced prick," she hissed.

Murmur wanted her alive, but apparently, he had no understanding of what was required to keep her that way. He would learn from his mistake the hard way, but that would be because she was dead.

She'd never wanted to die to prove a point, but this was almost worth it.

She shut her eyes. She didn't bother sitting up or loosening the painfully tight bandage. She didn't bother checking the locks to make sure everything was secure. And this time, when the despair crept in, she couldn't summon the will to defeat it.

At least if she died, she would thwart whatever plan this fucking asshole had, whatever it was he wanted her blood for. It was shit consolation for the absolute worst-case scenario, but it was all she had.

As the darkness rose up to claim her once more, before she drifted off into a deep slumber, she whispered his name.

She would curse him to eternal torment with her dying breath.

# 6

# Down in Flames

Murmur stumbled, and his knees gave out under him. They hit the ground, and he fell forward onto his hands. The knife he'd been holding clattered away, and the palm he'd cut with it smeared blood across the floor.

Black and purple smoke filled his library with an impenetrable gloom. The sharp scent of magic was still strong in the air, but it was already dissipating.

He fought to keep conscious, focusing on his breath while his head spun violently. If he passed out, he would lose control over his souls. They couldn't do much without his necromancy giving them power, but his territory would be vulnerable. His wards were still formidable, but the patrolling souls were how he'd gained his fearsome reputation. None crossed the Necromancer when they risked attack from a formless foe.

*Then again, it might be nice to pass out for a while. Enjoy the oblivion, forget your failures.*

"It won't be oblivion," he muttered to himself. "It never

is." He would just have the dream again and awaken in a cold sweat.

*Well, that's a poor excuse for escapism.*

"My point exactly."

He shook his head and tried to focus. It was hard to care about anything in light of current circumstances.

The spell had failed. Again.

He'd been so sure it would work this time. He'd gotten so far, so close that he'd *seen* the portal starting to form amid the black haze. The hellfire had burned exactly as it was supposed to. The blood sacrifices had gone perfectly.

But the spell still wasn't strong enough. *Why*? He had all the necessary ingredients; he was sure of it now. The witch's blood was so powerful, he was certain he'd barely scratched the surface of what it could do.

*Maybe it's not the blood's fault. Maybe you need to be stronger.*

"How? What can I do differently? What more can I give?"

He pushed every drop of himself into each casting, to the point where it took him days to recover, and he felt his body becoming colder and more lifeless with every failed attempt. He'd been certain that Suyin was the missing ingredient. No, he was still certain. He had studied Gamigin's research diligently.

He blew out a breath, forcing his eyes to focus. When he was exhausted like this, the souls' screams rose in volume. Without his will fighting them back, they overtook his mind, pounding at the inside of his skull like a thousand hammers.

Pushing into his palms, he sat back on his heels, tipping his head back to look up at the vaulted ceiling above. The blackened point of the tower's spire was so covered in cobwebs, it was hard to see the top.

The room started to spin, so he closed his eyes again. His body started to list to one side. He focused on keeping his spine upright.

*You need to sleep.*

"Shut up." He hated sleep. Not only because his defenses were down, but because his stupid death vision haunted him without cease. He could never get away from it. He could never truly rest.

He'd been awake for two entire cycles in Hell, which was equivalent to nearly five Earth days, though demons generally needed sleep every twelve hours, as humans did. And now, he'd drained himself attempting his spell, and the brain fog was making it difficult to form coherent thoughts.

*Not to mention the screaming.*

Always, the endless fucking screaming.

Somehow summoning the will, he climbed to his feet, stumbling over to the table to steady himself. He tried to think. To remember what he had to do.

*Need to check boundary wards.* He hadn't left his tower in days, save for his visits to Suyin's cell. *Need to repair sigil from failed attempt. Need to clean mess in library.*

Screaming filled his head. He shook it roughly.

*Need to gather ingredients for another attempt. Analyze failure and determine cause. Need to . . .*

Screaming.

*Need to . . .*

More screaming.

"Shut up," he growled at the infernal souls. "Shut the fuck up. Shut *up*!"

For once, they actually listened, and the din dampened to a dull ache at the base of his skull. He lifted his head and blinked, almost surprised to find himself alone.

*Need to sleep.*

Before he toppled where he stood, he stalked out of his library, leaving the carnage of the failed spell behind. He went down the dark hall to his chambers, slamming the doors behind him as he entered the gloomy room.

As he stripped off his clothes and dropped his weary body into bed, he thought of the witch in his dungeon.

*If you want me alive, you're going to have to feed me.*

He scowled. He knew humans needed sustenance to survive. It was partly why he despised them. Despite their short lifespans and multitudinous weaknesses, these were the beings that were the true rulers of creation.

Every rule angels enforced and every scheme demons concocted was for the purpose of influencing these mercurial creatures. Their whims controlled the state of the Earth. If they were evil, the world descended into chaos, and if they were good, the planet thrived.

How such witless lifeforms had secured this integral purpose was a mystery he would never solve.

He was well acquainted with the weaknesses of humans. He just hadn't expected Suyin to believe she had them. At first, he'd thought she was lying to trick him, but now he wasn't so sure. She'd seemed genuinely depleted when he'd visited earlier.

Could she actually die from simply *believing* she was starving to death?

He grimaced. He couldn't deny that it was a possibility. The power of the mind was formidable, and he knew better than to underestimate it.

*Just look at you. You've divided your mind into so many parts, you forget that the voice in your head is you.*

"Will you shut up, for once?" Murmur mumbled, sinking into the sleep he both craved and despised.

*He was burning alive. Agony seared every particle of his being, and the air was filled with his screams. Death was a mercy amid this unbearable torment, and he longed for it with everything left of him.*

*And then, a cool numbness descended upon his body, and*

*the glaring light faded blissfully away. The link between his consciousness and body snapped, and he let go. He eagerly awaited the dissolution of his essence, its merging back into the energy upholding creation.*

*That was how death worked for a demon.*

*Humans had souls. Those souls were what Heaven and Hell fought so hard to claim. When a human died, their soul was sent to either of the two realms. There they would rest or suffer until they were ready to begin a new cycle.*

*But a demon was a manifestation of the dark forces in creation, and a demon had no soul. This was accepted as fact. No one questioned this truth.*

*But when the tether to Murmur's physical body snapped, his consciousness . . . did not dissolve. He did not end.*

*Instead, he felt his formless self being drawn by a powerful force he could not resist. He was sucked toward an impenetrable cage. He cried out in despair, and his voice reverberated everywhere and nowhere at once. And it mingled with the others trapped with him. Thousands of others—*

And then he woke up.

His body covered in cold sweat, Murmur stared at the vaulted ceiling of his bedchamber. Just like his library, cobwebs crisscrossed the beams and coated the chandelier. He'd had this dream a thousand times, but it never failed to inspire the same bone-chilling terror. And that was because it wasn't simply a dream, but a vision of the future.

*His* future.

In the beginning, the vision had come sporadically. But now, it came every time he closed his eyes. He interpreted its increased frequency as an indication that the time for its realization was near.

Time was running out, and if he didn't find a way to make his spell work, he was going to find himself caught in the very prison he was trying to destroy. There would be no one coming to his rescue.

*Speaking of no one coming to your rescue . . .*

Unbidden, his thoughts returned to the witch he'd left crumpled on the cell floor. No one knew where she was, save for him. The dungeons of his lair were so vast, Murmur didn't even use half the space. That had made it easy for him to find a secluded wing to keep Suyin hidden from his other prisoners and even his own subjects. He trusted no one with his ingredient.

Murmur's lair had formerly belonged to Paimon, a powerful Queen of Hell and supporter of Lucifer. It was an impenetrable fortress, surrounded by high stone walls and full of hidden passages.

In the end, however, Paimon's defeat had come from within, at the hands of her prized servant, Mishetsumephtai the Hunter. Mist had been bound to Paimon by an unbreakable magical bond, and he had *still* found a way to betray and defeat her.

Yet another reason Murmur never trusted anyone with anything. Betrayal could come at any moment.

Paimon's old favorite spot, the Pit, was where she'd gathered spectators to watch her monstrous goraths consume whatever wretched prisoner she tossed to them. It was now empty.

Murmur did not feed the goraths, and he definitely did not host social events to watch them being fed. He despised social occasions. He despised other people, humans and demons alike. More than anything, he wanted to be left alone.

*You're never alone.*

"As alone as I can be," he amended, for the obnoxious voice in his head was right. He was never fully alone. His mind had splintered over the years. In his head, his souls screamed for mercy, and indecipherable visions played on loops. And he argued with himself, to top it off.

With a sigh, he tried to remember the many things he had to do. Instead he just felt tired. Tired but afraid of sleep.

And his thoughts kept returning to the witch in his dungeon.

# 7

# Starved Out

Suyin woke to cool liquid filling her dry mouth. It was bliss, and she swallowed hungrily. The liquid kept pouring, and she kept swallowing. But suddenly, she couldn't swallow fast enough to keep up with the flow, and it spilled everywhere. She choked, fighting for air.

"Swallow, witch."

She recognized that rough voice. Her eyes snapped open, and her heart skipped a beat as she found herself staring into those eerie bloodshot eyes. How could he be attractive when he looked like he'd just clawed himself out of the grave?

He capped the plastic water bottle he'd been pouring into her mouth, set it on the ground, and shot her an impatient look.

"Don't look at me like that."

She wasn't looking at him in any way. She was just trying to figure out what was going on.

She was lying on the ground. Right where he'd left her when he stole her blood. Not long after, she'd drifted into some woozy altered state that was halfway between sleep and straight unconsciousness, and she hadn't seen a point in pulling herself out of it, so there she'd stayed.

Until now. Because Murmur had come back.

"Yes, you win this round." His eyes narrowed. "Feel free to gloat."

She blinked. She was so exhausted it was hard to think, and every part of her body hurt. After what she'd been through in the last . . . however many days, the sight of the demon before her sent her pulse racing with fear and hatred. Mostly hatred.

She loathed him with a burning passion. Her dreams were going to be full of visions of his gruesome death for a long time to come.

But she was still afraid of him. And that made her hate him more.

"I will cater to your human needs, but don't think you've won my sympathy. I assure you, I have none to give."

Oh, they had no misunderstandings about that. He'd left her to rot and starve to death in a dungeon underground. She was under no illusions that he was sympathetic or caring in any way.

"You wanted food. So eat."

She frowned and forced her exhausted head to turn. In front of her on the floor was . . . She blinked.

A bag of apples. And a bag of carrots. And three plastic water bottles.

The sight was so bizarre—fresh, colorful produce, the inside of the plastic wet with condensation, amid this hellish pit of isolation—that she had to stare for several seconds before it sank in.

When it did, she sat up with strength she didn't know she had and snatched up the bag of apples. Her left hand responded to the movement with a pain so sharp, she cried out.

When she glanced down, her fingers were swollen and purple.

"F-fuck," she stammered, realizing she'd forgotten to loosen the bandage he'd tied on her. Her arm was going to fall off if she didn't get this fucking this off.

She lifted her head, pinning the demon before her with the fiercest glare she could muster, and held out her arm. "Take it off."

She hated how her voice shook. But she was weak and traumatized, and she was doing her best. She swore anew to kill this piece of shit for doing this to her, but for now she had to make sure she kept all her fingers.

"Take it off or my fucking fingers are gonna fall off," she snapped when he just stared at her with a slightly cocked head.

He looked down at her arm. "I wonder if they would regenerate." He was muttering again, like he was talking to himself. "Would be interesting to test."

"Take it off!" she shouted with a forcefulness she didn't feel.

His gaze snapped to hers and his brows rose. How did he have dark eyebrows and lashes, but white hair? The contrast was bizarre.

He reached out, and then those ice-cold fingers wrapped around her arm, dwarfing it against his skeletal hands. A shudder rolled through her at his touch.

He untied the bandage with creepy black claws, and she cursed colorfully as the blood rushed back into her throbbing fingers. It felt like she was being tortured by a mad acupuncturist and dipping her hand into boiling water at the same time.

Her teeth began to chatter, and her head spun. She didn't have the strength to handle pain on top of everything else.

She used her good hand to awkwardly tear open the bag of apples. Pulling one through the hole in the plastic, she sank her teeth into it, unable to stifle a moan as the sweet flavor filled her mouth. She took several more bites, lost in the deliciousness of the apple, until she suddenly became aware of eyes on her. She looked up and found Murmur watching her.

While she was preoccupied, he'd sat down across the cell, his back against the opposite wall, one arm draped over his bent knee. His enslaved souls were dimly visible in the gloom, moving like lingering smoke. He stared at her, but she could tell by the vacant look in his eyes that he was somewhere far away in his head.

She ignored him and went back to her apple, eating the entire thing, core and all. When she was finished, the feeling had returned to her hand enough for her to gingerly use it to open the bag of carrots.

She'd never particularly cared for raw carrots, but now they tasted damn near as good as the apple, the crunchy vegetables full of flavor and vitality. She swore never to turn her nose up at a carrot again.

After eating two, she forced herself to stop, though she was hungry enough to finish the entire bag. She wanted to ration her food since she didn't know when this fucker would deign to feed her again, and she didn't want to make herself sick by eating too much at once.

Murmur's brow was creased in a frown, and he was muttering something under his breath that she couldn't discern. He jerked his chin away, only to suddenly jerk it back the other way and snap, "That's ridiculous."

He shook his head roughly and growled, "Impossible."

Was he . . . arguing with himself?

His head suddenly snapped forward, and his gaze sharpened on hers in a way that told her he was actually paying attention now.

She swallowed the lump in her throat. She'd die before she let him see her weakness. "Where did you get the food?" she forced herself to ask.

"From my garden," he deadpanned.

She blinked.

He rolled his eyes. "I went to Earth and took it from a supermarket."

"Took . . . as in stole."

He looked at her like she'd just asked him if Hell was real. "Obviously."

She blinked. She wasn't going to thank him, and she didn't care if he shoplifted vegetables. Not if it meant she got to eat.

They stared at each other. She glared at him, her eyes full of hatred, and he just . . . watched her. Like he truly felt nothing. The same way he'd pushed through that crowd of people like they were inanimate objects, he watched her now with complete detachment.

In fact, before her eyes, she watched his eyes grow more and more distant, until suddenly, she knew he'd gone back into his head.

"Can't understand why it failed," he muttered, shaking his head. "All the ingredients. . . Everything in place . . . More blood needed perhaps? But how—"

"Your spell failed?" she asked.

He blinked, and suddenly he was back in the room with her. "Yes."

"Why?"

"I don't know." By the set of his jaw, he wasn't lying about that.

"That means you're going to keep me longer, doesn't it?"

"Yes." He didn't look smug, but he didn't look sorry either. He simply didn't give a shit.

*Bastard.* There was no chance of Stockholm syndrome with this one.

"How long?"

"As long as it takes."

"People are going to think I'm dead. No one knows where I went."

"That was the point," he replied easily.

She gritted her teeth against the wave of despair that crashed over her. She wouldn't give him the satisfaction of seeing her fall apart. Not that he'd care either way.

He was a demon. It wasn't like she'd expected anything different, but damn. She hadn't realized she could hate him any more than she already did, but somehow, she found a way.

"I must return to work now," he said, more to himself than her. But he didn't make any move to get up. And his voice suddenly sounded exhausted. "There's much to be done and little time left."

She frowned, trying to figure him out. "My blood is a key ingredient in your spell. What kind of spell? What are you trying to do?"

"That's not your concern."

"Maybe it should be. I'm a blood-born witch. Maybe I could help you."

His scoff made it clear he didn't believe her. And yeah, she didn't blame him. He was a god-knew-how-old demon who'd probably been practicing black magic longer than she could comprehend. She was a smart, powerful witch, but she couldn't match that.

"I already told you that trying to trick me won't work," he said, but she didn't miss the spark of intrigue in his eyes. Like he was enjoying watching her try.

"I'll be honest then," she said. "I'd do pretty much anything to keep from being left in this cell again."

His eyes narrowed, and she thought she might have surprised him with her candor.

"Maybe it's not smart to tell you that, but I need to make it clear that if you think I'm trying to manipulate you, it's only because I'm desperate."

"Why?" He looked around. "It's not that bad. I didn't even chain you up."

She shot him an incredulous look.

He shrugged. "You should see how I treat my other prisoners. Most are chained so tight they can't even lift a finger." A sickening glint lit his eyes, like he got off on that. *Of course he does.* "My most prized prisoner is decapitated regularly so he's constantly using all his energy regrowing his head." His lips curved at her expression of revulsion. "I'd say you have it easy."

"I'm not a demon. If you did that to me, I'd be dead." She gestured to the cell. "This is about as much as a human can take without dying. I need more than a bag of carrots once a week to survive, especially if you want to keep taking my blood."

He frowned, and her heart picked up. She might actually be getting through to him.

If she was going to figure out a way to escape, she needed to get out of this dungeon. There was no other way. In her starvation stupor, she'd come to a realization:

He was the reason she was in here, and he was also going to be the reason she escaped.

She wasn't deluding herself into thinking she could make him feel bad for her, but he had to have a weakness. All she had to do was find it and use it against him.

And she was pretty sure she already knew where to start.

"Look," she said, "I may not know enough about Sheolic magic to be of any help to you, but I do know a thing or two about blood sacrifices. And I know that a blood sacrifice willingly given is twice as powerful as one taken by force."

He stilled. For a moment, he didn't move a muscle. He didn't so much as twitch an eyelid.

She stared at him, heart pounding, willing him to take the bait.

"You want your spell to work," she continued. "I want to go home. Which means *I* want your spell to work, since you already told me you're going to keep me here until it does."

His eyes narrowed.

"Let me out of this cell. Give me free access to food and water and a proper bed. And a shower. Let me wander around your lair and get some exercise. Vow you'll let me go safely back to Earth after this is over. And in return, I'll give you as much of my blood as I safely can, whenever you want. Willingly."

There was no missing the look of intent in those creepy bloodshot eyes. He was actually considering her proposal.

*That's his weakness*. His need to complete his spell, whatever it was for, was his priority above all else. If she wanted something, she just had to convince him it was integral to his plan, and he could be persuaded.

"My lair is swarming with demons," Murmur said. "Many can't even shift into human forms, but even the ones that can are some of the ugliest creatures ever to grace the three realms. What do you think they would do if they found a living human woman wandering the halls, defenseless and alone?"

Okay, maybe she didn't want free reign of his lair after all. "They're your servants. Control them."

"I don't have time for babysitting. Keeping them contained here is enough of a job already."

"Let me stay with you then," she blurted.

His head reared back slightly, and his lip curled. With revulsion.

But that was why she'd suggested it. He spoke of his minions' intentions were they to find her wandering alone, but he obviously didn't share those urges. He had no desire to touch her, or he would have done so already, and he certainly wouldn't be looking at her like she was dog shit he'd accidentally stepped in.

Which suited her just fucking fine. To her, he was dog shit too. And she wanted nothing to do with him either, except perhaps to take a sword, separate his head from his body, and watch him bleed out.

But she had to keep such thoughts to herself. For now.

Murmur smiled suddenly. "You're hoping to convince me to let you out of your cell so you can find a way to catch me unaware. Perhaps you plan to take one of my weapons and incapacitate me. Then you'll wait until the potion I gave you wears off and take a hellgate back to Earth."

She didn't reply. Because yeah, that was exactly her plan.

She supposed it was pretty obvious. Bastard or not, he was obviously smart, and it wasn't a stretch of the imagination that she'd be planning an escape. There was no point denying it, and in fact, she got the sense he'd be more likely to give her what she wanted if she stuck with honesty.

"So what if I am?" she said. "You can't expect me to just sit back and accept my fate."

"Then tell me why you think I should grant your request if your escape plans are so obvious?"

"Because if I denied it, you'd never believe me anyway. And because you know I'm right. A willing blood sacrifice is twice as powerful as one taken by force. What if that's why your spell failed? What if that's all that's needed to make it work? Are you willing to take that chance, just to prove your point by keeping me locked up in this cell?"

His gaze was piercing, his eyes so unnerving, they made her skin crawl. Around him, the dancing shadows of his souls seemed increasingly restless.

Suddenly, he smiled. "All right. I'll bite. Let's bargain, witch."

Triumph filled her. She played it cool. She couldn't let him see how badly she wanted this. "My name is Suyin."

"I don't particularly care."

Well, that was nice.

"You were right to tempt me with your blood willingly offered," he said "You have indeed found something I want enough to be willing to negotiate. So here are my terms. I will provide for your human needs and agree to release you back to Earth when the time is right."

"How long will that be?"

"Who can say?"

She lifted a brow.

"However, time is short," he added. "I believe that if this doesn't happen soon, it won't happen at all. The stakes have never been higher."

She frowned, wondering again what he was up to. He was hardly offering a guarantee that she'd get out of here any time soon, but somehow, she believed he was telling the truth about the time constraint.

At least this way, if she could get out of this cell and have access to sustenance, she wouldn't completely lose her mind before this was all over. Or worse, starve to death.

"You have to let me go . . . *alive*," she added, realizing how careful she needed to be bargaining with a demon. If she let anything slip, he would use it against her, no question of it. "Alive and unharmed, for our entire time together."

His pale lips quirked. "Agreed. I will return you from whence you came in more or less the same condition I found you in."

"More or less?"

His brow cocked. "Perhaps with a pint or two less blood."

"I want out of this cell," she said. "I want somewhere safe where I can move about freely, away from demons. I want fresh air and sunlight, or whatever the equivalent is in Hell. I want a bed and a shower and access to food."

"There is no such place in my lair."

"Then make one. Those are my terms. If you want my blood sacrifice, freely given, you have no choice but to agree."

His eyes narrowed. "I could simply walk away and leave you to rot in this cell for as long as I have to. It would mean nothing to me."

She didn't doubt it for a second. There wasn't an ounce of emotion in those cold eyes. "But then your experiments might never be successful."

He turned his head away with a growl, and her heart raced. She had him. He was going to agree.

"Fine," he snapped, and it took everything she had not to let a victorious grin spread across her face. She pressed her lips together to hide it, but she could tell by the glare he shot her that he knew what she was thinking.

"You can have free reign of the empty floor below mine, in my tower. But you will not disturb me in my work unless I call for you, and if you value your life, you will not go wandering through the rest of the lair."

"Deal," she said easily. She had no intention of spending a second longer than necessary in his or any other demon's company.

"You will not attempt to escape, by hellgate or other means. You will not try to reach out to anyone for help. You will not attempt to harm me or betray our bargain. You will cooperate with me whenever I require your participation in my work."

She cursed mentally. He was careful, all right. With all those stipulations, he'd just obliterated all her potential plans of escape. She couldn't even *try*, and she definitely couldn't gut him with his own knife just to watch him bleed. If she agreed, she would be stuck here for as long as he wanted her.

But . . . she would be able to return home safely at the end. She would have access to food and water. She wouldn't have to rot in this dungeon, from which she had no hope of escape anyway.

In the end, there was only one choice.

"Fine," she said. "But you have to let me tell my friends and coven I'm okay."

"No."

"At least let me send a message—"

"No. On that, I will not be swayed."

She gritted her teeth. Her hopes hadn't been high, but it still pissed her off. "Fine. But you'll let the potion that blocks my magic wear off, and you won't give me more. I'm a witch. I want to practice while I'm here. Even if I can't use it to escape, I still want to use my time wisely."

"Agreed," he said more readily than she'd expected. She supposed it made sense they could relate in that, since he was obviously obsessed with his own spells and practice. One didn't earn a title like *the* Necromancer for nothing.

"And if something goes wrong with your spell," she added, "or it permanently fails, or something unexpected happens to you or your lair, then I'm free to leave."

If she wasn't mistaken, she swore she saw a flicker of approval in his gaze. Apparently, he was enjoying their negotiations. "If I give you permission to go, then you may go. Remember, your blood has value to me. If there's any chance of you being killed or seriously injured, I will take steps to prevent it."

She ground her teeth. "And what happens if your spell permanently fails?"

"It will not. But if it does, you're free to go."

"Fine," she said, because why not. She'd already come this far. None of his conditions were worth rotting in solitary confinement underground for.

"Lastly," he said, "when I do give you leave to return to Earth—unharmed, as agreed—you will never speak of my experiments or why you were taken to anyone. Even indirectly, by hints, symbolism, or inference."

"What am I supposed to tell people then?"

He shrugged lightly. "Be creative."

"Fine. But people are going to think I fucking died."

He looked blandly at her.

She shook her head. Obviously, he didn't care.

"Shall we swear in blood?" He lifted a hand, and she couldn't help swallowing at the sight of those long black claws.

She nodded and then flinched as he gouged them into his own palm. Blood welled and he didn't so much as blink.

"On my blood, I vow it," he said, speaking the simple yet powerful words of a binding blood contract.

Once they both swore, neither of them would be capable of breaking the terms they'd agreed upon. If he tried to kill her, he would find himself unable to strike the blow. If she tried to tell anyone about him, the words would stick in her throat.

He pulled a rag from his coat pocket and clenched it in his fist to soak up the remaining blood. Like he'd done this a thousand times. She supposed he had. Then he reached across the cell, holding out his other hand.

Swallowing, she stretched out her palm. She expected him to gouge her with his claws the same way he'd done to himself, but instead, he used the dagger to carefully prick the tip of her finger. A single drop of blood welled around the blade.

She frowned at him.

"I told you I wouldn't waste your blood," he said. "Now speak your vow, and let's be done with it. I have work to do."

She did, and he released her hand, wiping the dagger on the rag. He climbed to his feet and sheathed the weapon at his hip. Fuck, she'd forgotten how tall he was. He positively towered over her.

Without another word, he spun and stalked out of the cell, leaving her to scramble wearily to her feet and hurry after him or get left behind. Maybe she had to put her revenge escape plans to rest for now, but at least she was getting out of this dungeon.

# 8

# Room with a View

To her surprise, Murmur removed his coat and gave it to Suyin to wear as a disguise, before hustling her through his lair like she was escaping the paparazzi. Which she kind of was, considering she was a living mortal in Hell—not something demons saw every day.

The coat was so large on her, it swept the floor, and the oversized hood completely covered her face. She wrapped the massive thing around her like a blanket, surprised at the softness of the heavy black leather.

She cradled her bags of apples and carrots and the remaining two water bottles like the precious cargo they were, and she tried to keep up with Murmur's long strides without stumbling. Sure, she'd eaten and had some water, but she was going to need more than that to get back to full strength.

She was dimly aware of following Murmur down a long underground tunnel, climbing a winding rough-hewn staircase, and then passing through a high-ceilinged hall. Any time they crossed paths with other demons, all of varying shapes and sizes, the creatures folded nearly in half, chanting "Master" until they were out of sight. With their noses practically hitting the ground, it made it easy for Suyin to go unnoticed.

Murmur ignored them entirely. Either he wasn't into bowing and scraping, or he was just as coldly indifferent to his servants as he was to her. The notion was oddly reassuring. At least she wasn't the only one on the receiving end of that empty stare.

At the end of a long pillared hallway, they passed two sentries and began to climb another staircase that spiraled upward in wide circles. Creepy statues decorated the entranceways to the different levels, but Suyin barely noticed them. She was just trying to keep from falling on her ass. Or worse, into the enormous hole in the center of the stairwell. There was no railing, just a straight drop to the bottom.

She supposed for a winged demon, it would be a convenient way to ascend or descend the levels, and it had probably been designed that way on purpose. Then she glanced at Murmur's tall back in front of her.

He wore a loose shirt, and his long white hair was braided into a thick rope. Surely he had wings. Why climb the stairs then? He could have carried her easily.

She would have fought him tooth and nail though, and she figured that was probably the reason. She was exhausted, and though a part of her would have given anything not to have to walk, another part of her relished that tiny victory.

Making this demon's life worse than the hell he lived in was her new primary objective.

After several levels, the adjoining floors ended, and they continued climbing stairs around and around, suggesting that they were entering a freestanding tower of considerable height. Her entire focus narrowed to lifting one foot and placing it on the next step and then repeating the action on the other side.

She refused to show Murmur even an ounce of weakness. That alone gave her the strength to climb the rest of the way up.

Eventually, she saw a ceiling overhead and knew they were close to the top. The staircase passed through a hole to a landing with a single wooden door on the left. There was a statue of a centipede monster across from it, set into a small alcove in the stone. The steps continued ahead, but unlike the open stairs below with the death drop, these were enclosed behind the walls of the level they now stood on.

Murmur had stopped on the landing and was waiting for her to catch up. As she did, he frowned at her sweaty, flushed face like he didn't have a clue what was wrong with her. *Bastard.*

He unlatched the door, stepping into a short hall, and she followed him through. The tunnels underground had been low-ceilinged, and he'd had to stoop to keep from hitting his horns on the rock overhead. But here in the tower, everything was built for someone his size, which of course made Suyin feel positively miniature.

There were entrances on each of the three walls, and Murmur led her toward the one at the end. She was running on pure adrenaline at this point, and she could honestly say she'd never explored a castle in Hell before, so it was interesting enough to keep her awake. Everything was dusty and smelled faintly rotten. Like something had died here a while ago, leaving a putrid stench of decay permanently soiling the air.

She scrunched her nose up against the foul smell.

"These will be your quarters," Murmur said.

"Why does it smell like something died?"

"It's dust. I keep this level empty, and it doesn't get much use."

"It smells like death."

"You're in Hell. Everything smells like death." He pushed open the door. "Here's the bedroom. The other doors lead to the bathroom and study. Fresh water will be brought to you for bathing every day by the same demons who bring it for me."

She barely heard him. She was staring at the bed. It was a queen-sized mattress with a fresh duvet and sheets. "Where did you get this bed?"

Murmur looked at her like she was stupid. "What do you mean?"

"I mean. This is Hell. That bed looks fresh out of a hotel."

"Earth is just a hellgate away. And for demons who don't want to break the rules by visiting without sanction, anything one needs can be purchased at the Blood Market."

The *Blood* Market. Not the black market. How positively hellish.

"But the bedding looks clean."

"And?" He looked irritated now.

"You said the floor was deserted."

"My servants keep the linens fresh. Just because no one is staying here presently doesn't mean I'm going to leave everything to rot. Just because I'm a demon doesn't mean I live primitively or enjoy groveling in filth." He shot her a disgusted look, like he was insulted by her mere presence. "For a witch, I would have expected you to be less ignorant."

She matched his glare. "I was smart enough to keep away from demons, so forgive me if this comes as a surprise."

He rolled his eyes. "Get settled. I have work to do. You may use anything you find here, but you are not to go to the top floor."

She wandered over to the bedroom window and peered out, eyes widening at the view. They were at the top of the tallest point of the castle. The black-stone structure, which looked like something out of a nightmare, was surrounded by a high stone wall topped with spikes. A decrepit village surrounded the castle and lined the inside of the walls, and she could see the tiny shapes of demons milling about. In the distance, red, cracked plains reached the bases of tall craggy mountains.

There wasn't a drop of vegetation as far as the eye could see. The sky was red. *Red.*

She really was in Hell. It boggled the mind.

"Is that clear?"

She turned back. Murmur stood by the door all high and mighty with one eyebrow raised. He'd really mastered the sass, hadn't he?

"Don't disturb you. Got it." She added under her breath, "As if I'd want to."

"Do not enter the top floor under any circumstances, unless I explicitly permit it."

"I think you overestimate the pleasure of your company," she replied with a sneer. "I have no desire to spend any more time in your presence than necessary."

"Then we are in accordance. Now give me back my coat."

She was still wrapped in the thing like it was her favorite comfort blanket, wasn't she? Scowling, she set her cargo on the bed, removed the heavy coat, and held it out to him.

But he was all the way across the room.

He stayed where he was, holding out one of his creepy long-fingered hands and gesturing for her to cross the room and give it to him.

She didn't move.

His eyes narrowed. She set her jaw.

It was a battle of wills. Neither of them wanted to be the first to give in. Well, it certainly wasn't going to be her. He'd captured and half starved her; she wasn't going to make things easy for him.

"Give me the coat, Suyin." His voice was low. Full of warning.

"Come and get it," she replied, holding his stare. So what if her palms were sweating?

They glared at each other.

And then . . . he smiled. The chilling curve in the corners of his mouth caught her off guard, and she suddenly got the feeling he'd just changed the rules of their game. And she wasn't sure she wanted to play anymore.

But it was too late to back down, and her pride wouldn't let her anyway.

The smoke that danced at his feet began to churn with increased agitation. She swallowed. The shapes rose higher and seemed to thicken. Or . . . solidify.

And then the ghostly mass began to move. It crept across the floor, and she swore she saw the faint outline of hands, clawing their way across the wood planks, dragging their ethereal bodies toward her.

A wave of chills swept down her spine. The temperature felt like it had dropped several degrees.

Before her, a column of smoke rose from the floor, higher and higher, until the roiling black mass was equal to her height.

From the hazy gloom, a shape formed. Shoulders. A head. A . . . face. Sunken eye sockets, hollow cheekbones, strips of flesh hanging from an empty skull, rotted lips giving way to a mouth full of blackened teeth.

The specter stretched out a skeletal hand. Long bones, spindly fingers, decaying flesh clinging to it like cobwebs. It reached toward her. Closer, closer . . .

The hand curled around the coat still dangling in her trembling grip.

Instantly, she released the garment. Her blood felt like ice in her veins. The specter tightened its grasp on the fabric and actually *held* it. A ghost was holding onto a solid coat.

She watched the spirit drift back across the bedroom floor toward its master. The master who was giving it the power to do this and controlling its actions at the same time.

Murmur curled his fingers around the coat once it was within his reach. He shook it out and donned it, and the specter dissolved back into smoke. The dead face vanished, and all that remained were the faint churning wisps at Murmur's feet.

With a flash of that cold smile, Murmur spun and swept out of the room, coat billowing behind him. The last she saw of him was the tip of his barbed tail.

Alone, she stood frozen in place for several minutes, her heart pounding so hard she was amazed she hadn't passed out. She couldn't help but think, with an entire army of souls like that, he was essentially impossible to defeat. How could someone fight a ghost?

It certainly threw her own revenge goals for a loop. Not that she could do anything with the stupid vow binding her. But she'd still wanted to pretend, damn it, and that little display had pretty much ruined the fantasy.

Yet another reason to hate him.

She looked around her new quarters. The room was surprisingly comfortable and not at all what she'd expected, considering she was in Hell. But then, what did she really know about the underworld? Not all demons were mindlessly evil—some were cunningly evil, apparently—and it made sense that they would've found ways to acquire comforts from Earth.

She was too tired to care about it now, however. Unzipping and kicking off her boots, she pulled off her socks, pants, and jacket, leaving only her underwear and T-shirt on. She was dying to wash, but there was no way she was doing anything until she napped for a bit.

Moving her precious food to the small bedside table, she climbed into the bed and passed out in seconds.

Suyin awoke after a "nap" that had turned into a full night's sleep, her stomach gnawing with hunger. Apparently, a single apple and carrot didn't do much to quell one's appetite after starving for multiple days. Outside, the red sky seemed darker than it had before her rest.

She sat up in bed, grabbing a water bottle off the nightstand and drinking half of it in three swallows. Then she ate two apples and a carrot before her stomach declared that it wouldn't let her eat anything else acidic. In fact, she had to lay back down again and wait for the burning to stop.

While she lay there, she got good and pissed at Murmur, remembering that, in their bargain, he'd promised to feed her. Well, what she had wasn't going to cut it, and if he wanted her to stay put and shut up, he needed to cooperate too.

Once her stomach had calmed down, she got out of bed, all fired up to go upstairs and disturb Murmur, just like he'd told her not to, until he got her some more food. Some actual food.

She was halfway through getting dressed, stabbing her legs into her pants, when she noticed the pile across the room on the vanity.

She yanked her pants the rest of the way up and went to inspect. Fresh produce and colorful packaging in Hell looked no less bizarre than before, but she'd never been happier to see a loaf of bread.

There was a selection of veggies, sandwich materials, tortilla wraps, and more fruit. There was also a flat of water bottles. She wasn't going to find any typical comfort foods, but she didn't care. She didn't drink caffeine, and she didn't like sugar. Iris often joked that she was concerned for the sanity of anyone who didn't like chocolate or ice cream, but Suyin had always hated the syrupy taste of sweets.

She remembered Murmur mentioning that he had servants who would bring water and clean sheets, and she figured he'd also had them bring her food. She smiled evilly, imagining that prideful prick being forced to accommodate her human needs and send his servants on special missions on her behalf.

Good. She wished she were more high maintenance. Maybe

she should have him bring her entire makeup kit. She felt exposed without her eyeliner and dark lipstick.

But if his servants had dropped by while she was asleep—she tried not to be creeped out by the thought of demons sneaking around her while she was unconscious—that meant there might be fresh water to bathe. And that was worth investigating.

Sure enough, when she stepped into the hall and tried the first door, she found a bathroom with a stack of fresh towels and a big tub of steaming water. It wasn't quite bath sized, but she wasn't complaining.

Almost frantically, she stripped her clothes off and sank into the hot water, letting it soothe her aches and pains from days spent in the dungeon cell. She found a bar of soap and a comb, and she swore never to take such things for granted again. After washing her hair and scrubbing the remainder of her makeup from her face, she relaxed in the tub until it got cold. It wasn't like she had anything else to do.

When she got out, she used the soap and bathwater to scrub her filthy clothes, hanging them to dry over the edge of the tub and bathroom vanity. Then she tucked one of the towels tightly around her middle and decided to explore her new-and-improved prison cell.

Through the last door in the hall, she found a study with a fireplace, though all the furniture had been covered in white sheets. She busied herself pulling them off. Beneath the coverings, she found a sturdy desk built for a Murmur-sized demon, an equally large chair, and a claw-foot sofa and two armchairs facing the fireplace. Bookshelves were built into the walls, but they were all empty.

Once she'd made the room as homey as she could, the boredom set in. She dropped onto the sofa and stared at the fireplace's empty grate, shivering in her towel. The damn demon couldn't have left a single book on the shelves for her to read? She yawned and then figured she had nothing better to do besides sleep off her ordeal in the dungeon, so she went back to the bedroom, ate a light dinner, and went to bed.

When she awoke, the sky was dark. Not black, but it had deepened to a burgundy red the shade of dried blood. Which made no sense. She was sure she'd slept for at least eight hours, and she'd been awake for several before that. Shouldn't the sky be lightening?

There was no sun or moon or stars, making it impossible for her to track the passage of time the usual way. Combined with being stuck underground for what she presumed was several days, she was majorly confused.

It felt like time wasn't passing at all. Like she was living a waking dream, where things moved at both a snail's pace and break-neck speed at the same time.

She thought about the red plains and distant mountains and wondered if all of Hell had a similar landscape, or if there were forests and oceans like on Earth. She had to admit that the underworld didn't seem overly terrible. She was under no delusions about the vileness of demons, but as long as she kept away from them, she didn't think she'd mind exploring a little.

How many people could say they'd been to Hell and lived to tell the tale? Humans were terrified of the idea of Hell and demons. And in her mind, the best way to conquer a fear was to face it head-on.

After eating a surprisingly delicious wrap for breakfast, she found another fresh bath of hot water. She had to wonder how a demon hauled buckets of piping hot water up the tall tower, but then figured that was what minions were for. If she were a demon master with little servants, she'd have commanded them to bring her fresh water every day as well. Hell, she'd command them to go to plumbing school and rig up some state-of-the art pipes.

After her bath, she checked her clothes. They were dry,

thank god, so she dressed, and then went to the sitting room, sat on the couch, and stared at the empty fireplace.

With every passing hour, her boredom grew, and her curiosity grew with it. For a time, she lost herself in plotting idle revenge schemes and escape plans that wouldn't work because of their stupid vow.

Then she started to obsess over what Murmur was hiding upstairs.

He'd forbidden her from going up there, which meant there was something he didn't want her to see. Which, of course, meant she needed to see it. She'd always been hungry for knowledge and persistent to a fault. Once she got an idea, she fixated on it with single-minded purpose, to the detriment of all else.

Maybe whatever was up there could help her find a loophole in their bargain so she could escape. And maybe—and she hated the way this took precedence in her mind—she could find answers about Murmur's spell.

She wouldn't know until she looked.

# 9

# At Death's Door

Suyin's heart lodged in her throat as she climbed the dark staircase, sliding a hand up the wall beside her. The creepy centipede-monster statue outside her rooms had seemed like an ill omen, warning her that this was a terrible idea, but she'd ignored it.

Her footsteps were light, but they seemed amplified in the tight space. It was probably in her head, but damn it, it was nerve-racking.

At the top of the stairs, she stepped onto a narrow landing and found two looming double doors to her left. A simple latch held them shut. There was no lock or ward to pass through.

Apparently, Murmur really wasn't afraid of his people disobeying his orders. After all that bowing and scraping, she supposed it wasn't a big surprise. They obviously feared him, and now that she'd seen what his creepy souls could do, she didn't blame them.

She tried not to think about what he'd do to her when he found her. Because he was going to find her—she wasn't delusional enough to think otherwise. This was his domain. She

was only hoping to learn something about his plans for her before she got caught. And she was willing to risk it because she knew he wouldn't hurt her and risk wasting her precious blood.

Self-preservation had never been her strong suit. Or maybe she'd stopped giving a fuck when she turned fifty.

She lifted the latch and slipped through the smallest crack possible. Inside, she pulled the door shut behind her and then waited in the darkness. After a moment of silent breathing, nothing jumped out at her and no furious demon came charging out to punish her, and she relaxed. Infinitesimally.

Before her was a short hallway with a high ceiling. There were two sets of double doors, one at the end, straight ahead, and the other halfway down on the right.

The question was . . . which one to choose?

She tiptoed down the hall, relishing the fear for the punch of life it gave her. After rotting in that dungeon for days, it felt good to get her blood pumping again.

She stopped in front of the first set of doors. Staring at them, her heart raced, and they seemed to grow larger before her eyes. Something behind them called to her, and before she knew what she was doing, she'd reached out and curled her fingers around the handle—

She snatched her hand back.

Maybe her sense of self-preservation wasn't high, but she knew better than to blindly obey random compulsions, especially in Hell. She had a sneaking suspicion that whatever was behind there wouldn't be good for her health.

And there was still the second set of doors.

She stepped back from temptation and continued down the hall. When she reached the end, she opened the latch as carefully as she had the first. Whisper quiet, the doors seemed to glide open of their own accord.

And then she saw the library.

Her eyes widened and her mouth fell open. Staring in awe, she stepped inside and stood transfixed before the most incredible collection of books she'd ever beheld.

It was a witch's utopia. Heaven in the midst of Hell.

The outer walls of the crescent-shaped room were lined with floor-to-ceiling shelves. The roof was vaulted, pointed to the tip of the tower, which meant the shelves went so high up, they almost disappeared into blackness. Tall ladders on wheels were affixed to each section to make the highest levels accessible.

All the books were grimoires. She could tell by the Sheolic symbols and letters embossed on their tattered spines. She was standing in what had to be the largest collection of spell books on Earth or in Hell. It was an incredible sight to behold, and she stood rooted to the spot for several minutes just taking it all in.

Straight ahead, there was a gap in the shelves for a tall window, but the glass was so filthy and covered in cobwebs, it was almost impossible to see through. A fireplace faced it on the opposite side near the doors, and the glowing coals in the hearth told her the library had been recently occupied. The red sky was still dark, and the only source of light came from lanterns set periodically throughout the room.

Forget avoiding Sheolic magic. She wanted to uncover the secrets every one of these books contained, black magic or not.

The little wall space that wasn't covered in bookshelves was occupied by messy sigil sketches drawn directly onto the stone. Any gaps between books on the shelves were filled by jars of what appeared to be organs and small animals suspended in fluid, and there were bunches of dried herbs tied with string hanging wherever they could fit.

To the far left and right were two large worktables, and a desk stood underneath the grimy window. Every surface was covered in books and loose papers, which spilled over the edges and were strewn across the dark floorboards. Beside the desk, a hellgate was drawn on the ground, but the outside line had been disrupted to render it inactive.

The very center of the library was arguably the most mind-boggling sight of all.

There, a space had been cleared in the chaotic mess for the strangest, most complex sigil Suyin had ever seen. Once her gaze caught upon it, it was impossible to look anywhere else, even at the grimoire collection. She crept toward it, drawn by some unseen force, similar to how she'd felt standing outside the other door.

When she reached the edge, she crouched to look closer at the symbols. She didn't recognize any of them. This wasn't regular Sheolic magic. It had to be necromancy.

It was obviously an incredibly complicated sigil that required a high level of comprehension and skill to activate. She peered closer at the intricate lines, marveling at the expertise and care that went into them. They had been laid out in chalk and then painted over with a blackish substance she was sure was dried blood.

In the center of the sigil, there was a large empty circle, around which were more designs that appeared to have been scorched, blackening the surrounding floor. As if the lines themselves had burst into flame.

This had to be what Murmur was working on, the reason he wanted her blood. But what was the sigil's purpose?

She rose from her crouch and scanned the library again, searching for any kind of clue to the purpose of his spell. The sheer quantity of books continued to overwhelm her. She could spend months just exploring the room, looking at all the different titles and figuring out how they were organized, without actually reading anything.

Forget being bored. She would never run out of things to do with access to a place like this.

The desk by the window caught her eye again, so she wandered over to it, careful to walk around the outside line of the big sigil. She knew better than to step into an unknown spell, even one she was pretty sure was inactive.

The papers on the desk were covered in messy sketches, re-creations of what appeared to be sections of the sigil on the floor, and handwriting so messy it was illegible. Carefully, she sorted through the loose sheets, her curiosity burning.

As she moved a stack of papers aside, she uncovered a book that lay open. Only a small corner of one page was revealed, but it was enough.

She recognized it instantly. She'd studied that very same page many times.

Heart pounding, she moved aside the rest of the pages. And there it was. Just as she'd suspected but hadn't known for sure.

*The Book of Gamigin.* The book that had been stolen by a demon. *This* demon. Murmur had stolen her book, and then he'd stolen her.

She lifted her head and stared at the big sigil again. *What do I have to do with all this? Why me?*

Turning back to the grimoire, she began flipping carefully through the pages. At this point, she knew it like the back of her hand, but maybe there was something that Marie had missed in the scan, something she hadn't seen in her studies of it in the past, something that would give her some clue as to what—

"What part of 'do not enter the top floor under any circumstances' didn't you understand?"

Her head snapped up at the sound of a familiar gruff voice. A gruff, *furious* voice.

Murmur stood across the room, leaning against the closed doors, arms crossed. At his feet, the smoky cloud of souls churned with agitation.

His snow-white hair spilled over his shoulders and down his chest like an icy waterfall, his tall black horns rising proudly above. He wore a long black robe belted loosely at the hips. It parted at the center, exposing a strip of pale skin that contrasted sharply against the dark fabric.

It was a casual pose, but only a fool would miss the waves of menace rolling off him.

How long had he been there? Long enough, she supposed. And there was no pretending she hadn't been snooping.

She threw caution to the wind. She'd come this far; there was no point backing down now. "Why did you steal my grimoire?"

He didn't respond. Instead, he pushed off the wall and prowled across the room toward her. His steps were light, noiseless. No wonder she hadn't heard him come in.

Instinct had her shrinking back toward the window. Somewhere in her mind, she was frustrated by her show of fear, but a greater part of her recognized the danger this unhinged demon presented and warned her to tread carefully.

He came around from the side like he was intentionally herding her, trapping her with her back against the table. He didn't stop until he stood so close, she had to crane her neck just to see his face. The souls at his feet engulfed hers as well, and she fought back panic at their frigid caress. His proximity was bad enough without actual ghosts touching her.

"Give me one good reason why I shouldn't tie you up and throw you back in the dungeon right now."

When she didn't respond, he leaned forward, using his height to loom over her. The closer he came, the farther she leaned back, arching her spine painfully. He leaned farther still, propping his hands on the desk on either side of her.

She couldn't move. If she went any farther, she'd end up completely lying on the table, and she refused to take such a submissive position. Her spine protested at the crunch in her lower back, but if she straightened, she would bump into his chest.

A chest that rose and fell with steady breaths. A chest that was the same pale gray as his face and defined with lean muscle. Shadows clung to the indents above his collarbones and the line of his sternum.

She gathered her courage and dragged her gaze up to his. The skin around his eyes was darker than ever. His face was so gaunt, she could see the clear lines of his cheekbones. It was hard to think with him so close, blocking out what little light there was in the dusty library.

"Why do you need my blood?" she heard herself ask.

He stared at her, bloodshot eyes narrowing to slits. Time stretched. Every beat of her heart thudded in her ears.

"For a spell."

*No shit, Sherlock*. She was surprised he'd even answered. "What does the spell do?"

His head jerked infinitesimally toward the sigil on the floor. His tall horns exaggerated the movement. "You had a chance to study it for yourself. You couldn't decipher it?"

She noted the challenge in his bloodshot eyes. He wanted her to be clueless and stupid, she realized. Then he would be able to dismiss her. But she wasn't going to make any of this easy for him, not if she could help it.

"Knowing who you are and that it requires a blood sacrifice," she said, "it's likely necromancy. The lines are drawn in blood and chalk. That means they need extra fortification to keep from breaking, which implies there's strong resistance against whatever you're trying to do. The inner part of the sigil has burned away completely, suggesting hellfire was conjured in the process. Knowing that, if I had to guess . . ." Fuck, she was just spitballing here. In truth, she didn't have a clue, but she wasn't about to tell him that. "I'd say you're either trying to break a very powerful seal or create one."

His head tilted, locks of shiny white hair sliding over his shoulder. His lips drew together, but he didn't look displeased. More . . . curious?

He was difficult to read. It was hard enough to see past his unnerving eyes and the black shadows around them set into that pale face. And she couldn't think with him so close.

"So?" She forced her voice to remain level. "Am I right?"

"Which is it?" he asked. "Am I breaking or creating a seal?"

Her eyes narrowed. He genuinely wanted her to guess. And while a part of her wanted to tell him to go fuck himself and then see if she could reach up far enough to gouge his eyes out, another part wanted to prove to him that she wasn't the helpless little mortal he thought she was.

"Breaking," she decided. "You're trying to break a seal."

"Hm."

Her brows rose in expectation of a confirmation of her guess.

He smiled thinly. "I guess you'll never know."

*Dick*. She ground her teeth. "What do you want with me? Why do you have my grimoire?"

Ignoring her questions, he pushed off the desk suddenly and stepped back, and it was like all the air returned to the room. She sucked in a greedy breath and straightened out of her painful backbend.

Now that he'd given her space, she was pissed off at how much she'd lost composure. But that had been exactly his intent, hadn't it? He'd wanted to remind her that she was still afraid of him, and he'd succeeded. *Bastard. Prick. Asshole.*

"I specifically told you not to come up here," he said, staring at the sigil on the floor.

She said nothing. She had no way to justify herself. She'd known she would get caught too, but she hadn't planned out what to do once that happened.

"No one is allowed here." His voice was a low growl. "Those that disobeyed me in the past ended up on the tower spikes. As far as I know they're still there."

His head swung around, and he pinned her with a sharp look. He saw her confusion and jerked his chin toward the window.

Obeying his silent command, she unglued her rear end from the edge of the desk and took careful steps toward the dusty glass.

Pulling her jacket sleeve down, she smudged a tiny peep hole into the filth and then peered through the window. Outside she saw the black-blood sky and the shapes of distant mountains. She also had a clear view of the rest of the castle. There were several more towers, all lower than the one they were in. The tops were sharp spires. Atop those spires were bodies.

Demons had been impaled through their midsections and stacked on top of one another like a grizzly shish kebab.

She jerked back to stare at him in horror.

And he smiled.

Of course he did.

He was fucking disturbed. He had a torture dungeon and an army of dead humans enslaved to him. He impaled demons on his towers and had the audacity to smile about it. He'd left her to starve in a cell and only bothered to let her out because he needed her blood and didn't want her to die. Not only did he not care about her wellbeing, he got off on terrorizing her.

He was the enemy. He would not show mercy unless she forced him to. She had the distinct impression that he would seize any chance to betray those not careful to protect themselves in negotiations, simply because he could.

If she was going to survive this, she needed to be very careful.

"So?" That dark eyebrow arched again. "What's your excuse? Why shouldn't I treat you like every other person who disobeys me?" When she still didn't speak, he added, "Now would be a good time to beg."

His eyes burned with challenge. The corners of his mouth curved, like he was anticipating her groveling.

Instead she said, "How much more powerful would that spell be if I stood beside you while you cast it with my blood coming straight from the source?"

His smile dropped.

The silence was so charged, she swore she heard the crackle of energy.

"You have some nerve," he snarled, and he came toward her again.

She didn't move, though every instinct in her body screamed at her to run. She waited for his approach, expecting him to loom over her again. But he took it a step further.

This time, his cold hand curled around her throat. His touch was even icier than the specters brushing against her legs. He tightened his grip until she couldn't draw a full breath, the tiny bursts of air making her heart flutter with panic.

He stooped until they were at eye level.

"You're still trying to manipulate me. That makes you very brave or very stupid. Or both."

"I . . . can . . . help you," she wheezed through her constricted windpipe. His hand sent chills racing through her blood.

"How could *you* possibly be of service to me?" His pale eyes roved down her body like he was disgusted by the sight of her.

But he loosened his grip ever so slightly.

"I'll help you cast," she said quickly. Her voice was hoarse from being strangled. *Fucking zombie freak piece of shit.* She pictured stabbing a dagger straight into his skull. "I'll not only give my blood willingly, but I'll let you take it as it comes from my veins. I'll help you prepare. I'll do whatever you want."

His brow arched, and she realized he was waiting for her to tell him what she wanted in exchange. Because in his world, nothing was ever given freely. There was no such thing as generosity to a creature like him.

"In return . . . I want access to this library."

"No."

"I won't damage anything. I won't take anything. I just want to study."

His eyes narrowed. "Why?"

"Are you kidding?" Suddenly, she didn't care about the fact that the hand curled around her throat could snap her neck if he simply flexed his fingers. "I want to learn. I want knowledge, and I can't begin to imagine how much information is here. If I'm going to be stuck in Hell until you figure out your stupid spell, I might as well do something useful with my time."

He searched her gaze, eyes narrowed with suspicion. But he was actually considering her proposal, she realized, and her heart raced with anticipation.

She was well aware that if he gave her what she wanted, it wouldn't help her escape any faster. But until she came up with a better plan, she was trapped, and she wasn't going to pass up the opportunity to explore this library. She might never get a chance like this again in her life.

He straightened suddenly, releasing her throat. She sucked in a hungry breath. They stared at each other for a moment, and then he spun and stalked away, heading toward the door.

She expected him to leave without responding, but at the last second he turned back, looking over his shoulder. His tail flicked restlessly behind him. His souls churned at his feet like agitated smoke. She had to admit he was impressive, with that streaming head of white hair and those towering horns.

"You will not move anything from its original place. You will not damage anything—not so much as a creased spine or crumpled page. You will not interrupt or interfere with my work in any way. You will not look at or touch anything on my desk. And you will not enter the other room in the hall."

She nodded eagerly, scarcely believing her luck.

"And this time, if you disobey me, I will throw you back in that dungeon so fast, you won't have time to beg for mercy. There will be no provisions brought to you from Earth. There will be no special exceptions made. You'll be treated like any other of my prisoners, chained spread-eagled to the wall, hanging by your wrists. Do you understand?"

"Perfectly," she croaked.

He turned once more and made to leave. Just as his hand curled around the handle, she thought of one more way to push her luck.

"Wait."

He paused again, hand on the door handle, but he didn't turn back this time. He was pissed; she could tell by the tightening of his shoulders and the agitated swirling of his souls. But she soldiered on regardless.

"I need clothes. I can't be expected to wear the same outfit every day. I need to wash my clothes, and I have nothing to wear while they're drying."

He turned his head enough for her to see his straight nose in profile. She swore she could *see* his jaw grinding.

"And I'm going to run out of food and water soon. I'll need more."

"You don't *need* either of those things. Your ignorance has caused you to believe so strongly in human weaknesses that you manifested them."

She stared at his back. *What the hell does that mean?* Was he telling her she wasn't human? That was ridiculous. Absurd.

And yet . . . she was fifty years old and hadn't aged in

twenty-five years. She healed from wounds in hours instead of days. She was twice as strong as everyone else her size. She'd always assumed it was a highly unusual manifestation of a blood-born witch ability, but what if it was something else?

Could she really survive without food and water? And if she wasn't human . . .

Then what the hell was she?

Before she could ask Murmur, however, he pulled open the door and disappeared through it with a slam.

Alone, she looked around the goldmine of a library to which she now had unfettered access, her mind racing a mile a minute. Maybe, just maybe, the answers she sought about herself could be found here. And if not in a book, then in the mind of her captor.

Once again, her plans shifted.

She still wanted to kill him, still would visualize doing horrifically violent things to him on an hourly basis, but . . . he couldn't die. Not yet, at least. Not until he revealed everything he knew about her. Why she had these abilities. Who she was.

*What* she was.

He had answers. And she was going to do whatever it took to get them.

# 10

# Hell's Bel

"Don't eat that," Belial said, focusing on the knife in his hand as he chopped onions.

Meph ignored his warning, snagging another pinch of the parmesan Bel had just finished grating while continuing his endless chatter. Bel's brothers and their girlfriends had all decided to come over and keep him company because they were worried about him being alone in his big house.

They hadn't actually said that outright, because Bel would have killed them. But he knew what they were thinking, and it pissed him off.

Mist and Lily had gone to Ireland a few weeks ago, so at least they weren't around to add to the chaos. Although Mist was one of a very short list of people Belial allowed to help in the kitchen—because he actually *helped* and didn't just eat everything and make a mess—so maybe that wasn't such a good thing after all.

The rest of their dysfunctional family was outside on the patio, laughing and talking and making a whole lot of obnoxious noise. But at least they knew when to take a hint and give him some space—the whole reason he was in the kitchen right now.

"I'm just saying," Meph continued, "Iris's lease is up, and we need a place to live, and you've got like five spare rooms and a suite. It's a big fucking house, and you could use the company. I know I'd be bored shitless living here all alone. The silence would feel like it's pressing on my ears."

*You wouldn't know silence if it bit you in the ass*, Bel thought, grinding his teeth so hard his jaw cracked. His brother excelled at filling every possible silence with noise. If silence was golden, then Meph was a pauper. And there was no way in hell he was moving in here.

"Did you at least install some good speakers? If you had music playing, it'd probably make it feel less depressing in here." Meph snagged another pinch of grated parmesan, tattooed fingers reaching into Bel's workspace and disturbing his neat piles of precisely measured food prep. "At least in Hell, your lairs were never empty like this."

"Stop eating that," Bel growled.

Meph's fingers left a dent in the cheese gratings as he dropped the mouthful of parmesan in his mouth. "Back then, you had me and Raum to fuck shit up and keep things exciting. And then Ash was always lurking around too, though he wasn't much fun back then, always moping about his curse. But you had all your groveling legions trying to go to war for you, and all the demon ladies showing up to join your harem. Man, those were the days, huh?"

"Stop eating that," Bel warned yet again as Meph reached for more cheese.

"I mean, damn, you went from biggest badass in Hell to grumpy old chef in his lonely mansion. Kind of a demotion if you ask me. We need to get you a—"

"I said STOP EATING THAT!" Belial roared, and just like that, he snapped.

His knife slammed down onto Meph's hand, and then he burst into flames. Hellfire, to be precise.

As his world transformed into a roaring inferno, he distantly heard Meph shout, "Motherfucker!"

There was blood. There was fire. And there was rage. So much rage.

He was going to use that rage to burn down the fucking world. He was going to exterminate the stain that was humanity, end the pathetic race of struggling mortals. He was going to kill his brother. He was going to kill everything until nothing remained but blood and bones. And as every soul breathed their last breath, they would die knowing *he* had delivered their deaths. They would bow before him in subservience and fear as they bled out from their throats and watched their own bodies burn into—

A splash of ice-cold water hit him in the face.

Bel blinked and found himself back in his kitchen, still clutching a knife in one hand. Raum stood in front of him with an empty mop bucket that had contained the water he'd just thrown. A *mop* bucket.

But that wasn't the worst part. Oh no.

Meph was cursing him to Hell and back and cradling his hand to his chest, blood streaming all over his arm. Iris was beside him, screaming and swearing in tears and panic. Ash, Eva, and Sunshine hovered around.

It was a goddamn party.

And there were three tattooed fingers sitting in the middle of the parmesan cheese. Cheese that had turned red with Meph's blood when Bel had, apparently, chopped his brother's fingers clean off.

"Fuck," he breathed, staring at Meph's stumpy hand in horror.

"Yeah, fuck!" Meph shouted at him. "You cut my fucking fingers off, you fuck!"

"Oh my god, oh my god," Iris was saying, gripping her hair and looking a little too pale.

"It's gonna take me a week to regenerate, I have a fucking show in a month, and I need to work! I can't fucking work without fingers, Bel!"

Meph was pissed. Meph was never pissed.

Bel didn't think he'd ever seen Meph actually angry, in all the years they'd been brothers. Sure, he snapped occasionally, but he was always the first to bounce back.

"We need to stop the bleeding!" Iris shouted, gripping his shoulder. "We need to—"

"He's fine," Sunshine said, hurrying forward to take control. "Everything's okay."

"Those were my favorite finger tats!" Meph hollered, gesturing at the bloody mess on the counter.

Iris wailed, hands fluttering around Meph like she didn't know what to do with herself.

"They'll grow back," Sunshine assured her with a hand on her shoulder. "He's perfectly fine. Come, I'll close the wounds and bandage him up, and you'll see that everything's okay."

She gripped Meph's non-bloody arm and Iris's hand and practically dragged them from the room, leaving Bel and the others in a painful silence. A moment later, after giving Bel a long, penetrating look, Ash took the hint and led a shell-shocked Eva back outside, leaving Raum and Bel alone.

Bel stared down at the knife in his hand, still wet with his brother's blood, and then he tossed it onto the counter like it burned him.

"Fuck," he said again, and then he dragged a hand through his hair. He groaned when his fingers got stuck on the now-long strands.

His hair grew to chest length whenever he flew into a rage. He always kept it short because he hated being reminder of his anger when he looked in a mirror. But that meant he needed a haircut every time he lost control. He was so goddamn sick of getting haircuts.

"What happened?" Raum asked. He didn't accuse Bel or jump to conclusions. He didn't even look pissed on Meph's behalf. He just calmly stowed the mop bucket back under the sink and then straightened, propping a hip against the counter and waiting for Bel to speak.

Bel almost wanted him to be mad. He felt like shit. He felt like he deserved it.

"I was chopping, and Meph was pissing me off. Eating the cheese when I told him not to. And he was going on about how shitty my life was, living here by myself when I used to have a lair full of horny women and legions dying to go to war for me. And then . . . I lost it."

There was silence. Bel stared at the severed fingers among his ruined food. It was gross, but he'd seen worse. It was more the sight of his failure that he couldn't stand.

To his vast surprise, Raum chuckled.

Bel's gaze shot to him.

Raum chuckled some more and then caught his look and shrugged. "It's kinda funny."

"How is this funny," Bel growled.

"He kinda had it coming. Meph excels at pissing you off. It's his second favorite pastime after making freaky art. And you make it so easy for him. He can get under your skin like no one else."

Bel ground his teeth. "I should know better than to let him get to me."

Raum shrugged again, and that was all they said on the matter.

So much for his garlic-and-onion cream sauce. Now it was bloody severed-finger sauce.

He grabbed a mixing bowl from the cupboards and then dumped the whole mess into it.

"You haven't lost it like that in a while," Raum said.

Bel grunted in response, using a rag to swipe the last remnants of blood-soaked cheese into the bowl.

"I still think you should consider my theory."

Another grunt. This one slightly more on edge than the last.

"You know, I think that crazy succubus was right."

Bel stiffened at the mention of Naiamah. "What the fuck does she have to do with anything?"

The succubus Queen of Hell was his most well-connected contact in the underworld, and she'd long ago sworn to owe him a thousand favors—though he was down to less than a hundred now. But he despised her and would have released her from their arrangement centuries ago if she wasn't so useful.

The hate was mutual. Yeah, he wasn't proud of what he'd done to manipulate her into swearing those favors in the first place, but she'd done everything in her power to make his life hell for it ever since.

Every time he summoned her, she offered sex as payment so he could keep one of his precious few remaining favors. And he agreed because he told himself it was smart not to waste them, when, in reality, it was mostly because he'd always been stupidly attracted to her and unable to resist the temptation.

The problem was, when they had sex, she used her succubus powers to drain him of as much of his life force as she could, leaving him feeling like shit for days afterward. She'd enjoyed his misery and her power over him until recently, when he'd vowed to himself that he wouldn't touch her for at least six months.

He'd gone way over that time limit now, but he still wasn't sure if it had been a good idea or not. He felt more volatile than ever, and he'd underestimated how much sex had helped stabilize him. He fucking hated knowing that she had inadvertently been helping him control his rage.

"She said, 'repression never works,'" Raum replied, "and I think she's right."

"She's a bitch," Bel snapped. Of course she would say that. When he'd sworn off sex with her, she'd lost her favorite energy source and way of tormenting him.

"And you're an asshole," Raum said with a shrug.

Bel pinned him with a warning glare.

"I'm just saying, now that we're not in hiding anymore, I think you should consider paying a visit to Hell to . . . let off some steam."

"I'm not going to Hell," Bel growled, setting the bowl down and soaping up the rag to clean the blood off the countertop. "The rage is even worse there. It wouldn't help."

"Hm."

"What?" Bel snapped.

"I just think you should give it a try."

"And I think you should shut up. Are we done talking about this? I have to go dump our brother's fucking finger stumps in the compost bin along with fifty dollars worth of expensive fucking cheese, so forgive me if I'm not in the mood to introspect."

Raum held up his hands. Bel tossed the bloody rag in the sink, scooped up the bowl, and stormed out of the kitchen. Ash and Eva were suspiciously quiet as he passed them, and he pretended not to notice them.

He was so goddamn sick of everyone trying to fix him. Sunshine was coming in with her counseling, trying to convince him to open a restaurant like he wouldn't chop off the hand of the first human to piss him off—and they couldn't regrow that in a week. And everyone was dropping comments about how lonely he must be in his new house.

Well, fuck them. He'd chosen this house to get away from them. He was sick of their constant nagging. And they'd followed him here. None of them lived here, yet they always ended up in his kitchen anyway, giving him shit.

He didn't need fucking fixing. He just needed to be left alone. He just needed peace and quiet and some room to fucking breathe.

Fuck Meph and his constant needling. Fuck Raum and his psychoanalysis. Fuck Naiamah and her stupid assumptions about what did or didn't work for him. Fuck Sunshine and her perfect, charming temperament, pretending she gave a shit about him. And Iris for screaming like he'd killed a puppy.

By the time he made it to the compost bin, he'd worked himself halfway back into a rage. He lifted the lid and threw the contents of the bowl onto the pile so hard, it left an indent when it splattered onto the rotten food mush.

He dropped the lid and then tipped his face up to the sky, trying to slow his breathing. It was cloudy tonight. The air was warm, but it was humid, so it felt cooler than it was. Spring was well underway, but he didn't believe in any of that new-life bullshit.

He had to admit Sunshine was right about one thing, however. He did feel like he was toeing a line, and if he didn't do something soon, shit was going to change whether he liked it or not. And probably in a way he didn't want it to.

The last time he'd felt this out of control and sick of himself, he'd met Eva's human friend at a bar. She'd told him she'd sworn off sex for six months to regain control of her impulses, and he'd decided to follow her example. Well, he'd crossed that off his bucket list, and all it had gotten him was an even worse hair-trigger temper because of his constant state of horniness. Eva's friend was probably skipping off into the sunset with her newfound self-confidence, reforming her life, and achieving all her mortal goals in her eighty-year lifespan.

When was he going to learn that pretending to be human wasn't the answer? He wasn't just a demon. He was a fallen angel who fell so hard he'd turned into a demon. He was as old as the world. Literally older than dirt. He was so old he didn't even remember most of his life. And for as far back as his memory went, he'd been ruled by something he couldn't control.

That was all he'd ever wanted: to feel in control.

Ironic, considering who he was. He'd controlled a lot in his day—people, territory, wealth, power—but he'd never controlled himself. And wasn't that a bitch.

# 11

## Bats in the Belfry

MURMUR SNAPPED OUT HIS WINGS TO SLOW HIS FLIGHT and then landed lightly onto the courtyard outside his castle. The black stone gleamed with streaks of red. The sky was finally brightening, the long night coming to a close.

There wasn't a single sign of life around him. Nothing so much as breathed. But it didn't matter what his eyes saw. His nape prickled, and he checked over his shoulder. Twice.

Of course there was no one there. There never was. No one his eyes could see anyway. But he was starting to fear that what his eyes told him wasn't proof enough.

*Not believing your own eyes anymore? You're truly losing it. It's only a matter of time before you crack completely.*

"That isn't news," he replied to himself, striding through the barren courtyard.

So he was paranoid and possibly insane. Could one blame him after being haunted by dreams of his own death every time he closed his eyes? After being regularly sideswiped by visions of the future for millennia? After listening to the screams of haunted souls in his mind at all hours, never having a moment's peace?

He'd just been to check his territory wards. He had recently caught Raum sneaking around the perimeter after the demon had somehow gotten himself conscripted by Heaven into stealing *The Book of Gamigin*. He'd failed, of course, but he had managed to escape Murmur's dungeon with the help of an angel. Afterward, Raum had returned with an adequate peace offering—the dismembered body of the archangel Raphael—and a promise never to return, but the experience had left Murmur more trepidatious than ever.

His paranoia was not unjustified. He was secretly plotting the downfall of the High King of Hell. If Lucifer got so much as a whiff of what he was up to, he would storm Murmur's gates with a fury beyond anything he could withstand. Even his army of souls couldn't protect him.

The fact that Murmur had lasted as long as he had was a miracle in itself. Every time he attempted his spell, there was a disturbance in the High King's magical defenses. He was sure the only reason Lucifer hadn't figured out what was happening yet was because he'd grown complacent, drunk off power and the illusion of indestructibility.

Murmur had always been a recluse. Only the foolish dared disturb the Necromancer who lurked in his lonely lair, sealed behind powerful wards, decimating intruders with his ghostly army.

But everything had changed once he'd had the vision of the blood-born twins who would cause Paimon's downfall. It was the Queen of Hell who'd jumpstarted Murmur's slow slide into insanity, and he had sworn to take vengeance upon her ever since surviving her creative torture.

His mind may have been splintered, but he never forgot, and he never forgave.

He smiled to himself, picturing the look on Paimon's face

if she could see him now, sitting at the top of *her* tower, commanding *her* minions. Too bad she was currently somewhere deep underground, being digested by a gorath. And when the enormous centipede-like monster shit her out, she would regenerate in its feces, only for another to scent her flesh and eat her again.

She wasn't dead. But some fates were worse than death.

But now, as time ran out like the final grains of sand in an hourglass, his smugness at Paimon's fall was irrelevant. He had far bigger problems to think about.

Paimon had been Lucifer's most powerful and loyal supporter, and though it was known that the Hunter was the one to defeat her, when Murmur had taken her lair, he'd lost the obscurity he'd maintained throughout the ages. He'd become a threat.

How long until Lucifer got suspicious about what Murmur was up to in his new lair? How long until he had the presence of mind to check his defenses and sensed traces of the Necromancer's magic among them?

What if he already had? What if he was using his considerable power to spy on Murmur right now, plotting his attack at this very moment?

Murmur stopped and spun around, scowling at the dark courtyard around him. The dark, *empty* courtyard. But in his mind, it was crawling with spies, creatures hidden in the shadows, watching him—

"Stop this madness," he snarled at himself, spinning back around and forcing his feet forward. "This isn't the time to entertain delusions."

*The spies could be there. Lurking in the shadows, watching you right now.*

"They're not and you know it."

*Lucifer could already be onto you. He could know everything you're doing.*

"Be quiet, you incessant nag."

Well aware that he was insulting himself, he reached the grand entrance to the castle and gripped the ring handles, throwing the towering doors wide. Before him was the grand hall where Paimon had once sat upon her throne, her demon camel steed by her side.

Now it was empty.

Murmur had no desire to sit upon a throne or throw torture parties and delight in the humiliation of the disobedient. The disobedient were disposed of and forgotten. He didn't have time to spare with them. The hall had been empty since his takeover, and Paimon's vacant throne upon the dais did nothing but collect dust.

He bypassed the entire room, heading down a runner rug toward the exit at the far end.

"Master," the gargoyles guarding the doors greeted as he approached. He'd placed a rotating shift at every entrance since that angel had infiltrated his lair to liberate Raum from the dungeons.

The demons bowed deeply, and he paused before passing through. "Anything from the scouts to report?" he asked. These guards were also tasked with collecting information from all the others in order to update him.

"Nothing, Master. The territory is quiet."

Murmur's mouth twisted as he accepted this response. *If Lucifer's spies were there, some measly scouts wouldn't detect them.*

"But my souls would," he muttered.

*Would they?*

Silencing the mental voice with a shake of his head, he pushed open the doors and continued down another long hall. Offshoots led to passages underground and to the other towers in the castle.

Many of his minions roomed in those towers, and he never

disturbed their spaces. He had no desire to witness whatever slovenly hovels they occupied. So long as they obeyed orders when he gave them, he was content to leave them to their own devices. If he had his way, he wouldn't have legions at all. He preferred to be alone.

He took a turn and finally reached the entrance to his tower, the doors to which were guarded by another two gargoyles. They greeted him with subservient bows.

He stopped. The demons he entrusted with his tower security were ones who had managed to impress him with mild competency. It was well known throughout the lair that no one was to enter the master's tower, and those he entrusted with sentry duty knew never to abuse their privilege and encroach on his privacy.

The only demons allowed regular access to the tower were his cleaning staff, who came to change the linens, launder his clothes, and bring water to wash. But even they were forbidden from entering the library and were always careful to leave firewood and lantern fuel outside the door.

"Is there something you need, Master?" one of the guards asked as they straightened from their bows. Murmur usually blasted past them without a second glance, so he forgave them their question.

He couldn't believe he was about to do this.

"Which one of you went to Earth the first time to procure food and water?"

One of the demons straightened. A red-skinned gargoyle a good two feet shorter than Murmur. "It was I, sir."

Demons were only allowed to visit Earth when a King or Queen of Hell assigned them a human to influence, whose soul was ripe for corruption and thus claimable for the Nine Rings upon their death. Failure to comply with the rules resulted in punishment from Heaven.

The entire rivalry between Heaven and Hell struck Murmur as a complete waste of time, and he wanted no part in it. He didn't give a flying fuck about humans and their precious immortal souls.

And he'd stopped giving a flying fuck about the rules a while ago, too. After seeing Belial and his brothers make a life for themselves outside of the system, he'd become less wary of being caught. He could get away with a few short trips, and so could his minions.

"You will return to Earth and gather more food," he told the gargoyle. "And you will procure . . . clothing." He winced. Just speaking it aloud was embarrassing.

The demon blinked. "Clothing, sir?"

"Clothing for a human female roughly this size." He held his hand up to just below his chest, where the top of Suyin's head was when she stood beside him. Why he remembered that precise detail when he could scarcely remember to dress himself properly was a mystery.

"Black clothing," he added. From his time hunting Suyin, he'd learned that almost everything she owned was that color. Why he cared what color she wore, he couldn't have said to save his life.

Indeed, both guards looked at him like he'd lost his mind. But they were smart enough not to ask questions. That was why he'd chosen them as his tower guards. "Yes, Master."

"When you return with the items, give them to the cleaning staff. They'll know what to do."

"Yes, Master."

Without another word, Murmur swept through the doors into the spiraling stairwell. Forming his wings, he took flight, ascending the tower. It was awkward trying to fly straight upward, but it was still much faster than walking.

He landed on the stairs below Suyin's chambers. Folding and disappearing his wings, he started up the remaining steps, only to pause briefly and glance at the entrance opposite the gorath statue.

He wondered what the rooms were like now that Suyin had been living in them for a few days. Had she uncovered all the furniture? Did the bedsheets carry her scent now?

*Go in. Catch her unaware. Startle her and see if she'll scream.*

He rolled his eyes. "She'd be more likely to stab me again."

The idiotic voice in his head laughed as if it had enjoyed having a blade stuck in his jugular.

Shaking his head, he continued up to the top floor, stopping outside the entrance to his bedchamber. He'd spent the last six hours flying around his territory, and his attempts to sleep the night prior had been fruitless.

But falling into the bone-chilling terror of his death vision was the last thing he felt like doing at present, even if he was overtired to the point of barely functioning. He continued past.

*You're a wreck*, that stupid little voice reminded him. *You're so tired you can't see straight, let alone make actual progress with your work. If you tried to cast the spell right now, you'd pass out before you even summoned the hellfire.*

"Will you stop it?" he snarled, pushing open the library doors. He went to the fireplace and tossed another log onto the dwindling fire. "I'm sick of your pestering. If you're going to be in my head, couldn't you think of something useful to say for once?"

*I'm you. Tell yourself that.*

He gripped his hair in frustration as he crossed the room toward his desk, careful to avoid stepping on the sigil. He dropped into his chair and stared at the mess before him. "I know that. I'm aware. You've made it perfectly clear that I'm losing my mi—"

His head snapped up at a slight rustling sound, and he found himself staring into the dark eyes of his little prisoner.

She sat cross-legged on the floor on the far side of the room, her back against the tall bookshelves. There was a huge dusty grimoire in her lap and a stack of several more beside her. She stared at him with wide eyes, and he had the impression she'd been doing that since he walked in.

His ire rose, but their interaction the day before returned to his memory. He'd given her permission to be here, and she was doing exactly as she'd promised. Working silently out of his way, and other than the stack of grimoires beside her, she didn't appear to have moved anything.

She was still frozen, staring at him apprehensively. Probably because he'd been arguing with himself.

He was so used to being alone that he'd become accustomed to speaking aloud to the voices in his head. Talking to himself helped him organize his chaotic thoughts. He didn't care if it made the witch uncomfortable.

*Yeah, right. Your face is hot. I think you're blushing.*

"Shut up," he growled before he thought better of it.

"I didn't say anything," Suyin replied warily.

"Not you."

She looked confused. And concerned.

He rolled his eyes and focused back on his desk without actually seeing anything on it.

He already regretted making that stupid agreement with her. What the hell had he been thinking? She'd agreed to give him her blood willingly when he let her out of the dungeon. She didn't need to stand beside him while he cast the spell.

The difference between an unwilling and willing blood sacrifice was notable, yes. But the difference between a willing blood sacrifice being absent or present for the casting ritual was not. He'd convinced himself he'd agreed because every bit of extra power could mean the difference between success and failure.

*But there's more to it than that, isn't there?*

"There isn't," he muttered to himself, shuffling papers around with no real purpose.

*I think you're lonely. You like the idea of having someone around. Especially someone with actual intelligence, who is interested in your books.*

"You're delusional."

A sardonic laugh echoed around his mind, merging with the distant, ever-present screams of his souls. *Insult me all you want. You're just insulting yourself.*

He ground his teeth. Paper. He needed paper. A fresh piece. Every sheet here was covered in scribbles that had seemed terribly important at the time but were now meaningless. He didn't have the energy to read them and try to jog his memory about what they meant.

Feeling eyes on him, his head snapped up again, and he found Suyin still watching him. His eyes narrowed with warning. He was in a foul mood, and she was an easy target.

He hated that she'd so easily figured out what he wanted and used it to coerce him into giving her what *she* wanted. He was tempted to throw her back in the dungeon out of spite. He dared her with his eyes to challenge him now. See where it got her.

She stared back with a calculating expression that was not timid enough for his liking. But a moment later she dropped her gaze, focusing her attention back on her book.

He relaxed slightly. She was a pain in the ass, but at least she knew when to back down.

He returned his attention to the mess on his desk, continuing to shuffle papers around, looking for one that wasn't filled on both sides with scribbling. Somewhere here he had a stack of blank paper he'd been steadily working through. He was sure there were at least a few sheets left, but he couldn't fucking find them.

Growling with frustration, he continued sorting papers, his tail flicking with his growing irritation. He swept a pile onto the floor when he couldn't see properly, knocking over a cup of pencils in the process.

A light throat clearing had his head snapping up.

Suyin stood on the other side of his desk.

"What?" he snapped.

She lifted her hand. In it was the stack of blank paper he'd been trying to find. "I saw this on the other table and thought it might be what you were looking for."

He clenched his jaw and shot her the most furious glare known to man. To her credit, she didn't so much as twitch. There was no smug look on her face, no mocking smile, nothing to push him over the edge.

Slowly, he stretched out a hand and snatched the papers from her grip. He said nothing, waiting for her to react.

She didn't. She just turned and walked calmly back to where she'd been sitting, careful to avoid the sigil on her way.

He watched her lower herself to the floor and pull the grimoire back into her lap. She started to read, long black hair falling over her face. Several seconds later, she lifted a hand to tuck it behind her ear. An ear covered in piercings—rings and studs and all manner of metal things.

His head tilted.

She turned the page. The movement jostled the hair, and it slipped forward over her face like a curtain. She tucked it again, revealing that tiny decorated ear once more.

She was such an odd creature. So breakable. But strangely resilient at the same time.

She glanced up and caught him staring at her. Their eyes met, and hers flared slightly. She swallowed and tucked the hair behind her ear again, though it hadn't fallen forward yet. Color rose to her cheeks, subtle on her lightly tanned skin.

Her gaze darted back to her book, but he had the distinct impression she wasn't reading this time. She shifted positions slightly. She was too aware of him watching her to focus, and that gave him a measure of satisfaction. He liked making her uncomfortable.

Satisfied, he finally dropped his gaze to the stack of blank paper in his hand. He had no memory of putting it on the other table, and he could easily have spent an hour furiously searching before he located it.

His clouded, fractured mind was his own worst enemy, but he didn't have any way to correct it. He simply managed it as best he could.

He stood and grabbed one of the pencils from the floor, not bothering to pick the rest up. He felt Suyin's eyes on him the moment he moved, but she was careful to keep her head down as if she was still reading.

She was watching him, but she didn't want him to know it. Why this pleased him, he wasn't sure.

Sitting once more, he tried to force his scrambled mind to focus. The stress was tightening his shoulders, and the exhaustion made his eyes burn. In the back of his mind, as they always did, his souls screamed for mercy. He ignored them.

But they were still there. They were always there.

Suyin stared at the grimoire in her lap without reading it. Her lack of focus annoyed her. She hadn't had any trouble reading before Murmur had stormed in, arguing with himself. In fact, she'd been completely engrossed, her mind spinning with excitement as she dove into this incredible collection of knowledge.

There was so much information here, it would take a lifetime to go through it all. She didn't know how much time she had, but she knew it was limited. She ought to be using every waking second to absorb as much knowledge as she could.

But she couldn't focus for shit as soon as Murmur showed up.

Instead, she let her hair slide out from behind her ear and fall over her face, and she watched him work from behind it, hoping for any sort of clue as to what the hell he was doing.

He was currently muttering under his breath as he scribbled rapidly on paper. *The Book of Gamigin* was open on the desk in front of him. Occasionally he would crumple up the page he was writing on and toss it over his shoulder.

He was either a madman or a total genius. Perhaps both.

Either way, she was burning with curiosity—even more than before. Whatever he was up to involved *her* grimoire, the one she'd struggled in vain for years to make sense of. But now she knew for certain that *The Book of Gamigin* contained important information, and Murmur knew what it was.

Maybe it held answers about her mysterious abilities. Maybe she could finally figure out whether her father actually wrote it or had just acquired it somehow, and why. Or whether her mother had known what it meant, and if so, why she hadn't told Suyin.

Whatever it was, Murmur knew about it. But how to get him to open up? He was tight-lipped and disinclined to talking, unless it involved threatening her.

At that moment, he mumbled something incoherent, swept another crumpled page off the table, and then began flipping through the pages of another grimoire on the desk, still muttering grumpily.

If she'd met him under any other circumstance, even if he was in human form, she would have steered clear. Everything about him, from his haughty expressions to his unpredictable reactions, was one big red flag.

And not "red flag" as in Iris's shitty, toxic ex-boyfriends. "Red flag" as in potential serial killer with a murder room in his basement.

Which, technically, was completely true. She'd seen his dungeon.

Still, after watching him for a while, she had to admire his concentration. He continued reading and writing and muttering without looking up once. It was like he'd forgotten the world existed.

Maybe she ought to give it a try. She glanced at the grimoire in her lap and forced herself to focus once again. Maybe it was Murmur's intense concentration permeating the library, but before long, she got lost in her own studies again.

She'd always been resistant to studying Sheolic magic, but that was before she'd found this library. And been kidnapped by a demon. Every grimoire here was full of black magic, but she was starting to realize that she didn't care what it took—learning to protect herself was worth any risk.

Hours later, she looked up again, blinking when she remembered where she was. Realizing her legs were numb, she straightened them, wincing at the stretch of muscles that weren't used to sitting cross-legged for so long. Time to take a break.

She glanced at Murmur. He was still working. His hair fell over his face, and he tapped an idle claw on the desk as he read from a book. He hadn't moved once the entire time. She couldn't help but admire that kind of work ethic.

Making as little sound as possible, she lifted the grimoire off her lap and rose to her feet, her stiff legs protesting. Carefully and quietly, she returned every book she'd borrowed to its rightful place. She was dying to take one down to her room to keep reading without His Royal Craziness lurking around, but she didn't want to push her luck.

She was quiet enough that Murmur didn't appear to notice her leaving, and she closed the library door softly behind her, the latch making only the smallest click. Alone in the hallway, she let out a breath.

She'd been in his presence for a good four or five hours. He hadn't threatened her or done anything, but she'd been on edge the entire time anyway. Just being near him was draining, and she was ready for a nap.

Climbing down the steps, she headed straight to her room, only to stop short when she saw what was waiting for her on the bed.

Someone had left a pile of carefully folded clothing, all of it black. Beside it there was another flat of plastic water bottles—she normally hated bottled water and disposable plastic, but she doubted it was easy to find potable water in Hell—and more food. It was hardly a fresh-cooked meal, but she wasn't complaining.

In fact, a smile stretched across her face as she went through the clothes. There were two pairs of black leggings, a pair of sweatpants, two black tank tops, a T-shirt, a hoodie, and several pairs of underwear.

It looked like she was going to goth boot camp. She loved it.

Murmur had actually listened to her and sent his little minions on another Earth mission. And she couldn't help but wonder if the clothing was black for a reason. He'd been stalking her, after all. He knew how she dressed.

She thought of him sitting up there alone in his library, talking to himself while he worked, and though it probably made her stupid, her hatred of him lessened a little. A very little.

She'd never thought of herself as a forgiving person. The opposite, in fact. She was often too quick to cut people out of her life. One wrong move and they were gone, all ties severed, no second chances.

She'd never been broken up with in her life. All her ex-partners had been somewhat cruelly dumped the second she sensed clinginess from them or they wronged her in the slightest way. And sometimes she couldn't even use that as an excuse. In New York, she'd dated a girl for almost a year only to break up with her because she'd suggested they move in together.

So why was she standing here with the warm fuzzies because a demon had procured her some clothing and food? He'd only done it because he'd taken her to Hell against her will, where she had nothing to wear or eat.

*Maybe you're in danger of Stockholm syndrome after all.*

"Shut up," she said aloud, just to hear what it was like to talk to herself as Murmur did. She laughed. Honestly, it felt kinda good.

# 12

# MORBID CURIOSITY

DAYS PASSED—IT WAS ALWAYS DIFFICULT TO SAY HOW many in Hell—and the time for the next attempt of the spell was fast approaching. Surely having Suyin's willing sacrifice would be the extra boost Murmur needed to finally break through. It had to be.

Yet strangely, he found his usual driving urgency was lacking.

Currently, he leaned back in his chair, drumming his claws on the desk, watching Suyin work from the corner of his eye. The fire had been fed and burned brightly, permeating the library with a comfortable warmth.

After discovering the clothing his minions had procured for her, Suyin had come to the library and, instead of thanking him, spent an hour cleaning years of soot and grime off the window.

He'd pretended not to notice, but instead of focusing on his work, he'd watched her, strangely transfixed by the sight of her diminutive form scrubbing at the glass, lithe muscles shifting along her back and shoulders.

Afterward, the glow of the red sky entered the room and actually managed to brighten it. Suddenly, he could read his messy writing a little easier, and he found he enjoyed looking out the window while he tried to organize his thoughts.

So, after Suyin had returned to her rooms, he'd cleared off one of the tables for her to use. Not to express gratitude, he assured himself, but as an exchange of favors. So they were even.

He'd made it clear she wasn't to encroach on his workspace, but that table was being used mostly to store scraps of disorganized paper, and seeing her hunched over on the floor all day was distracting in its own right. It couldn't be good for her spine to have it bent like that.

Not that he cared. He just didn't want her distracting him.

Now, Suyin sat at her new worktable—for which she'd thanked him with a surprised look that made him uncomfortable—her nose buried in a book. And he watched her.

It seemed she hadn't lied when she'd told him she was hungry for knowledge. At first, he'd been convinced her desire to access his library was part of a foolhardy plan to soften him up.

But every time he came here, he found her diligently studying. She never said a word to him except to bid him good morning or night before she retired to her chambers—though he was sure she'd lost all sense of the time.

When Murmur had cleaned off the table, he'd left an empty notebook for Suyin to use for note-taking, and she'd already filled half of it. He wondered what she was working so determinedly on.

*She's probably searching every single book for the easiest way to kill you.*

He scoffed at the notion of a tiny thing like her causing him harm, but then his eyes narrowed suddenly. What *was* she up to?

She couldn't actually try to kill him, as per the terms of

their bargain, so he wasn't particularly concerned about mutiny. But she was in his library, reading his books, sitting at his table. He had every right to know what she was doing.

He rose from his desk suddenly, and she didn't so much as blink, remaining engrossed in her work. Silently, he stalked across the room and came up behind her.

Her thick hair cascaded down her back. It was pure black, no hints of brown. A good color as far as human hair went, he decided. His gaze moved to her tiny hands. She was currently copying a sigil into her book. The page opposite was filled with notes.

He leaned over to see what she was doing, and his lips curved slightly.

Anti-demon wards.

After he was done with her, she'd probably be even more paranoid than he was. Of course she'd want to learn ways to protect herself.

He nodded with approval at her careful but succinct note-taking. She was smart to copy down what she had. She wouldn't be taking any of his grimoires back to Earth, and this was a good way to ensure her memory stayed sharp.

Unfortunately, the book she'd chosen was elementary at best. He straightened and stroked his chin with a foreclaw.

He crossed the room to the furthest corner, left of the doors. Gripping the ladder, he rolled it over several feet and then climbed to the second-highest shelf. Trailing his claws along the spines, he scanned each faded title until he found the one he sought. He pulled it out and descended the ladder.

Coming up behind Suyin, he dropped the grimoire with a heavy thud onto the desk in front of her.

She jumped and her head snapped up. Twisting around, her eyes flared when she saw him standing behind her.

"If you want wards to keep out demons, you won't find a better book than that," he said, pointing at the volume.

She stared up at him, mouth slightly open.

He turned away and returned to his desk, flicking his claws in a dismissive gesture. "Marax is a buffoon, but his knowledge is vast." He dropped into his chair and smiled thinly. "I'd kill to see the look on his face if he found out how many of his grimoires I've stolen for my collection over the ages."

Suyin still watched him mutely.

With a shrug, he returned his attention to his work, picking up where he'd left off last night before falling asleep in his chair from exhaustion. He'd only woken up because Suyin had kicked one of the ladders loud enough to make a bang and then suggested he go to bed when he glared at her.

He was reviewing the incantation, ensuring everything was correct (though he knew it was) and that he'd used the most effective combination of syllables (though he knew he had). It was dull work, but every step of the spell had to be perfect.

After an hour or so, he looked up again, turning his attention outside. He hadn't been to check his boundary wards in days, and he was overdue. It was the last thing he felt like doing at present, but he felt like fighting off invaders even less. Such was the burden of controlling a large territory.

His eyes wandered over to his companion. They did that a lot. He'd lost track of how many years he'd spent working by himself. Having someone else here was strange.

But what was perhaps even stranger was how he didn't particularly mind it. But only because it was her. Anyone else he would surely have killed by now. As a rule, he detested the company of others. But Suyin was . . . tolerable.

He leaned back in his chair, suddenly wondering about what she wanted to study and how difficult it would be for her to find what she sought. If he were in her shoes, he'd want to learn every trick in the book to arm himself against demons. Especially after having been captured by one.

Suddenly inspired, he stood, chair scraping back with the

movement. Suyin remained focused and didn't look up. He returned to the far corner of the library and climbed the ladder again. Scanning the shelves, he withdrew a grimoire, climbed down, moved the ladder, climbed up, and took another.

He repeated the process until he had a stack of books up to his chin. He carried them over and dumped them on the corner of her desk. Just as before, she jerked upright and stared up at him with wide eyes.

"A collection of texts you might be interested in," he said.

She looked back and forth between him and the book stack. "Thank you."

His lip curled, her gratitude irritating him. He much preferred when she was pissed at him. Or better yet, terrified. "It's annoying watching you look in the wrong sections for things. The books you've been reading are rudimentary."

She pressed her lips together. "Well, thanks for finding me the good ones. I'm surprised you'd want me to learn how to fight off demons."

He shot her a bland look. "The day I would be concerned about your magic overpowering mine would be the day I deserve death."

"Pretty sure you already deserve that." Her eyes crinkled in the corners, and he realized she was teasing him. *The audacity.* "I shudder to think of all the terrible things you've done."

"Don't bother. You'll only give yourself a headache."

She laughed then, and he blinked, watching her face transform. He didn't think she'd laughed once since arriving here, unless it was out of bitterness. Strange how he was even aware of that.

Her laughter died quickly, however, and she stared right back at him.

Just as he was about to extricate himself from the interaction, she asked, "Where should I start?" Her gaze darted to the book pile. "Is there an order I should read them in? Which ones are the best?"

His eyes narrowed. He didn't have time for this. He needed to check his wards. Her curiosity meant nothing to him. Anything that stood between him and his plans needed to be eradicated. And yet . . .

*This is far more interesting than anything else you're doing today.*

Before he could convince himself otherwise, he leaned over and pulled a book from the middle of the pile.

"Start with this one," he said, setting it beside the grimoire she was already working on. "If you're going to practice Sheolic magic, you must first learn the dangers and how to circumvent them. That's outlined in here."

"Awesome," she replied, trailing her fingers lightly over the cover.

He grabbed another book from the pile. "Sheolic magic is sacrificial magic. This text covers suitable sacrificial materials, the importance of intention, and the process of selecting and utilizing a sacrifice. You need to have a firm grasp of this before beginning practice."

Her eyes lit up as he slid the book toward her, and she cracked the stiff spine, opening to faded parchment. "Damn," she breathed. "Does it explain how to make sacrifices without killing stuff?"

Murmur huffed. "Of course it does. While it's generally the most powerful form, death is still only one type of sacrifice. But of course it's the most dramatic, so it's the only one people talk about."

Her eyes remained fixed on the ancient pages as she turned each one carefully. He approved of her handling of the books. If she'd been rough with any of them, he'd have thrown her right back into the dungeon.

"And what kind of sacrifice do you prefer to use?" she asked.

"That depends on what I'm trying to accomplish." He propped a hip against the side of the table. "Generally, more powerful spells require a greater sacrifice. A personal sacrifice has the greatest effect. If the caster choses something that has great value to them, no matter how seemingly insignificant, that can have more power than a meaningless death."

She looked briefly up at him. "Like something that has sentimental value?"

"Yes. Or someone." He studied his claws. "Sacrificing a person the caster has bonded to is one of the most powerful offerings in all of magic. This is why an experienced practitioner avoids personal attachments. Because the moment they bond to someone, the object of their attachment becomes a powerful ingredient in a spell. And if the desire for the success of the spell is great enough, they will utilize it. If they do not, all their other sacrifices will never measure up to that potential potency, and they will unknowingly cripple themself."

"That's cold," Suyin said.

He met her gaze. "Power always comes at a cost."

She looked back at the grimoire and muttered, "And knowledge is power."

He smiled thinly. "Sheolic magic isn't what humans have made it out to be. Where Temporal magic uses the power of nature and celestial bodies, Sheolic requires personal fortitude. You must ask yourself, what are you willing to give up to progress?"

Her eyes lifted back to his. "What did you give up?"

He studied her for a moment, considering his answer. "Everything. I gave up everything, even my own mind."

She swallowed.

He tracked the movement of her throat, oddly transfixed by that slender column and the hollows above her clavicles.

The fire was warm, and she had removed her sweater, revealing more of her skin.

She didn't have the typical woman's shape of curves and softness. Her body was lean and slender with sharp angles—her jawline, her shoulder blades—and yet, she was graceful and lithe. Like a dancer.

A little dark dancer, with her black hair and piercing gaze.

Unsettled by his bizarre thoughts, he shook himself, pushed off the desk, and headed toward the door. There was work to do, and no time to waste in idle thought and conversation.

"Wait," she said, and for some godforsaken reason, he actually stopped and turned back. This was the third time he'd heeded that request, and it was starting to vex him.

He arched a brow.

"Are there any books on necromancy in the pile?" she asked.

He shot her a look. She was either clueless or an evil genius, because that was the one topic sure to gain his interest one hundred percent of the time.

"You want to learn the art of the dead?" he asked. "If Sheolic magic is dangerous, necromancy is even more so."

"It can't be worse than demon summoning."

He smiled. "And you wish to learn that as well, I presume? The risks are high." A demon resisted a summoning with every ounce of their being. The slightest mistake in the sigil or casting process and the demon would escape and slaughter the caster in retaliation for attempting to enslave them.

"Not really, to be honest," she replied. "And I don't know if I want to learn necromancy so much as understand it. I'm curious."

He pursed his lips and studied her with indecision for another moment. And then that cursed impulsive voice whispered at him again to give her what she sought, and like a fool, he heeded it.

He crossed to the opposite side of the room. Sliding a ladder over, he climbed several rungs and pulled a familiar grimoire from the shelf. He carried it over and set it on the table in front of Suyin.

"There." He tapped a claw on the cover. "This is the first in my own collection of texts and serves as a suitable overview of the fundamentals of the practice."

Her eyes widened. "You wrote this?"

He gave her a look. "There is an entire section of this library full of my grimoires. Yes, I wrote it."

Her brows shot up, and he was almost offended.

"I am called *the* Necromancer. Of course I've written grimoires, and of course I am the best source of knowledge on the subject. Who else would you expect to know more than I?"

Her mouth opened and then closed again. "No one, I guess. Still, I'm impressed."

He scoffed. "Your praise is meaningless."

She rolled her eyes.

Gritting his teeth, he strode away. Just days ago, she'd been cowering at the sight of him. Now she rolled her eyes blatantly before him.

"Where are you going?" she asked just as his fingers curled around the door handle.

He glared at her over his shoulder. She'd never asked him questions, and now suddenly, she was full of them and fearless in their delivery.

"I am a Duke of Hell," he reminded her haughtily. "I rule a vast territory."

"I know, but—" She paused and seemed to be reconsidering her question. But she pressed on. "What does that entail?"

"If you're trying to discover weaknesses in my defenses, I assure you—"

She scoffed, and his eyes narrowed at her impudence. "I don't care about that," she said. "We have a bargain. So as long as you're not trying to kill or torture me, we're good, remember? I'm asking because I'm curious, that's all."

"You know what they say about curiosity."

She shrugged. "The cat may be dead, but at least it lived a good life on its way out. I'd rather die curious than live in fear."

A laugh escaped him before he could stifle it. Only she would think that. He'd never met a more brazen person.

He found himself answering her question. "My souls patrol the boundaries of my territory, but I must regularly check the perimeters and refresh the wards so the magic remains strong."

"You don't have servants for that?"

"Demons are some of the most incompetent, witless creatures in creation."

"Not all of them." She gave him a pointed look.

Was she calling him intelligent? Of course he was. He didn't need veiled compliments to point that out. "The ones that aren't dim-witted are rulers of their own territories. Half the challenge of being among the Order of Thrones is managing the vacuous minds of one's legions."

"So you don't trust them with important tasks like monitoring your borders. You have to do everything yourself. But you still let them live here, free of charge."

She made it sound like he was performing a charity. He made a sour face. "They obey my commands when I give them. If they don't, I impale them on the tower spikes. Have you already forgotten what lies beyond the window you so diligently cleaned?"

She winced.

"Perhaps I should give you a tour of the rest of the dungeon to remind you what I do with people who challenge me," he continued. "I believe you missed some of my favorite rooms."

"Okay, I get it. You're evil and terrifying." She looked unimpressed, and that irritated him.

"I'll be commencing the first steps of the ritual tomorrow," he decided. It was time to finish this and return this recalcitrant witch from whence she came. "You will be available to assist me, as you vowed."

She nodded. "Anything I need to do to prepare?"

"Keep your blood in your body until I need it."

He turned and opened the door, but once again, her damned voice stopped him.

"Murmur?"

"What?" he snapped, annoyed with himself for listening to her as much as he was annoyed with her for stalling him.

"Thanks for the books."

His lip curled. "Mmph," was his response, and then he swept out of the room, the door banging shut behind him.

# 13

# THE FINGER OF RESPONSIBILITY

MEPH SHOWED UP AT THE HOUSE A FEW DAYS AFTER the incident.

A part of Belial wanted to slam the door in his face. He couldn't deny he was still a little pissed at his brother for riling him up and making him feel like shit about his life. But mostly, he just felt guilty, and he knew he owed him a conversation.

So when he saw Meph sheepishly grinning on his doorstep—his right hand wrapped in gauze—Bel stepped back and let him in.

"Nice hair," was the first thing Meph said.

Bel ran his fingers through it. He hadn't bothered getting a haircut after his last rage attack. He supposed he was tired of fighting the inevitable.

New mansion, long hair . . . Maybe he was having a midlife crisis.

He and Meph sat outside on the patio with coffees. The

silence was weighted, but it wasn't awkward. They'd spent too much time together for that to ever be an issue.

"So . . ." Meph shifted in his seat and stared at the pool like it was the most interesting thing he'd ever seen. "I wanted to say I'm sorry."

"Damn it." Bel propped an elbow on his chair's armrest and dropped his head into his hand.

"What?"

"I'm supposed to be the one apologizing. I was trying to work up the nerve, but you beat me to it."

"Nah." Meph fidgeted with his cup, spinning it in circles on the table. With his left hand, of course. The one with all the fingers still attached.

Bel lifted his head. "I chopped your fingers off."

"I know." Meph held up his bandaged appendage, that goofy grin appearing on his face.

"Why the fuck are you smiling?"

"Because, in hindsight, it's hilarious. I can't wait to tell this story a million times."

Bel shook his head.

"I shouldn't have said all that shit," Meph said, picking up his cup and staring at the coffee in it. "Ash came and tore me a new one after, and he's right."

"Ash did?"

"Yeah."

"I hardly even remember him being there."

"You know Ash. Always quiet in the corner, observing our idiocy, and then giving us shit for it later."

"True." Bel nodded knowingly. He may have felt like the burden of responsibility fell on his shoulders, but he'd always known Asmodeus carried a heavy load of his own. Especially back in Hell, when Bel had been even more unstable than he was now.

"I remember what it was like when I couldn't control my

demon," Meph said, "and I had to keep him caged with that sigil that kept me from shifting. That sucked." He looked at Bel. "But I guess it's worse with the anger, isn't it? Because there's nothing you can tattoo on yourself to keep it in. You just have to . . . force it to stay in check." He shook his head. "That sounds shitty."

Bel grunted noncommittally. It was. But there was no need for him to go on about it.

"So, yeah." Meph shifted in his chair. "I think it's cool what you've done here, getting set up in this cushy house and shit."

Bel cocked a brow.

"I do. Maybe I was a dick because . . . I'm a little jealous."

"Just buy your own house then, dumbass."

"Well. . ." Meph twisted his hands in his lap. "You know how Raum collected a fortune in Hell from all his stealing, and you and Ash are old as shit so you're just rich by default?"

"Yeah . . ."

"Well, I was too busy being . . . a demon. It's hard to hoard gold when you're a soul-sucking monster. I'm kinda broke."

Bel straightened. "What the fuck? Why didn't you tell me you need money? I'll—"

"No, thanks." Meph held up a tattooed palm. "I don't want any handouts. If I'm gonna do the human thing, I wanna do it without any free passes, you know?"

"Meph . . ." Bel made a face. "That's the dumbest thing I've ever heard. You're not human and you never will be. This isn't some kind of challenge. We came here to live."

"I know. And that's how I want to do it." Meph shrugged. "I'm making money selling my art. It's kinda awesome."

"And then you spend it all on shoes."

"It's my money," he replied with a grin. "I can do what I want with it."

Bel shook his head, but truth be told, he understood where Meph was coming from. He could imagine how it would feel to earn a living from actually doing something productive. Not just by raiding some poor fucker's lair and stealing his hoard.

In truth, he admired his brother. Meph had been dealt a shitty hand, and now look at him. Making his own way and building a real life for himself all on his own.

"You know . . ." Bel took a breath, unable to believe he was actually about to say this. "If you and Iris actually want to live here . . . you can." He winced, already sure he was going to regret making that offer. "*Temporarily.* Until you get your shit together and find something better."

Meph froze with his cup halfway to his mouth. He set it down. "You're serious?"

"Can't promise I won't lose it again," Bel added, taking his turn at staring at the pool to avoid his brother's gaze. "But I'll do my best."

"Are you sure you'd actually want us here? Wasn't the whole point of moving to get away from everyone?"

"Yeah." Bel blew out a breath. "You were being a dick, but you were also kinda right. Maybe being alone isn't the answer either. I'm just as on edge after a couple weeks of living alone as I was before."

Meph's eyes narrowed. "You're not just offering us a place because I told you I'm broke, are you?"

"Of course I am."

"Well, then, no. Thanks, but no."

"Don't be a fucking—"

"I don't need your pity—"

"It's not pity," Bel snapped, "and if you tell me I'm pitying anyone, I'll pop your eyeballs out with a rusty spoon, then make you swallow them and chase them down with your own blood. I don't do *pity*."

Meph's brows shot up. "Graphic. Even for you."

"I'm serious."

"Fine. But I told you I wanted to make my own way, and this kinda sounds like cheating to me."

Bel smiled suddenly as an idea occurred to him. "How about this? Instead of paying rent, you can work for me."

"Doing what?" Meph asked suspiciously.

"Cleaning the house and doing upkeep on the yard and pool. I need to hire someone, but I don't want some human traipsing around, getting into my shit."

"Wait. You want me to be your fucking maid?"

"Yep." Bel's smile was evil. "You said you don't want any handouts. Here's your chance to earn something in a completely human way."

"Well, shit . . ." Meph slumped back in his chair and blew out a breath.

"Plus, if you want Iris to stay with your lazy ass, it's high time you learned some basic life skills. Can't believe she still puts up with your shit."

Meph winced. "I'm working on it."

"Have you ever cooked her a meal? Unlike us, she actually needs food to survive."

He winced again. "I can order takeout."

"Wow," Bel deadpanned. "She must be totally impressed by your ability to use the Uber Eats app and spend all your hard-earned broke-ass artist money."

"Fuck," Meph groaned. "You're relentless."

"Just telling it like it is."

"What about Iris? What's she gotta do to pay her way if she lives here with me?"

"Nothing. You'll be responsible for both of you."

"What? Why? That's not fair."

"Because you're a lazy fuck, that's why. Life's not fair. Deal with it. Or rent your own place that you can trash, and see how long your woman stays with you."

Meph groaned again. "You're brutal, man."

Bel sipped his coffee, feeling smug. There was no way Meph would agree. He'd made a compromise, taught his brother a lesson, *and* managed to continue living solo, even after trying to make changes as Sunshine had encouraged. This way, he was absolved of all blame, and Sunshine couldn't say he hadn't tried—

"Fine," Meph said, sitting up straight again. "I agree."

Bel froze with his cup at his lips. "What?"

"I'll do it. I'll be your damn maid and landscaper and pool boy and whatever the hell else if Iris and I can live here." It was Meph's turn to look smug. "And I can tell by the look on your face that you thought I'd never actually agree, and you'd get to go back to loner living. So suck it."

"Damn it," Bel said.

"Which room's mine?"

"The basement suite. Better yet, the fucking crawl space."

"What, we can't have the room next to yours?" Meph's grin was evil now.

"No." Bel set his cup down and jabbed a finger in Meph's direction. "And if I hear you two fucking even once, I'll toss both your asses out the front door. My house, my rules, got it? I want this house spotless and the yard looking like a fucking Zen garden. No second chances. You don't make a mess. You don't touch my shit. And you don't eat my food until I say it's ready. And this is a *temporary* situation, got it?"

"Got it, boss."

Bel shook his head. He couldn't believe he was agreeing to this. "When are you moving in?"

"Iris's lease is up at the end of next month."

"Fuck my life."

Meph was still grinning. "You know Lily and Mist are gonna want to move in too when they get back from traveling, right? And there's only one suite."

"We'll cross that bridge when we come to it."

"They get home next week."

"When we come to it," Bel growled.

Suyin lay awake in bed, thinking. She'd stayed in the library for a long time after Murmur left. So long that she heard him return from checking his wards and then lock himself in his bedroom. She'd been immersed in reading and hadn't stopped until her eyes were closing. The books he'd chosen for her to study were fascinating, but she was most interested in the one he'd written himself.

Unsurprisingly, it was nearly as convoluted as *The Book of Gamigin*. His penmanship was atrocious, and he often went on long tangents until she'd forgotten what the original point he was trying to make was. But the more she read, the more she started to get a grasp of how his mind worked, and she had to admit it impressed her.

The book was packed full of information, and yet he'd told her there was an entire section of his library full of books he'd written. This was obviously only the tip of the iceberg. To say she was curious was an understatement.

And she couldn't lie . . . She was curious about Murmur, too. How his mind worked. What motivated him. What he'd seen and done in his impossibly long life. Why he was half mad and a control freak. Why he was so secretive. And most of all . . . what the hell he was planning with that damned spell.

She was nervous about the casting, though she wasn't entirely sure why. Perhaps it was because she'd had access to his library for several days now and she still hadn't found any answers to her questions. Or perhaps it was because Murmur seemed like an unstoppable force, yet even he seemed unsure of his success. That put her on edge.

She wanted answers, and she was running out of time to

get them. If the spell was successful and Murmur had his way, she'd return home without any idea what he'd done or why.

She sat up in bed suddenly, covers falling to her lap, as an idea formed.

Murmur had forbidden her from touching anything on his desk, which meant the information she sought had to be there. And Murmur was also currently asleep—a rare occasion, from what she'd observed. If she didn't start taking risks, she wasn't going to get anywhere. She'd decided to play nice so that when her chance came to learn more about herself, she would feel secure enough to take it, trusting that he wouldn't hurt her in retaliation.

Well, a chance had come.

She leapt out of bed before she lost her nerve, dressing in a hurry as the cool air prickled against her skin. She started to put on her boots and then changed her mind. Her footsteps would be quieter in just her socks.

She slipped out of her chambers into the stairwell and climbed the steps silently. At the top, she pushed open the door and padded down the hall, pausing outside Murmur's bedroom and listening for signs he had awoken.

Hearing nothing, she entered the library, grateful for the quiet door that whispered shut behind her. Everything was dark, just as she'd left it when she'd blown out the lanterns and let the fire die.

She didn't waste time. She'd come here with a purpose and knew what she was looking for. At Murmur's desk, she studied the array of scattered papers. The first time, she'd been caught before she could learn anything, and she was hoping to remedy that now.

She already knew that flipping through *The Book of Gamigin* would be fruitless, so she concentrated instead on reading Murmur's notes. She looked at his messy scrawl and grimaced. It was worse here than in the grimoire he'd written. She could barely tell if she was reading English or Sheolic.

She picked up a random sheet of paper and dropped into his chair, holding it in front of her face and trying to make sense of it. The only illumination came through the window from the red sky, and she didn't dare light a lantern in case she was discovered.

*Souls contained behind* . . . What the hell did that say? *Additional force . . . required?* She squinted at the page. *Form . . . portal?* But that didn't make sense.

And what *souls* were contained? Was he trying to get more for his army? But surely he already had a way to trap them. Maybe he'd lost his way of getting new souls somehow, and he was trying to get it back?

It might explain his obsession, since he derived much of his fearsome reputation from the ghosts who swirled at his feet. But something about that explanation didn't ring true.

She kept reading.

"Angel blood . . . outer layers. Added fortification." *Angel blood?* She glanced over at the sigil on the floor, the lines painted in dried blood. Where the hell would he get access to an angel? She wasn't sure she wanted to know.

She skimmed over the next section, which appeared to be a list of somewhat disturbing ingredients. *Pickled heart, liver, claw of winged demon, incubus semen*—gross—*blood of* . . . She peered closer at the last word, trying to decipher—

A howl split the quiet.

Her spine snapped straight, and she scanned the dark library. Chills raced up her back. That terrible sound of despair had come from very close by.

Another cry echoed through the halls. It finished in a hoarse groan, and she suddenly realized she knew that voice very well.

She was out of her chair running before her next breath.

# 14

# Arousing Suspicion

*That familiar burning engulfed Murmur's body. He knew this agony well, but every time it consumed him, he suffered anew. His screams of pain morphed to screams of terror as his body dissolved, and he found himself trapped with thousands of other souls, locked together in endless suffer—*

*"Murmur!"*

*He stilled. That was new. That had never happened before, and he was quite sure he—*

"Murmur!"

All of a sudden, he was thrust back into his sweat-soaked body, tangled in the bedsheets. The sensation of foreign touch on his skin—not the fabric of the bedsheets—reached his brain only a fraction of a second before he acted.

Before he was even fully conscious, he grabbed the intruder and flipped them under his body. He summoned his souls and used them as bindings, pulling the intruder's arms and legs apart and pinning them down.

With one hand, he supported his weight. With the other, he

gripped the intruder's hair and yanked their neck sharply to the side. His tail barb poised at the pulsing artery, venom welling at the tip, ready to strike at the slightest provocation.

The intruder went still.

And Murmur finally realized who was in his bed.

He blinked, certain his eyes were deceiving him. But no, as his vision sharpened with his awareness, he saw the dark eyes of his little witch. Her pulse beat so furiously, he could see it in her neck.

But she didn't move. She couldn't. He had restrained her completely.

A deep, primal satisfaction filled him, overriding the residual terror from the dream.

The sight of fettered limbs had always given him a depraved satisfaction. He wasn't ashamed to admit it. He enjoyed stringing his prisoners up, watching them try to pull their limbs free. He liked seeing the bindings that held them immobile.

But something about the sight of this little witch trapped was even more satisfying, to the point where he felt heat stirring low in his abdomen. But that didn't mean he wasn't angry. No, he was furious.

"Do you have no sense of self-preservation?" he snapped. "Do my commands mean nothing to you? I very clearly told you never to come into this room."

The fear hadn't left her eyes, but she replied hoarsely, "I thought you were dying, asshole."

"*You* could have died." He illustrated his point by waving his tail above her head in case she missed just how close it had been to her neck. "I thought your whole agenda here was to avoid that outcome."

She glared at him but said nothing. She wasn't nearly terrified enough for his liking.

His eyes were drawn down to her heaving chest, and he allowed them to wander over her neck, her jaw, and the pile of rich black hair still clenched in his fist. He'd never studied her this closely before.

"Besides, you should want me to die," he said. "If I'm dead, you can go home, remember?"

Her glare intensified. If she hadn't wanted him dead before, she looked as though she did now.

Then, she frowned. "What was that? A nightmare?"

"A vision," he found himself replying. Why, he didn't know.

He was too distracted, studying each individual eyelash around her eye. When he'd first taken her, her eyes had been covered in dark makeup. Now, they were bare. Her eyelashes were short but thick. She had slender eyes, but her dark pupils gave them an intensity that made them appear larger.

"Of what?"

"My death," he replied distractedly, still caught up in his detailed perusal of her features. He wasn't quite sure what was happening, but he wasn't in a great hurry to stop it.

"Your what?"

"I dream of my death every time I close my eyes." Why was he admitting this? He'd never told another living soul.

"Is it an actual premonition or just symbolism?"

"I'm a seer. I've had visions of the future for as long as I can remember."

"Can you change the outcome of—?" Her eyes widened. "That's what the spell is about."

"In part."

*Why* in the devil's name was he telling her this? But he was too caught up in this strange moment to care. He was chasing something he didn't understand, and perhaps didn't want to understand, but he didn't want to let it go yet.

"But you can't die."

He frowned.

She added, "Not until I've learned all your secrets."

Their eyes met, and he fought to comprehend the sensations overtaking his body. He wasn't used to feeling anything except perpetual coldness. He hadn't believed he was even capable after millennia of infusing himself with necromancy.

"Let me free." She pulled against the ghostly bonds still pinning her wrists and ankles down, and he noticed anew their positions. His much larger body was still over hers, his hips between her legs. He still gripped her long hair, tugging her head to one side and exposing her neck.

She struggled a little more, and the sight caused his lids to drop halfway down his eyes. His lips curved. "No."

"Murmur." She spoke through gritted teeth.

That heat pulsed low in his abdomen again. "Keep struggling. I enjoy it."

They stared at each other. He hated maintaining eye contact with anyone, yet he enjoyed it with her. Perhaps because he enjoyed the sight of her feistiness melting away as he overpowered her.

"Murmur."

The heat pulsed yet again at the sound of his name on her lips.

And then he felt it.

His body stirring. Awakening. *Hardening.*

And he suddenly understood what was happening, what rush he was chasing, what the sensation of heat filling him was.

His groin pressed against hers, and where before it had simply been an effective way to keep her pinned, suddenly, it was . . . more. Much more.

Her eyes flared, and she shifted. Friction. The heat pulsed. The blood pooled and throbbed. It was dizzying, hot. *Alive.* His head spun. His heart pounded.

Suyin made a tiny, breathless sound.

Her gasp broke the spell, and he lurched back, releasing his souls and freeing her fettered limbs.

"Get out." His heart was racing so fast he found it difficult to breathe. His chest was tight. Constricting him.

His body was supposed to be dead. It had died ages ago. His consciousness had been animating a lifeless corpse for centuries. A corpse that felt nothing—no sensation of pleasure or pain or desire.

*Apparently not.*

Suyin sat up, staring at him, eyes wide.

"Get out and don't come in here again." His voice shook with his unsteady breath.

She opened her mouth. She was going to speak. She wasn't running away. What the fuck was wrong with this woman?

"GET OUT!" he roared, and finally, she took the hint. She scrambled off the bed without another word and hurried out of the room, slamming the door behind her.

Suyin didn't stop running until she was back in the safety of her bedroom. She sat on the bed and brought her knees up to her chest, hugging them tightly.

*He got hard.* Their bodies had been pressed together, her limbs spread apart and held down by spectral hands. Yeah, that part had been disturbing, but the way he'd been staring at her, their faces so close . . .

*Keep struggling. I enjoy it.*

A low pulse of heat throbbed between her legs.

"Fuck," she said aloud. *No, no, we're not going there. Control yourself.*

It was one thing to decide she didn't want to kill him anymore. It was another to feel . . . this. He was a demon, for fuck's sake. An evil demon from Hell who practiced necromancy and commanded an army of human souls. She just wasn't that stupid. She *wasn't.*

The scene replayed in her mind again anyway.

The way he'd pinned her so fast, she'd barely seen him move . . . His weight above her, his piercing stare, his pure-white hair falling forward, those proud horns arcing up above his head . . .

And then he'd gotten hard. She'd felt him grow thick and long against her. Her thighs clenched together at the memory.

And then he'd . . . freaked out.

What was that about? She'd always assumed demons were horny perverts who would fuck anything. But Murmur had never once displayed sexual interest in her before tonight. And the shock in his eyes told her he hadn't expected his reaction either.

Had he never had an erection before? No, that would be ridiculous. He was a god-knew-how-old immortal. But maybe it had been a long time?

She'd compared him to a zombie multiple times. The few times he'd touched her, his hands felt like pure ice. Was it possible the necromancy he practiced had seeped into his body and changed him?

Was he dead, in a sense?

Except . . . nothing about him felt dead tonight. In fact, she very clearly remembered feeling heat pouring off him as he loomed over her.

*Keep struggling. I enjoy it.*

She pressed the heels of her palms into her eyes hard enough that she saw stars. That should not be a turn-on. It was not hot. He was depraved and liked the sight of someone weaker than him struggling to escape. That was sick and twisted. Not hot.

*Sick and twisted. Not hot.* She repeated it like a mantra, as if hoping she could rewire her brain.

Forcing her mind off horny thoughts, she remembered what had happened before she'd ended up in his bed. Just thinking of the piercing scream she'd heard sent a chill down her spine.

She was shocked to learn he was a seer, but it made so many things about his eccentric personality make sense. Who wouldn't be driven half mad by reliving their future violent death every time they slept?

A pang of sympathy shot through her. She'd read about blood-born witches with foresight gifts who had gone mad trying to interpret visions of the future. Murmur was unfathomably old, and he said he'd been having visions for as long as he could remember. Honestly, she was amazed he could still function at all.

That was what his spell was about. It made so much sense now. He was having visions of his own death, and whatever he was trying to achieve with that spell would prevent it.

More idiotic sympathy welled. God, could she get any stupider?

If she died down here, she would probably deserve it.

# 15

# The Grand Scheme

When Suyin rolled out of bed after a restless sleep, the sky was still dark, thanks to the painfully long nights in Hell. She knew she usually went to bed after twelve hours or so, but other than that, she had no way of tracking the passage of time.

She tried not to think about how worried everyone back home would be. She'd missed all her shifts at Le Repaire, and she was pretty sure she'd missed a coven meeting by now too. She wasn't a big social butterfly, but she also had some non-witchy friends who would be wondering why she wasn't answering their calls.

There wasn't anything she could do about it except ensure that Murmur's spell was successful. The sooner he accomplished whatever he was trying to do, the sooner she could go home.

After washing up, she dressed in black leggings and a hoodie and then zipped up her boots. She ate the last of her box of granola bars as she climbed the stairs, making a mental note to ask Murmur to get her some more food.

She entered the top floor but hesitated outside the library. She wasn't sure what to expect after what had happened last night. She still wasn't entirely sure what *had* happened last night.

It felt like everything had shifted between them, but she didn't know how Murmur was going to play it. Would he explain why he'd freaked and kicked her out of his room? Or would he just act like it had never happened? And which option would she prefer?

Probably the latter, she decided. Clinging to denial suited her just fine.

She couldn't avoid confrontation forever, so she took a breath and pushed open the door. Unsurprisingly, Murmur was there, crouched at the edge of the big sigil, repainting the lines with what had to be blood. If she'd needed a reminder of what he was, that was a pretty solid one.

The fireplace and lanterns had been lit, and the room was full of comfortable warmth and light. Murmur had braided his hair today, and the thick white rope lay down the middle of his back. His tail curled around his feet, the end flicking like a cat.

Just the sight of him made her stomach clench.

*Clinging to denial, remember?* She shoved the feeling away and came up behind him. "Is that what I think it is?"

He glanced over his shoulder. The moment their eyes met, whatever connection had awakened between them last night sparked back to life. There was an awareness of her in his eyes that hadn't been there before.

He arched a dark brow. "Since you went ahead and familiarized yourself with the contents of my desk, you should already know what it is."

Distracted as she was, it took a moment for that to sink in. When it did, she stiffened. He continued watching her with a knowing look—a *heated* knowing look.

He knew she'd gone through his desk, and . . . he didn't seem pressed about it.

She coughed. "Angel blood, then?"

He went right back to painting the line with controlled brushstrokes. She stared at his back, noting the strength apparent in the controlled movements of his shoulders.

"Correct," he said.

She waited with bated breath for him to chew her out, to threaten to throw her back into the dungeon, to warn her to never touch his shit. Instead, he just kept on painting. Several minutes of tense silence passed before she started to believe he was really going to let it go.

"Where did you get angel blood?" she dared to ask.

"From the angel chained up in my dungeon," he replied, still focused on his lines.

Her eyes bugged. "There's an *angel*— Who? How?"

"He was given to me as a gift. A peace offering of sorts."

She scrubbed her face, trying to digest that information. *That is so fucked up. This whole situation is fucked up, and I think I'm losing my mind.*

She probably should've started planning an angel rescue mission—because weren't they supposed to be the good guys?—but instead she was marveling at how Murmur seemed to be in a sharing mood. She wasn't wasting an opportunity like that.

She studied the back of his head some more. The memory of the night before resurfaced again, and her stomach flipped over.

She ground her teeth. She had to stop these stupid thoughts. He was her captor, and she obviously needed therapy in a bad way.

"Pass me the second bowl of blood from the table?" he asked. She did so, careful not to spill a drop, and he took it from her without looking away from his work.

She stared at the red fluid, noticing it showed no signs of clotting. "Did you use the same potion on the bowl that you used on the vial?"

"Yes. I use it every time I use a blood sacrifice. The recipe is in one of the books I gave to you. If you're going to be practicing Sheolic magic, you should learn it."

"I'll take a look."

He balanced the fresh bowl in one hand and continued painting with the other, still not glancing up. Was he that unaffected by what had happened last night? Or was he just skilled at hiding his thoughts?

It didn't matter. She forced her mind to focus on what really mattered: gathering information. She took a breath and asked, "Are you really a seer?"

"Yes."

"Do your visions always come true? Every time?"

"Yes." His tone was casual, but the subtle tightening of his shoulders said more than his words did. "From what I've seen, anyway."

"Have you ever changed a vision before? Prevented it from happening?"

"No."

There was silence as that sank in. Murmur kept working and Suyin stared at him.

"So what are you going to do?" She shouldn't care. He was right—his death would be the ultimate convenience for her, the easiest way to escape.

He set the bowl down and shot her a look over his shoulder. "I know what you're doing."

"Trying to learn as much as I can?" She shrugged. "Of course I am. I'm stuck here, and only an idiot wouldn't see the value in making the most of a bad situation. Not to mention, you can't blame me for being curious about a spell that involves *my* blood and *my* grimoire."

His eyes narrowed, but it seemed more deliberative than threatening. "I don't know for certain that the future I see in a vision can't be changed. In fact, factors suggest it can be. I can only hope that this time will be the exception to my past experiences. I've certainly never been as motivated as I am now."

She didn't know what to say to that. They were discussing his potential death, and he made it sound inevitable. Not only that, but he'd just revealed a critical weakness.

Before, he'd convinced her that assisting with his spell was the fastest way for her to get free. But if his spell was really a way to save his life, then technically, she could be motivated to stall his progress until the vision caught up with him. Then she would have both her revenge and her freedom.

But . . . she didn't want him dead anymore. Whether that was because she wanted answers and knew he had them, or for some other, much stupider reason she refused to consider, she didn't know.

"What happens if you can't change it?" she asked.

"Then I die, and I can only hope I've succeeded in changing what happens afterward."

"As in, after your death?"

"Mhm." He continued painting once more.

"But . . . there is no *afterward* for a demon. Everyone knows that demons don't have souls, so when they die, they just dissolve into energy."

"That has been the accepted explanation, yes."

"You're saying it's not the truth? That there's something more?"

He set the bowl and paintbrush down and rose suddenly to his full height. She blinked up at him towering above her. Somehow it always came as a surprise how big he was.

"Tell me," he said, tilting his head, "when did you acquire that grimoire of yours?"

"The one you stole?"

"Yes." He didn't even bother to look sorry about it.

"My mother gave it to me right before she died."

"And what did she tell you about it?"

Her mouth twisted. "Basically nothing. She told me it belonged to my father, it contained important information, and I was to guard it carefully."

He cocked a brow. "Didn't do a very good job of that, did you?"

She shot him a glare. "I kept it for over thirty years. And I might have taken better care of it if she'd told me what it was for. I read it a hundred times, and it was always gibberish."

"That's because you were reading it through the lens of your accepted reality."

"What's that supposed to mean?"

His head tilted the other way. "I still find it hard to believe you truly have no idea what you are."

She ground her teeth. She would have punched his perfect, dead face if she could have reached that high. "What I *am* is pissed off because I'm sick of people withholding information about my life from me. First my mother, now you. I was expected to protect some precious book without knowing why, and now I'm expected to open up a Suyin-exclusive blood bank for your stupid spell that you won't fucking explain to me!"

Murmur maintained that annoyingly calm facade. She glared at him, breathing heavily as her anger burned hot. She wanted to demand he acknowledge what happened between them last night and stop acting all cool and collected, like he wasn't thinking the exact same shit she was every time their eyes met.

"I don't have time for this," he growled, looking away. "This is not on my list of things to do in any way, shape, or form."

"What the hell does that mean?"

He stepped out of the sigil suddenly, fluid strides carrying him between the painted lines. Then he strode to his desk and dropped into his chair, beckoning impatiently for her to approach.

As she came up beside him, he pushed aside a few loose papers to reveal her grimoire and pulled it closer. "Right," he began. "I'm going to give you the briefest explanation possible because, as I said, I really don't have time for this."

She stared at the side of his face, scarcely believing what was happening. Was he actually going to tell her what she wanted to know?

He looked at her. By his movement, it seemed it was meant to be a quick glance, but once their eyes caught, they locked. And like before, that connection sparked instantly to life. Her blood heated and shivers raced across her skin.

He shook himself and turned back to the book. "As you surely know, demons and angels are created, not born. Angels have souls. Demons do not. Only beings with souls, like humans and angels, can procreate. Which is how the Nephilim, the forbidden human-angel hybrids, came into being."

"Fallen angels mated with humans."

"Correct." He flipped to the first section of the book, trailing a black claw over a diagram of some kind of aura surrounding a sketch of a person. She leaned over his shoulder to see more clearly. "These pages detail a soul's activating qualities and ability to conceive new life." He flipped a few pages ahead to another section. "And these show how the lack of a soul prevents conception."

"Oh my god . . ." He'd barely explained anything, and already her mind was blown. She'd stared at those diagrams for years wondering what the hell they were for.

"This model has been accepted as fact for all of recorded history," he went on. "Gamigin, however, was one of the first to question our established understanding of souls and study them. And according to his research, a demon can evolve a soul, in a way."

He flipped to another page of diagrams. They looked a bit like drawings of electrons mixed with mandalas. She'd always thought they were sigils, but clearly, she was wrong. "Here, Gamigin theorized how the soul is developed."

"Wait . . ." She blinked at the nonsensical drawings. "Demons can *develop* a soul? From nothing?"

He nodded. "After a very long time, a demon may acquire somewhat of a conscience—a sense of morality and a desire to improve themself. A soul evolves with it, though it's a bit of a chicken-and-egg scenario, since it's unclear whether a conscience births the soul or vice versa."

"But that would mean . . ." She trailed off. What would it mean?

"It means a lot of things." Murmur met her gaze. "Firstly, if an angel with a soul can procreate, shouldn't a demon with a soul be able to do the same?"

Her eyes widened.

"And secondly, any being with a soul must have a place for that soul to go after their death. Angel souls go to Heaven by default. Human souls are judged based on their deeds in life. But what about demon souls?"

"They go to Hell . . .?"

He nodded. "Theoretically, a demon's soul could be weighed on the scales of good and evil, just like humans'. But none have ever had the chance. They are all trapped in Hell, and unlike humans, they have no hope of rebirth and redemption in another life."

"That doesn't seem fair."

"No, it does not."

"But how do you know all this? If most people don't even know demon souls exist, how can you be sure they're trapped in Hell for eternity?"

He smiled thinly, like he approved of her line of questioning. "Because I know who's trapping them."

"What?"

"Gamigin may have been the first to study the evolution of a demon's soul, but he was not the first to have this knowledge. In fact, it has been known by one demon in particular for a very long time."

"Who?"

"Lucifer."

"Luci—" She coughed. "You're kidding."

"The High King not only knows of the existence of demon souls but has been making use of them."

"Making use . . .? What does that mean?"

"A soul is eternal, indestructible—immortal in the only true sense of the word. A soul is also pure, inexhaustible energy. An angel's soul is even more powerful than a human's, so it stands to reason that a demon's would be as well. Imagine the strength one could wield if they could find a way to harness that force."

"Like you did."

"I trap human souls and force them to work for me using their own strength. I'm talking about actually draining power from demon souls and funneling it into one's own essence."

"You're saying Lucifer . . ."

Murmur nodded. "The High King has a deep understanding of the physics of the underworld. He also has a vested interest in ensuring that he remains the most powerful being here. There are many who support an uprising in Hell. Wars are a constant, but many no longer wish to fight them. They're tired of Lucifer's tyranny and want stability. Lucifer represents the old ways, and many believe it's time for change."

"And you?" She was barely able to keep up with this conversation, but she was clinging to Murmur's every word all the same. "What's your stance on this?"

He lifted a shoulder. "Long ago, I had a vision that the High King of Hell would fall, so I've been arranging things to bring it about ever since. It is my calling, but also a matter of self-preservation. I want to ensure my own survival and that my immortal soul is not trapped in service to Lucifer for the rest of eternity."

There was an extended silence as that sank in.

"Your . . . soul."

He nodded, mouth twisting into a sour expression.

"*You* have a soul. You evolved and developed a soul."

He nodded again. He didn't look happy about it.

"How do you know for sure?"

"Because, again, I've seen it in visions. That's how I know all of this—how I learned about Gamigin's book and Lucifer's secret. I have the same vision every time I sleep, and it has made it very clear that my consciousness doesn't end after my death. I have a soul, whether I like it or not." His face made it obvious how he felt on the matter.

She searched his gaze. Standing at his side while he sat in the chair, they were at eye level. While the things that had originally disturbed her about his appearance were still there, now, she saw more. The ice-blue irises in his shadowed, bloodshot eyes were striking. His cruel mouth often quirked with humor.

"What happens in your vision?" she dared to ask.

His fingers flexed, claws digging into the desk, and he turned to stare out the window. The red sky was finally starting to lighten.

"I am burning," he said in a low voice. "The pain is excruciating."

*The scream.* He was experiencing how it felt to burn alive while knowing it was going to happen to him.

"And then, I die. It's a mercy, and at that point, I'm relieved." His jaw shifted, flexing a muscle at his temple. "But my consciousness doesn't end. My awareness remains. I am still *me*. And then, my essence is drawn toward a lightless chasm. I'm trapped there with thousands of other souls. We can never escape. There is nothing but endless black and the never-ending draining of our energy. The despair and hopelessness . . . It's far worse than burning alive."

"That's fucked up," Suyin breathed, not knowing what else to say.

"I have this vision every time I sleep." His voice was distant, his gaze still fixed out the window. "It used to come infrequently, but now I can't escape it. It's coming soon. Any day now, I believe."

"What are you going to do?"

"Lucifer has trapped the soul of every evolved demon who has ever died. I believe he keeps a list of demons he suspects have souls, and he actively hunts them, hoping to kill and add them to his collection. He will come for me soon, and when I die, my soul will go to his prison with the others, and I'll remain there for eternity."

He looked suddenly at her, and her heart skipped a beat.

"Unless I find a way to free those souls."

It was the last thing she'd expected him to say. She'd thought he would try to stop Lucifer from coming after him. Unless . . .

"Would he be too weak to kill you, then? Without all those souls?"

Murmur scoffed. "Hardly. They may be his greatest source of strength, but one does not hold onto the title of High King of Hell without considerable power of their own."

"So then how does freeing the souls prevent your death?" she asked. "Even if your soul is free, if Lucifer comes after you, you'll still be dead."

Murmur nodded approvingly. "You're asking the right questions, Suyin."

She wanted to kick the part of herself that warmed at his praise, but she was too riveted by what he was saying to care.

"The answer is simple: I plan to start a war. Lucifer will have more important things to worry about than me."

"A *war*? Why?"

"I have foreseen it, as I said before. The High King is destined to fall. If I'm successful, he'll lose his primary source of power."

"I still don't understand why he wouldn't come after you as soon as he knows what you did."

"Redirection. Lucifer keeps his prison hidden in the Nine Rings. The souls are entombed behind a door with a powerful seal. My spell will break that seal and create a portal so someone may enter the Rings and open the door. But that someone will not be me."

"Who will?" She was holding her breath. She'd never been so invested.

"Belial."

"As in Belial, the King of Hell? What's he got to do with this?"

"Everything. And he owes me a favor. Two, in fact." Murmur's lips curved wickedly.

She scrambled to make sense of everything. "So you're going to use Belial to open the prison and free the souls. Which will make Lucifer focus on him instead of you."

"Precisely. If Belial went against Lucifer right now, he would fail. The High King is too powerful. But, if I eliminate Lucifer's main power source, then things will really get interesting."

"You're really planning on starting an underworld war." She shook her head. "You're trying to overthrow fucking *Lucifer*. God, you really are mad."

"I'm motivated," he replied. "My life depends upon it, after all. And if my spell is successful, when I eventually die, my soul will be free to be judged and then go on to wherever it is I should go." He smiled grimly. "Make no mistake, I fully expect to rot in the lowest level of the Nine Rings, but I would rather suffer for thousands of years in the Rings than be trapped in limbo, in some lightless, inescapable prison, where my essence is used to feed the High King's power."

"That's . . ." She blew out a breath. "That's insane, Murmur."

His whole plan was. The scope was so grand, it was hard to wrap her head around it. Everyone knew Lucifer was the ruler of Hell. He had been since forever. To get rid of him . . . She had a hard time believing it was even possible.

And it was a hell of a burden for Murmur to bear. Her feelings about him were complicated. She still half hoped Lucifer would kill him. Murmur was a bastard, but damn it, she sympathized with him too. If he really did have a soul, she supposed that meant there was some goodness in him, and he deserved a chance to redeem himself.

Besides, he was *the* Necromancer. She couldn't imagine him not existing. It seemed against the natural order somehow.

"What about me?" she asked suddenly. "Where do I come into this? Why do you need *my* blood?"

"You still haven't figured it out?" A teasing glint came into his eyes.

"Obviously not, or I wouldn't be asking," she said through gritted teeth.

"Your mother gave you this." He tapped the page *The Book of Gamigin* was open to. "Where do you think she got it?"

"My father, but—"

"And how did he get it?"

"I don't know," she said impatiently. "My mother said he wrote it, but after what you've told me, there's no way that's possible. I can only assume he got it from the demon who wrote it, but I don't know—"

"Oh, my sweet, naive little witch." His lips curved into that cheek-crinkling smile.

She scowled at him. "Quit beating around the bush, Murmur. Just tell me already."

"Your father didn't get this grimoire from the demon who wrote it, Suyin. Your father *was* the demon who wrote it."

# 16

# Another Nail in the Coffin

It's like déjà vu!" Eva called out as she stepped around the corner at the end of the block. "Remember the first time we did this?"

Belial and his brothers—along with Iris and Sunshine—were waiting below the flickering neon sign for Bootleg, the club that hosted the Thursday-night jam Eva and Asmodeus frequented.

"I seem to recall that I was smoking," Ash said as Eva joined their group. He stooped to give her a kiss.

"Yeah, and then I told you how long it takes cigarette butts to decompose, and you looked at me like I'd grown a second head." Eva chuckled. "Thank god you quit."

"And then I asked if you were a closet lesbian because I didn't know you could see through Ash's curse," Meph said.

"Oh my god, I was so mad at you for that!" Eva chuckled. "I thought you were the biggest dick."

"So, not much has changed, then," Raum said.

Iris looked between them and laughed. “I have no idea what’s going on.”

“We’re just rehashing the first time I ever took the guys to this club,” Eva said with a grin. “It was right after Ash and I first met, before I knew he was a demon.”

The situation tonight was similar, but in Bel’s mind, things couldn’t have been more different. And their so-called family had expanded so much since then. Sunshine was holding Raum’s hand, smiling at everyone though she probably didn’t have a clue what they were talking about either. And Meph’s arm was slung over Iris’s shoulder, and the witch actually looked happy about it.

Eva transferred her gaze to Bel and smiled. “Should we go upstairs?”

His dysfunctional family had been trying to get him to go out with them for weeks, and he’d steadfastly refused. The last time he was in this club, he’d grabbed a human by the throat and nearly crushed his windpipe just for bumping into him. He wasn’t looking to repeat that experience, especially because this time, he wasn’t sure he’d be able to stop. Crushing a throat seemed like the perfect outlet for his pent-up frustration.

So why had he come out tonight?

He wasn’t entirely sure. Maybe he sensed he was close to a kind of precipice, and he’d come here hoping to recapture the hope and elation he’d felt after his last visit. It was that very night that he’d made his six-months-of-celibacy pact, after all.

Maybe, if he just kept trying, just kept pretending, things would fix themselves. Yeah, he’d never heard of that working for anybody ever, but fuck it, there was a first time for everything.

“Let’s go,” he told Eva.

They pulled open the heavy door and climbed the stairs to the dumpy old jazz club, pushing into the tightly packed throng of bodies. Being seven feet tall in human form, Bel towered over everyone. People took one look at him and got out of his way. Funny, because he wasn't even angry at the moment. Just mildly irritated, which was pretty much his constant state of being.

He was used to humans being afraid of him. He was an ancient supernatural being, and most mortals sensed that in some part of their subconscious. The only people who weren't afraid of him were those who viewed him as a potential sexual partner. And half the time, he was pretty sure they were still afraid of him too. It was just mixed with desire—a tantalizing combination for any thrill seeker.

The band was on stage, already setting up for the first round of jamming. "Skye has the night off and wanted to meet up," Eva called over her shoulder, half shouting to be heard over the house music pumping through the PA system. "I told her to save our usual table." She shot Bel a wary look.

"It's so loud in here!" Sunshine exclaimed, pressing her palms over her ears.

"Meph and I will get drinks!" Iris called out. She looked at Bel. "What do you want?"

"Something strong," he replied.

She saluted him with a grin and then grabbed Meph and dragged him toward the bar.

Bel and Raum flanked an overstimulated Sunshine as they followed Ash and Eva through the crowd. Poor Sunshine kept her palms over her ears, and her ever-present smile began to look slightly strained.

Raum shot protective glares in multiple directions. Their natural demonic allure meant Bel and his brothers were used to attracting attention, but Sunshine's otherworldly angelic aura drew just as many gazes. Eyes followed her all the way across the club.

"Sunshine, do you want some earplugs?" Eva asked when they reached the table. "I keep an extra pair of those foamy construction ones in my bag in case of emergencies."

"Yes, please!" Sunshine shouted, and Eva dug through her purse.

Bel took a seat on the narrow wooden bench against the wall, wincing when the entire thing creaked ominously under his weight. If it gave out under him, he was going to burn this place to the ground.

Raum sat beside him. "You good?"

"No," Bel growled. "Why did I agree to this again?"

"You used to like going out."

"Hm."

"Eva's friend Skye is here."

"Hm."

"Apparently, she asked Eva about you more than once. Ash told me."

"Is that so."

"I don't think Eva wants you to hook up with her though."

He didn't blame her. Eva's best friend was fully human, oblivious to the supernatural world, and not gifted with the Sight. Eva knew well how unstable Bel was and what happened when he lost his temper.

Raum shot him a look. "So, are you gonna go for it?"

Bel's jaw shifted. He didn't respond. He wasn't talking about this with Raum. Or anyone.

Raum shrugged and turned to observe Eva explaining how to use the spongy earplugs to Sunshine. When Sunshine continued to look confused, Raum stood and went over to assist. Bel watched with mild amusement as two different people demonstrated squishing the orange foam and shoving it into the ear canal while Sunshine looked mildly concerned.

A small human woman dropped into the chair across the table from him. She had tanned skin and shiny black hair, and Bel knew instantly who she was.

"Remember me?" she called over the loud music, a grin stretching her face. "We met one night like a year ago and—"

"I definitely remember you." He flashed a brief smile.

How could he forget? Skye was the one who'd inspired his self-inflicted celibacy in the first place. The night they'd met, she had told him she'd decided to forgo any sexual contact for six months. Bel, sick of breaking promises to himself and giving into Naiamah's manipulative sex bargains, had decided to join her. He'd left their conversation feeling like he was finally taking control of his life.

Now, he felt more out of control than ever.

In his peripherals, he saw Eva watching him with a frown. Asmodeus took her hand and led her toward the stage. She whispered something in his ear, and Ash shook his head and continued walking. Eva allowed herself to be led, but not without shooting another concerned glance over her shoulder.

"So?" Skye asked. "How did your pact go? Did you succeed?"

*Naiamah laughed in my face, and it turned me into a horny ball of rage instead of just a regular ball of rage. Now I've become a recluse because I'm afraid I'll kill a bunch of humans if anyone so much as breathes wrong around me.*

"I succeeded." *I'm still succeeding, even now, whether I want to or not.*

"Congratulations!" She laughed. "I succeeded too."

"And? How did it go for you?" Hopefully at least one of them got something productive out of those six months of self-inflicted torture.

"It was amazing! It changed my life. I feel like a new woman." She grinned, and he could see in her eyes that she meant it.

He tried to grin back but failed miserably. He was genuinely glad to see her thriving, but he was also a grouchy old bastard who'd forgotten how to make his smile muscles work. "I can tell," he said. "You look good." It was true. She did look good.

"Thank you." She tucked a strand of dark hair behind her ear. "You know, I was hoping I'd run into you at some point." She had to shout to be heard over the music. "I've seen Ash's other brothers a bunch of times since that first night we met, but not you."

"I don't go out much." Not anymore, anyway.

"Well, I'm glad you came out tonight."

"Me too," he replied, but he wasn't sure yet if he meant it.

He kept waiting for the urge to flirt to hit. Skye was attractive, youthful and lively, but with an edge that made it clear she wasn't innocent or naive. She was exactly the type of woman he would've gone for in the past.

The thing was . . . he was on edge around humans now. He couldn't help it. He didn't trust himself, and he knew his control was shit.

He glanced up and found Sunshine watching him. There might as well have been a spotlight on his head. *Gather 'round, folks! Belial is talking to a girl!*

Unlike Eva, however, Sunshine gave him an encouraging smile and a wink. At least someone believed in him.

Maybe she was right. Maybe he needed to get over himself and stop taking everything so seriously. Maybe he did have more control than he thought. He remembered well the hope for the future he'd felt after meeting Skye and making their pact. He hadn't felt anything like that before or since, and he wanted that feeling back.

"Are you still cooking?" Skye shouted across the table. "You told me when we met that you like to cook."

Bel took a breath. He could do this. It was just a simple conversation with a pretty human. And she was asking him about food. He could talk for hours about food.

"Yeah, I—" Unfortunately, he was interrupted by the house music cutting off and a guy on stage announcing that they were going to start the jam. A moment later, the band fired up, somehow managing to be even louder.

Iris and Meph returned with two armfuls of drinks and sat beside Skye. Meph grinned evilly at Skye, and Bel groaned internally. Sunshine looked thrilled by the music, and she dragged Raum into the crowd to be closer to the stage, smiling up at the musicians like they were heavenly angels come to Earth. Bel looked over and caught Skye watching him. Her gaze darted shyly away.

He picked up a shot glass from the table without asking who it was for and tossed it back. There were two more, so he drank those too. When he set the third glass down, he glanced up and found Skye now giving him a concerned frown.

Great. She probably thought he had a drinking problem. He was never going to get through this night with his pride intact.

Surprisingly, after some time, Bel found himself relaxing. He remembered what it was like when he'd first escaped Hell and he'd gone out to party with his brothers every night. While he wasn't up for that level of revelry now, he was starting to hope that maybe Sunshine really was right, and he hadn't given himself enough credit.

Maybe he could be around humans.

Whenever Eva and Asmodeus went up to play, the rest of them crowded the stage rowdily. It was fun to mess with Ash and watch him shoot glares at them out of the corner of his eye while keeping up with the band. Multitasker extraordinaire.

During their second set, Bel decided he needed a break. He slapped Meph and Raum on the shoulders hard enough that they stumbled, and then went back to the table. There was only so long he could stand having people pressed against him in a crowd before he started imagining tossing them through the air like sacks of grain.

He sat warily back on the wooden bench, and it groaned but held. There was another full shot glass on the table that he was pretty sure Iris had brought for him. He glanced up and saw her looking, so he raised the glass to her before tipping it back. She gave him a thumbs up.

Iris turned back to the stage just as Skye appeared beside him. She'd been with them in the crowd most of the night, but he hadn't gotten another chance to speak to her.

The look she gave him now told him she wanted to change that. "I'm hungry, so I'm gonna go grab something to eat," she said with a smile. Her gaze was direct. "You wanna come?"

He knew he should say no. Eva didn't want him hanging around her friend, and he should back off out of respect for her. But Sunshine's encouragement and the memory of his first meeting with Skye made him want to take a risk. Plus, the little human was the opposite of Naiamah in every way, and that was appealing enough on its own.

"Sure," he replied. Getting some fresh air and a break from the noise was probably a good idea too.

See? He could be smart about this.

"I'll text Eva and tell her where we've gone," Skye said, donning her coat. Eva was currently on stage, so she couldn't find a way to intervene, which suited Bel just fine. He stood, meeting Raum's gaze across the crowd. He was behind Sunshine with his arms around her and his chin resting on her head.

Raum cocked a brow in question, glancing pointedly at Skye. Bel rolled his eyes. Raum unwrapped his arms from Sunshine and pulled his phone out of his pocket. A moment later Bel's phone buzzed, so he checked it.

Raum's text said, *You got things under control?*

*Bite me*, Bel texted back.

Raum read the message but gave no outward reaction. He replied, *Eva will be pissed if you incinerate her friend.*

Bel shook his head. *Not fucking funny.*

*No one's laughing.*

He shot his brother a glare and pocketed his phone.

"Let's go!" Skye said. Pushing through the crowd, she ducked and weaved between bodies. Bel walked in a straight line behind her, and people moved out of his way.

Down on the street, he took deep breaths of fresh air and shoved his hands into his hoodie pocket. Meph had gotten him hooked on wearing them and he hated it, but damn it, they were comfortable. He had to order at least a 5XL which made his choices limited, but he let his clothing-addicted brother pick them out for him, so minimal effort was required.

He walked next to Skye, ducking under low-hanging signs and dodging crowds coming from other venues on the street.

"You're the tallest person I've ever seen," she said with a laugh when he was almost clotheslined by a string of fairy lights. "What are you, like, six-eight?"

"Seven foot," he mumbled.

"Damn." Her flirtatious grin was somewhat diminished by how far back she had to crane her neck for him to see it. "That's really tall."

"Yep." He cleared his throat and then inwardly cringed. Apparently, he'd lost all his game since becoming a recluse. The woman was trying to hit on him, and he was acting like an idiot.

"There's a taco place on the next block that I love," Skye said, mercifully changing the subject.

Bel mentally grimaced. *Fast food.* There was nothing he loathed more.

She flashed him a worried look. "Unless there's somewhere else you'd rather go?"

There was nothing on this entire street he would eat unless under threat of torture. "It's all right. I'm not hungry."

"Oh." She stuffed her hands into her coat pockets. "Is it weird for me to eat then?"

"Why would that be weird?"

"I dunno."

"It's not weird."

"Okay. Good." She coughed.

Shit, he was making this awkward, wasn't he? Truth be told, he was a bit nervous. He didn't want to fuck up. Not just because "fucking up" could result in Skye's untimely death, but because he actually enjoyed her company.

He wasn't even close to ready to go there, but he couldn't help thinking about his brothers and the happiness they'd found with their girlfriends. And maybe . . . though he'd never tell a soul . . . it would be nice to have that for himself. Maybe it would help him calm the rage somehow, the same way Iris had helped Meph make peace with his demon.

"So, what did you get up to during your six months of celibacy?" Skye asked, trying again to spark conversation. "How did you survive?"

"I cooked a lot. That's pretty much all I did." *Besides the near constant drama of trying to keep my brothers from ending up back in Hell, being stalked by angels, and trying not to burn my house down and kill people.* Damn, it was hard to be friendly when there was so much he couldn't say.

"Honestly, that sounds perfect because I swear I was starving the entire time."

He breathed a laugh. That, he could relate to. He was never actually hungry because he didn't need to eat to survive, yet somehow, he was always ravenous. Not necessarily for food, but just for . . . something. Food was just a distraction. But it was the best distraction there was.

"What about you?" he asked. "How did you get through it?"

"I focused on school. It was boring, but I've almost finished my degree now, so it paid off. I like your hair, by the way," she blurted before he could reply. "Long suits you."

"Oh. Thanks."

"You look like an ancient warrior or something. It's awesome."

He winced. Maybe he should get it cut after all.

"It's just across the street," Skye said, pointing. "Let's cross here."

When the pedestrian sign lit up, they stepped off the curb onto the crosswalk.

"It's kinda embarrassing," Skye said, "but I thought about you a lot after we last saw each other. I'm really glad I ran into you tonight because I wanted to ask you so many times how—"

It happened in the blink of an eye.

A car pulled out of a parking space, and the driver stepped on the gas, oblivious to the red light glaring in his face. Skye was slightly behind Bel, and he was looking over his shoulder at her while she spoke. Which was how he was able to see that she was directly in the car's path.

He acted without thinking. He spun, took a step toward her, and shoved her hard toward the sidewalk. She went flying. He braced just in time for the car to hit him.

If he'd been human, his legs would have crumpled, crushed at the knees by the bumper, and he would have flown onto the hood. He wasn't human, however.

The car came to a dead stop, the bumper dented so deeply, it looked like they'd driven into a streetlamp.

Distantly, he heard shouts and gasps from onlookers. He saw Skye on the ground all the way back on the sidewalk where he'd thrown her. The humans in the car that hit him sprang from the vehicle and rushed toward him, and so did some of the onlookers from the sidewalk.

But that was all distant. Because there was a roaring in his ears and a throbbing at the base of his skull that obliterated almost everything.

A fucking human had driven a car into him. And now the idiot was hovering around, making excuses and apologies when Bel could *smell* the alcohol on his breath.

Fucking humans were like filthy leeches, crawling around their precious planet, tainting everything they touched under the false illusion that they were the masters of the universe. They needed to be put in their place. They *all* needed to be put in their place.

"I'm so sorry!" the human was saying.

"Oh my god, the car—"

"How is that even possible?"

"Are you okay?"

"I saw the car hit him—"

"What were you thinking! The light was red!"

"I didn't see! I swear I thought it was green—"

The switch flipped. Bel snapped.

His vision became awash with red, and he knew his eyes had changed. And then he felt himself gaining height. With an ungodly roar, he turned and smashed both his fists down on the hood of the car.

The metal crumpled beneath his hands as if hit by two boulders dropped from a height. And then he grabbed the car underneath the folded bumper and threw it back several feet.

Instant, dead silence fell over the street.

He straightened, head hanging, hair in his face, fighting back the rage igniting his blood. He wanted to fucking kill everyone here gawking at him. He wanted to tear the heart out of that drunk driver's chest and make him eat it.

"Holy shit . . ." someone breathed.

Bel turned and stared down the driver until he blanched whiter than a sheet and stumbled, falling to the ground and holding his hands up. The preternatural fury in Bel's eyes told the human he was facing the kind of monster that was supposed to be imaginary.

Bel prowled toward him. The driver scuttled back. Tears collected in his eyes. "Don't hurt me, man. Please, I swear—"

Bel looked up. Skye was standing in the crowd of people who had gathered. Her features were stark. Full of terror. Just like everyone else.

She looked into his flaming eyes and stumbled back just like the other human had. And then she turned and sprinted down the street like it was the fucking zombie apocalypse and she was the last person alive.

The sight of her fleeing was the metaphorical equivalent to a bucket of cold water to the face. The red haze faded. The street returned to his sight. The sounds bled back in. Slowly, he fought to get his breathing under control and felt himself return to normal height.

Humans without the Sight could see the catastrophe he'd caused because there was nothing supernatural about denting a car hood. As for the hellfire in his eyes and his height increase, they may not recognize exactly what they'd seen, but their fear instincts were very real. They knew they were in the presence of something dangerous that shouldn't exist on Earth, and they were terrified.

Just like Skye.

He backed away from the stunned faces staring at him. If he didn't get out of this crowd, he was going to snap again. And this time he might actually kill someone. Probably that fucking drunk driver still cowering on the ground.

Bel stepped onto the sidewalk on the opposite side of the street. The people gathered there parted for him to pass, all staring at him like he was a green alien who'd just dropped out of the sky.

He strode down the block until he'd left the crowd behind.

No one followed him. Crossing the street again, he stopped outside the door to Bootleg and weighed his options. There was no way he was going back up there.

Looking around, he saw no sign of Skye. He'd probably scared her so bad, she was sprinting all the way home. She probably wouldn't come out for days. Eva was going to be pissed.

Screw the stupid feeling of elation he'd been chasing. Screw his stupid hopes of finding a pretty little girlfriend like his brothers. He wanted nothing to do with humans. He never wanted to make a woman look at him with that much fear again. It made him feel sick.

He'd come a long way from the evil, flaming bastard he'd once been. That fucker would have laughed with joy at the sight of mortals pissing themselves. Sunshine would say it was a good thing, but he wasn't so sure anymore.

*Fuck this.* He started walking in the direction of home. It was going to take him nearly an hour to get there at a normal pace, but he was still on a razor's edge, and there was no way he was trusting himself in a cab with a human driver right now.

He didn't want to talk to anyone. He didn't want anyone to talk to him.

So much for his control. So much for blending in. He'd done some Hulk shit on a random idiot's car and then given Eva's best friend nightmares for life. He supposed he should be glad he hadn't burst into flames, but damn, it had been close. Way too close.

# 17

# The Devil May Care

MURMUR LEANED BACK IN HIS CHAIR, WATCHING THE array of emotions flitting across Suyin's face. There was confusion, shock, denial, and finally, some kind of resentment, as though she were angry with him for daring to suggest that her father was a demon.

Strangely, he didn't mind being the target of her indignation.

He was the first to admit he didn't like humans. Even half humans. He didn't like demons either. He didn't like anyone. But Suyin was exceptional.

Her company was tolerable. Enjoyable, even. Her intelligence was refreshing. And her body, slender, lithe, graceful—

He quickly buried the arousal that stirred his blood as soon as he recalled the sight of her pinned beneath him. His body was dead. He'd made that sacrifice long ago. It had been a suitable exchange to master his practice. He'd accepted it.

*Well, it's obviously not dead anymore, is it?*

*It has to be*. If it wasn't, he didn't know what that meant for him. It had to have been a one-time thing. Nothing had changed. Maybe he'd imagined it.

*Denial hinders your progress and rots your mind. Accept the inevitable. The witch has roused your desire, and you should have her. Sate yourself in her. Take her again and again until you've fed this urge.*

*Be silent.* He shook himself and focused back on Suyin, still standing beside his chair.

"My father— No." Her head was down, her gaze fixed on the open grimoire on the table. "It can't be. He wasn't— His name was Samuel, not Gamigin, and—"

"Demons often use fake names on Earth when they're trying to blend in. And Gamigin's other name was Samigina. Look it up. Samuel seems like a reasonable substitute."

Her gaze shot to his, eyes wide.

"Did you ever meet him?" Murmur asked, genuinely curious. Much of Gamigin's life was a mystery to him.

"Technically yes, but he died only a few months after I was born, so I don't remember him."

"And what did your mother tell you about him?"

"I— Almost nothing." Suyin frowned. "But she said he was passionate about demonology, not that he was an actual demon."

"Well, she lied."

"Why would she do that?" She searched Murmur's eyes almost desperately, like she was still hoping for him to spring up and announce this had all been a trick.

"I don't know." He softened his tone. Seeing her in distress made him uncomfortable. He much preferred her hard shell and sharp edges. "If I had to guess, I would say for your own safety. She likely believed that you, and your father's legacy, would be safest if you believed yourself simply to be a blood-born witch. Then you wouldn't go searching for hints of your father's past and accidentally expose yourself."

"But—" She sputtered. "But I'm not aging!"

"You're immortal. Of course you're not aging."

Her eyes bugged. "I've been stressing about this for years. I thought I had some kind of super-charged witch ability that I had no control over, for fuck's sake. She could have prepared me!"

"As far as I know, you're the only Cambion in existence right now. She may not have known."

"The only what?"

"Cambion. A demon-human hybrid. Much like a Nephilim—an angel-human hybrid—you're immortal, you have special abilities, and your blood has powerful magical properties. Hence its usefulness in my spell. It was your father who gave me the idea to use it, actually. He has a whole section of his book dedicated to studying a Cambion's physiology and the magical properties of their blood. Another reason your mother may have kept you a secret."

"What do you mean?"

"Well, I'm sure your parents cared about their daughter, and the last thing they wanted was a demon like me hunting you down to use your blood in a spell." Murmur smiled without remorse. "So by keeping the truth hidden, even from you, it assured no one ever learned of you. I only did from a vision. Lucky me."

She ran a hand through her hair. "This is too much to process. I'm not even sure I believe you."

"The truth is not dependent upon your belief in it."

"*If* it is the truth, then what happened to him? My mother told me he died of an illness. But if he was a demon, there's no way that's true."

"It's not. It was Lucifer. As I told you, the High King seeks out demons he believes to have evolved so he can kill them and claim their souls for his power source."

Her hand rose to her mouth. "He was killed?"

"Gamigin broke the rules by escaping Hell and living as a human on Earth, so he was free game for Lucifer to eliminate without consequence. Many have tried to do the same, and all have failed. Then Belial and his so-called brothers came along. Somehow, they managed to persuade Heaven to allow them to live freely on Earth. But regardless of whether the rules have been changed, Lucifer will still kill them if he has the chance."

But Suyin seemed to barely be listening. "You're saying my father's—Gamigin's soul is trapped right now. By Lucifer."

"Yes."

"He's stuck in a horrible prison of endless suffering, like in your vision?"

"Correct."

"And if your spell succeeds, he'll be free? So he can go wherever he deserves to spend the afterlife?"

"Also correct."

"With . . . my mother's soul, maybe."

"Perhaps, yes."

To his vast surprise, Suyin's eyes filled with tears.

Murmur blinked at the sight. He'd done all manner of things to her—isolation, starvation, threats, terrorizing her with his souls—and never once had she shed a single tear. But now, at the mention of her dead parents, her eyes filled with emotion.

She turned around and leaned her back against the desk beside him, dropping her head into her hands. Her hair fell over her face, and she stayed like that, silent and unmoving, for long enough that Murmur began to feel mild concern.

"Suyin," he said gently. "As fascinating as the sight of your mental breakdown is, might I suggest you speed up the process a little? I'm rather bored."

Her head snapped up, and she pinned him with a furious glare. "You're kidding me, right? You just dropped this bomb on me, told me that my entire life is a lie, and you're *bored* by my emotional reaction? Fuck you."

He nodded with approval. This mood was much better. He preferred her anger to watching her shut down.

"You're an asshole."

"Yes. Are we done now?"

She pushed off the desk and seemed to shake the remnants of shock from herself. A strange sense of pride filled him. She kept surprising him, and he kept liking it.

He didn't regret telling her his secrets either. He wasn't entirely sure why. It served no purpose to him. If anything, it hindered his progress, wasting the time it took to answer her questions.

His death vision was drawing closer by the hour, but all of a sudden, he was in no rush to get back to work. Part of it was simply because it felt good to finally explain the inner workings of his mind to another. He'd never revealed his plan to anyone, and speaking of it for the first time brought a certain clarity to his unstable thoughts. Even the ever-present screams of the souls in his head had lessened in intensity.

Another part was that he liked how Suyin's mind worked. She reminded him of himself long ago, before the tormented souls and visions of the future had whittled away the edges of his sanity.

She was a distraction he didn't need . . . but perhaps one he wanted.

If his plan failed, he would die. He supposed that would cause anyone to behave a little recklessly. As long as it didn't completely derail his progress, he decided there was nothing wrong with enjoying himself a little. He'd certainly spent enough time being miserable and alone in his lair.

He smacked a palm on the desk suddenly. "We'll cast the spell tomorrow. I'll finish repainting the lines with Raphael's blood and then—"

"Raphael?" Her eyes widened. "*The* Raphael? The archangel?"

His mouth twisted. He hadn't meant to let that slip. The last thing he needed was Suyin trying to liberate his valuable blood source. Then he'd have to punish her, and he didn't feel like doing that.

A distraction was the best way to make her forget about it. Luckily, he knew just the thing.

"I have several more of your father's grimoires," he said. "If you want to learn more about him, you're welcome to look at them while I finish. I don't need you today."

His plan worked, and her eyes widened again. "He wrote more than one?"

"Yes. But this one"—he tapped the open book before him—"is by far his greatest achievement. And the only one that discusses the existence of Cambions."

"Can you . . ." Her gaze darted away and then traveled back to his. She seemed to be gathering her courage. "When you've finished your work for today, can we go through *The Book of Gamigin* together? I've read it a hundred times, and I never got a single iota of the information you just told me about it. I want to read it again and finally understand it."

He pursed his lips. *Wasting more time.* He couldn't. He shouldn't.

*She'll be gone soon, and you'll be all alone again. Enjoy her while she's here.*

Stupid impulsive inner voice. He could feel himself caving.

Suyin's efforts to persuade him weren't helping either. "If your spell fails or if you somehow can't stop your vision from happening, shouldn't someone be left alive besides Lucifer who knows all these secrets?"

He scowled. "You're trying to manipulate me again."

She shrugged unashamedly. "I'm just saying . . ."

He considered her point. If he failed at changing his vision, everything he'd learned from Gamigin's book would die with him. Lucifer would continue imprisoning demon souls.

The consciousness of Hell was changing, and Murmur had theorized that more demons would be developing souls than ever before. There would either be a great shift, or Lucifer would dominate, becoming more powerful than ever, and things would remain how they had always been.

"I don't care what happens to anyone else," Murmur said, to convince himself as much as Suyin. "If I die, it's irrelevant to me."

She frowned. She didn't like that answer, he could tell. She probably wanted him to save the world and all the little puppies and kittens too.

But instead of chastising him, she said, "Your vision is of your soul being trapped. That means that if you fail and die, your spell has also failed. So if you don't care about anyone else, you should at least care about that. If you show me what exactly it is you're trying to do here, I could try to continue your work even if you do die."

His brows rose. "Besides the obvious fact that it would take you centuries to be even close to powerful enough to attempt this spell, why should you care what happens to my soul, or the souls of any dead demons for that matter?"

"It's not just the souls of random dead demons. If everything you told me is true—"

"It is."

"—then it's my *father's* soul. I'm almost as motivated as you are to break them free. I don't think I'll ever be able to sleep at night again, knowing my father's soul is trapped in an inescapable prison in Hell."

"You never knew him. Why should you care?"

"I don't need to know him. He's my father. My mother loved him, and that's enough for me to know he was a good person. He doesn't deserve this."

"Fine." Murmur waved a hand. He was done arguing against something he'd already wanted to do. "You win. I'll tell you whatever you want to know."

Her eyes lit up, and her spine straightened. "Really?"

A funny lightness took hold of his chest, but he ignored it with a scowl. He'd given in far too easily, and he knew it. But he didn't have the energy to keep fighting her and the part of himself that wanted to give her what she wanted.

"Yes," he growled, "but not until tonight, when I've finished my work. And stop looking at me like that, or I'll change my mind and throw you back into the dungeon."

She rolled her eyes. The little witch rolled her eyes at him *again.*

"Now, get out." He dismissed her with a flick of his claws toward the door. "I have work to do, and you have proven to be the worst kind of distraction. Funny, because I distinctly remember you swearing to remain silent and keep out of my way at all times."

She smiled unrepentantly.

He scowled and jerked his chin toward the door.

She turned to go, her steps graceful despite the clunky boots she wore. Shaking his head, he rose from the desk and approached the sigil. He stepped over the lines to the section he'd been working on and crouched beside the bowl of Raphael's blood, picking up the paintbrush.

Suyin stopped at the door. "When's tonight?"

He glanced back with a frown.

"I don't understand how time passes here. Will it be dark out or do you mean in eight hours or so?"

"In eight hours."

"But it won't be night. So why would you—"

"In Hell, days are twice as long as on Earth, and nights are three times as long. But we track the passage of time the same way humans do."

"But . . ." She scrunched up her face. "That's so confusing? Why?"

He shot her a look. "Because in Hell, as on Earth, everything revolves around precious humanity. Now go, and don't come back until eight hours have passed."

The witch narrowed her eyes at him before finally slipping through the door. He didn't move, listening to her footsteps until they faded away.

He looked back at the sigil. The prospect of working didn't fill him with burning ambition and obsession as it always did. In fact, as he went back to repainting the lines, he barely paid attention to what he was doing.

Instead, he started planning how he would teach Suyin about her father's work and whatever else she wanted to know. He'd never had a student before. The idea of passing on his knowledge had never occurred to him, but now that it had, he was oddly fixated on it.

Gamigin's book was arguably one of the most important works in history, and as far as he knew, he was the only one alive who'd read and interpreted it correctly. He knew Heaven had been trying to get their hands on it, but he'd thus far thwarted their efforts.

He liked the idea of teaching Suyin what he'd learned. It would be a legacy of sorts.

*You really are losing your mind.*

"Don't start with me," he mumbled.

*Legacies are human concepts. Perhaps you only hate humans because you wish you were one. Imitation is the highest form of flattery, as they say. And you've sure spent a lot of time pretending to be civil and humanlike since your little guest arrived.*

"I said, *don't*," he snapped. "I don't have time for this right now."

*You should fuck her*, his mental voice whispered, doing a complete one-eighty.

He groaned. This was the last thing he needed.

*Pin her down, chain her up so she can't move, and then fuck her until she screams your name.*

His groan was for a different reason now as his head suddenly filled with erotic images.

Then he blinked and looked at what he was painting. His hand had been unsteady, and the line was the furthest thing from straight.

"For fuck's sake." Any mistake in a sigil this powerful had the ability to render the entire thing useless, or worse, create some catastrophic side effect. Where was his mind today?

*In the gutter, that's where. And if you don't get it out, you're going to fail, and Lucifer will find and kill you, and then you'll be dead, and you'll never—*

"You're either berating me for being distracted or telling me to fuck the witch. You can't have both. Which is it?"

His inner voice went suspiciously quiet.

Rolling his eyes, he dropped his paintbrush back into the bowl and stormed off to get a rag. The lines of each symbol had to be done without interruption. He'd need to repaint the entire section.

He cleaned up the area, but instead of recommencing, he let his eyes wander up and scanned the bookshelves before him. He was pretty sure he'd put Gamigin's other grimoires in that section, but maybe he ought to check? He'd also written a book of his own that recorded his learnings from Gamigin more concisely. He'd been sick of reinterpreting Gamigin's ramblings every time he needed to refresh his memory. Suyin would likely be interested in that as well.

Maybe he'd just grab the books quickly so he could stop thinking about it.

Stepping carefully out of the sigil, he crossed the room and climbed the ladder to one of the upper sections. He pulled the book he sought from the shelf, but before he could climb down again, his eyes caught on another grimoire.

*Hm.* Suyin might want to read this one too.

He pulled it from the shelf. *Come to think of it . . .* There was another book . . . *Right here, yes . . .* He definitely had to show her this one.

And so it went.

Three hours later, Murmur was buried behind a stack of books as tall as Suyin, and he'd completely forgotten about the unfinished sigil on the floor.

Suyin ate from her dwindling food supplies for dinner. She'd meant to ask Murmur to send his minions to Earth for her again, but she'd gotten a little distracted by all the life-changing revelations he'd dropped on her.

She was half demon. A Cambion. A creature considered a myth.

Her father was a demon. Not an eccentric man who'd suffered from delusions because of an unhealthy fixation with Sheolic magic. He was a powerful, genius demon who'd written a grimoire so packed with groundbreaking information that it took another powerful, genius demon to decipher it.

When Suyin thought of her mother lying to her about who he was all those years, not even telling her the truth on her deathbed, a wave of hurt and anger rolled through her. But at the same time, she understood it. She wouldn't have made the same choice, but she understood it.

Throughout her childhood, whenever Suyin had asked for details about her mysterious father, her mother's responses had been vague. Sometimes she had refused to say anything at all. But Suyin had always understood that her mother loved her father deeply, and her reticence came more from a place of grief, from holding a memory close to her heart that was too precious and painful to speak aloud, than from any attempt to keep her in the dark.

Had Fay and Gamigin known what would happen if he was killed? Had they known about Lucifer's prison? She didn't think so, but she did know that Gamigin escaping Hell and fathering a hybrid child was very against the rules, so they must've known there was a possibility of him being caught.

No wonder Fay had been so silent and closed off in her grief. Her husband, whom she'd loved enough to have a forbidden child with, had been murdered. Had he been killed before her eyes? Or had she witnessed him being caught and dragged back to Hell, holding on to some vague hope that he might somehow survive, only to finally be forced to give up and accept that he was gone forever?

Suyin would never know the answers to those questions. But knowing what Gamigin was now, she was surprised at how little it affected her beliefs about the man he'd been.

She trusted her mother—though it would take her some time to release her resentment over her lies—and had always seen her as a source of strength and inspiration. Fay had been strongly principled and steadfast in her beliefs. She had survived losing the love of her life and moving her infant daughter to a completely new country and culture. She had taught Suyin everything she needed to know about being a blood-born witch, while remaining a source of comfort and security for her. Even learning about her mother's dishonesty could not tarnish Suyin's gratitude for what she'd given her.

She firmly believed that if Fay had loved Gamigin enough to have a forbidden child with him, then he was worthy of it.

It fit with what Murmur had told her about demons evolving. Yes, demons started out as cruel, heartless harbingers of evil, but they could evolve souls and become something more.

And Gamigin had. He'd become so much more that he and Fay had fallen in love and had a daughter.

Her heart ached to think about the tragic end to their story. Gamigin's only crime was to want to better himself and be a husband and father, and he'd been killed for it, leaving Fay heartbroken and Suyin fatherless.

And he wasn't just dead. According to Murmur, his soul was trapped in an inescapable prison, his energy feeding the High King of Hell's power—the one who had killed him. And the prison was so terrible it had made Murmur scream that bone-chilling scream when he saw it in his dream-vision.

She remembered what he'd told her about it. *We can never escape. There is nothing but endless black and the never-ending draining of our energy. The despair and hopelessness . . . It's far worse than burning alive.*

She had to free her father's soul. Not only because he didn't deserve to suffer through that, but so he could reunite with her mother. Life had forced them apart, but they would be joined again in death. She wouldn't rest until Murmur's spell was done. There would be no peace for her until Gamigin was free.

Yet despite her tragic conviction, there was also closure to be had in finally learning who her father was. Who she was. *What* she was.

A Cambion. The product of powerful magic. Not some floundering witch with an inexplicable ability, but someone special, unique. Possibly the only one of her kind. The more she tried to wrap her head around it, to assimilate this revelation into her identity, the more she found herself bursting with questions for Murmur.

How fortuitous that she had come here—though she would never tell him that lest he become unbearably smug. Murmur was the only one who could come close to answering the unanswerable questions she had carried throughout most of her life. He was a veritable fount of knowledge when it came to her father's work and her own inconceivable existence.

Her plans had changed so many times since arriving in Hell, she'd forgotten where she'd started. But she was nothing if not adaptable. Now, there was no way anyone was killing Murmur. Not until he finished the work he was trying to do. And if she found a way to escape right now, she wouldn't even consider taking it. Rather, she would bleed herself out several times over if it made his spell work.

Funny how he'd resisted telling her what he was doing with her blood, but now that she knew, she was infinitely more motivated to help him.

But first, she needed answers. And Murmur was going to give them to her.

A few hours passed, and her anticipation grew until she couldn't stand waiting for another minute. Unfortunately, it hadn't been even close to eight hours since she'd left him upstairs.

Then again . . . she'd basically thrown his rules out the window lately, and he didn't seem to care. He wasn't even trying to be scary anymore. He would just glare or roll his eyes at her, maybe flick his tail or point a claw in her face, but that was it.

She smirked. She kinda liked their new dynamic. He was cute when he was grumpy.

*No.* Nope. She wasn't going there. Nothing about the Necromancer was *cute* in any way, and he'd probably string her up in his dungeon if she called him that to his face.

Still, she was too restless to wait any longer. She could use her dwindling food supplies as an excuse if he got mad.

Decision made, she left her chambers and climbed the stairs. She pushed open the library door but came up short when she saw that Murmur's workspace was empty. She stepped farther inside, scanning around, and then blinked.

Murmur sat on the wooden floor in front of the fireplace, a

bright fire crackling in the hearth, his back resting against the ratty old claw-foot sofa. It seemed odd that he would sit there instead of on the couch, but then, the couch looked like it was probably less comfortable than hard ground.

There was a teetering stack of grimoires beside him, and he was intently reading one open in his lap, legs stretched out in front of him. As always, the faint black shadows of his souls could be seen drifting around his form.

He tapped the edge of the book with a claw while he read, and his brow was creased with concentration. His long braid was pulled over one shoulder, and the orange firelight cast dancing shadows on his gray skin. His tail lay relaxed on the floor, the end flicking occasionally.

Why the hell was he suddenly so attractive to her?

She had a clear memory of thinking him hideous when she'd first arrived here. But try as she might, she couldn't see it anymore. His creepy eyes, pale skin, black claws, proud horns . . . all of it just looked stunning to her now.

*I am a brainless idiot.*

He glanced up suddenly, noticing her arrival. His eyes briefly traveled down her body, and her heart skipped a beat. She cursed herself to Hell, and then reminded herself she was already there.

"Good, you're here," he said. "Let's begin." When she didn't move, he beckoned her over. "Hurry up. I haven't got all night."

She frowned. Did he not realize that eight hours hadn't passed? She looked over at the sigil, and her frown deepened. Nothing looked different about it than before— No, wait. An entire section had been wiped clean.

He'd somehow made *reverse* progress.

"Murmur . . . ?"

Should she even ask? She wanted to help him, but—

"I found this book of mine," he said, looking at the volume

in his lap. "I interpreted Gamigin's notes in my own words. I thought it might make more sense to you, but now that I'm reading it, I'm thinking I'm as mad as he was. Maybe worse."

She laughed.

And just like that, she thought, *Fuck it*, and went over to him. He seemed to be in one of his rare sharing moods, and she was ready to learn. She wasn't going to waste this opportunity.

She sat down at his side, back against the bedraggled sofa, and leaned in to look at the book in his lap. She felt the cold caress of his souls against her legs, but she was growing used to their presence now. No matter how diligently she scolded herself for her newfound attraction, it sparked to life in close proximity to him.

"Here, I was trying to explain more concisely the correlation between a soul's evolution and the demon's development of consciousness. Generally, younger demons are more simple-minded than older ones, but with time, their intelligence grows. And according to Gamigin's discoveries, it continues to grow until they develop morals and a conscience."

Despite her intense interest in the subject matter, she couldn't help but notice the way Murmur's rough, gravelly voice made her skin prickle with awareness. Then he pointed to a line on the page, and she found herself studying his hands. His fingers were long and slender, but they were also graceful, and the way the tips faded from pure black to pale gray was mesmerizing.

"Obviously, that isn't a steadfast rule because, as mentioned here, there are plenty of highly intelligent demons that make no effort whatsoever to be good. But that leads one to question—did they skip the development of a soul, or do they have one and just choose to ignore it?"

She inhaled slowly, and her eyelids fluttered. Damn, he smelled good too. Like smoke and frankincense, mixed with that unmistakable manly musk that made women everywhere melt. Maybe it was his magic she was scenting, because she highly doubted he wore cologne, and that shit was potent.

He looked up suddenly, and she realized how close together they were. Their gazes met, his ice-blue eyes flicking between her dark ones.

All coherent thought ground to a halt. All of a sudden, she was unbearably attracted to him, to the point where she couldn't concentrate on anything else, and she didn't know how to turn it off.

"Are you listening?" he asked, frowning.

He even looked good making that annoyed face at her. His brows were these perfect, sculpted black arches. His lashes were so thick and long, and they framed his colorful eyes like liner.

She shook herself. She couldn't believe she'd lost focus so easily. "Yeah. I'm listening."

His eyes narrowed like he didn't believe her. She'd once found the dark shadows around them eerie against his whitish skin, but now it all just looked like a masterpiece.

Pretty guys had always been her weakness. Probably because she was bisexual. She liked seeing feminine traits like perfect cheekbones and full lips on men. She'd been wildly attracted to all the elves in the Lord of the Rings movies.

Murmur was like that, except kinda goth looking.

So, better. Way better.

*And fuck me, those horns.* What was she supposed to do with that?

"Can you repeat that last part?" she said, shaking herself. *Get it together, you horny bitch. Pay attention to what the hot dead guy is trying to say.*

She reminded herself that this was for her father, for his legacy, and for herself, so she could finally understand who she truly was. It didn't matter how fuckable her information source was. All that mattered was getting that information.

Murmur shot her a look, to which she responded with a weak smile. He knew she wasn't listening. Hopefully he didn't know it was because she was too busy thirsting after him while he was trying to explain complex theory-of-demonic-evolution shit to her.

*I am the dumbest dumbass to ever live and breathe.*

*But damn, he smells good.*

# 18

# Brush with Death

The minutes turned into hours as Murmur talked through his interpretations of *The Book of Gamigin* and Suyin asked questions. He couldn't lie—he enjoyed her interest in his studies.

"Does this mean I have a demon form like you?" she asked as they read through the section where Gamigin theorized about Cambion traits. He hadn't been able to confirm all of his hypotheses because he'd died before his daughter had grown, but from what Murmur had seen, his assumptions were mostly correct.

"Nephilim have an altered form that appears during moments of high emotion and stress," he replied, "so it would stand to reason that you'd have something similar."

She pressed her lips together. "I'm pretty sure I would've noticed if I sprouted horns every time I got pissed off."

"The mind is powerful. The false belief of needing food to survive caused you to feel more weakness than you should have. I wouldn't be surprised if not knowing you had an altered form and believing you were fully human was enough to keep it repressed. It's likely that if you'd felt the change coming, you would've fought it back unconsciously."

Her eyes were wide. "So how do I get it to come out? How do you shift?"

"It's different for everyone. Some demons find it hard to maintain their human form, while others find it as easy as their demon form. When I want to shift, I simply visualize it happening, and it does. Once I'm shifted, I can stay in that form for as long as I choose. It requires energy to shift forms, but not to hold them."

"I can't exactly visualize shifting into a demon form that may or may not exist."

"I suspect it will come naturally in a moment of high emotion. Now that you're aware of it, you'll feel the instinct, and if you choose to give into it, you'll shift. Each time will get easier after that."

"Huh." She looked back down at the book. "I guess I'll have to wait and see what happens."

She turned the page, only to uncover a spread of sketches that Murmur didn't particularly want to dwell upon. He started to flip to the next page, but of course, Suyin was too quick for that.

"Wait." She reached over him, pulled the book off his lap and into her own, and peered at the messy sketches. "What are these drawings about?"

Murmur tilted his head and studied her. She was acting differently tonight. She didn't shy away from touching him, yet a while ago, when she'd reached over to point at something on the page and their hands brushed, she'd jumped like he'd burned her.

Even stranger was how he continued to react to her himself.

He'd been practicing necromancy for millennia, but he still remembered a time before his body had started to change. Extended and frequent practice of black magic always left a mark on the practitioner, and necromancy was the blackest magic there was.

Long ago, his features had been fuller, the sclerae of his eyes had been white instead of red, and his skin, though still gray, had been warm to the touch. His body had begun to die over the years, until he'd finally sacrificed the last of its vitality.

Now, though his heart beat in his chest, the blood it pumped was lifeless. His skin was cold, his cheeks hollow. He'd become as dead as the corpses he could reanimate, and he'd lost all appetites and desires for pleasure.

But last night, with Suyin trapped beneath him . . . he hadn't felt dead. She had awoken some sleeping beast inside of him, and he'd started noticing things he wouldn't have a few days ago.

His gaze would catch on her small hands when she swept her long hair off her neck, and he'd find himself staring at her slender throat, imagining sinking his fangs into it. What would Cambion blood taste like? If its flavor in any way reflected the potency of its magical properties, it would be a delicacy indeed.

He leaned in slightly and inhaled, just to see if he could detect a hint of the taste.

She glanced up, and her eyes flared slightly when she saw his proximity. He shifted backward. He wasn't entirely comfortable with the idea of her knowing the direction of his thoughts. This was a new experience for him after so many centuries, and he wasn't yet able to control his reactions as he normally could.

"Murmur?"

"Hm?"

"I just asked you what these sketches mean."

He shook his head and forced his attention to the book. He saw the messy drawings of unnamed faces and remembered why he'd tried to turn the page.

"It's nothing of concern."

He reached over and tried once more, but she flattened her palm on it. "Why? These drawings are incredible. I want to know what they are."

"They're unrelated to the subject matter."

"Then why'd you put them in the book?"

He shot her a glare. He didn't want to discuss this, but Suyin had already proven to be annoyingly tenacious when she wanted something. The fastest way to get past this was to just tell her.

"When I have visions, I sometimes write or draw things. I'm not aware of what I'm doing at the time, and I can't control it. Sometimes it strikes in the middle of working or writing, which was the case here. It has nothing to do with the subject of this book."

She frowned at him. "Does it happen a lot?"

"Somewhat."

"That sounds like it sucks."

He nodded. An understatement.

She looked down at the page. "Do you know what these drawings mean?"

"Not these ones, no."

"These are incredible though. The faces are so detailed. Aren't you curious about who they are?"

"No. My visions aren't always useful to me. Many I simply ignore. Sometimes I see the fates of people I don't know or care about and would never make an effort to meet even if I could. It's a waste of time, really."

She snorted. "Only you would say that having visions of the future is a waste of time."

"It crowds my already overfilled head with images I can't place." Leaning back against the sofa, he looked toward the fire. Before he could think too much about it, he found himself speaking his mind.

"Sometimes I don't know if I'm remembering my own

memories or recalling old visions that had nothing to do with me. Sometimes I can't tell if the voices in my head are my bound souls crying for mercy or from visions I have yet to experience or have forgotten. Sometimes when I try to sleep, the voices get louder and louder until all I hear is a cacophony of screaming . . ."

He was suddenly aware of Suyin's stare. When he glanced at her, he found her eyes were soft. Suyin with soft eyes seemed paradoxical.

He scowled. "Don't look at me like that."

She shook her head and the expression vanished. "Murmur, that's messed up."

"I never claimed to be sane. Now, enough about me. Turn the page or I'll send you back to your room."

She glared at him. "I am not a child."

"Then don't act like one."

Her scowl deepened. And for some reason, the sight lessened his own discomfort, and he felt his good humor returning.

"You're an asshole," she said when he started to smile.

"We've been over this. Any new insults?"

"Dickhead. Prick. Bastard."

He faked a yawn. "Boring."

She punched him in the arm. He might have been mad if her tiny fist had managed to wound him, but as it was, he barely felt it. He laughed instead.

And then he pointed at the book. "Focus, witchling. Turn the page."

Her brows shot up. "Witchling?"

He shot her a smug look. "You're a witch, and you're . . . little. Thus, witchling. Now, focus."

"If you call me that, I'm going to call you Murmy."

The smile dropped off his face like it had never been. "Call me that, and I'll stuff a gag in your throat and chain you up so deep in my dungeons, you'll never see the light of day again."

They glared at each other for a moment.

And then she barked a laugh. "You almost had me for a second. I was quaking in my boots." She cocked a brow. "And then I remembered that you *need* me, and you would never do anything to jeopardize my precious blood for your precious spell."

He leaned in. "You're pushing your luck, witchling."

"Relax, *Murmy*." Her smile was full of challenge. "We're just having fun."

She thought she could best him? She thought she could meet him eye to eye?

*You've gone soft*, his inner voice mocked. *Allowing yourself to be challenged by a little hybrid? Shameful. Keep this up and next thing you know, you'll be traipsing around in your human form, trying to fit in on Earth with the weaklings.*

He hated when his own mind ridiculed him, but perhaps it was right this time. Perhaps he ought to remind Suyin who was really in charge here.

He didn't react to her taunt. He didn't so much as twitch. He just continued to stare at her. Wariness gradually crept into her gaze as she finally realized she may have pushed him too far.

Then he called his souls to rise. He allowed their faces to take shape—their haunting, screaming faces, lit by an unearthly purple glow. The mouths that constantly begged for salvation in his mind were open, revealing blackened teeth and decayed gums. Rotted flesh hung limply off their cheekbones, their eyes gaping, empty sockets.

Suyin's dark eyes darted around all the deathly faces closing in on her. Her fingers clenched the book in her lap so tightly, her knuckles whitened.

And Murmur felt . . . vaguely nauseated. Not triumphant.

The first time he'd done this to her, he'd wanted her to be terrified, and he'd enjoyed his victory. This time, however, it wasn't the same.

He didn't like the fear on her face. He didn't like how the good-natured defiance had bled from her expression. He didn't like how whatever camaraderie they'd had moments ago had shattered.

*What is happening to me?*

*You're weak*, the voice hissed. *And you're getting weaker.*

Disgusted at himself, he released the souls, and they disappeared, leaving nothing but faint, ghostly trails.

Suyin visibly sagged with relief. She looked at the fire, and he could tell she was fighting to slow her breathing and regain calm. He watched as her fear dissipated, only to be replaced with hot anger.

He stared into the flames beside her. Neither of them spoke for a time.

"Note to self," she muttered through gritted teeth, "Murmur can't take a fucking joke."

He wanted to tell her that he was the Necromancer, and of course he didn't take jokes, and it was her mistake to be foolish enough to provoke him. What had she expected?

But he didn't say that. He didn't say anything at all.

Instead, he climbed to his feet, and he saw her tense. He'd made her jumpy around him again. Wasn't that what he'd wanted?

He crossed the room to a dusty old cabinet in the corner, but her voice stopped him. "Are we done, then?"

He turned back. There was no sign of that softness in her eyes he'd seen only minutes ago. Instead, there was a burning indignation that was all too familiar. She was angry with him, but she wasn't leaving either. Her desire for knowledge superseded her wounded pride.

Yet another thing he begrudgingly respected about her.

"No," he replied. "Unless you want to be."

She glared at him and said nothing. But she didn't leave, which he supposed was answer enough.

Turning back to the cabinet, he opened the door and swept the cobwebs and dust aside, taking out a crystal decanter full of amber liquid. There were several cups too, but they were so covered in grime, it would take considerable scrubbing to make them usable.

He returned to Suyin and sat again beside her, holding out the bottle. A peace offering of sorts, though he would never admit it.

Her eyes narrowed, but she took it, grimacing at the filth on the outside. "What is this?"

"Alcohol."

She frowned. "Why are you giving me alcohol?"

"To drink." At her deepening look of confusion, he admitted, "You were frightened. And I suppose I feel somewhat . . . remorseful for being the cause of it. This will settle your nerves."

She ground her teeth. "You feel *somewhat* remorseful for using your creepy dead ghost army to scare the shit out of me. What a touching apology."

He turned away. Admitting to remorse was as far as he was willing to go. Really, she was lucky he'd given her that much.

She sighed like she knew it too. "You're an asshole. Why I'm even bothering with you is a goddamn mystery."

It was Murmur's turn to grind his teeth. It seemed she hadn't learned her lesson after being frightened by his "ghost army," after all. He was starting to think she never would. And he wasn't sure he wanted her to.

"Why does this bottle look like it came from a mummy's crypt?" she asked.

He glanced back. She was turning the grimy decanter over in her hands, studying it closely.

"That cabinet was here long before I arrived," he explained. "I don't think Paimon consumed alcohol often. It's likely been here for a century or so."

She uncorked the top and sniffed it. "Are you sure it's not poison?"

"These were Paimon's private chambers before they were mine. She wouldn't have kept poison here. But I'll take the first sip, if you'd rather."

"I like to live dangerously," Suyin said with a shrug, and then she took a swig.

And coughed.

"F-fuck," she wheezed. "That's strong as hell." She took another sip and coughed again. And then she held the bottle out to him.

He shook his head.

"Come on. Live a little."

"I prefer not to consume mind-altering substances. My mind is altered enough already."

He'd never understood humanity's fixation with alcohol. They voluntarily drank poison and enjoyed the way their brains slowly shut down. It was absurd.

"Just one sip," Suyin pressed. "You scared the piss out of me for no reason. You owe me."

He glared at her. And then he snatched the bottle out of her hand and took a sizable gulp. And coughed several times. "That's awful."

She laughed.

Fool that he was, his guilt lessened at the sound. He hadn't scared her so badly she wouldn't laugh in his presence anymore. That was good.

He took one more sip of the foul fire juice for the sole reason that Suyin wanted him to and it made her laugh. Then, with a grimace, he passed it back. "Don't ask me to drink any more of that."

She laughed again and took another swig herself. Silence fell for several moments as they stared at the fire. The alcohol sent warm relaxation trickling through his blood, making him aware of the tension in his muscles and giving him a chance to relax them. It was . . . pleasant.

"You took over Paimon's lair recently, right?" Suyin asked, setting the decanter down on her other side. He nodded. "So you haven't been here that long."

"Correct."

"Weird."

"Why?"

"I just have this image of you hiding away in this tower for centuries. Moving doesn't fit in with the picture." She looked around the library. "So you brought all these books from your old place?"

"I did."

"That's a lot of shit."

"It's not like I did it myself. What's the point of having minions if you can't make them do menial tasks? I kept a close eye on them. Anyone that disobeyed ended up on the tower spikes."

"How many people are up there?" she said, grimacing.

"A few." He smiled. "I think those spikes are my favorite part about my new lair. It's very convenient, and the demons are terrified of it."

She looked mildly disturbed but said no more. "I'm surprised you let them touch your precious books at all."

"They didn't touch them directly. They were carefully packaged first. No one but me touches them."

"And me," she reminded him with a smirk.

"Evidence my sanity has slipped."

"Oh, I think you've got plenty of evidence of that already."

He rolled his eyes.

"What was your old lair like?"

"Small. Empty. Quiet." He missed that quiet.

"Empty? You didn't have gargoyle minions running around everywhere?"

"You ask a lot of questions."

She shrugged. "I'm curious about how an evil demon in Hell lives his life."

He decided to indulge her. Maybe it was because he was enjoying the distraction. Maybe it was because he still felt guilty for terrorizing her. Maybe it was because of the alcohol he'd consumed. "I didn't have legions. I was one of the few demons in the Order of Thrones without them."

"What exactly do you mean by 'legions'?"

"Armies of lesser demon soldiers. They serve a master or mistress and go to war on their behalf to claim new territory or protect what they have."

"Why didn't you have them before?"

"I prefer to work alone, and my souls are formidable enough. My boundary wards were powerful enough to keep intruders out, and my territory was small enough that it wasn't particularly interesting to invaders. I don't trust others easily, and I can't stand incompetence. Lesser demons are some of the most dimwitted creatures in existence."

"So why'd you come here then? Why go to all the trouble of taking over the lair and all the stupid demons in it if you didn't want the responsibility?"

"Because of my plan. I needed a more secure place to perform my experiments and weather the coming storm. If my spell is successful, the High King of Hell will lose the primary source of his power. The most powerful demons in Hell actually uphold the stability of the realm. When Belial defected, the entire mountain range surrounding his territory sank into a crevasse that appeared in the landscape. Lucifer's fall will wreak even greater havoc."

Suyin's eyes widened, and he could practically see her sharp mind racing as she digested that information. "And why do you think you'll be safer here?"

"My old lair was perched on a cliff on the edge of the

Abysmal Sea. I enjoyed the view, but if there were an earthquake, the entire structure could fall into the waves."

"What makes this one safer?"

"The tunnels." His lips curved slightly. "There is a network of tunnels deep in the bedrock beneath this structure, created by gorath larvae. I've explored them at length, and I still haven't managed to map them completely. Even if the entire castle fell, there would always be an escape route underground."

"I'm guessing I don't want to know what gorath larvae are."

"Probably not," he agreed, thinking of the centipede-like monsters and their slimy, membranous offspring.

"Well, damn," she said, shaking her head. "You've thought of everything."

"I've certainly tried."

When Suyin didn't continue her interrogation immediately, he took the opportunity to relax further against the sofa and stretch out his legs. *Relax*. When was the last time he'd allowed himself such an indulgence? He couldn't even remember.

He shouldn't be allowing it now, but something about this moment of truce between him and Suyin seemed precious. He was reluctant to end it by returning to his never-ending cycle of work.

*Never-ending*. That was what it was, wasn't it?

Even if he survived and all his schemes went according to plan, he would still be locked in his tower, working on some impossible task. Because if he completed this objective, he would just find another, even more difficult one to strive for.

He would do it because if he stopped, if he allowed himself to rest for even one moment, the emptiness would seep in. The lack of purpose would reveal the gaping hole inside his mind that had been steadily growing for centuries.

That abyss scared him most of all. Possibly even more than the vision of his death. At least death would be something outside his control, something he had no choice in. That pit of emptiness was something else, something he guessed had come from the evolution of his soul.

He knew he had a soul, but he'd never thought much about *how* he'd gotten it. Gamigin had explained how demons evolved, developing emotional intelligence and moral compasses, and the soul grew with them during that process.

But Murmur didn't think he had much emotional intelligence—he was pretty cold and lacking empathy—and his sense of right and wrong was warped as well. He didn't give a fuck about anyone except himself, and he wasn't ashamed to admit it. So where had his soul come from?

Maybe the answers lay in the empty pit of darkness in his mind. But he feared that if he gave in and explored it, he might fall into some mire of despair that he'd never climb out of.

If he lost what gave his life meaning now, what would he have?

Reaching over Suyin's lap, he turned the page of the book and tapped the next section with a claw. "Read this. Tell me when you're done, and then I'll explain it."

"It's gonna take me a minute," Suyin replied, already concentrating on the page of text. "You have the worst handwriting I've ever seen."

"The effort it takes to decipher it will ensure you have a higher rate of retention."

She grumbled something about him making her life difficult, but he didn't bother listening. Instead, in a rare moment, he dropped his head back onto the sofa cushion behind him and closed his eyes. He felt Suyin glance at him, but he ignored her. As much as he was able, that was. He seemed to always be aware of her and where she was in the room, even when he pretended not to be.

It annoyed him. Where was his simple solitude? Why was he even thinking about this now? He certainly wouldn't have allowed himself this idle moment before she'd come along.

He had assured her that he wasn't manipulatable, but they both knew she had done just that, and he didn't even care anymore.

He hated that he didn't hate her. He hated that he didn't mind giving her what she wanted. He hated that she had the power to make him change his mind and bend his rules. He wanted to punish her for it, but then he hated the idea of her hating him again.

She might pretend she still did, but he knew she didn't. She was curious about him, that much was obvious. She was also hungry for knowledge and willing to overlook almost anything to get it. That was something he could relate to.

They were both using each other to achieve some aim, and that was a relationship he understood. Her motives were similar to his own, and thus, he was able to lower his guard with her in a way he never had with another.

So when his body suddenly felt heavy, he gave into the urge to relax. He didn't sleep. He just let his mind go blank and the tension in his muscles slacken, while his little witch kept reading at his side.

# 19

# Drop Dead, Gorgeous

Suyin got lost in the words scrawled in Murmur's chaotic penmanship. It was fascinating to follow his notes and see how his mind worked.

She'd never tell him to his face, but he was a bona fide genius. Sometimes he'd go off on a seemingly unrelated tangent for pages, only to jump back to the original subject, tying everything together in a way she never would've guessed otherwise.

"I don't understand what you're saying about the procreation ritual here," she said aloud after a while. "I get that Cambion conception isn't possible without doing the ritual first, but does it actually have to occur *during*—"

She broke off as she looked up from the book and over at Murmur.

His head rested on the couch cushion behind him, and strands of pure-white hair that had escaped his braid were fanned out around him. His eyes were closed, his lips slightly parted, his chest rising with steady breath. The smoky outlines of his souls moved so little, they were nearly invisible. Even the barbed tip of his tail lay still.

Damn, he looked good.

He was so big, and his tail and horns and skin were strange enough to keep her uneasy. Why that made him more attractive, she couldn't say. What that said about her, she couldn't say either, but it probably wasn't anything good.

"Occur during what?" he mumbled.

She frowned, completely forgetting what she'd asked. The silence lingered on. He still hadn't opened his eyes or lifted his head. Seeing him relaxed was such a bizarre sight that she couldn't tear her eyes away.

"You're staring," he said, and she tensed.

"Well, you're kinda freaky to look at," she said quickly to cover her tracks.

His half smile disappeared, and she immediately regretted her words. She'd gotten pissed when he'd commented on her appearance—calling her *little*, the bastard—but she'd essentially done the same to him. And she'd made it sound like she found him repulsive, which wasn't the case at all.

"I know how I look." His voice was low. "The last time I encountered humans, they recoiled at the sight of me."

"Well, you're a demon and they're human. They'd probably never seen—"

"They were blood-born witches, and they had come to Hell of their own volition. I found them in the tunnels of this lair, in fact. They had seen demons before. One of the twins was even in love with one. She came here to rescue him, and I helped her."

*Twins?* Blood-born witch twins were so rare, a prophecy had foretold Iris and Lily's birth. But he couldn't be speaking about them, obviously. This must've been a memory from long ago.

"That was uncharacteristically nice of you," Suyin said, hoping it would encourage him to elaborate.

"Oh, I didn't do it for free." His lips curved. "I got a new lair out of it, and then a load of gold when I sold them out to Valefor and had him steal your book for me. I arranged it all very carefully."

"Wait." Suyin straightened. "Valefor?"

"Mmm."

"But he's the one who's after Lily and Iris."

"That's what I just said."

"That doesn't make sense. Lily and Iris wouldn't come to Hell to *rescue* a demon. They hate demons. Valefor killed their parents."

"Yes, but he's dead now, and Iris and Lily have evidently gotten over their hatred. Just ask Mephistopheles and the Hunter."

"Who? What? That's not—" She shook her head. "How do you know all this?"

He opened his eyes and turned his head over to meet her gaze. She knew he was being intentionally vague—she'd already learned that he enjoyed dangling information in front of her like a carrot and making her jump through hoops to get it. It was fucking annoying.

"You'll have to ask your witch friends when you get back to Earth," he said. "You three should have lots to talk about."

"Nuh-uh." She jabbed a finger at him. "I'm not letting this go that easily. What the hell do Mephistopheles and the Hunter have to do with—" She broke off, and her eyes bugged. "Meph."

Murmur smiled as she put it together.

"You're kidding me. No, that can't be— It has to be a coincidence."

"It's not."

"You're telling me my best friend is dating a demon? A fucking *demon*. She loathes demons with a burning passion. She despises them with every fiber of—"

And then she remembered their recent conversation. Iris's lies of omission and seemingly nonsensical certainty that she was safe from Valefor.

"Is Valefor really dead?"

"Yes."

"How? How did he die?"

"As far as I know, Belial killed him."

That was why Iris was so convinced she was safe. She'd known. "Nice of her to tell me," Suyin grumbled. She and the coven members spent hours every week keeping that damn cloaking spell going and it wasn't even necessary. "Fucking hell. I can't believe her boyfriend is a demon."

"Lily's too," Murmur tacked on, his cocky little smirk telling her he was enjoying her disbelief.

"How did it happen? How did she even meet a demon and not try to immediately kill him?"

"You'll have to ask her that."

"Just tell me now."

His lips quirked. "You can't make me talk, Suyin."

They stared at each other. She saw the stubbornness in his eyes and wanted to kick him. He wasn't going to tell her anything for the sole reason that she was dying to know. It was his favorite game, and they'd been playing it from the moment they met. *Asshole.*

"Why are you always so cagey anyway?" she snapped. She wasn't going to beg for answers, and he was right: She'd be able to find everything out once she returned to Earth. Rest assured, she and Iris would be having a nice, long chat. "What purpose does it serve keeping all these secrets from me? I've already said I want to help you. You're only hurting yourself by keeping me in the dark."

"Maybe I enjoy it."

"Why?"

"Maybe it's all a game to me," he replied, echoing her very thoughts.

"A game where you make all the rules and call all the shots."

"My favorite kind."

That wicked smile . . . He was a dick, but she swore it was a form of foreplay just looking at him.

She groaned internally. It had been her master plan to insert herself into his life and get under his skin until he cracked and told her everything she wanted to know. But that plan was a double-edged sword, because the closer she got to him, the harder it got to remember why she was trying to manipulate him in the first place.

"I hate you," she muttered, more to herself than him. Just as a reminder. Because she did.

"Do you?" His eyes were full of challenge. He didn't look offended.

The longer they stared at each other, the more she felt herself caving.

"I *should* hate you," she corrected, mentally kicking herself. "I keep reminding myself to hate you."

"But you don't."

Her upper lip curled. He smiled, finally lifting his head off the couch and angling his body toward her. As if this was a conversation that interested him enough to command his whole attention.

"Why should you hate me?" he asked as if he didn't already fucking know.

"Hmm, where to begin?" She crossed her arms and shifted toward him too. She'd all but forgotten the book in her lap.

"Maybe because you kidnapped me, locked me in a dungeon, and then left me to starve to death. Or maybe because you scared the piss out of me with your creepy souls—*twice* now. Or maybe because of all the times you half strangled me, threatened me, insulted me, and traumatized me with your stories about the horrible things you've done to demons, humans, and even angels."

He laughed. He actually laughed. "You're being dramatic."

"Dramatic? I can't even—" She shook her head. "If I had more energy, I'd punch you."

There was that grin again. This time it flashed his fangs, and the sight of them sent a tiny pulse of heat throbbing through her traitorous body. *No, we are not doing that.*

"The way I see it," he replied, "I've treated you like a queen."

Her brows shot up so high, they probably disappeared behind her fringe. "I never knew you were delusional as well as psychotic."

"You were *supposed* to be a prisoner," he said, choosing to disregard her comment. "And yet, somehow, you now have private chambers in my tower and servants to bring whatever you desire from Earth."

"That's only because—"

"And if that wasn't enough, you are the one and only person ever to be allowed access to my library. There are demons currently impaled on the tower spikes just for entering this room or daring to touch a single book. And yet, I granted you complete, unfettered access to everything here after only knowing you a short time."

"That's great, but it's hardly a justification for—"

"On top of *that*, I am now sitting here, putting aside my important work, upon which my life quite literally depends, in order to teach you about your father's grimoire and your origins." He shot her a challenging look. "Tell me, how is it that you still believe I treat you badly?"

She opened her mouth to reply . . . but nothing came out.

*Shit, he's kinda right, isn't he?*

"You would have let me starve to death," she said, aware she was grasping at straws.

"You wouldn't have died. And I didn't realize your strength was influenced by food and water, since that's not the case for me. I corrected my mistake though, did I not? Look at you now." He lifted an arm and gestured to her before letting it drop into his lap. "I've never seen a more ungrateful person. I've half a mind to throw you back into the dungeon so you remember how good you have it."

"I don't even know what to say to that."

"How about, 'Thank you, Master, for your benevolence'?"

*Is he fucking serious?* She looked sharply at him. Humor danced in his eyes. The urge to punch him rose anew.

It didn't escape her notice that she was trying to convince the bad guy that he was the bad guy. Of course he disagreed with her. Villains always felt justified in doing the terrible things they did.

So why was she letting him persuade her? Why was she listening to his point of view at all?

"None of this changes the fact that you took me without my consent and refused to allow me to tell people I wasn't dead. You really want to prove your point? Let me go home and tell my friends and coven I'm okay. Then I'll stop hating you. No more arguments. No more fights."

The humor bled from his gaze, and it hardened. "No."

"I'll come back. I won't try to escape. I'll even swear a vow."

"No."

"Come on, Murmur."

"No. We'll cast the spell soon anyway. With any luck, it'll be successful, and you can return to Earth for good."

She ground her teeth. He had a point, but she was still goddamn frustrated. Just when she thought they were making headway, something always reminded her what he was capable of.

Maybe he was right, and he wasn't treating her badly, but at the end of the day, he'd abducted her, and he wasn't letting her go until he was finished with her. Her wants and needs were irrelevant. And that was something she could not overlook.

Facing the fire again, she looked down at the book in her lap. Her blood felt hot with her rising ire.

She needed to focus on the plan: help Murmur free her father's soul and get as much information out of him as possible in the meantime. That meant not pissing him off so much he made good on his threat to throw her back into the dungeon. That meant swallowing her pride. Not insulting him or telling him how she really felt.

But damn, he made it hard, sitting there all smug, proud of himself for having bested her, with his gorgeous hair and regal features and eerily beautiful eyes. *Damn him.*

"So?" His voice filtered into her thoughts some time later. "Are we going to continue the lesson, or you would prefer to stew in misery instead?"

And just like that, the short fuse of her temper blew.

"You know what?" she snapped, forgetting all the reasons she should keep her mouth shut. She closed the book in her lap and set it aside. "I've had enough. You can take your precious information and shove it up your ass. I don't need anything from you. I don't *want* anything from you. I know you think I'm so desperate for information, I'll take anything you throw at me. But honestly, I'd rather not know than put up with your—"

His hand shot out of nowhere and wrapped around her neck, limiting her air supply enough that she broke off midsentence with a choked sound of surprise.

"Enough," he growled. His relaxed posture was gone, and his souls churned restlessly in response to his agitation. He leaned forward, using his size to loom over her. His tail snapped restlessly. His horns towered above her.

"You come into *my* lair and start making demands. You distract me at every given opportunity with your questions and your sharp little mind. Wherever I turn, there you are. Even when you're quiet, your presence is screaming at me, and it drives me mad." His voice deepened. "You beg me to teach you, and when I do, you make further demands of me. And then you have the audacity to shout in my face about all the injustices I've committed against you."

Instinct screamed at her to get rid of the grip on her throat, even if her pride wanted her to act like it didn't affect her. Her hands shot up to claw at his fingers, trying to pry them loose. She wasn't actually asphyxiating, but the limit on her oxygen was making her panic. Especially with the look of unhinged fury in his eyes. She'd pushed him too far, and now there was no telling what he'd do.

"Let me tell you here and now and for the last time: *I don't care if you don't like me.* I don't give a fuck if you don't like how I treat you. I don't give a fuck if your friends on Earth are worried about you. I. Don't. Give. A. Fuck."

He was so close, their noses almost touched.

"Is that clear?"

She didn't respond. His hold was loose enough for her to choke out a few words or nod her head if she wanted. But she didn't. She glared at him instead, with all the fury consuming her body from the inside out. She let it burn her alive.

"I said," he repeated, his voice a deep growl, "is that clear?"

She opened her mouth, on the verge of telling him to go fuck himself. But he met her defiance with an intensity she'd never encountered before.

Suyin exuded forcefulness. In every other interaction in her life, she bulldozed people who stood in her way. She was diminutive in size, but she made up for it with a ferocity of will and an almost unhinged fearlessness.

There was never a challenge she didn't meet. There was never a gauntlet she didn't throw. And she never backed down from a fight.

She had never met anyone who could match her will. Man, woman, or otherwise.

Not until now.

Unbidden, a throb of heat pulsed between her legs. Electric shivers traveled down the back of her neck and arms. *No, you are not doing this, Su. You are not going there. You can control yourself. Do not give him what he wants. Do not—*

She . . . nodded.

The movement was subtle, but she knew he felt it against the hand beneath her chin. Victory flashed through his bloodshot eyes. Triumph transformed his features from stern to cocky self-assurance.

It pissed her off. It turned her on. She didn't know what the hell was happening.

"Say it," he said. "I want to hear it."

No, that was too far, there was no way she—

"I . . . understand."

His lips curved. "Good girl. I'm glad that's cleared up." And then he released her throat.

She gulped in air, her eyes filling with tears at the sting on her windpipe. Other than that, neither of them moved.

Another pulse of heat raced through her veins. Attraction sizzled in the inches between them.

And then because she was an idiot with no sense of self-preservation or impulse control, her hands shot out and gripped his coat.

After that, she wasn't sure who moved first. All she knew was that one second, they were staring at each other with the promise of death in their eyes . . .

And the next, their mouths were fused together.

Tiny tingles and simmering urges ignited into a powerful wildfire, one Murmur wasn't sure he could stop. He slid a hand into Suyin's hair and pulled her closer, pushing deeper into her lips and losing himself in her taste.

It wasn't close enough. If he could have, he would've crawled right into her skin and consumed her from the inside out.

Suyin seemed to feel the same. Her grip on his clothing was tight, pushing him to the edge of his tolerance, but he allowed it. Their heads tilted in opposite directions, and their mouths opened wider so their tongues could keep twisting between them.

He'd thought he might detest even the pressure of her tongue, the slight restraint of her lips pressing against his, but that wasn't what happened at all. Instead, every stroke, every mingling breath, added more fuel to the fire.

The space between their bodies felt like an ocean. The clothes between them felt like barriers that he needed to tear down immediately. He needed her underneath him, trapped and unable to escape.

He transferred his grip to her waist and lowered them to the floor, rising over her and using his body to pin hers. A gasp escaped her as her back hit the ground, but she didn't try to break his hold.

He took a moment to appreciate the sight of her beneath him. Her skin was flushed, her chest heaving with rapid breaths, her hair spread out on the floor like a midnight halo.

She was small, but he was beginning to recognize a fierceness inside her that could not be conquered. He wanted to conquer it anyway. And in this moment, with her trapped below him, her eyes clouded with desire, he felt closer to his goal than ever.

One of his hands supported his weight, and the other dove back into her hair, clenching it in a fist. Then he dropped his head, and their lips crashed back together again.

She reached up, sliding her hands into the hair at the base of his loose braid, and that was when he hit the boundary in his head. His skin crawled at the invasion, and his pulse skyrocketed.

He lurched back, snatched her wrists, and then pinned them to the floor above her head with one hand. More hair slipped free of his braid, and it fell around his face above hers, blocking out the rest of the room.

As soon as her arms were trapped, he calmed, so he dove back into the kiss with renewed vigor. She moaned as their tongues tangled, arching her spine off the floor and pressing her breasts into his chest.

With his free hand, he reached down and cupped her ass. She tried to hook her leg around his hip as he ground their bodies together, but he stopped her with a growl, gripping her thigh and pushing her leg open. She didn't seem to mind, her tongue still dueling with his until it caught on one of his fangs. It was a light scrape, but the sudden coppery, sweet flavor of her blood made his head spin.

He could feel the heat between her legs, and it was quickly making him lose all sense. The taste of her blood was the final straw—he was seconds from biting into her tongue again to draw more. Or better yet, sinking his fangs into her throat.

But he dragged his mouth away suddenly.

As their gazes met, a thousand dark urges charged through his head like raging bulls. He couldn't place a single thought or organize the tumbling chaos. All he felt was an unquenchable desire of epic proportions erupting from the center of his being.

He wasn't entirely sure what would happen if he gave into

it, but he knew it would be dark and twisted. Like everything else in his mind. Like everything else in his life. He also knew he would no longer be in control, and he wasn't sure he was ready to let go to that degree. There was no telling what would happen.

He searched Suyin's dark eyes. He saw desire reflected back at him, but he also saw wariness.

He understood. She was right to be afraid. She was right to be unsure.

"I'm giving you the chance to leave now," he said, his voice sounding strange to his own ears. "I won't stop you. I won't chase you." *No matter how badly I might want to.*

Her eyes flared slightly at the word "chase."

He wasn't sure why he was warning her. Shouldn't he want to take what was offered now, before she had a chance to reconsider? Shouldn't he want to feed whatever dark beast she'd awakened while he had the chance?

And yet the idea of taking something from her that she wasn't sure she wanted to give was repulsive. No matter that he'd stolen her from her home and stolen her blood. This felt different. He didn't want to steal this.

"If you stay, I can't guarantee I'll be able to stop. This is your chance to go."

She swallowed visibly. And he saw the moment his warning fully penetrated. The haze of desire faded enough from her gaze for it to sharpen with understanding.

He released her wrists and pushed off of her, dropping back against the couch. He closed his eyes, flexing and releasing his hands, and fought to get his urges under control. They were strong enough even to drown out the wailing of his souls. It should have been a reprieve, but it was far from that.

"Go." His voice was a growl.

She didn't move, lying frozen on the floor as if begging to be leapt upon and ravaged.

"Go before I change my mind," he snapped.

Apparently, she knew better than to ignore that. Without another word, she scrambled to her feet and hurried from the room. The door banging shut was followed by her echoing footsteps down the hallway.

Alone, he dug his claws into the floorboards at his sides and gritted his teeth, fighting to get whatever monster had crawled out of him back in its cage. Not long ago, he'd been feeling content and relaxed for the first time as far back as he could remember. Now, he was anything but.

He swore that one of the reasons he'd survived as long as he had was because he'd transmuted the sexual urges that ruled so many demons. He'd never been controlled by sex. The most powerful succubi in Hell had never been able to get a rise out of him.

And now this. Reduced to a raging monster of primal urges.

He took deep, calming breaths. He flexed his power over his souls, just to remember what control felt like. He reminded himself what was at stake, and why he couldn't afford to lose focus now.

But the inner battle raged on.

# 20

# The End of the Road

As predicted, it had taken Belial over an hour to walk home from the club. His new neighborhood was ritzy and full of mansions, and as a result, the streets were dead silent, save for the occasional car passing by. It was oddly calming.

When he got home, he ditched his clothes on the bedroom floor and stood under the scalding spray of his shower for over half an hour before sprawling out on his enormous bed.

The house was so quiet he could hear the ringing in his ears.

It was late, well after two in the morning. The room was dark. But he wasn't even close to sleeping.

Instead, he lay on his back and stared at the ceiling. He couldn't get the terror in Skye's eyes out of his head. Eyes open or shut, the sight of her backing away from him was burned into his retinas like he'd been staring at a too-bright light.

His phone rang on the nightstand. He would normally never answer a call this late, but he had a feeling he knew who it was.

"Bel, are you okay?" Eva asked immediately when he picked up. "What happened?"

"Don't ask *me* if I'm okay," he replied. "Ask your friend."

"What happened?"

"I scared the shit out of her." He spoke through gritted teeth. "She took off running like the hounds of Hell were after her."

Eva cursed.

"Have you spoken to her?" he asked. "Did she make it home?"

"I talked to her."

He waited for more. The silence was suspiciously weighted. "And?"

"And . . ." Eva took a breath. "You're right. You scared the shit out of her."

"What did she say?"

"Um . . . well, I don't know exactly what happened, because she couldn't really explain the supernatural shit. So she kinda translated it into thinking you're a big, terrifying red flag."

Bel winced. "She's not wrong."

"What exactly happened?"

"A car almost hit her. Some drunk idiot running the red light. I tried to shove her out of the way, but I pushed her too hard and she went flying."

"Oh, damn," Eva said.

"That's not all."

"Uh-oh."

"The car hit me instead. I got . . . pissed. Lost my temper a little. Smashed the hood in."

"With what?"

"My fists."

"Oh my god."

"Bunch of humans saw me."

"Shit. Was there fire?"

"No. But it was close."

"Shit." Eva was personally acquainted with the phases of Bel's temper tantrums. First, his eyes flickered with hellfire, then he started to gain height. The air around him would waver with heat waves, and then he'd burst into flames.

But that was only the beginning.

"You got hit by a car though?" Eva asked. "Are you okay?"

"The car was in worse shape than I was."

"Well, that's kinda badass."

He snorted. "Ask Skye how badass it was."

"She thinks you have like, next-level anger issues."

"Again, she's not wrong."

"And . . . she's inexplicably, irrationally terrified of you."

"What?"

"Yeah, I had to help her through a near panic attack just from talking about you. I think the supernatural stuff made her instincts go haywire. She doesn't even understand why she's so scared."

"Fuck." He really had traumatized her. This was exactly why Eva hadn't wanted him hanging around her. Maybe he ought to foot the bill for all the therapy Skye would need to cure her sudden crippling fear of tall blond men. "Eva, I— Shit."

"It's fine, Bel. Actually, I wanted to say I'm sorry. I didn't mean to glare at you from across the club like this was some stupid high-school drama. I was just worried—"

"You were looking out for your friend. There's nothing to be sorry for."

"I know, but I don't want you to think it's because of you. I mean, it is kinda, but you're a great guy, and—"

"It's fine. And please never call me a 'great guy' again."

She snorted. "My apologies. What I mean to say is that it has nothing to do with you personally. I just don't want Skye to get hurt. She's human, and she doesn't have the Sight. I just don't want her to get caught up in all this."

"Eva. I get it."

She sighed. "Did you have fun at Bootleg at least? It was great to have you out with us again."

"Yeah, I did." He dragged a hand through his hair and then dropped it back onto the bed. "But I think it's safest if I stay away from humans for a while."

"You live on Earth, Bel. Humans are kinda par for the course."

"I know."

But his slip-ups were piling up. First Meph's fingers, now this idiotic display. How long until he lost it and did something really terrible? But he couldn't force himself to stay at home all the time and expect not to lose his mind either. He didn't know what to do.

That was the problem with his celibacy pact. Sex had always been an outlet for his temper. When he'd stopped, he'd cut himself off from one of his primary forms of release without offering an alternative.

Naiamah was right, that bitch. *Repression never works.* Knowing she had called that from the get-go, back when he'd been all optimistic about his new life plan, pissed him off. Just once, he'd wanted to do something different.

He'd wanted to *be* someone different.

"Look," Eva said, "maybe I could talk to Skye, explain to her that—"

"No. You were right before. She's safest far away from all of us. If it'll help her feel better, you can tell her I said I'm sorry for losing my shit, but that's as far as I'll go."

She blew out a breath. "Fine. I hate this though. It would be nice for you to have some company, you know? You're a catch, Bel. What woman doesn't want to sit and drink fancy wine while you cook her a five-course meal? That's the dream."

He grunted. It was a nice fantasy. But he was pretty sure it wasn't "the dream" to date a flaming rageaholic who blew up every time someone looked at him sideways. He wasn't about to make some poor human risk her life every second she was around him in case he tried to push her out of the path of a moving car and ended up launching her halfway down the block.

And that wasn't even touching on why he hadn't started having sex again after reaching his six-month goal. He would rather die than lose control and flambé someone in bed. Just knowing that he had to worry about that was enough to kill his desire.

"I should go, Eva."

"Yeah, me too. It's so late, I feel like my eyes are bleeding."

"Thanks for inviting me tonight."

"Aw, of course. It's never as fun without you there. We all miss you when you're not around."

"You're starting to sound like your mother, you know."

"She wants you to come over for dinner again."

"Of course she does."

"Night, Bel."

"Night." He hung up. And then, because he was feeling sorry for himself, he chucked his phone across the room. It was vaguely satisfying to see it smack the wall.

Then he groaned. If he'd dented the drywall of his fancy new house, he was going to punch himself. He wouldn't mind if his phone broke though. Then he wouldn't have to endure any more awkward conversations.

# 21

# Curiosity and the Cat

Several hours later, Suyin lay awake in her bed, staring at the ceiling. Her bedroom was directly below Murmur's, and she couldn't help wondering . . . was he up there now? Trying to sleep and failing as she was?

When she'd returned to her rooms after what happened in the library, she'd found another pile of food waiting on her bed. Murmur had sent someone to get her more supplies before she'd even had a chance to ask. Or maybe he'd told the demon to replenish her stash whenever it ran low. Either way, it showed a level of thoughtfulness she hadn't expected from him, and she wasn't sure what to make of it.

She couldn't stop thinking about how he'd looked above her, his eyes heavy-lidded with desire, his snow-white hair falling like a curtain around them. And she'd confirmed it this time: There was nothing cold about him when he kissed her. Maybe he was normally cold to the touch, but when he was turned on, he was like a furnace. The heat of his body seared through her clothes to her bare skin, making it burn with desire.

She wasn't even trying to lie to herself anymore. She was wildly attracted to a mad necromancer demon. She wanted him. Badly.

But she'd still left when he gave her the chance.

She may have given up on denying her attraction, but that didn't mean she had to stop fighting it. She *had* to fight it. She'd never been religious, despite knowing of the existence of Heaven and Hell. In her mind, it was actions and intentions that determined a person's worthiness for Heaven. It had nothing to do with how many lifeless sermons they sat through.

But surely, having sex with a demon was a surefire way to doom a soul.

Then again . . . Iris was doing it.

Suyin smacked a palm to her forehead. She couldn't be that person who got kidnapped, taken to *Hell*, and then fucked her captor within an inch of his immortal life. Over and over. For hours. On the table. On the floor by the fire. In his bed. In her bed.

With a groan, she rolled over, facing the red sky outside. A moment later, she rolled back the other way. She rolled one more time before blowing out a breath and sitting up with a jerk. *Fuck it.* She was way too restless to sleep right now.

Climbing out of bed, she pulled on leggings, a hoodie, and a pair of warm socks, not bothering with shoes. She tiptoed out of her bedroom and climbed the stairs. Murmur's floor was quiet, the hall torches extinguished. In the distance, faint howling could be heard from god knew where, but otherwise, all was quiet.

She started down the hall toward the library's double doors at the end, only to stop outside the doors to Murmur's room. She stared at them.

Choosing to stop things earlier had been a rare moment of clarity. She needed more moments like that, and she sure as hell wasn't going to find them in Murmur's bed. The worst thing she could do would be to bring sex with her captor into the already incredibly complicated picture.

So why was she standing there, staring at his closed door? And why was her heart suddenly racing with excitement?

The subtle creaking of his bedroom door opening pulled Murmur out of the mire of his thoughts. He wanted to say he'd been mulling over his many complex plans, double-checking every aspect of his spell, but in reality, he'd been replaying the moments with Suyin in the library. How her body felt under his, the way she'd looked at him with so much desire in her eyes.

As such, he sensed her presence immediately.

He stilled, listening with every fiber of his being. Tiny footsteps padded across the floorboards, and he found himself holding his breath.

She stopped at his side, her form a dark outline in the shadowed room. The window drapes were drawn, and only the faintest hint of red glow escaped around their edges. It wasn't enough to properly light her features, but he could still see her eyes on him.

He turned his head on the pillow to meet her gaze. He didn't try to pretend he was asleep.

"You shouldn't be here," he said into the dark.

"I know." She spoke with a resignation that told him she knew exactly what she was getting into. "I couldn't sleep."

Neither could he.

He sat up, and with one rapid motion, he wrapped his hands around her waist and flung her down onto the mattress. He rolled over top of her, and the sheet that had been covering his naked body tangled around him in a way that normally would've made his skin crawl, but he was too distracted to care. Gripping her wrists, he pinned them down on either side of her head so she wouldn't try to grab him again.

He'd expected her to let out a cry, for that apprehension to seep into her expression once more, for her to struggle to escape.

But she didn't do any of that. Instead, she relaxed in his hold. She didn't pull at her wrists. Her body didn't squirm with discomfort. She let him pin her down. She gave him control.

They watched each other in the darkness. This close, he could make out her features clearly, those sharp eyes peering up at him with expectation.

"I gave you a chance to leave," he reminded her. "You took it."

"I know."

He arched a brow. "So what do you think you're doing now?"

She took a breath and seemed to be building up to something. Then she whispered, "I changed my mind."

Part of him wanted to push her away—she'd had her chance, so why should he give her another? Another part wanted to descend upon her with savage ferocity, to slake the desire that had been building since the first moment he'd touched her.

Still another, twisted part wanted to make her suffer. To punish her for doing this to him, for making him feel this way. He'd never asked for this.

He leaned in, running his mouth lightly over hers. Her head tipped back, and her lips parted. He did it again, and her breath gusted out. He trailed his mouth along her jaw toward her ear, and he felt her tremble beneath the grip he still had on her wrists.

When he reached her ear, he growled softly into it, "I don't give second chances, Suyin."

He intended to push off of her and demand she leave. He intended to do anything to maintain the upper hand.

But the witch beat him at his own game. Again.

Before he had a chance to pull away, she turned her head sharply, and their mouths collided. The softness of her lips against his, moistened by her tongue, stole his awareness.

That quickly, he was lost. He forgot all about his plans and his pride, all too eager to forget himself in her.

He kissed her with a desperation that infuriated him, so he poured that into the kiss too. Her tongue reached out, seeking his, and they tangled together. Twisting, stroking, thrusting.

He released her wrists, wanting to touch her. Her hands immediately went into his hair, the strands slipping between her fingers as she clenched her fists against his scalp.

Immediately, he froze. "No."

She stopped, lowering her arms back to the mattress. "Let me touch you."

"No."

"Why?"

He ignored her question, dropping his head and dragging his mouth along her tender throat, imagining sinking his teeth into it.

"Murmur . . ." She moaned as he bit down lightly on her throat, careful not to break the skin. "I want to—"

"Take this off," he growled, fisting the fabric of her hoodie. He wanted to touch more of her, taste her bare skin.

She started to sit up, and this time he let her move, leaning back as she worked the material over her head. She wasn't wearing anything underneath—no undershirt or bra. He liked that.

His gaze wandered over her bare upper body. Her breasts were small, her nipples dark, her skin supple. She looked vulnerable like this . . . until he looked into her eyes. There was nothing vulnerable about the hungry way she watched him.

He reached for her, and their mouths met once more. She gripped the sheet still caught around his hips, trying to pull it away, but he caught her wrists and pulled back with a warning look.

"Let me touch you," she panted.

He searched her face. Was he going to allow this? For so long, he'd despised even the lightest sensation of being restrained, and that included another's hands on his skin. His bedsheet ended up on the floor more often than not because he couldn't stand the feel of it wrapped around his legs.

Even now, so long after his time as Paimon's prisoner, the feeling of being shackled in any way sent him into a cold sweat, the old memories crawling out of some dark inner hovel to haunt him.

But . . . this was Suyin. And he wanted to know what it would be like to let her touch him. He wanted it badly.

Slowly, he released her wrists, holding his open hands above hers for an extended pause and giving her a warning look. If she pushed him too far, he would retaliate.

Logically, he knew there was nothing she could do to him that he couldn't stop immediately. There was no way she could overpower him. But this aversion wasn't logical; it was psychological. And if there was one enemy Murmur couldn't defeat, it had always been his own mind.

As Suyin pulled the sheet aside, his hand dove into her hair, tangling with the silky strands. He tightened his hold, drawing her head back. With his other hand, he gripped her jaw, his thumb and forefinger pressing into her soft cheeks, though he was careful not to cut her with his claws. She was so small compared to him, he had to be careful.

She moaned as he kissed her again, but her little hands didn't stop until they wrapped around his hard shaft. It was his turn to moan. *Fucking hell*, that felt incredible. How had he gone so long without this?

He lost control of their kiss as she stroked his shaft with a firm grip, and he could do nothing but breathe against her lips. His head spun with pleasure.

"Lie back," she whispered.

He shook his head mutely, too lost in the movement of her hands to form words.

"Murmur . . ."

Her grip tightened, and for a second, the panic rose. His spine stiffened and he pulled back. She released him immediately, and from the frown on her face, she was beginning to figure out his hang-up.

They stared at each other. He didn't want her to stop. He just didn't want to feel restrained in any way, and he sure as fuck didn't want to explain that to her.

"Lie down," she said again.

"No," he growled.

Her eyes narrowed. "What if I told you I want you to lie down because I want to suck your dick?" Her lips curved into a wicked smile. "Would that convince you?"

His mouth opened and then closed again. His gaze fixed on her lips, and he imagined them parting as she took him into her hot, wet mouth—

*What do you know, I'm convinced.*

Still, he moved cautiously, never taking his eyes from her. He leaned back, resting onto his elbows. Her dark eyes lit with satisfaction and the promise to make it worth his while. He didn't doubt her for a second. *Little witch.*

Then her eyes traveled over his naked body. "Goddamn," she breathed. "You're a work of art."

He arched a brow, but he had to admit to feeling a certain satisfaction that she was pleased by the sight of him.

She crawled closer, and he bent one knee up to make room for her between his legs. She lifted her eyes to his. He tried to disguise how desperate he was for her to continue, but he wasn't sure he could mask his thoughts right now.

He reached down to thread his fingers into her hair, clenching them just tightly enough for her to feel the sting in her scalp. He could have stopped her if he'd wanted, but he didn't.

She bent her head, and her fingers curled around the base of his shaft, standing it up until the head was inches from her mouth.

Heat flared between their locked gazes. Her lips parted, her little pink tongue snaking out. She licked once, from the underside of the head over the top of the slit. He groaned, long and deep, and dropped his head back, hair falling behind him.

She closed her lips around the head and sucked him right into her mouth. He cursed, and the hand in her hair tightened.

Once again, he was riding the very edge of his tolerance for contact. But this was worth it. And the twinge of discomfort added another layer of excitement. At any moment, his warped mind might decide it was too much, and he would have to stop. He would enjoy every second of this that he could.

Suyin's hot lips slid off the tip of his shaft, her tongue twirling around before she took him back into her mouth. His vision blacked out briefly. He lifted his head again, forcing his eyes open so he didn't miss a second of the visual.

This was indescribable. He knew right then she had created a monster. An insatiable one. He wanted this every day, forever. He wanted only this for hours on end. He wanted—

"Fuck!" His hoarse shout pierced the air as her wet mouth slid halfway down his shaft, and he hit the back of her throat. She'd taken him as deep as she could, but she made up for the distance with her hand, moving up to meet her lips in the middle.

She moaned, and the vibration against his cock made him see stars. She looked up, meeting his eyes, her lips sliding back to the tip and then sinking as deep as she could go again. When he hit the back of her throat, his hips thrust up of their own accord. She gagged, choking around his girth, and he groaned at the sight.

He released her hair and wrapped a hand around the back of her neck. He pushed her down again, and when he bottomed out in her mouth, he flexed his fingers and growled, "Swallow."

She did.

Tears gathered at the corners of her eyes, but she swallowed. Her throat opened, and he sank another inch deeper. "That's it," he praised on a low moan. "You can take me."

He held her like that and began a steady rocking of his hips, pulling out just slightly and then sinking farther. He continued encouraging her to swallow, and she kept obeying him.

She made a tiny helpless sound around him, the hum going straight down his shaft.

Heady, intoxicating pleasure flooded his bloodstream. For the first time in as long as he could remember, perhaps ever, he became nothing but an extension of his body. His mind switched off, the voices and screaming souls silenced, and he gave himself over to his primal urges.

Keeping a firm grip on Suyin's neck, he increased the pace of his thrusts. Nonsensical praise streamed from his mouth, most of it unknown to him. But the way she moaned and fought to take him deeper pleased him to no end.

"That's it," he panted. "You're doing so well, little witch. Take more."

He worked her faster, holding her head in place while he thrust into her wet mouth. Saliva ran down his shaft. Suyin choked, but when she glanced up, her eyes were full of pleasure. Drugged with it.

It was that sight that pushed him over the edge.

"Oh, fuck—" His attempts at speech dissolved into a long groan as he spilled into her mouth.

Her eyes widened, and he glimpsed her throat working as

she drank him down. He swore the sight of it made him come again, before he'd even finished the first time. Or maybe it was one long orgasm that didn't seem to end. Making up for all the centuries he'd deprived himself.

His head spun, and his heart pounded so hard he swore he could hear it. He collapsed onto his back. Either his eyes were shut or he'd gone blind, because he saw nothing but blackness with a thousand brilliant colors dancing around like flashing lights.

He meant to speak. He meant to praise Suyin, to tell her how she pleased him, but his head wouldn't stop spinning and the pleasure didn't let up. He suddenly couldn't tell which way was up or down, or whether he was lying on his back, standing on his feet, or floating through space.

The world kept spinning, and he had no choice but to let himself spin with it, until he flew right off the edge of consciousness into the dark.

# 22

# Shot in the Dark

SUYIN SAT BACK AND WIPED HER MOUTH WITH THE BACK of her hand, and it came away wet. She'd swallowed as much of his release as she could, but more had leaked out of the seal of her lips.

She'd never heard of anyone having an orgasm for that long. Knowing Murmur, it had probably been a while. To say he needed it was an understatement. She'd never met a more high-strung person.

"Damn," she breathed, not knowing what else to say. That had been hot. Easily the hottest oral sex she'd given, to a man or a woman. She generally preferred oral sex with women. They were more responsive, and it took a lot more effort to get them to climax, so it was more rewarding.

But Murmur was . . . She didn't know. But there was something extremely satisfying about making this super control freak unravel.

Then she frowned. There was still no movement from said control freak.

She crawled up beside his large naked form to peer at his

face, and a laugh burst out of her. "You're kidding me," she muttered.

The fucker had passed out cold.

She laughed again. It was flattering, honestly. She'd made him come so hard, he straight-up lost consciousness. She'd never given anyone that great of an orgasm before.

She dropped onto her back beside him. Her hoodie was gone, thrown somewhere in her haste to get skin on skin with him, but she was still wearing pants. He hadn't even gotten her fully naked before he passed out, the bastard.

She turned her head on the pillow so she could enjoy him like this, all sprawled out naked and sexy. She wasn't over how good he made "pale and dead" look. He wasn't built, but his lean strength was clearly defined, even lying on his back. The line down the center of his abs was hot as hell, and she wanted to trace the V-shaped muscles pointing to his cock with her tongue.

She bit her lip when her eyes landed back on that cock. Semi-hard now, it lay against his abs, looking heavy and delicious. She wanted to suck him off again. Even better, she wanted to climb on and go for a ride.

She wasn't sure he'd let her, however.

She hadn't missed the way he caught her hands every time she tried to touch him. He didn't seem to like being touched, though he definitely hadn't minded her touching his dick. But she also hadn't missed the way he'd taken charge of her giving him head.

He obviously had major control issues, but was that a surprise? If someone had tried to tell her Murmur was vanilla in bed, she would have laughed in their face. He was a freak in everyday life. Of course he'd be a freak in the sheets too.

Shit, though, she was so turned on. She shot him a glare. Fucker was still dead to the world. Damn him for passing out and leaving her in this state.

She smiled suddenly. Maybe she could get revenge.

She slid her hand into her pants until she found the wet mess she'd made in her underwear. Her fingers shot to her clit like it was a magnet, and she started to rub, her gaze fixed on Murmur the whole time.

So she was jacking off while staring at an unconscious demon. Her soul was definitely doomed. But then, she was half demon, so she'd probably been doomed from the start. She might as well enjoy the journey.

Her gaze feasted on his defined jaw and the graceful arch of his collarbones. She stared at his freaky claws and barbed tail, and most of all, she stared at his cock. She imagined it in her mouth again, and then she imagined him sinking it into her.

She came on a hard moan, her thighs shaking, her spine arching off the bed. Her hand was soaked with her release, and by the time she finished, she was nearly ready to pass out herself.

She pulled her fingers out and held them up. The tips glistened faintly in the low light. Then she sat up. *Time for revenge.*

She traced her wet fingers down the length of that thick gray cock, and then, grinning evilly, she ran them over his lips. With his heightened demon senses, he was going to scent her the second he woke up. Perfect.

She stroked a few strands of hair off his face—refusing to analyze her motives for the affectionate gesture—and then climbed out of bed. She searched around in the dark for her hoodie and then pulled it on.

Standing at his side of the mattress, she looked down at him. Maybe it was stupid, but she was glad she'd come. She was sick of fighting herself. It was starting to seem like her best option was to just give in to her impulses and worry about picking up the pieces later.

Cleanup rather than prevention.

And then, because she was an idiot, and he just looked so darn cute all sprawled out and unconscious, she bent and kissed him on the cheek.

His skin was still warm.

Murmur awoke to the smell of Suyin's arousal. *Little witch.* This was no accident. Her scent was all over him, and he hadn't even gotten a chance to taste her last night.

His eyes popped open as the rest of the night's memories flooded his mind. He wasn't quite sure how to process this new turn of events. He'd been without sex for centuries and hadn't thought twice about it. Now, he was obsessed.

He hadn't even penetrated her yet, but he already knew he *needed* to. And he didn't just need to do it once. He needed to do it for hours. Over and over until he passed out from exhaustion. And then he'd wake up and repeat the cycle again.

He leapt out of bed and dressed in a rush, halfway across the room before he'd even properly gotten his pants on. He threw a robe on, not bothering with a shirt, and pulled the mess of his hair out from beneath the collar.

He stopped dead with his hand on the door handle, suddenly realizing . . .

He had slept. Uninterrupted. Without the death vision. Without any vision at all, not even a distant, fragmented dream.

It was the first time in years he'd slept deeply. And he felt fucking fantastic. Energized. *Awake.* No wonder everyone was so obsessed with sleeping. He was already looking forward to trying again, if this would be the result.

*Just need to have more sex first. Lots of sex.*

He nodded eagerly, for once fully in agreement with himself.

He threw open his bedroom doors and strode into the hall, only to realize he'd forgotten shoes. He spun back around with a curse and grabbed his boots, stuffing his feet in as he half walked, half jumped on one leg toward the library.

Once there, he stoked the fire in the hearth and lit the lanterns, though the room was already much brighter since Suyin had cleaned the window.

She was evidently still asleep. He wondered when she'd left last night. A part of him wished she had fallen asleep with him so he could have woken up and gotten a mouthful of that enticing scent before he went about his day.

Standing over his desk, he arranged his sketches and lists in preparation to cast the spell. Except he couldn't motivate himself to focus. He was far too distracted by other things. He planted his palms on the desk, trying to force his mind to work.

"What's the first order of business today, boss?"

His head snapped up.

She was beside him, having snuck in while he was lost in his thoughts. She had a wicked little smirk on her face.

He narrowed his eyes. *Forget focus.* It would be an affront to let such a challenge go unmet.

*Here we go*, Suyin thought, two seconds before Murmur grabbed her.

In a flash, he pulled her against him and then pressed her back against the desk, planting his palms on either side of her and leaning in.

"Turn around," he growled.

*That's how he's gonna play it, huh?* It was first thing in the morning. She'd barely eaten breakfast.

She didn't let her partners boss her around when it came to sex. She wasn't submissive, and she wasn't normally attracted to dominant partners either. If anything, *she* was usually the dominant one.

It wasn't that she had a need to be in control. It was just that everyone else was incompetent. And that wasn't just in bed. Every time she delegated a task, she was unsatisfied with the results. Whenever she could, she preferred to work alone.

It was worse when it came to sex. She always ended up issuing command after command because her partners inevitably proved incapable of giving her what she needed. She'd give so many instructions, it'd feel like an incredibly specific sex-ed class instead of a mutual exchange of pleasure.

So she took control. She dominated because it was easier to take matters into her own hands than to sit back and watch someone fumble around and embarrass themselves until she lost all attraction to them.

Harsh, but true.

But here was this seven-foot-tall demon glaring down at her, telling her to turn around—probably so he could bend her over his desk and fuck her stupid. He didn't stutter. He didn't have that look of hesitation in his eyes that told her she could steamroll him if she just uttered a few well-placed criticisms. In fact, he looked like he *wanted* her to defy him so he could make her pay for it.

"Now," he said in a low voice. His tail swung lazily behind him. One claw pointed at the desk in question, its surface covered in papers covered in his messy madman scrawl.

She needed this experience. She needed to know what it felt like to submit to someone who could actually match her will.

So she turned around.

Immediately, he pressed into her from behind, and she felt his hardness against her lower back. Her stomach clenched in anticipation. Distantly, she felt the sensation of his churning souls against her lower legs, but it didn't bother her. If anything, it increased her excitement.

He hooked a claw into the waistband of her leggings and snapped it lightly against her back.

"Take these off."

She caught her pants and underwear together and shoved them down to her knees. The cool air of the library mixed with Murmur's heat against her bare ass made her pulse race. He began to push up her hoodie, his big hands sliding up her sides, sending shivers over her skin. She pulled it the rest of the way off, tossing it away.

He stooped, sliding a hand into her hair to draw her head to one side so he could drag his teeth up her throat. His other hand reached around to cup her breast. She was enveloped by him, and this time, she was the naked one while he was fully clothed.

Releasing her hair, he pressed a palm between her shoulder blades and pushed her forward. She bent over the piles of loose papers and open books on the desk. His heat seared her, his big hands stroking down her spine, the ends of his soft hair tickling her skin.

Arching her back and leaning on one elbow, she pulled her own hair over one shoulder so she could see him behind her. He loomed like a shadow. His eyes were burning.

A jolt of arousal shot through her like a lightning bolt, and she felt her core flooding with heat. Just feeling his eyes on her, knowing she was exposed to him, was making her body go wild.

"Flat on the table," he said with a growl that made the hairs on the back of her neck rise.

She hesitated briefly. There was some inner wall erected in her mind that she'd have to temporarily dismantle to give him this much control. She wasn't sure she was ready for that. She wasn't sure she wanted to give him any more power than he already had.

And yet, before she'd even finished the thought, she found herself flat on her chest on the table, her cheek against the rough texture of loose papers.

She saw him crouch in her peripherals. His palms landed on her ass cheeks, and he spread her all the way apart. She was so open, and he was so close that she could feel his breath against her slit. At this point, she was so wet, she swore it was about to start running down her legs.

*Told you, bitch. This demon is a fucking genius.*

And then he licked her.

An ungodly moan rolled out of her, like no sound she'd ever made before. She was barely aware of herself, her attention fixed on the hot bursts of pleasure between her legs.

"You taste fucking delicious," he snarled.

He held her open and feasted on her like he was a starving man, his tongue spearing through her sensitized flesh, grinding against her clit in *just* the right way, and—

"Oh god—!" she cried, slapping her palms onto the desk beside her head and clenching her fingers hard enough to crumple the paper under them. *Where did he learn to do that?* She swore her clit was a goddamn vault that no one but her could open. If so, then he was fucking Houdini.

The big hands on her ass squeezed, his claws pricking her naked flesh. "You've created a monster, Suyin."

"You . . . were already a monster," she panted, black spots dancing in her vision as pleasure made her head swim. Her climax was so close, she could taste it.

"Look at you. You're so wet you'd have made a puddle on the floor if I didn't lick it up."

She moaned again. "Murmur."

"What do you want, little witch? Use your words."

"Make me come! Fucking god, just make me—"

He penetrated her with his tongue, and she broke off with a cry. And then he went back to her clit, circling around it with precision. A few rubs on the top, and she flew over the edge into ecstasy.

She definitely made a whole bunch of uninhibited noises.

Her thighs, ass, and legs all clenched with the rhythm of her core, and she pressed back and ground against his face. He flattened his tongue against her clit and let her ride it out.

Just as she crested over the orgasm's peak, her muscles beginning to relax, he pulled away. She couldn't have opened her eyes or lifted her head to save her life, and she could only wonder what—

And then she felt him. Thick and hard, pressing against her entrance. She gave thanks for the Cambion-conception ritual she'd read about—an accidental pregnancy was the last thing she needed right now—because she didn't think she had the presence of mind to stop this.

The head of his cock met resistance against her opening, and for a moment, she didn't think he would fit. The blunt head pushing against her felt way too big, and she remembered how her jaw ached after having him in her mouth.

But then he pushed harder, and there was a stretch—*goddamn*, was there a stretch—and the head slipped inside her.

"Fuck—!" Her spine arched.

He bent over her, planting his big hands on the table beside her shoulders.

She looked down at them and time froze for a second. *I am being fucked by a demon in Hell*, she thought. *And I love it. I'm going to come again, and it's going to blow my mind.*

"Murmur," she cried. All of a sudden, she felt strangely panicked. Probably because he could tear her clean in half if he wanted to. But there was more to it than that.

She was letting go of restraint. She was handing him control. Of her body. Of her mind. Of her choices.

But somehow, this half-mad demon with questionable morals knew exactly how to soothe her. He leaned down, his big body pressed against her naked back, and he stroked her hair off her face with one hand, dragging his claws lightly against her scalp.

"That's it," he praised in her ear. "You can take me, can't you?"

"Yes," she found herself moaning. "Yes, I can take it. I want it—"

Her speech faltered as he gave her more, sinking another inch deeper. The stretch bordered on painful, but this was the kind of pain she wanted more of.

"You're squeezing me so tight." His groan sounded unhinged, like he was losing himself to this as much as she was. "Can you take more?"

"Yes! Fuck, yes—"

"You're so good, bent over my desk, begging to be fucked. I'd kill anyone you asked me to. I'd start another fucking war to reward you."

She moaned desperately. He fed her a little more and then pulled out partway and started working her slowly, easing in and out with subtle strokes. She was so wet, she could feel her arousal coating the insides of her thighs.

"That's it." He pushed a little deeper. "I'm almost halfway."

*Almost* halfway? "Oh my god," she moaned.

His hips started to move as he fucked her in long, slow strokes. Every inch of his thick girth made her body scream with pleasure. Her eyes were screwed shut, her teeth gritted against the intensity.

And he wasn't going easy on her anymore. His pace increased, and he pushed deeper with each thrust until she felt him bottom out inside her. Her moans turned to cries, each more uninhibited than the last.

Her palms were flat on the desk beside his, and in an action that surprised her, he gripped them, winding their fingers together. His hands dwarfed hers, and it reminded her just how drastic their size difference was. He was nearly two feet taller than her.

Demon and human. Wrong size. Wrong coupling.

Wrong . . . but so damn right.

She pushed against him and threw her head back with a cry as he thrust still deeper. He dropped his head and fixed his teeth over her shoulder, hips working against her ass.

He had her pinned, and he seemed to really fucking like that.

His moans and growls became more and more feral, and she knew he was close. Driving this demon over the edge was her new favorite hobby, and the closer he got to his orgasm, the more her own excitement revved up.

He gave a hoarse shout, a curse, and a moan at the same time, and she felt his cock swell inside her. The damn thing got even bigger. Every pulse of his shaft and the searing hot release filling her up from the inside was too much, and she climaxed too.

The world spun like they'd fucked on a Tilt-A-Whirl. Every stroke of his dick was like fucking heaven, and she swore his cum was a healing elixir, because the hot wetness suddenly spilling out of her soothed the aches of being stretched.

His movements slowed to a gentle rocking as they came down together. His frantic growls turned to lazy ones, like a satisfied lion.

And finally, he stilled. Silence descended on the library, save for his heavy breathing as it gusted past her ear, blowing strands of her hair into her face.

He untangled their hands and stroked her hair back, tucking it behind her ear. "You," he purred, "are proving to be quite the distraction."

She breathed a tired laugh, which only made her pussy clench, and they both moaned. "You're the one commanding me to bend over desks and get naked."

"You're the one obeying." There was so much satisfaction in his voice, she could practically taste it.

"You like it."

"You have no idea. As I said, you've created a monster. I think I might have to add some new conditions to your prison sentence, or I'll never get any work done."

She tensed slightly. "What does that mean? You said I'd be free to go after your spell was completed."

"I did say that."

"You can't go back on your word, Murmur."

But he wasn't listening. And suddenly, neither was she, as he slowly withdrew from her body. He was still semi-hard, and now that they were past the peak, she had no idea how the hell he'd fit inside her. She moaned at the sudden release of pressure as more of his release spilled out of her.

"Fuck me," he groaned, and she figured he was enjoying the view. She didn't bother looking. Her cheek was plastered to the papers, and she was too relaxed to open her eyes. "Maybe I'll make you stay like that for a while."

"Don't you dare, Murmur . . ."

Another drop of his cum slid out of her. They both moaned.

Okay, maybe she'd stay for a bit. Just a tiny bit. As long as he stood there staring at her.

"Spread yourself open for me," he said.

She did it. She reached back with both hands and pulled herself open, causing more of that hot fluid to leak out of her. Being fully exposed with cum all over her legs felt equal parts erotic and embarrassing.

She heard Murmur shift behind her as he crouched, and then his hands were at her core, spreading her labia apart, careful not to catch her with his claws. She moaned.

And then he trailed his tongue through her soaking wet flesh once more.

He licked up her pussy, tasting his own cum, and then traveled back down and swirled the tip of his tongue around her clit.

"Oh my *god.*" Her toes curled inside her boots.

"No god here," Murmur said between long licks. "Just me."

It didn't take long before she started to come. It was a lazy orgasm, like her muscles were too tired to bother with the full deal, but it still jolted through her system like a shot of ecstasy injected through her clit.

"You're dirty," she breathed as he stood again.

"And you're dripping," he purred, bending over her to whisper in her ear. He straightened. "You can stand now, witchling."

She planted her palms on the table and stood. Her knees immediately buckled, but he was there, scooping her into his arms. She was a mess. His cum was still running out of her and probably all over him. And her pants were still bunched at her knees. Again: embarrassing.

But apparently, she didn't have the capacity to experience that emotion right now, because she just looked into his eyes and asked, "Are you going to take care of me now, demon?"

He smiled in response, already striding out of the library. Her heart warmed when he turned into his room instead of continuing down the stairs. She refused to consider why.

# 23

# Bound and Determined

Murmur crawled over the witch in his bed. He'd stripped her pants and boots off before laying her down, and he let his gaze feast on every delectable inch of her naked body. Her lightly tanned skin, her dark nipples and small breasts, her midnight hair spread across the pillows . . . She was exquisite.

She reached for him, so he let his souls rise, their cold hands seizing her wrists and pinning them down above her head. He smiled as she struggled to break free, her eyes going from wide to heated when she saw how much it aroused him to restrain her.

"Methinks you have a kink, Murmur," she teased, relaxing into her ghostly bonds.

He lowered himself over her, kissing her and teasing his tongue against hers. "You're naked and wet and completely at my mercy. Can you blame me?"

She groaned as he fit himself between her spread thighs, and whatever reply she might have given was lost beneath her pleasured cry as his hardened shaft slipped into that perfect notch.

"Are you sore?" he asked, barely controlling himself from thrusting forward.

"Yes, but—"

He groaned in dismay, but he wouldn't hurt her. The pleasure he felt was solely because it was her pleasure too. There would be no enjoyment if she wasn't right there with him.

"—I don't care," she finished on a sigh, restoring his hope.

He stilled. "Are you sure?"

"Yes. Fuck—!"

He didn't wait for her to change her mind. Her body was already open and wet for him, and he slid in far easier this time. He went slowly, however, conscious of her tenderness.

"You feel like fucking nirvana," he growled, dropping his head to bite her shoulder.

"Oh my god." She squirmed beneath him. "Wait. Fuck, I— Oh, *fuck*— Wait."

He stopped, lifting his head and frowning in question. "Did I hurt you?"

"No, it's just . . ." She pulled again at her bonds. "Can you make them let me go? I don't like the idea of them watching."

"Who? My souls?" He chuckled at the thought.

She scowled. "Can you blame me? They're ghosts. I don't want them to see us fuck."

He laughed. "Suyin, I control them. Their screams are in my head because that's the only place where their free will remains. I see through their eyes and feel through their hands, and they only have the senses that I allow them. They're an extension of me."

"They're still ghosts," she muttered. "And they're restraining me."

"I know." He smiled wickedly. "I'm enjoying it very much. But if you insist."

He released the tethers, and she used one of her freed arms to reach up and stroke her fingers through his hair. He tensed but allowed the contact.

"Why don't you like to be touched?" she asked.

He flexed his hips to remind her he was still inside her. "Ancient memories that I allowed to rule me for long enough that they became a personality trait."

She moaned as he continued his lazy thrusts, but she seemed determined to get her answers, as was her way. It was one of the things he liked most about her, frustrating as it was at the moment. "What . . . does that mean?"

He wasn't in the mood to talk, however. He much preferred to focus on what their bodies were doing. "Does it matter?" he said against her ear, nipping lightly on the edge, moving his hips in a steady rhythm.

"I'll—" She gasped as he surged a little deeper. "Oh god, that's so good. I'll let you use your souls to restrain me if you tell me."

He lifted his head, stilling his movements, and searched her gaze. She was always negotiating with him, always quick to find a way to use his aims to achieve her own.

She smiled, sensing victory. "Tell me why, and you can go back to using your freaky ghosts instead of chains."

"Or I could just find some chains," he supplied.

"But you like the idea of the ghosts more," she shot back. "It turns you on, doesn't it?"

"You think you're so clever," he growled, thrusting deep, causing her to arch off the bed with a moan. "You think you can manipulate me."

"I'm just . . . negotiating— Fuck, Murmur!"

"You're a clever little witch, aren't you?"

"Yes, yes . . . Oh, god—"

He stopped suddenly. "I'll agree to a compromise."

She blinked through the haze of pleasure.

"I'll use my souls to restrain you now and then tell you what you want to know later. I'm not in the mood for talking at present."

"Fine. But don't think I'll forget to ask, because I won't."

She looked smug at her victory, so he showed her who was really in charge by binding her wrists and ankles with shadowy tethers and spreading them apart on the mattress.

Her eyes widened and she pulled against the restraints, but she didn't fight to break free.

He stooped to kiss her again, picking up the motion of his thrusts. Her body tightened around him, her wet heat an inexhaustible paradise. After so long in a deadened state, this much sensation was beyond intoxicating.

He loosened the hold on her ankles, using his ghostly hands to catch her behind her knees instead. He lifted her legs up toward her torso, exposing her dripping core and allowing for deeper penetration. His cock barely fit, but he fucking loved the sight of it sinking inside of her, knowing he was filling every inch of space she had to give.

He formed more bindings at her ankles and spread her legs up and open, thrusting deeper. Her moans turned to cries, and she pulled on her wrists, but he allowed no give in her bonds.

He kept one palm planted beside her head, supporting his weight, and the other he let roam down the soft skin of her side, over her slender waist to the delicate flair of her hip.

"If you don't like it, tell me and I'll stop," he said before forming another spectral hand in between their bodies. He let it creep down her abdomen slowly, giving her plenty of time to react.

Her eyes shot wide and her body tensed, but she didn't tell him to stop. He would show her that she'd made the right decision.

The hand slipped between the folds of her labia, circling the slippery wet nub of her clitoris. Her cry became a stream of foul curses that would've made him laugh had he not been using most of his concentration to keep himself from spilling prematurely.

He could imagine how the icy touch would feel against her heated flesh. The phantom fingers worked her faster while he thrust harder, pushing a little deeper each time, forcing her body to stretch to accommodate him.

Her eyes were squeezed shut against the intensity of sensation he unleashed upon her. He sensed she was close. He needed to push her over the edge because it wouldn't be long before he couldn't hold himself back anymore.

"Suyin," he moaned.

She jerked, pulling at her wrists again.

"Open your eyes."

She did, but they rolled in their sockets, lost to her ecstasy.

"Look at me," he growled.

Her dark eyes snapped to his and held his gaze. He let the ghostly hand at her core push her just a little harder, and he felt the moment she went over. Her body locked up, and her core muscles rippled around his shaft like they were trying to massage his release right out of him.

And they succeeded. With a hoarse shout, he fell into his own climax, head spinning. His heart pounded in his skull and in his shaft as he released inside of her, the hot fluid spilling out of her core.

Her cries were replaced by soft moans as her body eased down from its peak. He released her bonds and slid out from between her legs. Leaning back, he took a moment to appreciate the sight of her well-used sex, and then he dropped to her side.

"I can't believe I let a ghost rub my clit," she mumbled.

Some time later, Suyin yawned and stretched to wakefulness. She enjoyed her body's pleasure-sore state for a moment before sitting up and peering into the room.

There was no sign of Murmur, and the space on the bed beside her was cold. She figured he hadn't stuck around after she passed out from the exhaustion of being thoroughly fucked. Just the thought of what he'd done to her made her face heat and her lips curve.

She scanned her surroundings, trying to see where he'd tossed her clothes, but it was too dark. Pulling the bedsheet off and wrapping it around herself, she padded over to the window and threw back the heavy drapes. The sky was at its brightest now, and its eerie red glow filled the bedchamber.

She turned around to take it in, and her eyes widened.

Seeing Murmur's room in proper light for the first time meant she could see that the walls were covered in drawings. There were faces with haunting eyes that seemed to watch her. There were half-drawn sigils. There were endless, illegible writings, in English and Sheolic, sometimes a phrase or two, sometimes multiple paragraphs.

On top of that, there were claw marks gouged into the stone, and the wood of the headboard and bed frame looked like it had been mauled.

She approached the closest wall, leaning in to study the drawings. There was one of a half-rotted face, its mouth open in a silent scream. It looked similar to the faces of Murmur's souls when he materialized them. Lines of Sheolic script circled its head like a halo. The word "screaming" was written below it, but the G trailed off into a bunch of messy scribbling.

The scrawling lines traveled down to the floor and stopped abruptly. When she looked down at the floor beneath the last line, there was a small piece of charcoal, left right where it had been dropped.

She picked it up. It was worn to a stub, and it immediately stained her fingertips black. Setting it back down, she went around the bed and studied the walls on the other side. Most of the faces were similarly creepy and weren't something she'd want staring at her while she slept.

The bedside table was covered with pages of still more sketches of faces and sigils. In fact, every available surface was covered in papers and shredded notebooks. And she already knew the bed had been a mess before they got into it, as if when Murmur slept, he tossed and turned endlessly.

A chill raced down her spine. This was not the dwelling of a normal person. It looked like the scene of the villain's domain in a horror movie. The place where the stupid teenagers would be lured to and killed. Their blood would probably spatter over the walls dramatically in the climax.

It was a reminder that Murmur was . . . multifaceted. She had seen a side of him that she doubted many had. He could be playful, naughty, and oddly sweet. He could also be cold and cruel, and he slept in a murder room.

Turning back to the bed, she sat on the edge of the mattress and scooped up a stack of loose pages from the nightstand. The sketches were actually quite beautiful. He managed to capture the vibe of whatever scene or face he was drawing with a few well-placed pencil strokes.

She uncovered the next paper in the stack, and her eyes widened.

It was her.

It was so clearly her, she could have paid a professional artist to draw a portrait and not gotten a better result. Her head was half turned, her chin lifted, which gave her a fierce, prideful look, and her eyes were subtly narrowed as if she was suspicious of the world and everyone in it. An accurate portrayal.

He had told her he'd found her because of a vision, but she hadn't realized he'd seen her face this clearly. A sudden suspicion had her uncovering the next sketch and the next, sifting through the rest of the pile. As expected, they were all of her.

In one drawing, she was glancing over her shoulder, her hair blowing as if she was moving quickly. In another she was reaching back to tuck her hair behind her ear, glancing sidelong at the artist. In the last one in the pile, she was running, and her heart stuttered in her chest when she realized what it was depicting.

She was rushing down a dark alley, brick walls rising on either side of her. She was stooped slightly as she ran, as if chasing something. Beneath her grasping hands was a quill scribbling illegible letters.

It was her own damn dream.

She'd forgotten about that stupid dream until now, but here was a chilling reminder of what her intuition had been trying to tell her. She'd been chasing something she couldn't read—knowledge, *understanding*—and it had led her to Murmur. The one who had all the answers she sought. The explanation couldn't have been more obvious.

This whole experience was starting to feel a lot like destiny.

She shook her head. She needed to get a grip.

Putting the sketches back, she rose from the bed. There was no sign of her clothes anywhere, so she crossed the room to the tall wardrobe and pulled it open. The inside was a mess. Clothing was stuffed into every possible crevice and hung out of drawers that barely closed.

She breathed a laugh. The damned demon was walking chaos.

Opening a random drawer, she found a long, tunic-like shirt. She donned it and laughed again. It was enormous and fell to her knees. The fabric was so thin, she could see her nipples through it, and the cut in the neck was so low on her, she was in danger of falling out of it.

She shrugged. Murmur had seen her naked. There was no need for modesty now.

Exiting the bedroom, she headed toward the library. For

some reason, her stomach felt fluttery. She supposed it made sense to be nervous to see Murmur after what had happened between them. This was uncharted territory for her.

When she slipped inside, the air was warm and the fire burned bright. Murmur stood by the window with a book in one hand, his head down as he read, hair falling over his face. He wore only a silken black robe, belted at the hips.

Her heart gave a little kick at the sight of him.

Then she shook herself. That was not what this was. They'd had great sex, and she no longer hated him with a burning passion, but that was as far as it was going.

He looked up, sensing her presence, and his lips curved. Setting the book on the desk, he held out a hand. "Come here, witchling."

She crossed the room and went to him without hesitation.

To her surprise, he scooped her up and rested her against his side like she was a goddamn toddler. She would have been pissed except he held her with a hand on her ass and there was nothing remotely paternal about the way he looked at her.

"I see you helped yourself to my wardrobe," he said, hooking a claw in the neckline of the loose shirt and taking a shameless peek inside.

She swatted his hand without any real effort. "You stole my clothes."

His smile was wicked. "I was hoping you'd show up naked."

"Your bedroom is freezing. And you don't have any blankets. When was the last time you lit a fire in there?"

His smile dropped. "Never, since I moved here anyway. I try to spend as little time there as possible."

She took a breath and said with false casualness, "Interesting decor."

He frowned.

"The walls are . . . unique."

He shut down fast, like she'd expected. She could tell he was about to change the subject, so before he could, she quickly said, "Are they all from visions?"

"Mostly, yes. And sometimes, my souls project things at me while I'm sleeping. Seeing as they were mostly the scum of the earth while they were alive, their thoughts are unpleasant, to say the least."

"So why keep them around? Why not send them to the Nine Rings where they belong?"

"Power, Suyin." The way he said it, he might as well have added "duh" at the end. "It's always about power."

She nodded, saying nothing, because she couldn't argue with that. If she'd lived in Hell, she would have been obsessed with power too. It was likely the only way to stay safe.

They fell silent for a time, and she allowed herself to relax in his grip, though she must have looked absurd. Her hair was a mess, she was wearing the largest shirt ever made, and Murmur was holding her against his side with one arm like she weighed nothing. She probably looked like a manic doll.

And then Murmur said, "The sigil is ready."

She stiffened and glanced at it. The last she'd seen, he'd erased an entire section. But when she looked now, she saw that he had indeed finished repainting the lines. Everything looked fresh and new. She must have been asleep for several hours for him to get that much done.

She looked at him with a frown. This was a good thing. If the spell was successful, she could finally go home, get back to her life, and assure everyone she hadn't been murdered. The coven needed her. There was still so much she wanted to explore in this library, but nothing mattered more than getting back to Earth.

And yet, a moment later, she heard herself say, "You owe me an explanation. You can't do the spell until you've fulfilled your end of the deal."

*You better not be stalling, Su. There's no way you're that stupid.*

Murmur carried Suyin to the couch and sank into the worn cushions, positioning her on his lap so she straddled him. "In answer to your question," he said, diving right in, "allow me to first clarify that it's not that I don't like touch, but rather that I don't like to be restrained." The sooner he got this conversation over with, the better.

"I kinda figured that," Suyin said. "Does it bother you for me to sit like this then?"

"A little," he answered honestly, "but I can control it."

Her brow furrowed. "I can move."

"Stay."

"But—"

"I'm aware it's not a rational response, and I can control it to an extent. And I want you here. So stay."

"Okay." Her soft smile did something to his insides. "So are you gonna tell me why?"

"It's boring."

"I somehow doubt that."

He lifted a hand and studied his claws. "Long ago, Paimon, the former ruler of this lair, captured and imprisoned me for a decade or so. I was restrained and tortured until part of my mind fractured, and I've been that way ever since. Eventually, I escaped and swore I would one day exact revenge. And I did." He dropped his hand. "And now, here we are."

Suyin shook her head. "Yeah, no, that wasn't boring."

"It's boring because it's average. Find me a demon that has never been captured and tortured in his immortal life, and then I'll be impressed."

She snorted. "Fair enough. But it's still pretty fucked up."

"It was a very long time ago."

"But you're still affected by it."

"As I said before, after I escaped, I allowed the memories to control me for long enough that they became part of my personality. Mortal or immortal, we are all the sum total of our experiences—on Earth or in Hell."

She pursed her lips like she suspected he was making light of things. But what could he say? That he was ashamed that even now, a thousand years later, he still shuddered every time his bedsheets became tangled in his legs or his clothing was too restrictive? That he'd stabbed people just for daring to touch him?

It was a weakness, and he supposed it was only logical to want to hide it, even now when she'd forced him to expose himself.

"Why did Paimon capture you in the first place?" Suyin asked, showing once again how quick she was to get to the heart of the matter.

"I wasn't always the loyal supporter of Lucifer that I am today."

She blinked. "Is that a joke?"

"Yes, Suyin, it's a joke, seeing as I am currently plotting to overthrow him at this very moment."

She rolled her eyes. "So you've tried before."

"I put my support behind another who did."

"Who?"

"Her name is Naiamah, and she's a Queen of—"

"Oh, I know who Naiamah is," Suyin said. "When I lived in New York, I was friends with a group of witches who practice black magic and serve Naiamah. They were always trying to get me to join their coven."

"Why didn't you?"

"They're big into male sacrifices. They like to catch creeps and sacrifice them for power rituals and shit. I'm not necessarily against killing rapists, but I wasn't sure I wanted to be the one doing it."

"Not even to have access to a formidable power source?" Murmur smiled thinly. "There's nothing quite like the boost you get from a human sacrifice."

She made a face. "I'm just not big into murder, okay?"

"I suppose that's your choice to make."

"Tell me more about Naiamah."

"It was she who first suspected that Lucifer had an additional power source. We were long-time acquaintances—there's no one better at procuring unusual items in Hell. She's always despised Lucifer, so when she told me of her assumption, I was naturally curious. She asked for my help breaking into his inner sanctum to potentially uncover his secrets, and I agreed."

"What was your beef with Lucifer?"

Murmur shrugged. "He is a colossal prick who's been drunk on power for far too long. And, as I've told you before, I'd seen in visions of his fall for some time. Since I never knew when, I decided it was smart to get ahead of the game. Unfortunately, Naiamah and I were both caught. Paimon took me, and Lucifer took Naiamah. We paid a steep price for our betrayal, though I do believe Naiamah managed to escape several years before I did."

"She didn't come back to help you?"

"She didn't know. My job was only to get past Lucifer's wards, which I did. It was my own fault Paimon caught me. She sensed my magic and knew I was plotting against Lucifer, but she didn't know how. She tried to torture it out of me, but I said nothing. As far as I know, no one ever connected me to Naiamah's attempted break-in, and that is the way we both want to keep it." He gave her a sharp look. "And if you value your life, you'll keep that secret yourself."

She shot him a look. "Obviously. Does Naiamah know what you're planning now?"

"Of course not. I trust no one, least of all that conniving succubus. As I told you, I've been very careful to keep it secret, lest word reach Lucifer's ears. I'd be dead before I ever got a chance to try my spell. Honestly, every hour that passes I'm amazed he hasn't figured it out yet. If he were paying attention, he'd be able to sense my magic attacking his defenses. He could piece it together at any moment."

Suyin looked rightly unsettled by that statement. The only reason Murmur didn't have a similar reaction was because he was good at compartmentalizing. He'd sealed his fear and doubt in an inner vault where they couldn't interfere with his progress.

"Let's get this spell over with then," she said.

He nodded, mentally chastising himself for feeling reluctant. It was her fault. She had bewitched him with a false sense of contentment. The sooner he got this over with and got her out of his life, the sooner things could return to normal.

"Yes," he agreed. "I've drawn this out for long enough. I'm ready to be done."

He stood, lifting Suyin with him, and then set her on her feet. She craned her neck to look into his eyes, and he smiled faintly at the sight. When had her delicate form become something he enjoyed? He distinctly remembered seeing her as weak when he first brought her here. Now, he knew she was anything but.

Just another way she had bewitched him.

"Come," he said, leading her around the sofa toward the sigil on the floor. He picked up the freshly sharpened knife he'd laid out on the desk, turning it over in his hands. The blade was coated in the same anticoagulant potion that he used on his vials and bowls.

"That's what you're going to use?"

"Yes. You'll stand here"—he pointed to a circle at the edge of the design—"and make sure your blood flows into the bowl. We can't let a single drop fall outside. We must be very precise."

She nodded decisively.

"When I've finished your part," he said, "you need to step away as quickly as possible. The final sacrifice is my own blood, and once I make it, the sigil will erupt into hellfire. The spell is both a key and a gate, so if we are successful, the hellfire will give way to a portal. That portal leads to a door inside Lucifer's territory, which must be opened by hand once the seal is broken. All that is to say: Make sure you're away from the sigil when the portal opens, or you may be sucked through."

"Got it."

"Good." His gaze wandered over her body in his shirt. Through the thin fabric, he could see her nipples and a hint of the dark triangle of hair between her legs. "Are you warm enough?" He couldn't have his secret ingredient cold, could he.

"It's toasty, thanks to the fire. Plus, I feel like this is a good outfit to make a blood sacrifice in. Very witchy, don't you think?"

His brow arched. "I *think* that I'd like to tear it off and fuck you again."

Her lips curved wickedly. "Well, then I'm definitely not changing."

He shot her a look and turned away, shaking himself out of his sex-crazed delirium. This behavior was absurd. He was truly losing his mind.

"Come," he said. "Bring the knife and bowl. It's time."

# 24

# Death Trap

As they went through the final stages of preparation for the spell, Suyin couldn't help noticing how differently Murmur acted toward her now. Occasionally, he would ask her to pass him some ingredient or read something off his notes. She even asked questions, and he answered readily, as if eager to share his thoughts. It was a far cry from "If you disturb me or get in my way, I'll throw you back into the dungeon."

Most of the prep work had been done in advance, and before long, he was beckoning for her to bring the knife and bowl into the sigil's outer circle.

She handed the tools to him, and he had her hold out her arm. Rolling her sleeve up past her elbow, he wrapped a hand around her forearm—his hands were so big his fingers met on the other side—and stopped, looking her in the eye.

"Are you ready?" he asked.

She nodded once.

"You'll be safe."

"I'm not scared." For herself. She couldn't help worrying

about Murmur, however. The stakes had never been higher, and she hated the thought of anything happening to him during the ritual.

"Make sure every drop of your blood goes into the bowl and nothing escapes. If it does, tell me immediately."

She nodded.

"When I tell you, leave the circle quickly without stepping on any of the lines."

She gave him a look. "I know that, Murmur." Not stepping on the lines of an active spell was pretty much the first thing a witch learned.

He gave her one right back. "Humor me. We're going over every detail to ensure everything goes perfectly and we don't have to do this damn ritual again."

"Fine. You may continue to mansplain."

His look of confusion made her laugh.

"Never mind," she said, waving a hand.

"Back away from the sigil when you're done." He pointed over to the farthest worktable. "There are rags there. Use one to bind your arm. I also made you a healing accelerant. Drink that and your wound will heal quickly."

Sure enough, there was a jar of some nasty-looking green liquid beside the bowl of water and rags. In the midst of preparing his spell, he'd taken the time to gather supplies for her to care for her wound.

"Thank you," she said.

He looked vaguely disturbed by her gratitude.

"Lastly, and I want you to listen closely," he said, "if the spell is successful, the portal will appear in the center of the sigil, as I said. But if anything goes awry or I'm incapacitated in any way, I want you to take the hellgate and return home. I've linked it to the gate I used to take you from Earth. It will drop you in an empty apartment several blocks from your own."

"But—"

"It was part of our bargain, remember? I must return you safely to Earth. We swore a vow."

She wasn't thrilled about the idea of jumping ship and leaving Murmur alone, but she also understood the importance of protecting her own ass. If something went horribly wrong, it was probably wise to get the fuck out as fast as possible.

"Fine. If unforeseen circumstances arise, I'll take the hellgate and go home. You'll know where to find me."

Murmur began lighting the candles he'd placed periodically around the outside of the sigil and then returned to her side. Herbs in a bowl on the table were lit, set upon a glowing piece of charcoal, and soon, a smoky scent filled the dark room. She could already feel the tingle of magic in the air.

He began muttering incantations under his breath as he pulled grayish masses from a jar and set them on the charcoal to burn with the herbs. The smell of burning flesh overpowered the sweet herb smell quickly, and she grimaced, trying not to gag.

When the candles and incense and weird body parts were finished with, he beckoned Suyin closer. She held out her arm, and he passed her the bowl to hold with her other hand beneath it. He grasped her palm with an ice-cold hand—none of the warmth he'd had earlier remained—and turned it face up, exposing the underside of her forearm.

He held the knife over the skin and then met her gaze.

His eyes already looked extra bloodshot, and if she wasn't mistaken, the shadows under them had darkened. Was the magic affecting him physically already? If so, she didn't want to think about how the rest of the spell would go.

His brows lifted in question, and she nodded firmly.

He was quick and efficient, and the blade was deathly sharp, but it didn't stop her from hissing from the pain as he cut a line across her arm. She gritted her teeth as her blood welled around the wound and began to overflow, running into the bowl. Murmur wiped the blade carefully with a rag and set it down on the table.

As she bled, the room darkened until even the red sky turned black. The lines of the sigil began to glow with an unearthly purple light. The air filled with smoke, and the smell of the burning flesh and herbs made her head spin.

Finally, her part was done, and Murmur took the bowl and gestured for her to step out of the circle. He didn't speak or look at her, and she guessed it was because even the slightest lapse in his concentration could cause the entire spell to fail.

Somewhat disoriented, she wrapped her free hand around her forearm and put as much pressure on the injury as she could, ensuring no more blood spilled. Then, she backed quickly away, careful not to brush against any of the ingredients or candles.

At the table, she cleaned and wrapped her wound and then took a swig of Murmur's healing accelerant. The foul liquid made her choke, but immediately, some of her dizziness faded, and she could feel her arm tingling as it started to heal. She'd have to ask him how to make it later because damn, it was effective.

Wound taken care of, she turned around and peered into the gloom, trying to see what Murmur was doing.

He stood at the edge of the sigil, holding the bowl of her blood out over the outside line. As she watched, the bowl burst into flames. *Hellfire.* The scent of magic suddenly sharpened, sending prickles down her back. It was a cold, stale smell, like a rotten building in wintertime, and all her instincts screamed that it was *wrong*.

Something unnatural and dark that was better left alone.

Murmur set the still-flaming bowl on the table beside him, picked up the knife, and then pressed it to his own palm, gouging it deeply. Blood welled around the blade, spilling between his fingers like he was squeezing an overripe fruit in his fist.

Unlike with her blood, he wasn't careful to catch it in a bowl. It spilled everywhere, the drops splattering on the ground, pooling at his feet. But as his blood hit the ground, it was pulled by an invisible force toward the sigil, drawn down each line toward the center of the circle.

All of a sudden, the entire sigil burst into hellfire, the lines burning like they'd been painted with gasoline.

Suyin's arms rose to shield her face against the roaring fire, though she was a safe distance away, as Murmur had warned her to be. Her hair whipped around her as a phantom wind gusted through the library, sending loose papers flying.

Black smoke filled the room until she couldn't see anything except the light from the flames. And then it got even darker, and she swore she heard screaming, faint and far away.

The wind and smoke seemed to condense into the middle of the circle, like the eye of a storm. Faint purple light emanated from it. *The portal*, she realized. It was working.

Disembodied screams reverberated around the room, and Murmur's unholy chanting mingled with them. The darkness grew so impenetrable that even the flames became invisible, and she could see nothing but the swirling black portal, getting thicker and denser.

The magic in the air was so strong, she couldn't breathe, and her throat felt like there was an invisible noose around it. Her skin crawled, and her eyes felt like they were going to burst in their sockets.

And then suddenly . . . everything stopped.

The darkness dissipated, the flames were extinguished, the wind died, and the familiar sight of the library returned. The smoke was still so thick, she could barely see, but she felt the magic fade and knew the spell was over.

Coughing and waving a hand in front of her face, she peered into the gloom, searching for Murmur. She caught a glimpse of a dark figure, listing to one side. As she watched, his legs folded, and he sank to his knees. He swayed, about to fall.

Without thinking, she ran forward.

She dropped, catching him just before he fell. But the damn demon was huge, and she would have fallen too if he hadn't found awareness from somewhere and steadied himself at the last moment.

He gripped her shoulders. His head lolled, hanging forward, but he was semi-conscious at least.

Slowly, he lifted his chin, his long hair a mess from the gusting wind. His clothes were singed but he looked otherwise unharmed. That was until she saw his face.

He met her gaze, and she gasped.

His eyes were solidly black. Dark veins spread out around them and spidered down his cheeks. His face looked extra hollow, his skin so pale it was nearly as white as his hair. His lips were bloodless and stained black at the same time. If he'd looked eerie before, it was nothing compared to now.

His claws tightened on her shoulders, and he leaned in. Or maybe he was still swaying on his knees, fighting to stay awake. But when he drew near, she heard him very clearly whisper.

"The spell . . ."

"What? What happened?"

"Failed. Again."

And he slumped forward, unconscious.

# 25

# Cold, Cold Heart

When Murmur's mind crept back to consciousness, he heard the crackling of the fire. He felt warm, which was a rarity for him. He was always cold. He was so cold, he'd just *become* the cold so he didn't feel it anymore. But he felt warm now, and it was pleasant.

He opened his eyes. He was lying on the rug by the fireplace in his library, covered by a blanket. He turned his head and saw Suyin, fast asleep. She sat beside him on the ground, leaning against the couch, which she'd pulled closer to the fire. There was a book open in her lap, but she'd nodded off while reading, and her head slumped to the side. He smiled a little at the sight.

His gaze dropped to her forearm, resting carefully over the open book, and his smile faded.

Blood soaked her bandage.

Blood that hadn't fucking worked.

*Why* hadn't it worked? He'd been sure her sacrifice would be strong enough. But obviously, he was still missing some crucial step, and he didn't know what it was.

He was running out of chances to try. Every time he failed, it drained him of power and took him days to recover. This time, he'd gotten further than ever before, and it was only a matter of time before the High King figured out what he was doing and incinerated him with hellfire.

Even with Suyin's willing blood sacrifice, he wasn't strong enough to break through the final barrier of protection around the Nine Rings. Reinforced with the archangel's blood, the outer lines of the sigil had held, and there was more than enough strength in the hellfire. But something was lacking to complete the portal.

He needed more. An even greater sacrifice. It was the only explanation.

But he had already taken twice as much blood as he needed from Suyin to make the offering. And she was as willing as it was possible to be. She knew exactly what he was doing, and she wanted to help of her own free will. Why wasn't it enough?

Slowly, the truth sank in, and with it, his blood ran cold.

There was one terrible form of sacrifice he had not yet considered. One very final, terrible form.

And, given his fondness for the witch, he could only conclude that it would be an astoundingly powerful one. More than powerful enough to do what he needed it to.

Murmur turned to one side, pushed into his palms, and sat up. His head spun and his stomach churned from his realization. He felt like death warmed over. He always did after practicing strong necromancy, and this was easily the most difficult spell he'd ever attempted. But this time, his epiphany made him feel worse than the magic.

He'd told Suyin to leave if anything went wrong, and him face-planting after the spell finished was easily classifiable as a complication. Yet she had stayed. And she'd somehow dragged his unconscious body over to the fire, though it must have been difficult.

Whenever she was around, he became fixated on her presence, whether she was arguing with him, sitting in the corner reading quietly, or offering her body to him and obeying his commands. He had made compromises for her. He *never* compromised, but somehow she had convinced him.

She was fucking with his head. And while he couldn't lie and say he didn't enjoy being fucked with—especially when it involved bending her over his desk—it was making it harder to think clearly, clouding his judgment.

His souls still screamed at him, and his multilayered plans grew more intricate with every complication. His impending death still loomed on the horizon.

Suyin distracted him from his goals and hindered his progress. He'd come this far, after so many long years, and he couldn't throw it all away now. This was bigger than either of them. He had to do whatever it took—*whatever* it took—to finish this. The very fate of the underworld depended on it.

And now he wondered, if he hadn't allowed her to distract him, would he have figured out his mistake, identified the missing link, much sooner? Because a part of him balked at the idea. A part of him rejected it the minute it rose to mind. A part of him wanted to refuse to even entertain it.

But the spell had failed, and now he had no choice but to consider it. And as he did, he knew it would work. In fact, he'd been a fool to think a spell this powerful could succeed without it. He had allowed his attachment to her to distract him from the truth.

He'd said it himself, not long ago, when he'd been teaching Suyin about Sheolic magic.

*Sacrificing a person the caster has bonded to is one of the most powerful offerings in all of magic . . . If the desire for the success of the spell is great enough, they will utilize it. If they do not, all their other sacrifices will never measure up to that amount of potential potency, and they will unknowingly cripple themself.*

That was what he'd done, hadn't he? Crippled himself. By forming a bond with Suyin, he had sabotaged his own spell. And now, to make it work, he had to sever that attachment in the most final, irrevocable way.

Time was running out. It was now or never.

This time, he would do what had to be done.

He closed his eyes, found the part of himself that he'd given free reign these last days—the part that was full of desire, the part that allowed him to relax and feel contentment—and he sealed it away behind an impenetrable mental wall. Just as he'd done to his fear and doubt. Just as he'd done to all the weakest parts of himself.

When he was done, he opened his eyes and reached out, jostling Suyin gently back to wakefulness.

She jerked upright, eyes snapping open. They widened when they saw his face.

"Suyin—"

"Shit, Murmur!" To his vast surprise, she tossed the book aside and launched herself into his arms, seizing him in an embrace so tight, he nearly fought to draw breath. "Thank fuck."

Stunned, he slowly wrapped his arms around her, completing the strange embrace and patting her back awkwardly. His stomach suddenly felt like a sword had been stuck through it.

She seemed to sense his discomfort and pulled back a moment later. "You're okay."

"Yes." He set her apart from him, needing distance.

"Your face looks fucked. Jesus."

"It always does when I do powerful magic."

"Do you pass out every time you attempt that spell?"

"No. I'm often weakened, but this was the first time I've lost consciousness." He scowled. "It should have worked."

"Why didn't it?"

He hesitated, jaw shifting. "I'm still missing something."

"Do you know what it is?"

"No," he lied, frowning at the way his stomach churned. "I need to do more research."

"Still?" She blew out a breath. "Fuck. Where do we even begin researching that? Who would even have the kind of information we need?"

His jaw clenched. "There will be no 'we' this time."

She blinked. "Why not?"

The furrow in her brow, the confusion in her eyes . . . She truly looked dismayed by his words. *Foolish witch. Didn't they teach you never to trust a demon?*

"I've decided to grant your request, Suyin."

"What request?"

Their blood vow prevented him from doing what needed to be done, but he knew a way to circumvent it. "I recognize that you can't stay here indefinitely, much as it might convenience me. I will allow you to return to Earth so you may assure your coven you're okay. And when I've solved this problem and am ready to try again, I'll come for you."

"I— But—" She swallowed and searched his gaze. "Are you sure you don't need my help?"

"Careful," he warned, unable to quell the strange nausea still roiling in his stomach. "By that tone, one might think you *want* to stay here with me."

Her features froze in an unreadable expression. Then she shook her head. "No, you're right. I need to go back. I need to tell everyone I'm alive before they plan my funeral." She smiled, but it didn't reach her eyes.

"Go now and gather your things. I'll return you to your home."

"Okay."

They stared at each other.

"Are you sure you're okay?" she asked softly. "Your eyes . . ."

He was seized with another gripping spasm in his gut. "I'm fine. Get your things. We'll leave now."

Suyin almost couldn't believe it as they stepped out of the hellgate into an empty apartment. The drywall had been mostly torn out, and wherever it wasn't, it was riddled with holes. The kitchen in the next room had been gutted down to bare wires and pipes. The old hardwood floors were scuffed and filthy.

But she was on *Earth*, and it was glorious.

"How did you find this place?" she asked Murmur, turning to face him where he stood behind her. She flinched slightly when their eyes met. Or at least, she thought they met. She couldn't tell where he was looking.

"It wasn't difficult," he replied distantly.

He was even creepier now with his solid-black eyes and those spidery veins cascading down his cheeks. She was worried about him, if she was honest. He looked even deader than usual, and he'd been strangely detached since waking up. He probably needed to take it easy for a few days to recover, but she knew he had no intention of doing so.

*You're a fool, Suyin.* Fifty years old, and she was still falling prey to the I-can-fix-him mentality. Murmur could take care of himself. He'd been doing it for millennia, longer than she could even conceive of.

"How do we get outside?" She looked around for an obvious exit. Surely he hadn't been using the front door.

"Follow me." He strode toward the kitchen, beckoning with his claws.

They stepped over rotted floorboards and chunks of drywall. He slid aside a loose piece of plywood covering a broken window, and they climbed through onto the balcony outside.

The air in the city was hardly fresh, but the moment she was outside, she gulped in great lungfuls. The apartment was moldy and dusty, and she hadn't noticed the difference from

Hell. But now that she was outside, it felt like she hadn't breathed fresh air in weeks.

"There are no stairs," she said, eyeing the precarious metal roof of the garage below them.

Murmur answered her question by suddenly unfurling a massive pair of leathery black wings. They spread as much as the confined balcony would allow, and her eyes widened.

They were exactly how she'd imagined his wings would look. The black skin stretching between the slender bones appeared supple and soft. The top of the wing, the "thumb," had a curved black claw, much like the ones on his hands. The bones separating the segments looked delicate and strong at the same time.

He held out a hand, and without a second thought, she placed hers in it. Sometime during her little escapade in Hell, she had started to trust him.

Time would tell if that got her killed or not.

He pulled her closer and wrapped an arm around her, making her feel positively miniscule. And then he picked her up, climbed over the edge of the railing, and leapt off.

His wings snapped out, and he pumped them several times before landing gracefully in the alley below. Anyone in the surrounding apartments could look out a window and see her standing beside a seven-foot-tall demon with horns, a tail, and bat wings.

"Can you shift into human form?" she hissed, looking around for signs of people.

"No," he replied as if offended by the suggestion. "You know how the Sight works, Suyin. Humans can't see me anyway."

"Unless they have the Sight, yeah. In which case, you'd terrify the ever-living shit out of them."

"Sounds like a good day to me."

"Murmur . . ."

He smiled, but it faded quickly. "Can you return safely to your apartment from here or should I walk with you?"

She already recognized the neighborhood, and after living in New York, she would never worry about safety in Montreal. "I'm fine alone."

"It's probably for the best. There are certain demons in this city who I'd rather not run into."

"Iris's boyfriend?"

"And his so-called brothers, yes."

"Why can't they know you're here?"

"Because we made a bargain. It's a long story."

She looked up at him. "Okay."

"Okay."

There was a pause.

"One more thing," he said. "You don't have to worry about a police investigation or your friends throwing you a funeral." He reached into the pocket of his coat, pulled out her phone and keys, and held them out to her. "When I first took you, after I stung you the second time, I used your thumb to unlock your phone and then returned to Earth and sent messages to all your regular contacts."

She snatched the items from his hand. "You what?"

"I told them you were going on a vacation."

She opened and closed her mouth. "You're kidding me, right?"

"No, I'm not—"

"For fuck's sake, Murmur! You could have at least told me! I was stressing about it this whole time, so badly I could barely sleep! Why the hell would you keep that a secret?"

"It didn't strike me as important—"

"Not important?" She threw up her hands. "I told you how worried I was about my friends and coven thinking I was dead. How could you think it wasn't important? I asked you multiple times to let me go back. You didn't think telling me that would have been smart?"

He crossed his arms. "You barely asked. I didn't think you cared."

"That's not— How could you— You frustrate the hell out of me, you know that?"

His lips pursed. "The feeling is mutual."

"For fuck's sake . . ." She shook her head.

"I fail to understand the importance you place on your earthly friendships. All humans die. The death of a human should never come as a surprise."

She was exhausted at the thought of even trying to explain that to him, so she didn't bother. "Whatever. Just . . . what did you tell them? They would never believe I'd just leave—"

"I told them you needed some time alone to practice your wards in a quiet place, away from the interference of so many other minds."

She opened and closed her mouth. "Shit." He was a genius. Because that was exactly something she would do.

Pocketing her keys, she looked at the device in her hand and hit the power button. The screen stayed dark. *Duh.* It had been weeks, surely. The battery was long dead.

She looked up.

"Remember our blood vow, witchling?"

"You return me home unharmed, and I don't tell anyone about you or your spell. I know."

He nodded once and then turned to go. Just like that.

"Wait!" she said as he unfurled his wings.

He turned back with a brow lifting in question.

"How can I get in touch with you? In case I need anything . . ." She trailed off, wincing as he continued to stare blankly at her.

"I will come to you when it's time to complete the spell."

"I know, but how do I . . ." She shook her head. "Never

mind." She was being ridiculous. She didn't have any reason to contact him, and she didn't need to worry about him not coming. He needed her blood.

He frowned.

"I'll wait for you to come get me," she said with a dismissive wave, forcing herself to sound unaffected. "You've proven you can track me down easily enough."

He searched her gaze for a moment. Then he gave her that little half smile again and said, "See you soon, witchling."

She lifted a hand in farewell.

He crouched and sprang, and with several pumps of his powerful wings, he was airborne. He flew up to the balcony and then was gone.

Alone, Suyin clutched her jacket over her heart. What the hell was wrong with her? Why did she feel like this?

*I think . . . I might have feelings for him.*

She closed her eyes. Surely she was not that stupid.

Swallowing the lump in her throat, she transferred her bag of food and goth-boot-camp clothes to the other shoulder and looked down the dark street. It was time to go home and pick up the pieces of her life after Murmur had broken it.

When Suyin made it home, she stood in the hot shower for at least thirty minutes. She thoroughly scrubbed her hair and then let the hot water pummel her shoulders until the stiff muscles started to loosen.

After blow-drying her hair, she threw on her *Night of the Living Dead* T-shirt and climbed into bed. She plugged her phone in at her nightstand, and when the battery charged enough, she fired it up. The first thing she did was check the date.

She cursed. She'd been gone for a whole month. It simultaneously felt like far longer than that and no time at all.

The same text with minor adjustments had been sent to all her regular contacts, which included Iris, a few of her friends, and members of her coven. Her parents were gone, and she had no living relatives that she was aware of.

In a way, she was just as much of a recluse as Murmur, wasn't she?

All his creepy stalking had paid off too, because he'd known exactly what to say to make her friends not suspicious of her disappearance.

Iris had sent a reply, telling her to enjoy her time away and let her know when she was back in town. Her coven members assured her she was well deserving of some time off and they would cover her shifts at the shop as long as she needed. A few had emailed asking for help with their studies, but they all said their questions weren't pressing and urged her to take her time and respond when she was ready.

And Murmur, that devious fucker, had phrased her messages exactly in her tone. Was he that masterful at impersonating her, or did they both just suck that terribly at communicating?

She hated that she didn't know.

She hated that she'd been snatched off the face of the earth and thrown into a dungeon, and no one had been worried about her. She hated that one text message was all it took for the people in her life to forget her completely.

She'd done such a good job keeping everyone at arm's length, there wasn't a single person who would miss her if she disappeared. If Murmur had killed her, how long would it have taken them to start wondering where she was? Several months? A year?

It was a depressing thought.

The first person she replied to was Iris. She hadn't come close to forgetting what Murmur had told her about Iris's boyfriend.

*I'm back. We need to talk*, she texted.

There was no response, and Suyin wasn't in the mood to catch up with everyone at the moment, so she put the phone down and pulled the covers up to her chin.

She was back in her home where everything was familiar, and yet it might as well have been a stranger's apartment. Because *she* was different. Finding out what she was, and what her father was . . . She hadn't really processed it yet, and she was only becoming aware of that now in the quiet of her bedroom.

It would take time, she told herself. One did not simply reconstruct their self-identity overnight. Things would work themselves out. And her life didn't need to change at all if she didn't want it to.

What did being a demon-human hybrid really mean to her anyway? How was it going to affect her life? She kept waiting for some sort of existential crisis to hit, but if anything, she only felt a sense of peace in finally having the answers she had so desperately been seeking.

Demons weren't necessarily evil. Gamigin proved that. Hell, even Murmur proved that. His morals were questionable at best, yes. But he wasn't evil. He just needed a little coaxing toward understanding, but she believed he could get there if he wanted to. She had seen it in the way he looked at her.

So no, she wasn't particularly broken up about being half demon, even though it surprised her that her beliefs could change so drastically in so short a time.

But her father—his legacy, his intelligence, his research . . . She was proud to be his daughter. She was proud to be a part of his work.

And she was glad Murmur had found her and opened her eyes to all of this, even if he'd made her suffer to get there. She still hadn't forgotten that he'd locked her in a dungeon and left her to starve, and she'd probably still be down there now if she hadn't been quick-thinking enough to bargain with him.

She rolled her eyes. Fucking Murmur.

*Fucking* Murmur. Now that was a nice thought. Maybe the venom in his tail had given her brain damage, because there was no way her mind should have flip-flopped from remembering his dungeon to being in bed with him. And yet images of his big body covering hers quickly filled her head, all that shiny, gorgeous hair caressing her skin, the burning intensity in his ice-blue eyes . . .

She thought about the way he called her "witchling," and how he'd told her to stay on his lap while he told her about his past, even though he hated feeling restrained. And she thought about how he'd taken time from his work to teach her about Gamigin's book, and how he'd trusted her enough to share the true purpose of his spell.

Whether it was foolish or not, her heart gave a pang. Because she missed him already. Because she had feelings. She couldn't deny it. She'd finally escaped Hell, and her first night home, she wished she was still back there. *So, so stupid, Suyin.*

The phone rang.

She snatched it off the nightstand, banishing the unwelcome revelations from her mind. Iris's name was on the screen, and as soon as Suyin accepted the call, she started talking.

"You're back! How was your trip? How come you didn't tell me you were leaving?"

"It wasn't planned."

"Why did you go? Is everything all right?"

She took a breath. "Yes. And no. Listen, can we talk? In person?"

She lowered the phone and checked the clock. It was one in the morning. Fuck, her sense of time was way off. Was there such a thing as Hell jet lag? Because she had it.

"Want to meet tomorrow?" Iris asked. "I'm just about to go to bed."

"Sure."

"We could meet at the cafe by—"

"Let's meet at Le Repaire. I want to show you something." *And corner you so you can't run when I confront you about lying.*

"Um . . ." Iris hesitated.

"There are no demon detection wards up right now," Suyin said.

"Oh, okay. Well, that's fine. It wouldn't matter if there was. I mean, I don't care about— Well, anyway. Yeah, let's meet there."

Damn, Iris was a terrible liar. How had they avoided this for so long?

Suyin felt isolated, but maybe it was because she was isolating herself. If she'd really been available to Iris as a friend, it would have been impossible for Iris to keep up this charade.

If she wanted someone in the world to care about her disappearing for a month with only a single text, then maybe she needed to start reaching out to people. Being there for them on a deeper level than just her physical presence.

"How's eleven a.m. sound?" Iris asked.

"Perfect. Night, Ris." She went to hang up.

"Su?"

She lifted the phone back to her ear.

"I . . ." There was a pause. "Just glad you're home. That's all."

"Me too," Suyin replied. But as she hung up, she wasn't sure if it was a lie or not.

# 26

# Bad Blood

Suyin showed up half an hour early for her meeting with Iris. First, she checked in with Marie-Thérèse, who was working upstairs at the shop, letting her know she was back in town and asking how things had gone while she was away. After a short conversation, Suyin headed downstairs to the coven's basement meeting space.

She took one look at their paltry library and sighed regretfully. She'd once been proud of the collection they'd amassed. It seemed laughable now.

While she awaited Iris, Suyin settled herself at one of the worktables with a few old grimoires, trying to see if they contained any useful notes on Sheolic magic, though her hopes weren't high. She'd changed her opinion pretty drastically about it since meeting Murmur and learning she was half demon herself. Unfortunately, she wasn't going to find much in books written by human witches on Earth.

Iris arrived only a few minutes late, her smile forced. "Hey." She slid into a chair at the table opposite Suyin and ran a hand through her bright blue hair.

"How are things?" Suyin asked, taking a moment to look over her friend. Besides her obvious apprehension about being here, Iris looked good. Relaxed.

"They're good." This time, her smile seemed genuine. "Really good."

"Glad to hear that."

"Yeah. We're thinking about moving actually."

"Where?"

"I told you Meph's brother bought a house, right? Well, my lease is expiring soon, and we were thinking of moving into his place. There's a nice basement suite that's empty. I mean, the house is huge, way more space than he needs for himself, and we're honestly kinda worried about him being a total recluse living alone. Which sounds stupid, but—"

"What's your boyfriend's real name?" Suyin interrupted.

"Um." Iris swallowed. "Meph."

"Yeah, but that's a nickname, right?"

"Yeah."

"So what's it short for?"

"It's more that he changed his name. He doesn't like to be called—"

"What's his real name?"

Iris narrowed her eyes. "Why are you asking?"

Suyin leaned back in her chair and crossed her arms. If she was going to interrogate her best friend, she might as well play the part. "Answer the question, Iris."

"He doesn't like using his real name, so I don't. Out of respect for him."

"Hm." A convenient answer. "And Lily's boyfriend? What's his real name? Because I seem to recall you telling me Mist was a nickname as well." She remembered wondering if they were all gang members, and that was what Iris had been lying about.

Iris winced. The silence stretching between them was weighted with tension.

"Where were you?" Iris asked suddenly. "It's not like you to just drop everything and leave on a whim. And you didn't even tell me where you were going. I was this close to calling the cops, honestly, especially since you told me you thought you had a stalker. It was keeping me up at night, wondering if you were in danger and I was being a terrible friend. You can't do that to people, Suyin."

"Don't try to turn this around on me. I know you're avoiding my questions—"

"You always keep everyone at arm's length. Honestly, it's exhausting being your friend sometimes. I love you, but it's true. When I was angry and hateful, we worked because you just let me stew, and you never tried to encourage me to heal. I thought at the time it was because you accepted me for who I was. But now that I'm on the other side of that anger, I kinda wonder if it's just because you didn't care."

It was Suyin's turn to fall silent and avoid the perceptive green eyes of her friend.

"I didn't expect you to fix my problems for me," Iris continued, "and I'm glad you didn't waste your energy trying. But I was . . . toxic. And I can't help but think that the only way to endure that kind of constant anger was to keep me at a distance."

Suyin glanced back at Iris. "You accuse me of being detached," she said coolly, "and maybe you're right. But I'm not the one who has been lying to my closest friend."

Iris flinched.

"So why don't you start by answering my questions and then we'll go from there."

"You wouldn't understand," Iris said in a small voice. "I *can't*."

"I think you'd be surprised by what I understand."

"I can't, Su." To her credit, Iris's eyes were sad. "It's for the safety of the people I love. It's so important that if not telling you means we can't be friends anymore, then I'll have to accept that. I'm sorry, but I can't risk it."

Suyin took a breath. She was angry, but if she put herself in Iris's shoes, she understood. Maybe if she told a couple secrets of her own, Iris would be more inclined to open up. And the only way to find that out was to just do it. No more second-guessing.

So she opened her mouth and said, "I wasn't on vacation. I was in Hell." She was riding the edge of her vow with Murmur by saying this, but she'd been over their bargain carefully in her head. She'd only agreed not to talk about his work and him, not that she wouldn't tell anyone she went to Hell or what she'd learned while there.

In one blink, Iris's features went from apologetic to shocked.

"You wanna explain . . .?" she ventured when Suyin remained silent.

Suyin took a breath. Part of her was dying to tell Iris whatever she could about the absolute madness she'd lived through for the last month, but she couldn't help but hesitate.

"If I tell you my secrets, will you tell me yours?"

"I can't— What secrets do you have? What's going on? Are you okay?"

"Yeah, I am." Suyin paused, realizing that what she'd just said was completely true. "I actually feel more okay than I have in a long time."

"Why? What changed?"

"I found out who—*what* I am."

Iris could not have looked any more confused if she tried.

"I know you've been lying to me, but I've also lied to you." Suyin folded her hands on the table and stared at them. "About my age. I let you think I was in my thirties and just hated birthdays. But the truth is, I turned fifty this year."

Iris made a nervous laugh that died quickly at the look on Suyin's face. "Wait. You're serious?"

"One hundred percent. I just turned fifty."

"But . . . I mean. Wow. You're aging really well. I mean, not that that matters but—"

"I'm not aging, Iris. At all."

"What? But— Does that mean you have a special ability like Lily and I?"

"It's not an ability. It's just happening."

"Well, if you're practicing life-prolonging magic, I don't see why you'd hide that. Lots of powerful witches do it, and you're definitely—"

"I haven't done anything, Iris. The opposite. I've been checking the mirror every day for the last ten years, hoping to find a single wrinkle."

Iris frowned. "So . . . what did you find out?"

Suyin inhaled deeply and then just spat it out. "I wasn't on some solitude retreat. The truth is, I was taken by a demon and brought to his lair in Hell."

Iris's jaw dropped.

"I convinced him to let me out of his dungeon, and we kind of . . . became friends over the last month."

She winced. It sounded ludicrous when she said it out loud, and she hadn't even gone into the part where they blew each other's minds with out-of-this-world sex.

"Anyway, eventually, we started studying together, and he told me a lot of stuff. Including who my father was." The vow wouldn't let her talk about Murmur's spell or why he wanted her blood, but she could talk about herself.

"Who your— What?" Iris shook her head roughly. "You didn't know?"

"I thought I did. I mean, I knew what my mother told me about him, but apparently, most of it was lies."

"Who was he then?"

"A demon."

Iris did a slow blink. And then another. Suyin could

practically see the gears churning in her head. "But that's not possible. Demons—"

"Are created, not born. They're sterile, yes. I know. But . . ." She took a breath. "Shit, this is hard to explain. Basically, demons can evolve."

Iris didn't look as surprised or incredulous as one might have expected.

"After enough time spent being evil," Suyin continued, "I guess they start to wonder what they're doing or question why they're doing it. They develop emotional intelligence and a conscience. They start to care about stuff. They—"

"Develop souls," Iris whispered.

"Exactly." Suyin frowned. "How did you know that?"

But Iris shook her head. Suyin figured she'd just keep talking. She was going to lay it all on the table, and then she was going to force Iris to tell her everything, even if she had to tie her to the chair and interrogate it out of her.

"So, my father discovered that demons who evolved souls actually *can* reproduce, and that's how I—"

"Wait." Iris suddenly stiffened, holding up a palm. "Wait, wait, wait. Demons can't have children. That's the way it is."

"Like I said, that's true, but not with demons who have evolved."

"You can't know this."

"I *can*, considering it's how I exist."

"Whoever told you that was lying. You can't be half demon because there's no such thing."

"He wasn't lying. It's all in my father's research. I can show you the book myself and explain how it's possible. But I didn't need to prove it to believe it. My whole life I've been trying to figure out why I'm different, why I heal faster, why I'm stronger, and now, why I'm not aging. This is the only thing that makes sense."

Iris stared at her. Her face was blank, her eyes wide. Every few seconds she blinked as if hoping when she opened her eyes, all this would have gone away.

"So you're saying . . . demons with souls . . . can have children."

"Yes."

"They're *not* sterile."

"Yes."

Iris leapt to her feet. All of a sudden, she looked quite green. "No."

"Yes. And my father proved it." Suyin gestured to herself. "That's how I—"

"Oh, fuck." Iris folded at the waist. "Oh, no—"

"Iris, what the hell?"

"I can't be pregnant!" she suddenly shouted.

Satisfaction filled Suyin. Finally, *finally* . . . a confession. But she was also slightly concerned. Iris wasn't taking this well at all.

"I just got my life together!" she cried. "I just barely learned how to take care of myself! Two years ago, I could hardly remember to eat because I was so obsessed with revenge and so fucking angry all the time!" She was half in tears. "I love Meph, I love him to death, but I *cannot* be pregnant right now! I'd need like ten more years to even consider—"

"Iris!" Suyin figured it was time to intervene. "Iris, calm down. You're not pregnant."

"You can't know that. I've been having unprotected sex. This morning! I did it this morning! Oh my *god*—"

"Iris! Calm down. According to my father's grimoire, Cambion conception involves complex magic for it to be possible. It's extremely difficult."

"You're . . . sure?"

"Yes. It can't happen by accident. There's no way. If you don't want to get pregnant, you won't."

Iris took two wobbly steps back to the table and dropped into the chair. "Oh, thank god. Thank the lord on high and all the dickish angels." She sat up and jabbed a finger in Suyin's direction. "You scared the living hell out of me! Don't *do* that!"

Suyin couldn't help but smirk. "So, you're not really into the idea of motherhood, huh?"

"Fuck no. Babies scare me." Iris laughed. "Not saying I'd never want them, because things change, but honestly, knowing Meph couldn't was a relief because then it wasn't my choice, and I'd never have to—"

She broke off suddenly and stared at Suyin, evidently just realizing what she'd admitted to.

"Relax," Suyin said, rolling her eyes. "I already knew."

"W-what?"

"I know about your demon boyfriend."

"How!"

"Seriously? How could I not? You're a terrible liar, and what kinda name is 'Meph' anyway?"

Iris groaned and buried her face in her hands. "I told them they needed fake names, but they refused to listen. It was all some big joke to them, picking out stupid names and then making fun of each other instead of using them. They're idiots, the lot of them."

"How many demons are in Montreal right now, Iris?"

Iris lifted her head and winced. "Five."

"All Meph's brothers?"

She nodded weakly.

"And Lily's boyfriend, Mist, is one of them?"

Another nod. "You can't tell anyone, Suyin. They're not evil. I know it sounds crazy, but you have to believe me. They just want to live on Earth and be left alone. They're not even breaking the rules anymore. They got permission since Raum's—"

"I'm not going to tell anyone, and I already know they're not evil."

"You do?" Iris looked incredulous.

"Wasn't I just explaining to you how they evolve souls?"

Her eyes narrowed. "Why aren't you freaking out? I was the world's biggest demon hater. You went along with all my harebrained revenge schemes. You listened to me rant for hours about the evilness of demons and how they should all be exterminated. And now you're just accepting that I'm in love with one and we're all besties?"

Suyin laughed. Because yeah, she got why Iris was confused. It sounded ridiculous even to her. And what she was about to say was even more ridiculous.

"I'm not surprised because I kinda made friends with my own demon."

"The one that took you to Hell?" Iris dragged her hands down her face. "Shit, how did we skip over that part? What happened? Who was it? How did you escape?"

"I didn't escape. Like I said, we became friends." *Friends who fucked each other's brains out.* "He let me come back because . . ." She trailed off, the words sticking in her throat when she realized she'd reached the limit of what the blood vow allowed her to say.

"He *let* you? After he kidnapped you?"

Suyin winced. "He isn't great at boundaries, and he doesn't particularly give a shit either. But it's hard not to like him anyway." She rubbed her face. "Shit, I sound like you, making excuses for all your shitty exes."

Iris snorted. "I used to hate myself, didn't I?" She smacked a palm on the table. "Don't change the subject! Who is this fabled demon with a complete lack of boundaries and respect who somehow still managed to worm his way into your cold, dead heart?"

Suyin snorted. "I can't tell you. I swore a vow."

"A demon took you for some nefarious purpose, and he made you swear a vow you wouldn't tell anyone about him or why he wanted you?"

"Sounds about right."

Iris narrowed her eyes for a moment. And then, slowly, they grew wide. And then she sat up straight and said, "Oh my god, it's Murmur, isn't it?"

Suyin didn't even have to say anything. She stared at her friend in shock.

"Shit, it is!" Iris banged her hand on the table again. "That creepy, lying, backstabbing son of a bitch! No, no, you can't be friends with him."

Well, the cat was out of the bag. She hadn't even tried to hint at his identity, and Iris had guessed it anyway. "Why not? How do you know him?"

"Did you know he made a bargain with Mist that he wouldn't betray us, and then he went and did it anyway? He found some loophole in his promise and sold us out. It's because of him that Meph and I were taken by Valefor and brought to Hell where I was nearly fucking killed."

Suyin winced. Murmur had told her this story. From Iris's perspective, however, it was pretty incriminating. *Damn it, Murmur. Do you have to make it impossible to defend you every single time?*

"Valefor was a sick fuck, and Murmur sold us out to him in five seconds, all so he could get his hands on your precious book—"

"Wait— You knew?" It was Suyin's turn to get bug eyes. "You knew about *The Book of Gamigin* and didn't tell me?"

Iris looked sheepish. "Well, I knew Murmur took it. But I didn't know why he wanted it or what it's about. But everyone seems to be talking about that damn book lately. First Murmur, and then Sunshine wanted it, and apparently, she was on a mission for some big head honcho in Heaven—"

"Heaven? An angel?"

"Yeah, Raum's girlfriend, Sunshine. She's an angel."

Suyin groaned. "This is so fucked up. An *angel*? Jesus Christ."

"Su, I'm serious. Murmur isn't fun, sexy evil like Meph. He's just *evil* evil. All he cares about is whatever diabolical master plan he's cooking up. He'll lie, cheat, steal, or kill anyone to get what he wants. I don't know what he told you to convince you that you're friends, but he was lying. You can't trust him."

"Damn it, Iris. Why couldn't you have told me all this a month ago? I could have used this information when I ended up in a dungeon in Hell with no idea who he was. I had to figure everything out the hard way."

"I'm sorry. I really am. But I'm glad to hear you agree. I'm serious when I tell you not to mess with him—"

"I agree that he's diabolical and will do anything to achieve his goals. I don't think he's evil though."

"Su . . ." Iris's tone was pitying, and it made Suyin's skin crawl.

But was she doing what Iris thought she was? Making excuses for someone who didn't deserve them because she'd blinded herself to his true nature?

If so, it would be a first. She'd always been detached, even from the people closest to her, and usually, she preferred solitude over enduring an unworthy person's company.

She knew Murmur was morally ambiguous. She knew he'd done and would continue to do questionable things to achieve his aims, and he was never going to be sorry about it. But she'd also seen him show empathy, and she knew he felt something for her, in whatever capacity he could. He had a soul—therefore, he had the potential to be good. And in her eyes, none of what he'd done was inexcusable.

That was until Iris told her that he'd almost gotten her

killed. His side of the story had conveniently left out that tidbit of information.

Which in turn made Suyin wonder . . . how many other things had Murmur done that she didn't know about? She'd thought she'd made a clear judgment about him based on her observations, but could she really make an informed decision without all the facts?

"Look," she told Iris. "I'm not making excuses for Murmur. I mean, he left me in a cell for days with no food or water. But—"

"He *what?*"

*Probably should have skimmed over that bit.* "But he and I swore a binding vow. Even if I don't trust him, I know he has no choice but to stick to that at the very least."

"How careful were you in your negotiations? Because I'm telling you, I saw him swear on his own blood that he wouldn't come after me, Lily, and Mist, and he wouldn't tell anyone where we were going or send anyone after us. And yet, somehow, Valefor showed up here saying Murmur sent him. He found a way around that vow, and I still have no idea how."

Okay, that was a little freaky. "He has no reason to kill me. In fact, I can't tell you why, but he has a vested interest in keeping me alive."

"He could lock you up in his dungeon forever."

She grimaced. That did sound like something he'd do.

"Su, I'm serious, this is dangerous. We should go to Meph and his brothers right away and see what they can do—"

"No." She held up a hand. "That'll just piss him off, and that's the last thing I want. We have a weird kinda friendship right now, and I'm choosing to trust in it."

Iris was shaking her head, but she knew Suyin well enough to know that when she made up her mind, there was no changing it. They were both stubborn like that.

"So . . . are you really half demon?"

She suddenly smiled at her friend. For the first time in her life, all her secrets had been aired. Iris knew everything there was to know about her. "Yeah. Crazy, right?"

"You're going to have to tell me about your family and why you didn't know. You've never really talked about your mother. And I need to hear every detail of the conception ritual so I can make sure to avoid it at all costs."

Suyin chuckled. "I think you secretly want little demon babies running around. A whole brood of them, tugging on your pant legs, demanding peanut butter sandwiches—"

"Stop it!" Iris waved her hands frantically. "I've already got one man-child. I don't need another."

# 27

# Something Wicked This Way Comes

Suyin spent the rest of the day with Iris. They stayed downstairs at the coven for at least four hours, catching up and reading *The Book of Gamigin* on the computer. When they got hungry, they went out for a late lunch before finally walking together back to Suyin's place.

It felt like the friendship Suyin had so valued was re-building. Now that they were free to speak openly again, she remembered why they'd become close in the first place. Iris was fiercely loyal to those she cared about, and Suyin admired her dedication to protecting her loved ones.

When they reached the base of Suyin's staircase, they stopped.

"Want to come up?"

"Nah," Iris replied, "I should get back. I kinda blew off Meph to catch up with you. He's gonna be mad jealous." She grinned like she liked the thought. "It was good to see you, Su.

I mean it. I hated not speaking to you. It sucked, but I thought it was what I had to do."

"It's all right. I get it."

They smiled at each other. Neither of them had ever been the touchy-feely type, and this was about as intimate as they got. But it was enough. Suyin saw the apology in her friend's eyes, and she let her friend see the forgiveness in hers.

"Are you going to tell him?" Suyin asked suddenly.

"Who? About what?"

"Meph. About everything I told you today. About Murmur."

Iris winced. "Yes. I'm sorry, but I have to. I'm going to be completely honest with you because I'm sick of lying. I lied to Lily for years, and then I lied to you, and now that everything is finally out in the open, I never want to lie to anyone ever again."

It was understandable. Iris had hidden that fact that their parents been killed by a demon from her sister for years, and Suyin knew their relationship had suffered as a result.

"And I tell Meph everything," Iris continued, "so I'm going to tell him this. And he's going to tell his brothers because Murmur poses a potential threat they need to be prepared for."

"What threat?"

"I mean, they can't be forced back to Hell now that they have permission from Heaven to live on Earth *and* an angel on their side. But Murmur is dangerous. I don't know what he's up to, but it's wise to be prepared. Plus, Bel owes him two favors, and I think they're all waiting to see what those will be."

Suyin winced. She knew what one of them was, but the vow prevented her from telling Iris about it.

She'd also learned today that Belial was Meph's "brother"—along with Asmodeus, Raum, and Mishetsumephtai. Small world. Or something like that.

"He's a backstabber, Su," Iris continued. "I already told you how he sold me and Meph out. But he also swore another vow to Belial that he wouldn't fuck with him, his brothers, or anyone important to them. And then not a month later, he showed up here and took you."

"Did Belial specifically say my name in that bargain?"

"Well, no, but—"

Suyin had to laugh.

"Why is that funny?!"

"Murmur probably went into that negotiation already planning to take me and being careful to word it in a way that he could still do it without violating the terms. You have to respect that kind of forethought."

Iris's mouth dropped open. "Oh my god."

"What?"

"You like him."

"Well, yeah, like I said—"

"No, you *like* like him. You're into him!"

There was an awkward pause.

"It's not like that," Suyin protested weakly. Except she was pretty sure it was.

"It so is. I can see it in your eyes. Oh my god, did you sleep with him?"

Suyin winced.

"Holy fucking shit!" Iris shouted so loud that someone walking past on the opposite sidewalk shot them a concerned look. "How could you— He's creepy as hell. He looks like a vampire. He's like a giant, undead goth elf, with that white hair and those freaky eyes, and— Okay, never mind. I totally get why you're attracted to him. But still!"

Suyin shrugged. "It wasn't planned, trust me."

"Lemme get this straight. He knocked you out, dragged you to Hell, locked you in a dungeon . . . and then you slept with him."

Suyin mentally added, *Starved me, threatened me innumerable times, scared the living daylights out of me with his creepy soul army . . .*

Instead of voicing that, however, she pinned Iris with a bland look. "Are you slut-shaming me?"

"What? Fuck no, I'm not slut-shaming you. I'm worried for your goddamn sanity!"

Suyin crossed her arms. "You don't get to tell me it's not hot to fuck a seven-foot-tall monster with horns. I don't know what Meph's demon form looks like, but I bet he's not any prettier."

Iris visibly winced.

"So don't act all shocked that I would be attracted to Murmur."

"I'm not, but—"

"I'm not saying I think he's some great guy, because believe me, I know what he's like. He's part psychopath, part evil genius. But I learned more about magic from him in the month I spent in Hell than I have almost my entire life. On top of that, he's great in bed." She lifted her hands. "What's a girl to do?"

"Murmur. Is great in bed." Iris raised her brows.

"Let's just say . . ." Suyin took a breath. "I'm used to calling the shots. But he's the biggest control freak I've ever met, and apparently . . ." She shrugged.

Iris shook her head. "Well, I'll be damned. You learn something new every day."

"What?"

"I always thought you'd have dominatrix vibes in bed. I mean"—she gestured up and Suyin's form—"look at you."

She laughed. "I'm not a dominatrix."

"Apparently not, if you want Murmur to boss you around." Iris waggled her brows and then dragged a hand down her face. "I'm having a hard time picturing it. I've only seen him once, but all I remember is him decapitating a shitload of gargoyles, being totally covered in blood and wielding a sword, acting like a complete lunatic, and making a bargain with Mist that he wouldn't come after us—which he promptly ignored."

"You're only making him sound hotter to me."

"You're fucked in the head." But Iris laughed.

"So are you." They exchanged knowing grins.

"Look, I gotta go. Are you sure you're going to be okay home alone? No demons coming to kidnap you?"

"Yeah, I'm good. I'm just gonna crash early."

"All right, just . . . call me tomorrow? I gotta hear more details about you getting demon dick."

"That goes both ways, slut."

Iris laughed. "We'll see."

Suyin turned to climb her stairs but stopped, glancing over her shoulder. "Can you do me a favor?"

Iris raised her brows in question.

"I get you have to tell your man. But if they decide to go after Murmur, can you let me know first? Give me a chance to warn him?" Because of the damned vow, she couldn't explain to Iris that she wanted Murmur to have time to finish his spell and free her father's soul. And maybe she wanted to protect Murmur too, no matter how absurd that notion was.

Iris frowned like she was still concerned for Suyin's sanity, but she nodded. "All right. Bel's gonna be pissed he twisted the terms of their contract. Again. But I'll keep you posted." She turned to go with a smile, waving a dismissive hand. "Murmur, though? Really?

"Says the girl dating the fuckboy," Suyin shot back with a grin.

Iris scoffed as she strode away, calling back, "You need therapy!"

"So do you, bitch!"

Laughing, Iris raised her middle finger over her shoulder.

Suyin's apartment was still covered in expired wards from before she was taken, but she couldn't be bothered to clean them up yet. She wasn't going to reactivate them. If her demon came back to grab her, she wasn't interested in keeping him out. She'd be more likely to greet him at the door with a smile on her face. Naked.

She spent the rest of the evening trying to read and getting nowhere. She'd picked up a book on defensive Temporal magic last month and had been excited to dive in, but that was before her stint in Hell. As she leafed through the pages, she found that she already knew most of what they contained, and her thoughts kept returning to Sheolic magic, where everything was still so new.

She went to bed earlier than usual, trying to recover from Hell jet lag. She didn't feel tired at first, but she was eventually lulled to sleep by the sound of wind in the trees through the open window.

She woke late in the night as she felt a weight dip into her mattress. She blinked and found herself staring into ice-blue eyes.

"Murmur."

In the darkness, his white hair gave off an ethereal shimmer. He sat on the edge of her bed, twisting to lean over her.

"Witchling," he purred, and the sound of his gravelly voice made her pulse race.

She drank in the sight of his features—those high cheekbones with dark shadows beneath them, his proud nose and full mouth. She could see that he'd recovered from the spell. His face was back to its normal complexion, and the black veins beneath his eyes were gone.

She couldn't deny that she'd missed him. They'd spent every waking moment together for a month, and after only one day apart, she was happy to see him again. She'd never felt that with another person in her life, and frankly, it scared her.

The air crackled with their connection. He bent his head, and she didn't hesitate, pressing her lips to his as soon as he was close enough. He tasted amazing and smelled even better, and she groaned as he deepened the kiss.

And then she took a chance. Pulling her arms out from under the blanket, she reached up and slid her fingers into his hair.

He stiffened immediately and pulled away.

"Let me," she whispered.

He stilled, watching her with narrowed eyes, and then leaned back in. Her fingers dove into his hair, and this time, though the tension in his body was evident, he allowed her to touch him. Knowing what he fought for her made her heart swell.

He kissed her again, his dexterous tongue sliding between her parted lips. Her fingers tightened in his hair, and a low growl rumbled up from his chest.

Feeling mischievous, she stroked the silky strands back with both hands, gathered them into a bunch at the base of his neck, and fisted it loosely in one hand. She gave it a light tug. This time his growl was more of a warning. She smiled against his lips.

A second later, he snatched her wrists and pinned them down to the pillow above her head.

He pulled back. "Don't play with me, witch."

She smiled devilishly, her body stretched out beneath him. "But it's so fun."

Tingles of awareness raced over her skin, and she felt every inch of his heat pressed against her. He lowered his head until their mouths hovered inches apart. Unable to disguise her desire, a moan escaped from the back of her throat.

"Careful," he said softly against her ear. "Or I might think you missed me."

*I did. More than I should have.* Iris's warnings suddenly echoed through her head, and she scrambled for a distraction. "Did you figure out what you needed for your spell?"

He hummed an affirmation while kissing up her neck.

She couldn't think straight with his mouth on her. "Then are you here to take me back to your lair?"

His head shook.

She frowned. "Then why—?"

"Always with the questions, Suyin."

"Always with the evasive answers, Murmur."

He raised his head, eyes full of heat. And then he released his grip on her wrists and lifted off her. Just as she started to move, she felt the icy shackles of his ghosts encircle her arms and pin her back down.

She pulled on them, but they held fast. "Damn it, Murmur—"

He yanked the blankets back, exposing her body to the cool air. Her baggy T-shirt was bunched around her waist, her lower body exposed. That was what she got for sleeping half naked.

"What have we here?" His smile turned wicked.

Leaning in, he gripped the sides of her shirt and drew it over her head, tossing it away. Then he shifted down and wrapped his hands around her ankles, pushing her legs up and apart. He spread them wider and wider, until her inner thighs were stretched to their maximum.

Her labia parted, and she felt the cold air on her core. Murmur sat back, taking his sweet time enjoying the view. He was fully clothed, while she lay naked and open in the most vulnerable way.

What was it about being exposed to him that made her body light up like kindling on a bonfire? Her inner muscles clenched just from the feel of his eyes on her, and she felt wetness leaking out of her already.

His eyes were full of dark promise. "Tell me to stop if you want to, and I will."

She said nothing. Nothing would make her want to stop this now.

With a liquid grace, he slowly moved, dropping his head between her open thighs. And then his hot, wet tongue trailed down her center, and she threw back her head and moaned.

"The most delicious thing I've ever fucking tasted," he growled, taking another hungry lick and driving her wild.

His mouth sealed over her and sucked. Releasing her ankles, he spread her flesh farther apart, revealing her clit, which he circled with his tongue. His *black* tongue. Somehow she hadn't noticed that little detail until now. The sight of that tongue, combined with the sensations it was giving her, started to drive her toward climax.

She pulled at her wrists, trying to get closer to him and pull away at the same time.

His tail came out of nowhere, the tip of the sharp barb trailing along her inner thighs while he continued working her clit with his tongue. She cursed and moaned, equally alarmed and turned on by what he was doing.

He lifted his head. His lips, shining with her arousal, curved into a smile.

And then the sharp barb of his tail traveled over her still-spread pussy, hovering right over her swollen clitoris.

"Murmur, no," she panted, suddenly struggling anew in her bonds. She tried to snap her legs closed, but he caught her ankles and pushed them apart again.

"Do you trust me, Suyin?"

"Fuck no!" She struggled harder. "You're completely fucked in the head if you think I'm gonna let you stab me with that thing."

He laughed. "Not even if I promise you'll like it?"

Like an idiot, a complete and total fool, she stilled. "How could I possibly like being stung in the clit with a venomous barb?"

"I can control how much venom is in the sting. A lot will paralyze you. A little will give you a rush like you wouldn't believe."

"What? How?"

"Trust me or not. Decide."

She stared at him. She wasn't really considering letting him do this, was she? Nah, there was no way she was that stupid—or horny enough to act like she was.

Which made it pretty surprising when she nodded a second later.

His tail flexed and he struck. Fast, like a goddamn scorpion. Hot burning started right in the middle of her clit, and next thing she knew, she was screaming. In a good way. A really good way.

If she'd had any sense, she would have worried about the volume of her voice concerning her next-door neighbors and possibly ending up with the cops knocking down her door.

But she went completely out of her head. She launched into outer space and traveled at light speed through the galaxy of orgasms.

Searing pleasure shot through her veins, centered around the powerful heat in her clitoris. Her eyes went blind, the blackness littered with colorful spots, and she lost all comprehension of where her body began and ended. It felt like she had ruptured into a thousand particles.

And then an intense invasion into the very center of her had her consciousness shooting right back into her body. Her sight came back, and she found herself staring into piercing bloodshot eyes as Murmur thrust his thick shaft into her still-pulsing core. He was still dressed, his pants shoved down just enough for him to get inside her.

She cried out as he pushed past every barrier of tightness. As she continued to ride out her orgasm, each flex of her inner walls contracted around him, while each release allowed him to sink deeper.

She thrashed on the bed, tugging at her wrist bonds, crying out with complete abandon as he filled her again and again with thick, heavy thrusts. Her knees were bent up and open, and there was no way to escape the depth of his movements. His hair fell into her face and all around her, blocking out the world.

Winding around her thigh, his tail tightened like a lasso, and one of his hands reached down to hold her hip, securing her in place. He moved in a hot rocking motion, his hair swaying around them, his breath coming in harsh pants through his open mouth. In the space between his parted lips, she could glimpse the tips of his sharp fangs.

"I'm going to fill you up with my fucking cum," he growled. "And then spread it all over you until you're soaked in it."

"Oh my god!" she screamed as her body shook with ecstasy.

His claws tightened around her hip. His pace increased until hints of pain mixed with her pleasure as he stretched her with every hard thrust.

And then he started to come. She knew the instant he did because she felt him swell inside her. He pulled out of her throbbing core, and, jacking his thick cock with one hand, he kept coming. Just like he'd promised, it landed all over her, and it was the hottest thing she'd ever seen.

Still bound by the souls, she had no choice but to lie immobilized and enjoy the view as he covered her. The hot liquid ran between her breasts, down her stomach, and over her thighs.

Finally, he dropped to her side on his back. Her head spun. She didn't need oxygen yet was gasping for it at the same time.

His eyes shut, and his breathing slowly evened out. Until it was almost too even, and she started to fear he'd fallen asleep.

"Murmur?"

He cracked an eyelid and turned his head to meet her gaze.

"You gonna let me go any time soon?" She pulled on the bonds at her wrists.

His lips curved. "I'm tempted to say no."

"You like me being tied down, huh?"

His eyes darkened. "Then you can't escape."

"I wasn't trying to."

"But you still couldn't, even if you were."

She had to smile. She wasn't complaining, that was for sure.

Nevertheless, her icy bindings dissolved. She lowered her arms, wincing at the stretch in her shoulder muscles. Murmur rolled onto his side facing her, satisfaction written all over his face as he surveyed the mess he'd made on her.

"I need a shower," she said.

He climbed off the bed with surprising quickness and straightened his clothing, and then, to her surprise, he bent and scooped her into his arms. He held her close as he stalked down the hall, ducking to fit under the doorway.

"You're way too big for this house," she remarked. "You should just shift to human form."

He glanced down at her with a curled lip.

"I've seen your human form. You look good."

"I look *human*."

She laughed. "I take offense to that. And right now you're so huge, your horns are nearly scraping the roof."

He shot her another look, and before her very eyes, his horns retreated into his skull and disappeared. "Problem solved."

He still had to stoop to enter the bathroom. Shifting her to his side and holding her with one arm, he bent and turned on the water. Or tried to. It seemed he didn't have much experience with how showers worked. He kept trying to twist the lever instead of pulling it up.

"Let me down," she said, chuckling. "I'll do it."

He straightened, letting her slide down until she stood on her own. Once the shower was hot, she stepped under the spray on wobbly legs. Murmur propped a shoulder against the wall, tail flicking lazily behind him.

Tugging the curtain closed, she got busy washing, scrubbing extra hard, considering she'd taken a bath in demon jizz. "So, what did you mean about not taking me back to your lair?"

"I'm ready to cast the spell, but I don't need to bring you back with me. I found another way."

She peeked around the curtain at him with a frown. "What way?"

"In addition to your blood, I also need to draw on your energy—your vitality, or innate magic. Luckily, there's a seal that allows me to take power from you at a distance. I'll put a mark on your skin, collect your blood here, and return to Hell by myself."

"But . . ." She stared at him, but he wouldn't meet her eyes. She couldn't deny the sting of disappointment she felt. She didn't actually *want* to go back to Hell, did she?

Her rational side said no, but she couldn't pretend she hadn't been daydreaming about their study sessions in the library. God, maybe Iris was right, and she needed to rethink her position on all of this.

"I thought you'd be happy to hear that," he said.

She ducked back behind the curtain, taking a moment to disguise her emotions before she replied. "You're right. I am glad."

"Liar," he said in a low voice.

She didn't respond to that, because she wasn't sure what to say.

"If you wanted to return, you shouldn't have told your little witch friend about me."

She stuck her head back around the curtain again. "How did you know about that?"

He just smiled that creepy smile. "I can have eyes anywhere if I wish."

*His souls*, she realized. How lovely to know she'd had ghosts tailing her for the last two days.

"She figured it out on her own," she said.

"Were you hoping the other demons would protect you from me? You didn't even activate your wards."

She snorted. "I figured there was no point trying to keep you out. And I'm not afraid of you anymore, remember? We have a deal." *And maybe I wanted you to come back for me.*

"I always keep my promises."

She made a face into the stream of water as she washed her face. "Like when you promised Mist, Lily, and Iris you wouldn't trace them back to Earth?"

"*I* didn't trace them. My spell did."

"That's such a twisted interpretation."

"Mishetsu was at fault. He should have been more careful in his negotiating, but he was weak from blood loss and torture, and I took advantage."

"You *tortured—?*"

"*I* didn't torture him." Murmur scoffed. "Paimon did. In fact, I did him a favor by raiding her lair and leading the twins to the Hunter to rescue him. If not for me, they would both have failed. They ought to be thanking me, but instead they chose to fixate on the fact that I made a deal with Valefor in order to retrieve my book."

Well, that was interesting. "Why couldn't you get it yourself?"

"Because then it would have been known that I wanted it." He said it like it was obvious. "I always disguise my true intentions. Had I not done this over the years, my plan would have been discovered a long time ago, and I would likely be dead."

"You're paranoid."

"Yes."

She bent and turned off the shower. Climbing out, she grabbed a towel and wrapped it around her middle. They returned to her bedroom where she threw on a robe. "So are we actually going to do this here? I don't mind going back to Hell. I want to see your spell when it's successful."

"What if I change my mind and decide not to let you go?"

"I'll find a way to escape."

He smiled, but it faded quickly. Suddenly, he wouldn't meet her eyes. "As much as I enjoyed your assistance, this is something I must do alone."

He crossed the room and picked up his coat from a chair, where he must have discarded it while she was still sleeping. He pulled a holster from beneath it that contained a long knife. Then, from a pocket inside the coat, he pulled out a narrow, cylindrical jar.

"So how does this seal work?" she asked, eyeing him warily. "I'm not sure I like the sound of you sapping power from me from a distance."

"It's simple. I'll carve the mark into your skin, and then I'll carve the matching one into my own when I return to Hell. A drop of your blood applied to my mark will activate it."

She sat in the chair his coat had been draped over. She couldn't deny that she felt uneasy about the whole process, but she reminded herself again that Murmur had vowed not to harm her. Whatever he was planning had to fit within the terms of their contract.

Still, something about this didn't feel right. "Are you sure I shouldn't go back with you?"

"It's safer for you to remain here. I told you what will happen once the spell is complete. It's better this way, Suyin."

His words were reassuring, but while he spoke, his gaze remained fixed on the vial on his hand. She wished he would look at her, but more than that, she wished his attention didn't matter so much. She'd never felt like this about anyone before, and not knowing if he returned her feelings was agonizing.

But her pride wouldn't let her ask. It would barely let her admit those feelings to herself.

She took a breath. "All right. Let's do it." She rolled up her sleeve and held her arm out, but he shook his head.

"The sigil must go over your heart."

# 28

# Absence Makes the Heart Grow Colder

The sky was blood red when Murmur stepped through the hellgate back into his lair. As he smudged the outer line of the sigil, faint flickering on the horizon caught his eye.

Frowning, he hurried over to the window, peering out at the cracked plains and dark mountains towering in the distance. The orange flickering he saw came from the foothills—the edge of his territory.

It was fire.

*Fire, fire, fire.*

He closed his eyes and focused on the souls patrolling the boundaries. Sure enough, they had alerted him to a breach over an hour ago; he'd just been too distracted to notice.

Either legions had gathered with torches, or a massive wildfire had been lit. But both meant one thing: His territory was under attack. And there was only one person who would have the audacity—and the cause—to attack the Necromancer out of the blue.

Lucifer was coming for him.

*The end is nigh. It's do or die now. If the spell fails this time, you're going down.*

Murmur's last attempt had gotten so close to success, odds were that Lucifer had sensed him attempting to penetrate his magical defenses. Now the High King had come for retribution.

Heart in his throat, Murmur spun away from the window and hurried to his table of supplies, taking the vial of Suyin's blood from his pocket and then removing his shirt and coat and tossing them on a nearby chair. Things were about to get bloody.

He'd been expecting Lucifer to catch on at some point and had spent every moment since Suyin left working to prepare the spell. Despite the dire circumstances, however, he could barely focus on what he was doing.

He kept thinking back to Suyin. To the trust he'd seen in her eyes as she let him carve one of the deadliest symbols in magic into her skin. It made him feel sick.

The way she'd looked when he bid her farewell, her eyes sad like she didn't want him to leave, like she didn't want this to be their goodbye . . .

He braced his palms on the desk and dropped his head, his hair hanging forward. His breathing was ragged. It felt like he couldn't breathe at all, in fact. It felt like someone had placed a thousand-pound weight on his chest.

*Losing your edge, Necromancer? I thought you were willing to give up anything and commit any atrocity to achieve your precious spell?*

"Quiet." He needed to shake this feeling. He had one purpose, and that purpose was greater than anyone or anything else. It always had been.

He shook his head roughly and pushed off the desk, straightening. If he kept his body moving, if he didn't give any attention to the gnawing at his insides, then maybe he could do this.

No thinking. No feeling. It was the only way he was going to succeed.

*The High King is coming for you—unless you can give him something else to focus on.*

Murmur picked up the vial of Suyin's blood and . . . paused. Cradled it in his hand carefully. Once he activated the mark, she would be gone. This was the last vial of blood he would ever take from her.

*Gone, gone, gone forever. You'll be all alone. No one will ever miss you. No one will ever care about you. How could they, when you're such a piece of shit?*

His fingers curled around the glass. They trembled slightly.

"Master!"

The frantic knocking at the door had his head snapping up.

"Master, I know we're not to disturb you in your tower, but the territory wards have been breached. I believe we're under attack! What are your orders?"

A low growl rumbled in his chest. Time was of the essence, now more than ever. If he performed the spell now, Lucifer would have much greater problems to focus on than Murmur. If he hesitated, the High King would come, and everything would be lost. There wasn't time to waste directing his legions and managing his territory.

"Master? Are you in there?"

He said nothing. His minions could take care of themselves. Until he had finished this casting, he could not afford to be distracted.

A moment later, the demon's footsteps faded as he ran back down the stairs, having concluded that his master was not present. He was smart enough not to open the library door to check, and for that, he would be spared impalement.

Murmur strode into the circle at the edge of the sigil, uncorked the jar, and poured the contents into the waiting bowl. Setting the empty receptacle down, he readied the rest of his casting ingredients.

Several times he had to stop and wipe the sweat off his brow, though the room was cold. His chest felt so tight he couldn't breathe, and his stomach flipped over and over, forcing him to pause frequently to close his eyes and breathe through the nausea.

*Weakness. Your attachment has made you weak.*

Attachment. That was what this was, wasn't it? He had formed an attachment to the witch.

*You said it yourself. The day you allowed yourself to form sentimental bonds would be the day you met your end.*

"It has to be this way," he muttered. "I swore to do whatever it took."

*That's right. She has to die. Not just for the spell. But to purge this weakness from your mind.*

Half the point of this spell was to avoid his own death. But the other half was for a purpose greater than his own life. A foreseen destiny that was his responsibility to bring to fruition.

He would not fuck it up now. He couldn't.

Too soon, he was ready to make the sacrifice. Standing in the center of the sigil, he unsheathed his blade and carved the second mark into his own forearm. Blood ran around the blade, over the muscle and down his wrist.

He didn't feel the cut. It was nothing compared to the pain in his chest.

The sigil was simple, but its practice was not, nor was it always a practical solution, since the sacrifice usually resisted the inscription of the mark. They would have to be restrained so the mark could be inscribed, but then, what was the point?

If they were restrained and helpless, it was easier to just kill them then.

But it did have its uses in special circumstances—like say, instances of treachery and trickery—and this was one of them.

Murmur's sacrifice had not resisted him. Murmur's sacrifice trusted him. Or at least, she trusted in the vow he'd sworn to protect her. She wasn't aware of the loophole in their arrangement that he'd found and exploited. And he'd been counting on that.

He had sworn to let her go alive, returning her from whence she'd come in the same condition he found her in.

He had done that. He had fulfilled his word. He could not harm her while she was here.

But he had never sworn he wouldn't harm her from afar after she was home.

Perhaps she might have realized this if she hadn't foolishly allowed herself to soften toward him. But she had, and he had done what any villain would do: used it against her.

She'd sat still and allowed him to carve the death mark onto her chest, right between the breasts he had enjoyed in the throes of pleasure minutes before.

He was the villain. The evil liar, cheater, and killer. He knew this.

He didn't care.

*Liar.*

He *didn't.*

*Liar, liar, liar.*

"Be quiet. I need to focus."

When this was done, there would be no more sidelong looks beneath silky black hair or intelligent questions or sharp eyes. No more snarky comments or prodding jokes or tireless ferocity.

*She'll be gone, and you'll be alone. You'll be alive, but you'll hate yourself.*

"I said be quiet," he snarled at his own mind.

Sheathing his still-bloody knife with a jerk, he picked up the bowl of Suyin's blood. He dipped a finger in and then held it up. All he had to do was touch the bloodied finger to the mark.

The magic would activate. Her sacrifice would be complete. The spell would work. His work would be finished. His life would be spared. Lucifer's destined fall from power would begin.

Suyin would be dead.

*She'll be gone forever, and an immortal being knows that forever is a very long time.*

"It doesn't matter. The spell comes before any personal attachment."

He tried to draw his finger toward his arm, but his body was frozen as though he were paralyzed. He couldn't move a single inch.

"I have to do this," he snarled, fighting harder against the phantom force immobilizing him.

*You will never forgive yourself. You will despise every single day of your existence. To live and breathe will be a curse.*

Sweat gathered at his brow. Veins bulged in his arms as he strained against the invisible tension. "I can't keep her here with me anyway, so what's the point? She's half human, and she would never be content to be locked in my library forever. I must do this!"

*She will be dead. And* you *will have killed her.*

He emitted a low growl—a sound of exertion. Still, he fought.

*You will be the one that drains the life from her eyes. You will be the one to snuff out her light.*

His body shook, a sheen of sweat forming over his skin. Fighting against himself felt like forcing together the opposing sides of two powerful magnets. No matter how hard he tried to move, he couldn't beat the resistance. Because it was coming from his own mind.

*Her slender body will topple to the ground, her skin cold, her eyes empty. She won't bleed. Her heart will seize inside her chest, and nothing will be able to restart it again. You will have killed the only person that has ever meant anything to you. You will have destroyed the most valuable thing you've ever possessed.*

"Fuck!" With a shout, he dropped to his knees onto the floor, his arms falling at his sides. His muscles shook from exertion. That fucking nausea swirled harder and harder until—

He grabbed a nearby empty bowl and retched. Nothing came up.

"Fuck." This time his voice was tired. Resigned.

He couldn't do it.

"Why can't I do it?"

*You care for her.*

He couldn't deny it. He liked her company. He liked her endless questions, her thirst for knowledge, her indomitable will. He liked her dark eyes, her silky hair, her soft hands.

*You formed a bond with her, just like you swore you never would. And you just tried to kill her—the only person you've ever cared about, and probably the only one who's ever cared about you.*

He couldn't deny that either. Lucifer's legions were on their way now, and here he sat, unable to do what he needed to complete the spell. Unable to finish what he had started because of his attachment to one half-human witch, even if it meant facing his own death.

*You value her life above your own.*

"That can't be true." He shook his head. He didn't possess the ability to care for anything that deeply. His own ambitions had always been his only motivation. He had no care for others; he never had. It was simply not his nature.

*You have a soul. You told Suyin what happens to demons who develop souls—they develop consciences as well. Did you think you were the exception? Did you think you were different? Hate to break it to you, but you're not. You're just as much of an idiot as Raum and his simpering brothers, desperate to protect their precious females.*

"Suyin is special," he growled. "She is worth protecting."

*Is she special enough to die for? Because that's what you need to do to complete the spell.*

"That's absurd. There is no way to complete the spell without her. A life must be sacrificed with the blood offerings in order to—"

He broke off suddenly.

*A life must be sacrificed.*

The spell required a death sacrifice. He had concluded that with certainty. It would never have the strength to push through Lucifer's defenses without it, and his bond with Suyin had turned her life into an even more powerful offering.

But there were *two* blood sacrifices in the casting. Suyin, and himself.

And therefore . . . two potential deaths.

Sacrificing Suyin despite his attachment to her would greatly increase the power of the offering. But he hadn't considered the other alternative.

Sacrificing *himself* to save her would be ten times more powerful. One hundred times.

There was nothing more potent than a selfless sacrifice in all of magic. It was so incredibly rare to harness in a ritual that it was almost unheard of. But when circumstances aligned, and a selfless sacrifice could be made, free of duress . . .

The power was immeasurable.

His spine shot straight as he realized exactly what he had

to do. On his knees at the edge of the sigil, the culmination of years of work, the peak of his achievements, he faced the end.

It would work, too. He would summon Belial with one of his favors, forcing him to step into the portal and open the door. Murmur didn't technically have to be present for the task to be completed.

No, he wasn't actually contemplating this, was he?

*You've formed an attachment*, that stupid fucking inner voice informed him. *A powerful bond. Accept it. Do what must be done.*

"No." He shook his head.

*You love her. That's why you can't kill her. That's why you have to do this.*

"No." His heart skipped a beat. "No, I do not. I cannot *love*— I'm not capable of such a thing."

*You think of her in every spare moment. You enjoy her company, and you wish you could keep her here forever. You feel sick at the thought of hurting her.*

"Wrong!" he shouted at the empty room. "You're wrong—"

*You felt sick carving the death mark into her skin because you hated betraying her trust. You wanted to be worthy of her. You despised the idea of hurting her.*

"Stop it. Just . . . stop."

*You went there with the intention of taking her life. Then you enjoyed her body and the sight of her pleasure-drunk eyes. And then you lied to her and left her to die.*

"I said *stop*."

*You betrayed her. And you love her. And now you hate yourself.*

He dropped his head in his hands, forgetting the blood still staining his finger. He really was mad, sitting here arguing with himself. Incapable of completing his spell.

*That's not true. You know what you have to do, and you're more than capable.*

"Yes." He slowly lifted his head, looking around his library. "Yes, I do know."

Empty. The room was so empty and lightless. Full of knowledge, but what had it amounted to? At the end of the day, he was alone. What was so special about his life anyway? He was driven to survive by nothing but pure selfish ambition. At the end of the day, he meant nothing.

*You're going to do it.*

"Yes." He took a breath. "I am."

As soon as he spoke it aloud, as soon as he made the decision, the knot in his gut unclenched and the nausea eased. The weight lifted off his chest, and suddenly he could breathe. Everything felt lighter. *He* was lighter.

He scrambled up, grabbed his knife from the table, and slashed across his forearm, right over the mark. Rendering it useless.

The weight lifted even more. He felt so light, he was surprised he didn't float off the floor. He smiled at the thought of his own fucking death. Like the lunatic he was.

*A fitting way for the Necromancer to go, I believe.*

Indeed it was. Surrounded by the most powerful magic he'd ever attempted, his life would be the catalyst to complete his spell and begin the High King's downfall. It was poetic, in a way.

He leapt to his feet. Before he could die, there were several steps he had to take.

Hurrying to his desk, he rifled through the mess of papers, shoving them off the edge until he found a blank piece. And then he began to write.

When he finished the letter, he folded it in three and then sealed it with melted candle wax, pressing it flat with his own fingerprint. Crossing the room, he found a clear spot on the floor, withdrew his knife, and slashed his arm open again. It wasn't wise for him to waste so much blood before attempting the spell, but since he didn't plan to survive, he wasn't particularly concerned about that now.

He drew a demonic summoning seal on the ground. A demon could only summon another demon when there was a debt sworn between them. Twice, Belial had agreed to owe Murmur an unspecified favor. He had stipulated several conditions—Belial was no novice at negotiating—but Murmur knew how to work around them.

Now, however, instead of summoning the demon he wanted to speak to, he added a few tweaks to the sigil and then tossed the letter into the center. He activated the spell, and flames shot up around the outside of the sigil. When they died down, the letter was gone.

He hurried back to his desk. Now that the letter was sent, he needed to get the spell done before the recipient had time to show up demanding answers. The last thing he needed was a flaming, raging interruption at this crucial moment.

But there was one more thing he had to do.

He ran around the library like a madman, collecting books from various locations. Then, he penned a second letter and set it atop the stack. His gaze caught on one of the books in the stack, and he froze as something occurred to him. A tiny spark of hope lit in his chest.

Then he shook himself. The sacrifice would not be selfless unless he was fully committed. This was the only way. He had lived long enough.

Still, he couldn't stop himself from ripping a tiny piece of paper and putting it between the pages as a bookmark. So subtle it was basically invisible. It could be years before it was discovered, and by then, it would be far too late.

He stashed the books in a secret place, left a discreet trail he was sure his witch's discerning eyes could find, and then repaired the outside line of the hellgate so it could be reactivated. He knew Suyin well enough to guess she would come to confront him with a vengeance once she learned what the mark did. He needed to leave an open gate for her to do that.

When that was done, he hurried back to the sigil and readied his supplies to pick up where he'd left off. He looked down at his bare chest and swallowed. What he was planning . . . It wasn't a particularly pleasant way to die.

Then he thought of the trusting look in Suyin's eyes, her soft smile when he'd scooped her into his arms and carried her. Guilt and self-hatred felt like a sword in his chest. On the other side of his denial, he couldn't believe he'd even considered trying to kill her, let alone taken it as far as he had.

He was doing this for his vision of the future. For himself and his life's work.

But he was also doing it for her. Not only so she would live, but so she could rest easy knowing her father's soul would be freed.

He turned the knife toward his own chest and began to carve a necromancy sigil into his skin.

A demon could only be killed by decapitation and then complete incineration by hellfire. Any remaining piece would regenerate if it was not burned to ash.

But a demon with a soul . . .

Besides Gamigin, no one had studied this phenomenon. All rules and understandings of demons applied only to soulless demons. Once a demon evolved, the rules changed. The life force of a being with a soul was tied to their soul.

And without it, they would die.

Necromancy was the art of animating soulless bodies . . . and controlling souls who had already left their bodies. Which meant Murmur knew exactly how to make the perfect sacrifice.

When he finished the sigil, the cuts covered his entire torso, from his collarbone all the way down to his navel. He was weak from blood loss now, lightheaded, his skin clammy with a thin layer of cold sweat. The world spun around him as he dropped to his knees.

He was bleeding out, but that alone wouldn't kill him. But what he was about to do next would.

The knife fell from his fingers, his grip too weak to hold it. He swayed but forced himself to remain upright as blood poured from his chest, pooling on the floor.

And then he began the incantation. He spoke the syllables of his precious spell and watched his blood being drawn down the lines of the sigil toward the center. The hellfire ignited. His voice rose in volume though he couldn't find the strength to raise it himself. The magic amplified it. It built higher and higher the longer he spoke. The winds began, gusting around the room as it was plunged into smoky darkness.

And then, at the very center of the sigil, the portal began to solidify.

*It's going to work.*

The sacrifice was working. He could feel the magic pulsing out around him in great waves. It was powerful, so powerful that there was plenty more to spare. He could feel it drawing his soul from his body, using his sacrifice to push through the final barrier.

Somewhere far away, Lucifer's seal weakened and then broke completely. Murmur felt it happen right before he lost the strength to remain upright, toppling to the ground.

*Tired.* He was suddenly so tired.

His consciousness slipped from his blood-soaked body.

And then, suddenly . . . he was living the death vision.

The very fate he'd fought so hard to prevent came regardless. He hadn't altered his destiny after all. No matter what he did, he was always meant to die burning alive.

Flames surrounded him, scorching his essence. But they weren't hellfire, as he'd always assumed. They were not physical at all. They were *white*. Purifying. They seared to the core of his being, and he screamed in terrible agony.

And then . . . nothing. Blissful nothing.

He forgot who he was or what his mission was. He felt . . . release. He felt freedom. He felt—

*Trapped.* Suddenly, a powerful force was drawing him back, a dark tether sinking hooks into his essence and sucking him down, down . . .

Blackness surrounded him. Haunted cries echoed around him. He reached out to test the boundaries of his prison, but he had no form to utilize. He could sense the confinement, but it was as though he was paralyzed, trapped in a formless body encapsulated in ice.

All around, he heard screams.

# 29

# Be Still, My Beating Heart

A sudden tightness in her chest woke Suyin just after dawn. She sat up in bed, trying to place the strange feeling. She hadn't had any dreams that she remembered, but it wasn't normal for her to wake up beset with . . . sadness? Grief? She wasn't sure what it was.

More likely, it was the uneasiness about Murmur's spell that she hadn't been able to shake since he'd left last night.

Throwing her robe on, she padded into the kitchen on bare feet and flicked the kettle on for some herbal tea. She needed something calming. All night, the mark on her chest had burned, and it was still burning now. The skin stung from being cut, yes, but it was more than that.

The mark burned with dark magic.

She could feel its deadly power searing her from the inside, until it took all her self-control not to claw at her chest as if to scratch it off with her nails. What the hell had Murmur done to her? And why had she let him?

She stood by the window, watching the tree in the backyard swaying in the wind. But what she was really thinking about was the look on Murmur's face while he'd carved that mark on her. He'd looked sickened, even paler than usual. Was it because he hadn't liked harming her? He may have had a soft spot for her, but she wasn't sure he was even capable of that kind of empathy.

Afterward, he'd avoided meeting her eyes, and he'd left in a hurry, barely bothering with a goodbye though it was potentially the last time they'd ever see each other. She'd been fighting panic at the thought, and he'd been unable to get out of there fast enough. And now she couldn't help thinking . . .

He was hiding something.

She knew him well enough by now to sense he was lying. He'd never bothered lying to her before. Before she'd convinced him to open up about his plans, he'd simply ignored her questions or refused to answer them.

God, how could she have been so stupid? She'd let him sex her into complacency last night. And then she'd let him carve a sigil directly onto her skin, and she'd taken his word on how it worked instead of asking him to prove it first. She'd told him she trusted him, but that was taking it a little far.

He'd fucked the sense right out of her, evidently.

She dragged a hand down her face.

"If you fucked with me, Murmur," she muttered to her silent kitchen, "I swear to god I'll make you regret it."

First, she had to figure out what the mark actually did. Maybe he hadn't lied, and she was being paranoid and overly suspicious. It was possible. She wanted to believe in him, and she wanted to give him the chance to prove that he was worthy of her trust But she had to take care of herself too.

After her tea steeped, she went back to her bedroom, stripped off her robe and T-shirt, and then used her phone to take a picture of the mark on her chest. She zoomed in, studying it closely.

The skin was already scabbing over, thanks to her accelerated healing. It struck her as strange that she hadn't felt Murmur use the mark already. The sigil's power would fade as it mended, so whatever purpose Murmur had for it, he should have acted on it right away.

Had he done the spell already while she was asleep, so she hadn't felt the drain on her energy? If so, there was no point researching this. But instinct told her to keep digging.

She copied the mark onto a piece of paper in her notebook so she didn't have to tell anyone that she'd let a demon carve it into her chest. Then she snapped a photo of the drawing and sent an email to a certain black-magic coven in New York.

The head of the coven, Moira, was an eighty-year-old witch who looked forty, thanks to frequent youthfulness animal-sacrifice rituals, and that was who Suyin contacted directly. She attached a photo of the drawing and asked if Moira or anyone she knew recognized it.

Luckily, she didn't have to wait long for a reply.

She'd just gotten dressed when her phone buzzed. Heart racing, she opened the message immediately.

*Hi Suyin,*

*Where did you see this symbol? You need to be extremely careful. Do not put this mark anywhere near your bare skin. I would even be careful touching it without gloves on—it's that powerful.*

*This is a Sheolic death mark. Once carved into the skin, it can be triggered from anywhere. It's used for sacrificial magic when the sacrifice isn't present for the ritual. The caster cuts a second symbol on herself and then uses the blood of her sacrifice to activate it, which will cause the sacrifice to die instantly, channeling his life force into her spell.*

*If you're planning to attempt it, the challenge is getting the mark into your sacrifice's skin. You need him to trust you enough to allow you to carve it, or he would need to be drugged or restrained.*

*This is not a low-level casting. Chances of failure are high, even if you follow all the steps correctly. I would recommend considering a simpler method for a male sacrifice.*

*Please don't hesitate to reach out if you have any questions. Last I heard you were hesitant to learn Sheolic magic, and now you're casting death marks! Something tells me we have lots to catch up on. ;)*

*Moira*

Suyin reread the email five times. Each time, her heart beat faster, and it grew harder to draw breath. She dropped into a chair, clutching her phone with a white-knuckled, shaking hand. It took all her self-control not to find a knife and slash through the sigil right then, but she knew better than to break the line before learning the consequences.

She clutched her sweater tightly over her heart. Over the death mark.

The *death* mark.

The Sheolic death mark that Murmur had carved into her skin.

*Do not put this mark anywhere near your bare skin. I would even be careful touching it without gloves on—it's that powerful.*

Well, it was carved into her fucking chest.

And just like the stupid male sacrifices Moira was talking about, Suyin had sat back and let Murmur do it. She remembered his averted gaze, his softened tone as he avoided her questions . . .

*Do you trust me, Suyin?*

She had. She'd been trying to, anyway. Trying to overcome her habitual distrust of people for his sake, because she'd believed he deserved it. At the very least, she'd trusted in their blood vow to protect her.

But now, replaying the conversation in her mind, she recalled exactly what he'd said, and she realized she'd been duped. *I will return you from whence you came in more or less the same condition I found you in.*

He had returned her home unharmed, as promised. He'd never sworn not to kill her from afar once he did.

Her phone clattered to the floor as it slipped from her hand. She tore her sweater and shirt off and stepped in front of the mirror. There, topless, she stood looking at her body with that physical manifestation of betrayal carved into her chest.

Right over her fucking heart.

She screamed. A primal scream of rage.

And then she felt it . . . The shift.

She'd completely forgotten about the possibility of having an altered form until this moment, but when she felt the dark energy bubbling up inside of her, she recognized it immediately. And she realized she had felt it before in the past, but just as Murmur had said, she had unconsciously repressed it, believing she was keeping her emotions in check.

She didn't repress it this time.

Sharp black claws grew from her fingertips. Her canine teeth lengthened into deadly points. Her eyes washed over with pure black. And while she stayed the same size, her skin took on a faint purplish hue. The increased strength she'd had her entire life augmented until it felt like she could snap bones with her bare hands.

Any other time, her mind would have been blown. But right now, all she could think about was using her newfound weapons—claws and teeth and strength—to rip Murmur's heart out. Just as he'd done to her.

She'd trusted him. She'd let herself soften toward him. She'd been vulnerable with him, in a way she'd never been with anyone before. And now this.

"You fucking *bastard*," she snarled. "You backstabbing piece of shit. You fucking *liar*!" Her nostrils flared, her chest heaved, and her demonic eyes were black pits of rage. Her reflection in the mirror looked crazed—an apt description, because she fucking was.

This wasn't just a betrayal. Murmur hadn't just lied or cheated.

This was a literal knife in the back. Because he was going to fucking *kill* her.

She hadn't been stupid enough to believe he was some reformed "good" demon just because they'd bonded, but she'd thought they had an understanding. They'd had sex multiple times, and she'd thought he cared for her in whatever twisted way he was capable of. She'd thought they had a bond.

Wrong. *Wrong, wrong, wrong.*

She seethed. The anger felt like pure fire running through her veins. The betrayal burned like acid in her stomach.

She needed to find a way to deactivate that fucking mark immediately. If she'd thought it would work, she would've used her newly formed claws to gouge it off right then and there. But she didn't understand how the spell functioned enough to risk it. And knowing what she did about black magic, she had a terrible suspicion that once the mark had been on her skin for several hours, the damage had been done.

She ran to pick her phone up off the floor. With shaking hands, she fumbled to reply to Moira's email, her claws scratching at the screen.

> *Once the mark has been applied, is there a way for the sacrifice to deactivate it?*

Back in her bedroom, she donned her shirt and sweater and then she sat on the bed, trying to figure out what the fuck to do. She tried to drag her hands through her hair only for her claws to get caught in the tangles. There wasn't time to waste, but she needed to know what to do to save herself first. If there was anything.

Moira's reply was swift.

> *No, not from the sacrifice's end. That's what makes it so deadly.*
>
> *The only way to deactivate it is if the caster interrupts a line of her seal. Or, if the death mark is never activated, the sacrifice's mark will heal, and the magic will fade with it.*
>
> *Hope that helps and good luck. :)*

Suyin leapt off the bed. Maybe there was hope after all. She'd lasted this long. If she could just find a way to stop Murmur from activating the mark, she'd be golden.

She had two options: She could begin a period of diligent study or even ask Iris's boyfriend and his brothers for help in trapping Murmur. But that would require trusting a bunch of unknown demons, and it would take time she didn't have. It had been hours since Murmur had put the mark on her. She didn't know why he hadn't activated it yet, but she figured she didn't have long.

Which left her second option: go to Hell, find him, and stab him until he bled out.

Was it stupid? Reckless? Probably. If he was willing to kill her, he truly felt nothing for her, which meant he'd be ruthless if he caught her. On top of that, the odds of him having left the hellgate in his library open were low.

She probably wouldn't even be able to get there, but it was

worth a shot. Considering her options were do or die, she was inclined to take risks.

Mind made up, she hurried into her living room, which was still taken over by her expired paranoia wards. She grabbed the mop from the kitchen and washed a clean spot on the floor. Then she called up an old text saved on her computer for reference, grabbed some chalk, and began inscribing a hellgate sigil.

With a bit of walking around, she could have found the empty apartment Murmur had used, but again, that would take time she didn't have.

As a blood-born witch, she was naturally able to travel through gates, while witch practitioners had to consume demon blood first. That had led to the age-old rumor that blood-born witches were descended from demons, something Suyin had always scoffed at.

She wasn't laughing now.

According to her father's research, blood-born witches were the descendants of Cambions, so they did indeed have demon blood in their veins. Which was why they could use hellgates. Go figure.

When the gate was finished, Suyin activated it, visualizing the gate she wanted to connect hers to and hoping like hell Murmur had left it open. Then she ran back into her room, dug out one of her ritual daggers from her closet, and strapped on the worn leather sheath. The blade was far sharper than anything in her kitchen.

She was going to stab Murmur in the back, just as he'd done to her.

# 30

# HELL HATH NO FURY

"WHAT'S HE PLAYING AT?" ASH SAID, DRAGGING HIS fingers through his shiny black hair.

"I have no idea," Belial growled in response, but he was getting sick and goddamn tired of the Necromancer popping up all the time. "I think it's time to kill him."

Mist frowned. He and Lily had returned a day ago from Ireland to this mess. Bel figured they should've stayed away.

"I thought you formed an agreement that he wouldn't bother you or anyone you cared about," Mist said.

The demons were gathered in Bel's living room to discuss what to do about their recurring necromancer problem. Iris had spent the previous day with her friend Suyin, only to tell Meph afterward that the witch had recently returned from Hell, having been captured by Murmur for some unknown purpose.

"I did," Bel said. "But I didn't think to specify every single one of Iris's fucking friends, and that slimy fucker took advantage of that." He ground his teeth. He couldn't believe he'd been outmaneuvered in a bargain by Murmur. He was *Belial.*

He was supposed to be the one outmaneuvering people. It was embarrassing.

"Do you think he was telling the truth about the Cambion shit?" Meph asked, crossing his tattooed arms. He and Raum sat on one sofa, Bel sat on the other, Mist lurked in the corner like a shadow, and Ash sat at the grand piano, elbow propped on its polished black top. Sunlight streamed through the tall windows, casting golden rays across the hardwood.

"If he is, the implications are . . ." Ash trailed off.

Bel finished the sentence in his head. *Enormous. Mind-boggling. Catastrophic.* Demons who could reproduce? It was absurd. It went against everything he'd ever understood about the world.

But he couldn't deny it made sense.

Sunshine's mentor Adriel had already confirmed that they had evolved souls. And it was always understood that demons couldn't procreate because they were soulless. The soul was responsible for the inherent gift of creation. A demon with a soul was already an anomaly. So why not demon offspring?

"I still think we should kill him," Bel grumbled, stewing over how Murmur had played him. That kind of slight could not go unpunished.

"We need to find out what he's up to first," Ash said. "What did he want with Suyin? He made her swear a vow not to talk about it. That means it's important."

"Maybe he just wants to study her or some shit," Meph offered. "I mean, even I'm pretty curious. Does she have a demon form? Or is she like Eva and she just kinda gets bigger and scarier? And on that note, does her blood have magical properties like Eva's does?"

"Maybe that's why he wanted her," Mist said. "For her blood."

"I think we should get Suyin over here and ask her ourselves," Ash suggested.

"She's not going to tell us any more than she told Iris," Meph interjected, "and Iris already told me everything she said."

"Yeah, but Iris was probably too busy panicking at the thought of having your deranged demon babies to pay attention," Ash shot back.

Meph snorted. "I can't blame her for that."

"I can't believe Gamigin was her father." Raum shook his head. "I always thought he was a bit weird, but I never would have guessed that."

"I gave that necromancer fuck *two* favors," Bel growled. "Then we gave him Raphael as a peace offering, and he's still fucking playing us. He needs to die."

"Bel, you sound like a broken record," Ash said. "We aren't even talking about Murmur anymore. Were you even listening?"

"He's got a one-track mind," Meph said. "Kill, kill, kill."

His brothers chuckled, looking at him with amusement. Bel's fingers tightened around his coffee cup. "This isn't a goddamn joke. Murmur is a problem, and we've let him go unchecked for too long."

"That's because he's fucking powerful," Ash said. "It's not as simple as marching into his lair and tearing his head off. He's got an army of souls at his command. How are you supposed to fight ghosts?"

"Can confirm it's impossible," Raum mumbled.

Bel stood suddenly. "I don't give a flying fuck about his shitty ghosts. He hides behind his spells and magic because he's weak. If I can get close to him, I'll wring his neck till his head pops off and cremate him with hellfire."

"And how are you planning to do that?"

"Yeah, you've never been big on stealth."

"Stop telling me what I can't do, you little shits." Bel jabbed a finger in each of his brothers' directions. "I would wipe the floor with all of you. And if one of you makes another comment about how I can't kill a measly necromancer, I'll rip your arms off and beat you unconscious with them to prove a point."

Meph held his hands up. "No one's questioning your badassery. We're just concerned for your safety."

"Fuck safety! And fuck all of you. I don't need your goddamn coddling. Why don't you go open a fucking daycare if you want to baby someone."

Ash barked a laugh. "Now there's a good image."

Meph chuckled. "Can you imagine it? Demon daycare. Moms dropping off their little kids with us delinquents."

"Raum would be good at it. He's already babysitting the puppy dogs."

While his brothers continued with their ridiculous fantasy, Bel spun with a growl and stalked out of the room. Back in the kitchen, he tossed his coffee cup into the sink a little too forcefully, and it shattered. He didn't stop to clean it up.

He needed space from his brothers until he got his temper back under control, so he strode down the hall to the office he never used. Locking the door behind him, he sank into the cushy leather office chair and stared out the window overlooking the backyard.

He was pissed his brothers weren't taking him seriously, but he knew that was stupid. His brothers never took anything seriously. It had nothing to do with him.

But he wasn't joking around about killing Murmur. He'd had enough of the damned Necromancer.

It was at that moment, in a cruel twist of fate, that the air on the other side of the desk suddenly burst into purple flame. There was a small explosion of light, and purple sparks showered down like fireworks. And then it was over, as quickly as it had begun.

In the aftermath, a summoning sigil appeared on the floor,

having formed from the ashes of the explosion. In the center of it was a folded piece of paper, sealed with purple wax.

"You've got to be kidding me," Bel said, staring at it. Because he already knew exactly who had sent him that letter.

"You're dead, Necromancer. So fucking dead."

He stood, pushing the chair back and walking around the desk. He approached the sigil warily, bending and picking up the letter. Slipping a finger under the wax seal, he popped it open and unfolded the paper in slow motion.

As he began to read, his suspicions were confirmed.

The Necromancer had called in his first favor.

Miracle of miracles, the hellgate worked.

The world turned on its axis and shook her around, and then Suyin stumbled out the other side, head pounding. As the room stopped spinning, she saw the familiar shapes of Murmur's library and knew she'd made it. Murmur had actually left his gate open, a careless act that seemed totally unlike him.

But she didn't have long to dwell on that.

She'd stepped out of the hellgate . . . into an apocalypse.

The room was full of a thick black smoke that she promptly started choking on. It was so dark it was hard to see anything, save for an orange glow flickering through the window outside. A glance through the glass showed fire burning all across the plains surrounding the castle. There was a distant roaring and a low rumbling on the ground like thousands of pounding footsteps.

But she only spared a moment looking out the window, because what was in the room was far more shocking.

In the center of Murmur's spell, surrounded by swirling gusts of black smoke and wind, was a vortex. Purple and black, it filled the entirety of the circle Murmur had drawn in blood around it. The presence of that portal meant only one thing:

The spell had succeeded.

But if it had succeeded, then where was Murmur? And how the hell was she alive?

Nape prickling, Suyin ventured farther into the room, squinting into the darkness to make out her surroundings. She was still in her altered form, and she flexed her claws in readiness for any surprise attacks.

If she could sneak up on Murmur and stab him before he ever noticed her, she would gladly do so. She'd rip his throat out with her claws first and then sink her blade into his chest. Anything to appease the hurt and rage burning in her chest.

Except . . . as she got closer to the sigil and spinning portal, she saw a dark shape sprawled at the far edge, next to the ritual table.

Heart in her throat, she tiptoed a little farther.

The gleam of white hair caught her eye, and she knew it was him.

Vengeance momentarily forgotten, she rushed forward, dropping to his side. He lay on his side, half over the outside line of the sigil. One arm was stretched out, and the other was trapped under him. His silvery hair fell over his face, hiding his eyes, but it was immediately obvious that he was unconscious.

And he was surrounded by a huge pool of blood.

Suyin wasn't squeamish, but the sight of this much blood made her stomach churn a little.

"What the hell?" she muttered. This wasn't what she'd expected to find at all. His upper body was bare, his white-gray skin even more deathly pale than usual. No breath from his nose ruffled the hair over his face.

She ought to have been relieved. He couldn't kill her if he was unconscious. She'd made the right call, coming here without getting anyone else involved. Now all she had to do was find where he'd carved the mark on himself and cut a slash through it to break the magic. Then she'd keep watch and make sure he didn't wake up and try to re-carve his mark before her own skin could heal. She should have been rejoicing. She would live.

Instead, a cold sense of dread rose within her.

She gripped Murmur's upper arm, his skin ice-cold under her palms, and then pushed as hard as she could, rolling him onto his back. He flopped over, arm draped across his middle now, hair still over his face.

She gasped when she saw the marks on his chest.

His entire torso had been carved up with some sort of sigil. The dark red of his blood against his pale skin was grisly and made her cringe with unwilling sympathy. She gently swept his hair off his face. His eyes were closed, features slack. Those same black veins she'd seen before snaked out beneath his shadowed eyes.

"What did you do, Murmur?" she whispered.

He would regenerate. A demon couldn't die from blood loss, even to this degree. He would wake up, and she needed to focus on doing what she'd come here to do.

*The mark*. She didn't think the giant sigil on his chest was it. Moira had said it was simple, and that one was extremely complex. There was nothing on the stretched-out arm, so she lifted the one bent over his abdomen.

She gasped. There, in the highest part of his inner forearm, was a mark nearly identical to the one on her chest.

Except for the fact that there was a slash carved through it.

Her breath caught. He had interrupted the mark himself. He'd planned to kill her and then changed his mind. Setting his arm down, she stared at him, trying to understand, her mind reeling.

She'd been so ready to hate him, to despise him for eternity. She'd never felt an intensity of betrayal so deep as when she'd realized he planned to kill her. Her skin burned just thinking of it.

But here he lay in a pool of his own blood, having done some terrible unknown magic to himself. Having slashed over the sigil that would take her life.

She didn't know how to feel. She couldn't forgive him that easily. Regardless of whether he'd had a change of heart, he'd still come to her house and had sex with her in her bed, while planning to kill her. That was too fucked up. She couldn't let that go.

But this . . . if this was what it seemed like to her . . . it meant something. It wasn't enough, but it meant something.

Almost against her will, her hand stretched out, and she stroked the back of her claw along his cold cheekbone.

"Why did you do it?" she whispered. "Why do you make it impossible to be on your side?" She took a breath and then admitted what she never would have had he been awake to hear it. "You had me. You won our game. I would have done anything for you. I would have given you whatever you wanted. But you had to go and ruin it, didn't you?" She shook her head. "It was probably for the best. I don't think you'd even know what to do with emotions if you had them."

She pulled her hand back and then stood, wincing at the blood that had soaked into her pants and stained her boots. She looked at him sprawled out on the ground, cold and alone, and her heart ached.

Then she turned and walked away.

She went to his desk, sitting in his well-worn chair and sorting through the mess of papers. If she wanted to figure out what had happened here, she needed to look for clues, and she had to do it fast. However he'd done it, Murmur's spell had succeeded. Which meant Belial was going to show up soon, use the portal and open the door, and shit was really going to hit the fan. She needed to be long gone before that happened.

It only took a moment of searching for her to be sure there were no answers on Murmur's desk. But they had to be somewhere. One thing she'd learned spending time with Murmur was that he wrote everything down. It helped him make sense of the chaos in his mind.

Blowing out a breath, she slumped back in the chair, staring at his still-unconscious form, sprawled in the middle of the sigil, surrounded by blood. Even as mad at him as she was, she hated seeing him like that.

She pushed back the chair, leaned forward, and buried her face in her hands, trying to make sense of the myriad of emotions in her head. Rage, confusion, fear, heartbreak, longing . . . She couldn't even try to name them all.

And then she spotted it.

A tiny trail of blood drops.

# 31

# Red Letter

Suyin sat up straight, following the blood drops with her gaze until they disappeared into the smoky gloom. They seemed to lead toward the far wall of bookshelves.

She stood and followed the trail. It led her all the way to the back of the room, stopping in the center of a long line of towering shelves.

She scanned the books, first peering at her own height and then crouching down and looking lower. And then, using the shelves like the rungs of a ladder, she climbed up a couple of rows and scanned the books there too. Nothing jumped out at her.

As she was climbing down, she saw it.

A tiny piece of paper, stuck to the side of a nondescript book spine. The paper said, *Suyin*.

Her heart leapt into her throat, and she stared at the book. At the top of the spine was a very small sigil that could have just been a decoration on the cover.

But she didn't think it was.

Jumping off the shelves, she pulled out the knife holstered at her hip and used the sharp tip to prick her finger. Then, sheathing the blade, she climbed back up the shelves and pressed the drop of blood into the sigil.

Immediately, the entire shelf lurched.

With a yelp, she tightened her grip on the shelves, and only her quick reflexes kept her from toppling onto her back.

The entire shelf unlatched and shifted open. *A hidden door.* Of course there was a hidden door in here. Why was she even surprised?

She jumped off the shelves again, sucked the blood off her fingertip, and then gripped the edge of the big shelf and hauled it the rest of the way open. It was stiff and took a lot of strength, but she finally pulled it wide enough to slip through.

It was pitch-black inside, so she pulled out her phone and switched on the flashlight. Her battery was precariously low though it had been fully charged before she left. Unsurprising—hellgate travel always messed with electronics, and being in Hell probably did too.

The light illuminated a small table with a big stack of books, maybe a dozen or more. There wasn't much space in here for more, and she figured it was more of a hiding place for valuables than any kind of room.

The books were old grimoires, their covers worn and faded. On top was a folded piece of paper. Holding her phone up with one hand, she smoothed it open with the other, her heart racing when she saw her name at the top, written in Murmur's familiar scrawl.

> *Suyin,*
>
> *The contents of my library are yours. I can think of no other I would give them to. What that says about me, ~~I'm not sure~~ I don't care. Take whatever you want, but the books in this stack*

*are the most valuable in my collection. I want you to have them. Left here, they will fall into unworthy hands.*

*I couldn't do it. I guess it doesn't matter why anymore.*

She read and reread the note several times, each time trying to convince herself it didn't mean what she thought it meant. But each time, she only grew more certain it did. Her heart sank deeper and deeper until it felt like it plummeted out the bottom of her.

She picked up her stack of books and slipped out of the dark room, using her back to push the door shut. Placing the books and her note carefully on Murmur's desk, she approached his still form. She moved slowly as if dreading what she was going to find, though she already knew what it would be.

He hadn't moved. His wounds hadn't closed. He wasn't healing and regenerating.

"Why?" she whispered, staring at his features. Demons couldn't die without hellfire. It couldn't be possible.

*I couldn't do it.* He was talking about the mark.

"I don't forgive you," she tried to whisper, but the words caught in her throat.

A banging on the library doors startled her, and her head snapped up.

"Master!" a muffled voice shouted.

Her eyes widened. Murmur's subjects couldn't know he was . . . indisposed. She was certain any kind of weakness would send the entire castle into a frenzy. And then there were the fires on the plains.

"Master, the defense wards are down, and the legions draw closer! I know we're not to disturb you, but we must know what to do."

She scrambled to her feet, racing over to the window and peering out over the territory below. The fires in the distance were *demons*. And not just any demons. Legions—armies. And they were approaching Murmur's lair.

"Fuck," she breathed. This was not her problem. She needed to get out of here. But . . .

She spun around and stared at Murmur. She wasn't leaving him. Surely he wasn't actually dead, and she couldn't leave him here in the middle of an approaching battle. She'd go back to being angry once this was over.

"Master, are you here? I know we aren't to disturb you in your tower, but I will come in to make sure you're okay if you don't respond!"

Mind made up in a flash, she ran across the room to the door, and then cracked it open, giving thanks that she'd somehow managed to hold on to her altered form this whole time. With her creepy eyes and claws, the visitor wouldn't realize she was half human.

Outside, a short, red-skinned demon with stubby horns and leathery wings wrung his hands nervously. He stared up at her in obvious surprise. That made sense. She wasn't supposed to be here. No one was supposed to be here.

"Where is the master?" the demon asked, leaning as if trying to peer around her shoulder.

"He's . . . busy," she said, still racking her brain for a way out of this.

"I must speak with him," the demon said. "It's urgent. The territory is under attack."

She narrowed her eyes, trying to figure out how much to give away and how loyal Murmur's subjects were to him. Did they hate him for his obvious neglect? Were they bored and wished he sent them out warring?

Then she figured she'd just ask him outright. "How loyal are you to Murmur?"

The demon's eyes bugged. Immediately, he looked nervous. "Very loyal. Extremely loyal. The most loyal."

Okay, he was probably mostly afraid of being impaled if he answered wrong, and she didn't blame him.

"Do you prefer him as a master to Paimon?" Murmur had told her that Paimon's subjects had automatically become his as soon as he took over her territory.

The demon nodded empathically. "Oh yes, our master is the greatest master."

"You don't wish you were out . . . fighting? You know, conquering new territories and shit?"

"No, no." The demon waved his hands, and this time she had the sense that his response was genuine. "We're tired of fighting. All we ever do is fight, fight, fight, for centuries. But we're tired. We want to rest. Master doesn't make us fight. Master lets us stay here. As long as we obey his rules and leave him alone in his tower, he doesn't hurt us, he doesn't make us battle, and he doesn't feed us to the goraths for sport. We are *very* loyal to Master."

Weren't demons supposed to love fighting, for the sole fact that they were demons? Wasn't violence and bloodshed supposed to be the entire purpose of their existence? And yet, these demons were tired and wanted to rest. They were *grateful* Murmur neglected them.

She would never have believed it before she'd spent time here herself, but now . . . the idea of demons who just wanted to be left alone didn't seem so outlandish.

She took a breath and decided to trust this little red fucker.

"Listen closely," she said, and immediately the demon leaned in. "Murmur has performed a very difficult spell to . . . increase his power. So he'll be twice as strong as he was before."

The demon's eyes widened. That was a crock of shit, but she wasn't about to let word get out about what had really happened. And Murmur could thank her later for boosting morale with his subjects. *Because he's not dead. It's not possible.*

"But because of this spell," she went on, lying through her teeth, "he's indisposed while he recovers. He left me in charge in his absence."

The demon nodded. "You are his consort, the only one to ever receive gifts from the Master and be allowed within his treasured library. This is wise. The Master always has a plan."

His *what now*?

"What should we do?" the demon asked. "The boundary wards are down, and enemy legions are running freely across the plains."

"Just . . ." She wasn't a demonic battle general. This was way outside her pay grade. Still, the demon said he didn't want to fight anymore, so she'd go with that. "Stay inside the lair where it's safe. Organize your defenses and protect the castle, but don't bother charging out to meet them. You'll be exposed out on the plains."

"Yes, mistress. Thank you, mistress." He bowed.

"Whatever happens, don't let anyone come up here. No one can disturb Murmur's tower, okay?"

"Yes, Mistress." The demon hurried away to fulfill her orders, and she slammed the door, leaning against it to catch her breath.

This was so fucked up, but she had her priorities. And as much as that awkward little demon had suddenly made her care about the state of Murmur's territory, she had to take care of herself first.

She locked the door behind her, knowing it wasn't going to keep out any real intruders. Murmur had given her his entire library, and she was taking the responsibility seriously. *Even though he's not dead.*

As such, she found a piece of chalk and spent several minutes drawing a ward on the back of the door. Murmur would probably be able to break it with ease, but regular lesser demons wouldn't, and it was better than nothing.

Then she went back to his prone body, crouched down and hooked her arms under his, and tried to drag him.

In a low squat, she managed to move him halfway to the hellgate before she had to stop and rest. She was strong, but damn, he was heavy. How much did seven feet of solid-boned demon weigh? Bastard was going to throw her back out.

Didn't matter. In the distance, the plains outside the lair swarmed with more demons. She hoped the ones here would be able to hold the walls of the lair. She hoped the library would be safe. But she needed to get Murmur the fuck out of here. No one could see him like this, wounded, unconscious, possibly dea—

"Shut *up*," she snapped at herself, and then she bent and grabbed him again. "Almost . . . there . . ." With a grunt of exertion, she hauled him up and shuffled the rest of the way. She dragged his deadweight across the hellgate . . . which of course smudged the lines and deactivated it.

She cursed, and her breath caught as her eyes filled with tears. She was teetering on a razor's edge of falling apart.

Taking deep breaths, she left Murmur, grabbed another piece of chalk, and set about fixing the lines. She retraced them all around his motionless form and then had to forcibly roll him to each side to repair the lines beneath him.

Finally, it was done, and she was able to reactivate the gate and link it back with her apartment. She tossed the chalk piece, stepped into the gate, reaching to grab Murmur's hand—

And that was when she remembered that an unconscious person couldn't travel by hellgate.

Which was why she was pretty damn surprised when, a moment later, the world turned on its axis and spun her around like a kernel in a popcorn machine. She found herself standing in her living room on Earth, bending over to clutch Murmur's ice-cold hand as he lay too still at her feet.

An unconscious person couldn't travel by hellgate. But a dead one could.

Because a dead person classified as extra baggage. And people could take items through hellgates as long as they were touching them with some part of their body.

Her blood went cold, but she shook her head firmly. "He's not dead," she said aloud, not believing the words coming out of her mouth.

But she reminded herself there was such a thing as a temporary death for a demon—they could regenerate from mortal wounds so long as they weren't inflicted with an angel's consecrated weapon. It was too early to know for sure.

Even though there were no mortal wounds on his body. Even though the wounds he did have hadn't even begun to heal, though it had been hours since she'd found him.

"No, no, no," she whispered, her chest tightening so much it hurt to breathe. But she couldn't allow herself to think about it yet. She still had one more thing to do.

With monumental effort, she managed to drag Murmur's body out of the hellgate. Then she found her chalk, repaired the smudged lines once more, and traveled right back to the library. The portal still spun around in the center of the spell, just waiting for someone to step into it.

She ran to Murmur's desk and picked up the stack of books he'd given her with the folded note still on top. And then she carried the load back through the hellgate to Earth, setting it down quickly and sinking to the ground.

With her final task complete, the adrenaline began to leave her bloodstream, and the shock took over. Her claws morphed back to human hands with blunt nails. They shook visibly. Her skin returned to its natural shade, and her sharp fangs became short, dull points.

She stared at Murmur's expressionless features. At the sigil carved into his chest that still hadn't healed. All of her was shaking now. The silence in her house felt oppressive. She wanted to scream to fill it, but she couldn't find her voice.

*I couldn't do it. I guess it doesn't matter why anymore.*

The tightness in her chest turned to pain so sharp she gasped. *Is he really dead? Am I really sitting in my living room with Murmur's dead body?*

No, this couldn't be how it ended. It *couldn't*. He wasn't gone. She refused to accept it, to even consider it a possibility. There had to be something—

*The books.* Maybe there was something in the books. Another note, perhaps.

She grabbed the bottom spine, dragging the entire pile closer to her. She didn't stop to wonder if her actions were rational. All that mattered was keeping her mind busy so she didn't have to think about the truth or listen to the terrible silence.

She snatched the first book off the top, and her heart lurched when she immediately recognized it. *The Book of Gamigin.* Guess she hadn't needed to fight to get it back after all.

That book came too close to making her think about the things she couldn't face, so she quickly set it aside and grabbed the next, and then the next. She flipped through each with increasing desperation, refusing to acknowledge the absurdity of her hope that she'd find another note from Murmur tucked in their pages, assuring her he would wake up shortly.

A few of the volumes were an overview of Sheolic magic, more thorough than anything she'd find on Earth. There were a couple grimoires full of complex spells she'd need to spend hours studying just to figure out what they did. One tome was a book of curses with a blackened cover that made a chill race down her spine just from holding it.

The next one she recognized. It was the book on necromancy that Murmur had given her to read the first day they'd stopped actively antagonizing each other. And this was the first volume of several, she saw, noting the rest of the books in the pile.

In the past, she would have dropped these books like they'd burned her, so determined was she to stay away from anything black-magic related. And necromancy was the blackest magic of them all.

But if her time in Hell had taught her anything, it was that things in life were more in shades of gray than black and white. Maybe Murmur had enslaved human souls, but he only took souls who were destined for Hell anyway, and he gave them a choice. They knew what they were signing on for when they were bound into his service, and they had no one to blame but themselves.

As for raising zombies like something in a cheesy horror flick, Murmur had scoffed when she'd asked about it, calling it a rudimentary practice, something she had found amusing. Most humans were terrified at the thought of the walking dead. But the demon capable of making them thought it was a waste of time and too easy of a task to be considered any real accomplishment.

Her throat seized at the memories, and she choked on a sob. She shook her head roughly, blocking the feelings before they exploded out of her, and grabbed the next book.

Murmur had once told her that animating a soulless being was the easiest part of necromancy, and the true masters were more concerned with souls. As she hurriedly flipped through the different volumes, organized in order of difficulty of practice, she began to understand why.

The first books focused mainly on animating the soulless dead. They were not alive, but they walked and followed their master's command with mindless obedience. The next were about communicating with bodiless souls. And the final ones, the advanced ones, were about controlling bodiless souls, just as Murmur had done to amass his ghost army. They were soul zombies, in a sense.

A soul could only be trapped when it was in a state of limbo. Once it had passed on to its rightful place in Heaven or Hell, it generally could not be called on, though there were exceptions. But a soul in limbo who hadn't severed its attachment to its body, clinging on because of anger, fear, or unfinished business, was free game.

As she turned the pages of the final book, she noticed a small piece of paper sticking out of the middle. Her heart began to race as she quickly opened to that spot, hoping to find another message from Murmur. Something. Anything that could delay her facing the truth a moment longer.

But there was nothing. Just that tiny scrap of unmarked paper.

Then again . . . none of the other volumes were bookmarked like this, and the torn piece seemed fresh, the edges still sharp. She hurriedly scanned the page it had led her to.

The messily scrawled heading read, *The Truest Form of Resurrection—Reanimation by Returning a Soul to Its Body.* Several pages were required to list all possible dangerous side effects and things that could go wrong, but Suyin's eyes slowly slid out of focus as the meaning of what she was reading sank in.

Her head snapped up, and she stared at Murmur's body. His *dead* body. He really was dead. The Necromancer was gone.

Then she looked down and fingered the torn piece of paper. And she knew.

He'd left her this book with this page marked on purpose. He'd wanted her to find it. He'd wanted her to find and read it because he was dead.

And he wanted her to bring him back.

There was no message. No easy assurance that he was fine

and would awaken shortly. And in fact, if she hadn't been hunting through these books in desperation, she never would've found that tiny piece of paper at all.

She couldn't even think about him being gone forever; it hurt too much. But she was also furious that he'd expect her to perform complicated black magic to resurrect him after how he'd betrayed her. She seethed at him for trying to kill her, lying to her, and then going and fucking *dying* without giving her a chance to stab him first, leaving her alone with the agony and memories of him.

Then she started to wonder . . . if he'd really wanted her to bring him back, why hadn't he mentioned it in his note? Why had he only left a tiny shred of paper? For something as critical as this, shouldn't he have written some highly detailed instructions?

And then she remembered what she'd just read—that a soul couldn't be controlled once it had passed on to its place in the afterlife. That meant that if Murmur's soul wasn't in purgatory, it would be impossible to bring him back.

Which, in turn, meant that once Belial opened the door, broke Lucifer's prison, and the demon souls went free, the window of opportunity to resurrect Murmur would close.

Belial could be opening the door any minute now. There was no way Murmur would have allowed any delay in completing the spell's final purpose, not when he'd sacrificed himself to make it possible.

Finally, she started to realize that he might not have written instructions because he didn't *want* to ask her to bring him back. Because he understood that he'd betrayed her and knew she'd be angry.

So he left the choice up to her. He'd left the information for her to find and asked for nothing.

Allowing her to choose whether he lived again or stayed dead forever.

If that wasn't an extremely backward, fucked-up way of asking for forgiveness, she didn't know what was.

There she sat with his lifeless body, a detailed manual on how to resurrect him, a limited timeframe in which to do it . . . and a serious choice to make.

Yet in the end, there was no choice at all.

Despite what he'd done, her heart screamed with unbearable pain if she even considered the idea of him being dead. It hurt so bad, it felt like her ribs were collapsing and crushing the air from her lungs. In his own fucked-up way, Murmur *had* cared for her. He'd wronged her, but in an even more unhinged way, he'd also tried to make amends.

She didn't have to forgive him, but if she did this, they'd be even, and she wouldn't have to face the anguish of losing him forever. He'd died so she could live.

And now she was going to bring him back.

# 32

# Damned if You Do, Damned if You Don't

THE MOTHERFUCKER HAD THOUGHT OF EVERYTHING.

The following morning, Belial sat alone in his bedroom and reread Murmur's letter for the hundredth time. After he'd received it the day before, he'd pocketed the piece of paper and returned to his brothers in the living room.

He'd sat in stunned silence and listened to them debate what to do about a problem that no longer mattered. Sensing something was off, they'd asked him repeatedly if he was okay, and he'd had to reassure them that he was fine, just tired, stressed, blah, blah, blah.

Because Murmur had specified in the letter that he couldn't tell anyone.

That fucking letter had told him he couldn't do a lot of things, in fact.

He couldn't hesitate to fulfill the request—a clause he had already pushed the limits of. He justified it by telling himself he needed to take time to ensure he understood every aspect of his task before acting, but he could feel the terms of the contract tugging at the edges of his mind, and he knew he couldn't put it off much longer.

He couldn't ask for help, even if he didn't tell the person what he was doing. He couldn't ask someone else to do it for him, which left out using one of the ninety-seven remaining favors Naiamah owed him. He couldn't injure himself or provoke someone into injuring him to avoid doing the favor. The favor was still valid in the event of Murmur's death. And if Murmur wasn't dead, Bel couldn't kill him—for fun or out of spite.

When Belial had first agreed to owe the favor, he'd stipulated that Murmur couldn't ask him to do anything that would put him or anyone he cared about in danger. Murmur had justified it in the letter by saying that his task in itself was perfectly safe. Any danger that followed—and there was a hell of a lot—would follow after the completion of the task. Since Belial hadn't specified *indirect* danger, there was therefore no violation.

No matter how carefully he read the contract, he couldn't find a single loophole.

But one thing that struck him was the careful wording of the conditions in the event of Murmur's death. Because it almost sounded like the Necromancer expected himself to be dead.

*Good*, Belial thought. Because if he wasn't dead, Bel was going to kill him after this. He'd known what he was getting into when he'd agreed to owe Murmur two unspecified favors. He knew it better than anyone. Some of the shit he'd forced Naiamah to do over the years still made him feel guilty when he thought about it now, centuries later. But he'd never expected this. He'd underestimated Murmur. By a lot.

He'd always suspected the Necromancer was up to something big, but this . . . What Bel was about to do would change his life as he knew it. In fact, it had the potential to change the life of every single being in Hell. And he was sure Murmur had been planning that all along.

The underworld war that Belial had been trying for millennia to avoid? Murmur wanted to kick-start it. And once Bel did this task, he would have. Whether or not he was dead, the Necromancer would succeed in his objective. And what a legacy to leave behind.

Hell was about to face a shitstorm of biblical proportions.

And Belial would be at the center of it.

It took Suyin sixteen hours of nonstop work to finish preparations for the spell.

Her entire living room was stripped bare, and she'd scrubbed away every scrap of evidence that she'd ever done magic there. Then she'd begun drawing the necromancy sigil and collecting the necessary ingredients.

There was a bird cage by the window with half a dozen pigeons in it. That was the part she felt the worst about. The spell required a death sacrifice of some kind, and Murmur's grimoire had recommended any number of animals. But not only was Suyin not keen on killing a goat or a sheep, she didn't want the large amount of blood those animals were sure to have spilling all over her apartment.

So after doing careful research in Murmur's books, she'd determined that she could swap one large sacrifice for several smaller ones. Pigeons were populous enough in this city, and the world wouldn't miss a few of them.

A baited trap on the roof of her apartment building had made the process easy, and she'd gotten all the birds she needed throughout the course of the day while she was busy with the rest of the prep.

But damn, she felt sick every time she looked at the cooing birds, awaiting their fate in blissful ignorance. She vowed that after this she would feed pigeons for the rest of her life to make up for it. Murmur could pay for the bird food.

As for him, she'd washed the blood from his skin and combed the tangles out of his hair. Even though she knew he couldn't feel it, she put a small pillow beneath his head and covered him with a blanket, leaving his face uncovered so he appeared to be resting.

*Just resting. Yeah right. This is fucked up on too many levels to count.*

Though his wounds remained and black veins still spidered out from his eyes, his body still showed no signs of decay, and she figured it never would. Apparently, though a demon with a soul could die by having it removed, their body still wouldn't disintegrate without hellfire.

She figured Murmur must have guessed this would happen, which was why he'd left her the way to bring him back. He always thought of everything.

After the long, sleepless night, she straightened from staring at the book on her desk, grimacing as she stretched her stiff back and felt it crack. She looked around the room and then back down at the book, and her eyes widened as she realized she was actually ready. She'd gathered all the supplies and triple-checked that every part of the sigil had been executed properly.

Now she just needed some extra manpower. Or *woman*-power, as it were.

Prepping the spell was only half the battle. To actually do the casting, she would need to focus with great intensity, visualizing the sigil in her mind with such clarity, there would be nothing else in her thoughts. She would also need to chant the Sheolic incantation Murmur supplied in the grimoire, over and over, with increasing intensity.

But even then, she didn't think her power alone would be enough. This was the highest level of necromancy, and if she wanted to be strong enough to complete the spell, she would need a couple of powerful witches backing her up.

Luckily, she knew just who to ask.

She fired off a message to both Iris and her twin, Lily, asking them to meet her as soon as possible. Luckily, both sisters were available, and they made plans to convene at a nearby cafe.

After eating a quick breakfast, Suyin said goodbye to Murmur and her bird sacrifices—well aware of how absurd that was—and then headed to the cafe, rehearsing her story again and again, hoping like hell she'd be able to convince the twins.

When they arrived, their friendly smiles dropped as soon as they saw Suyin, their expressions morphing into concern.

She could guess what she looked like. She hadn't combed her hair in days, and she was pale with dark circles under her eyes from lack of sleep. And despite her usual aversion to caffeine, she was sipping the triple-shot espresso in her hands like it was the elixir of eternal life.

"Hey," Iris said warily, sliding into the booth across from Suyin while Lily offered a small wave. She could tell they were both dying to ask what was wrong but were too polite to jump right into it.

"I need your help," Suyin said immediately. "And it has to be now." There was no point beating around the bush.

"Sure," Iris said immediately. "What's up?"

"First . . ." She took a breath. "I need you to swear you won't tell anyone until after. Especially your demon boyfriends and their brothers."

The sisters exchanged glances.

"Um . . . why?" Iris asked.

"I can't tell you until you agree."

"We can't promise to help you with something and not tell anyone what we're doing if we don't know what it is," Lily said gently.

"All I can say is that it's magic related, and the spell won't put you or anyone you care about in danger—beyond the expected dangers that come with practicing highly advanced magic."

The sisters exchanged glances again. They had that psychic-twin-bond thing going on, Suyin noticed, which wasn't something they'd had in the past. She figured that since Iris had come clean to Lily about how their parents died, they'd gotten closer. She was glad for them both. They deserved to have that connection.

"Su . . ." Iris made an apologetic face. "Look, I'm guessing this has something to do with Murmur, which is why you don't want us to tell the guys. While I understand you believe you have some kinda friendship or whatever, I don't think it's wise for me and Lily to get involved in anything he's doing."

They probably thought she was trying to get them involved with Murmur's latest murder plot. Unfortunately, it was far worse than that.

She took a breath. "I really didn't want to have to do this, because I don't want to view our friendship as a transaction, but . . . I have to."

The twins frowned.

"You both owe me, and I'm calling it in."

There was a pause as that sank in.

Suyin pressed on. "When I heard that you guys were here, looking for another blood-born to lead the coven and help you maintain your protection spell, I dropped my entire life in New York and came to you. And I've been maintaining that cloaking spell ever since, even when you lied to me about still needing it. I didn't do it as some sort of exchange, but if I have to use it that way now to get you to help me, I will. I *need* your help, and you both owe me."

Lily pursed her lips. Iris looked a combination of guilty and exasperated.

"Can we tell the guys about it after we're done . . . whatever it is?" Lily asked.

"Yes."

"And it won't put anyone we care about in danger?"

"No."

Lily searched Suyin's face for a moment with narrowed eyes, and then she nodded. "All right. I'm in."

"Lil," Iris hissed out of the corner of her mouth. "You sure?"

"Yes. She's right. She did us a huge favor, and now she's asking for help, and I think we should give it to her."

"But what about Murmur?"

Lily shrugged and glanced at Suyin. "She said we won't be in danger."

Iris looked at Suyin.

"I swear," Suyin said.

Iris blew out a breath. "Does it have to be right now?"

"Yes." Every minute they waited was a minute closer to the window of opportunity closing. For all she knew, it had closed already.

"All right. I'm in too. But I'm telling Meph about it as soon as we're done. I don't like keeping secrets."

"You can write a whole book about it if you want. I hope it's a bestseller."

"Fine. So what do you want us to do?"

Suyin took a breath. "I think it's better if I show you."

Bel stood in his office staring at the summoning seal still inscribed on the floor. He'd kept the door closed since leaving the room yesterday, and his brothers knew better than to snoop in his house behind closed doors.

No one but him knew it was here. No one but him knew what he was about to do.

He pulled Murmur's now-crumpled letter from his pocket and tossed it onto the desk. "I swear to god I'll kill you for this," he growled at the paper, as if the writer himself could hear him.

And then he stepped into the seal.

The world spun and flipped over, and then Bel found himself standing . . . in chaos.

He was in a library, but that was the least of his concerns. The room was black, save for the orange glow of fire that shone from the tall window across the room. As if the world outside was on fire. Roaring could be heard in the distance, and there was a faint rumbling that felt vaguely like an earthquake approaching.

But again, that was the least of his concerns.

There was a complex sigil in the middle of the room, surrounded by a shitstorm of scattered paper and spilled blood. Some of it had been used to draw the sigil, and plenty more had pooled around the outside.

In the center of the design was a giant black-and-purple spinning vortex.

*The portal.*

Cursing inwardly, Bel took two steps toward it, intending to get this over with as quickly as possible, so he could return home and prepare for the aftermath. But he stopped abruptly.

He was in Hell for the first time since he'd escaped with his brothers. Mist, Meph, and Raum had all been back briefly since they'd escaped, but Bel hadn't. He blew out a breath and felt some of the ever-present tension leave his shoulders.

The air was foul, the sky was red, and there was nearly constant war and violence, but . . . it did kinda feel good to be back. Just knowing he could lose control and burst into flames without the same consequences as on Earth was a relief.

It didn't matter now anyway. He was about to shake things

up in a major way. After today, all the shit he'd been worrying about for the past year was going to be the least of his concerns.

He took a breath and continued toward the spiraling vortex of doom. *Let's get this over with.*

The three witches stood in Suyin's living room, two of them with their mouths hanging open.

"Oh my god," Lily breathed, staring at the enormous sigil, candles, herbs, cage of pigeons, and "sleeping" demon on the floor.

"What in the fuck?" Iris said. "Is that—"

"Murmur," Lily gasped.

"Is he . . . asleep?"

"He's dead," Suyin said, and they both stared at her.

It was almost comical, the way their bugging eyes jumped between her and Murmur's body.

"That's impossible," Iris said. "The only way to kill a demon is to cut off their head and burn the pieces with hellfire."

"The only way to kill a *soulless* demon," Suyin corrected.

"What does that mean?"

"A demon with a soul will die if their soul is separated from their body." She gestured to Murmur. "As evidenced." To another, her unemotional demeanor might have seemed cold, but that numbness was the only reason she'd made it this far. If she'd allowed so much as a glimmer of despair or grief to break through, she would've lost it.

"But— Oh my god."

"Wait. Murmur has a soul?" Lily whispered.

She nodded.

"And how did he end up . . . like this?" Iris asked.

"It's a long story."

"We're gonna need an explanation, Su."

That was fair enough. And honestly, it would be good to get this off her chest. The shit she'd been carrying around for the last couple days was too much for one person to handle alone.

So she took a breath, and she told them everything. Murmur's death had voided their blood vow, and she found she could talk freely. She even told them how he'd carved the death mark into her skin.

When she finished, the sisters looked like they'd seen a ghost. Or a dead necromancer about to be resurrected.

"Are you sure you want to bring him back?" Iris asked. "I mean . . . Fuck."

Suyin knew exactly what she meant. "It's fucked up what he did, but he also died to avoid killing me. I owe him this at least. When it's over and he's alive again, he'll go back to Hell, and I'll never see him again. But he sacrificed himself for me. I have to do this."

"I can understand that," Lily said, but Iris was still staring at the demon on the floor suspiciously.

"It's just . . . I'm not sure I think it's smart to bring him back," Iris said. "He's been causing trouble for Meph and his brothers since we first got mixed up with him."

"I know you don't trust him, but I owe him, Ris. It doesn't matter what he's done or what he still might do. I have to do this to get a clean slate so I can move on with my life. I'll never be able to let this go if I don't."

"I'm in," Lily said. "I'll help you."

"Lily." Iris winced. "You're always so quick to put your faith in people. I just don't think it's so simple this time."

"It is. Yes, Murmur betrayed us, but he also helped us. We never would have been able to rescue Mist from Paimon's lair if he hadn't shown up."

"But—"

"I believe in second chances," Lily said. "And I also believe in forgiveness." She gave her sister a pointed look. "I think you of all people should recognize the value of those things."

There was a weighted silence.

And then Iris sighed. "You're right, I do understand the value of forgiveness. I don't like it, but I'm choosing to trust your judgment, Suyin." She clapped her hands. "So? Where do we start?"

Suyin took a breath. "First, we chant. And then I have to kill a bunch of pigeons."

# 33

# Free Spirit

The second Belial's foot touched the edge of the portal, it sucked him straight into its vortex. But this spell wasn't like a hellgate. It wasn't a rough ride. Instead, it felt like his body briefly vaporized into tiny particles, only to reform again on the other side.

This spell must have required untold sacrifices and magic to penetrate straight through Lucifer's ironclad defenses and into the center of . . . wherever this was. Of course it didn't function like a normal gate.

Bel looked around.

For the most part, everything was blackness. He was standing in a long tunnel, the purple glowing portal still swirling around him.

Ahead of him was a stone door. On that door was inscribed a seal. The lines had been drawn in blood, and at one time they would have glowed red with Sheolic magic. But thanks to Murmur, the magic had been broken. Now they were only faded and cracked lines, the old blood already flaking away.

All Bel had to do was walk forward and open that door. Then his task would be complete and he would be free to go. Judging by the absence of anyone in the library and the chaos reigning outside, Bel suspected that the Necromancer was indeed dead, though he didn't know how or why. His second favor would never have to be fulfilled. He would be free of Murmur forever.

He would also have Lucifer after him and way bigger problems to deal with, but he'd cross that bridge when he came to it.

He stepped forward out of the portal, and paused for a moment to look behind it. A tunnel stretched before him, leading into darkness. His nape prickled. A suspicion arose, but it was too inconceivable to believe.

Curiosity got the best of him. He turned, careful to inch around the edge of the portal so he didn't get sucked prematurely back to the library, and then he walked down the tunnel.

The faint purple glow of the portal was the only source of light, and as he moved farther past it, it faded to complete darkness. He guided himself by keeping one hand on the wall. A voice whispered in his head that he was fucking crazy for walking down a black tunnel with no idea where he was going, especially when his task was back in the opposite direction.

But he had to know.

With his next step, the ground dropped out beneath him.

His foot landed on empty space, and he was halfway into transferring his weight forward before he lurched back. He swayed briefly over the steep drop before correcting his balance, heart pounding.

A fall like that wouldn't kill him—he was a demon with wings after all—but nobody liked the sensation of a sudden, unexpected plummet into an abyss.

Despite the impossibility of it, he suddenly knew exactly where he was.

He stepped back to the edge of the precipice, leaning out as far as he could, and looked down.

Sure enough, far below, he could make out a flickering orange glow. A lake of fire, filling the entire bottom of the chasm he was peering into. He twisted and looked up. The edges of the enormous pit rose for what looked like miles. High above, he could see the faintest smear of the red sky.

The longer he stared, the more his eyes adjusted, until he could discern faint smoke spiraling around the inner walls of the chasm.

Souls.

He knew how this place worked. After death, human souls were judged. Those who were unworthy were sent to Hell to face penance for their evil misdeeds. They were sorted into nine levels. Nine layers of suffering, worsening depending on the amount of evil staining the soul.

Belial was standing somewhere in the Nine Rings.

No one was supposed to come here. Not even Lucifer.

The giant chasm of the Nine Rings was in the center of Lucifer's territory. No one dared even fly over it, lest they be sucked into the vortex of souls below. The Rings were guarded by reaper-like beings who oversaw the souls within. Those beings never left the pit, and no one who wasn't supposed to be there entered. If they did, they never returned to tell the tale.

The High King's lair surrounded the Rings, and it was his job to guard it, ensuring no one trespassed into the forbidden chasm, and that the souls who went in didn't come out until they were ready for reincarnation.

All that Murmur's letter had told him was that he was to take a portal to Lucifer's territory and open a door. But he hadn't mentioned anything about the Nine-fucking-Rings. Why would there be a door with the High King's seal on it here of all places? And what was behind it?

Belial backed away from the edge.

He couldn't answer the many questions he had, but he could get himself the fuck out of here. He wasn't supposed to be here, and he feared that if he stayed too long, the guardians would find him.

His blood cold, he made his way back down the tunnel until the faint glow of the portal reappeared. He sidestepped it carefully once more and approached the forbidden door. The door that Murmur had evidently died trying to gain access to.

*Why?* He supposed he was about to find out.

The door had no handle and no hinges, and was in fact just a huge block of stone set in front of an opening. It would take impossible strength to move, but Lucifer had that in spades.

Bel reached around to grasp it, but the stone was larger than his arm span. He gritted his teeth. He was too small to reach it in human form. Of course he was.

He stood back. Closed his eyes. Curled his hands into fists. And then he breathed out in a long, deep exhalation.

And he gave into the rage.

The internal walls he'd built around it fell away, and a fiery ecstasy charged through his veins. His vision was overtaken by fire. Everywhere he looked he saw flames, and it was fucking glorious. He wanted to burn alive in it. He wanted to destroy everything in his path. He wanted to bathe in blood and stand atop the crumbling ruins of the world, knowing he had brought about its end.

Through the intoxicating rush of his inner darkness, he maintained a tenuous grasp on the present. He was so tall now, his head hit the roof of the tunnel. And he could have gotten much bigger, had he the space.

He reached out, wrapping his arms around the heavy block of stone. In this state, the stone felt light, and he gripped it easily. He turned, hefting the enormous piece of rock, and with a roar, chucked it down the tunnel, past the portal, and into the chasm beyond.

At his back, he felt an ice-cold blast.

He spun around. The opening before him was pitch-black, but he could hear moans and screams within. And then suddenly, there was a rushing sound, like a river breaking free from a dam.

And then souls came.

They blew past him, shooting with powerful force down the tunnel. Their essences brushed against him, offering him glimpses of their lives and memories . . . and he knew.

He knew exactly what Murmur had done.

From the depths of the lightless chasm, the soul cried for release, his cry mingling with the others. Thousands of haunted, voiceless screams, were trapped in this blighted place. There was no release for them, no end to their suffering. The great dragon sucked their essences, draining them like water from a punctured vessel. They knew only darkness.

To them, death had not meant release, but enslavement.

But then . . . everything changed.

The door was opened. And there was freedom at last.

Suddenly, the soul was rushing toward some unknown destination. Thousands of other souls went with him, all chasing their long-sought salvation.

But then he felt a tug. A tether, drawing him back.

Not back in the direction of the prison, but . . . somewhere else. To a place that had once meant everything to him but now seemed like a distant memory. Did he want to go back there? He could sense that if it fought hard enough, he could snap the tether and continue on.

But . . . something called him back.

Some voiceless, faceless longing told him that he had unfinished business. It told him that there were wrongs he had to right, mistakes he'd made that he had to atone for.

So he surrendered, and he let the tether take him.

He was sucked backward. He slammed into a confined vessel, his formless essence imprisoned by atoms and molecules. Rushing rivers of blood deafened his inner ear. The throbbing pulse of life beat like a drum.

And then he sucked in a breath . . . and opened his eyes.

Soaring through burning skies, high above the scorched plains and bone-littered mountains, the High King of Hell let out a mighty roar.

Ahead, the Necromancer's lair loomed, its stone spires like a dark crown. He'd been flying rapidly toward it, planning to take that castle apart piece by piece until he found the traitor within, feasting on the flesh of any creature who stood in his way.

Instead, he froze midflight. It could not be. Surely he was mistaken.

And yet . . . Suddenly weakened, his wing beats faltered, and he plummeted toward the ground below. Just before he made impact, he managed to gather his wits enough to pump his wings and bring himself back to altitude. But his mind continued reeling.

In the heart of his fortified territory, in the deepest, darkest depths of the Nine Rings . . .

A door had opened.

His secret source of power had been compromised. The souls he had imprisoned were rushing out, finding the freedom he had denied them.

The High King opened his throat and roared with impossible fury.

It was a roar so great, the entire underworld shook. The plains trembled, cracks snaking along the hardened surface. Boulders tumbled from the tops of lifeless mountains.

Demons from all across the land screamed and covered their ears. Some fell into the fissures opening in the ground. Others were crushed by falling rock and debris.

Lucifer angled his wings and turned his great body around, flying back toward his territory with all the speed he possessed. But he already knew what he would find. He already knew who had fired the first shot and rekindled an ancient feud. He was the High King, and he could sense the presence of his oldest, greatest enemy within the center of his territory.

Belial wanted a war? Then he would get one.

With a startled gasp, Suyin lurched back, away from the body she knelt beside, falling onto her hands. Behind her, outside the sigil, Iris cursed and Lily muffled her scream with a palm.

Murmur's pitch-black eyes had opened. His chest rose and fell with breath.

Suyin waited, her heart slamming in her chest. Would he speak? Would he recognize her? Everyone knew the consequences of necromancy could be disastrous. He was awake, but that didn't mean their spell had been successful.

It happened in a blink.

One minute she was staring at his vacant expression. The next, he was moving. *Fast.*

He lurched upright and his arm shot out, fixing around her throat. With a single, fluid movement, he slammed her down onto the floor and loomed over her. Her breath rushed out as she hit the ground.

"Where am I?" he snarled into her face. If he was in fight-or-flight, he'd gone with *fight*.

But the sound of his voice triggered something, and it hit her suddenly. That gravelly, deep voice, always rougher than she expected . . . It was *him*. He was really here.

"You're alive," she whispered, her throat tightening with emotion.

He blinked and went still.

Slowly, she lifted a hand to his chest, not daring to believe she'd feel a heart beating beneath her palm.

But it was there, thudding steadily.

"Suyin—" Iris's panicked voice cut through the haze.

"I'm fine," she replied, careful to keep her voice soft. "Don't come closer."

Murmur's grip tightened on her throat, and he glanced over to where Iris and Lily stood. With his eyes solid black, she could only tell where he was looking because his head turned. The twins obeyed her request and didn't approach, but their faces were full of shock and disbelief.

Suyin could relate. They'd done it. They'd actually brought Murmur back from the dead. It was going to take a while for that to sink in.

But he was obviously confused. Did he know who she was? Had he suffered some kind of brain injury because of the time his body was in stasis?

"It's me," she said. "You were dead, but we brought you back."

His frown deepened, drawing a line between his brows.

"Do you remember what happened? When you died?"

His face scrunched up, like he was struggling to remember.

"You did a spell to free Lucifer's trapped souls. You were successful, but you had to sacrifice yourself in the process. You left me those books, and I found the marked page and figured out how to resurrect you."

He continued to stare blankly at her. She had no idea whether she was getting through to him or not. She had no idea if he even knew who she was.

"Murmur? Do you remember me?"

"Yes, I—" He squeezed his eyes shut as if in pain. "The voices." His eyes snapped open again.

She frowned, trying to understand.

"The voices are quiet."

"What voices?"

"Where are the voices?"

"What voices are you talking about?"

"Where are the voices?! They're always there, screaming. They never stop."

He shook his head roughly and then released her throat and sat up, gripping his hair tightly and hunching forward. "Can never have a moment's peace. Can never be alone. Can never sleep. Can never rest."

Suyin sat up, looking over at Iris and Lily, who were still frozen. She shook her head in response to their unspoken question. She didn't have a clue what to do.

Looking back at Murmur and feeling some nurturing instinct she hadn't known she possessed, she reached out and placed a hand on his back. His skin was cold, but not as cold as she'd expected. "It's okay," she whispered. "You're okay."

He shivered at her touch but didn't throw her off or erupt into violence like she'd feared. He appeared to be cognizant enough and didn't seem to be turning into a flesh-eating zombie or whatever could've happened if the spell had gone wrong.

"I'm so tired," he whispered.

"It's okay. You can rest now."

"I've been tired for centuries. Can never sleep. The voices are always screaming. Now they're quiet. Can't tell what's worse."

She stroked his cool skin, wishing there was some way to comfort him. But he seemed lost to his thoughts, to the turmoil inside his head.

"It was so dark there. Never-ending darkness. Darker than black. And so cold. I'm always so cold."

He was obviously in shock. He'd been dead and stuck in Lucifer's horrible prison. He'd told her of the screams he heard in his visions, so whatever that place was like, it was obviously torture. He would need time and rest to get back to himself, and he probably wouldn't be able to relax with Lily and Iris here.

She looked up at the twins. "You guys should go."

Their expressions indicated reluctance to leave her alone with the unstable, freshly resurrected demon.

"I'll be fine," she assured them, speaking softly lest she upset Murmur. "He just needs to sleep it off, I think."

"He's actually alive," Iris whispered, eyes wide. "We did it."

Suyin nodded, and the three of them exchanged glances. Despite everything, they couldn't help but share pride in what they had accomplished. She was sure they were one of a very limited number of witches who had ever succeeded at magic of this level.

"Are you sure we shouldn't stay?" Lily asked.

Suyin nodded again. "I think he'll come out of it quicker if we're alone."

"Just . . . keep your phone handy," Iris said. "Call me if he does anything weird."

"If he decides to get stabby," Lily muttered, "she may not have time to call."

Murmur stiffened. And then he slowly lowered his hands and looked up. His hair hung forward, shadowing his face. With his eyes pure black and those dark veins spidering beneath them, he looked terrifying. And he was looking at Lily and Iris with pure murder in his expression.

Suyin needed to get them out of here for their own safety.

"I'll be fine," she assured them, sincerely hoping that was true. "I'll call if I need help, okay?"

The twins were briefly petrified by the sinister glare Murmur was giving them. He looked like something straight out of a horror movie.

"I don't think he'll relax until you're gone," Suyin said.

Lily finally nodded and pulled Iris toward the door. "We both have our phones."

"I want hourly updates," Iris said. "If you miss one, I'm bringing the cavalry."

"Thank you," Suyin told them before they left. "I couldn't have done this without you both."

Iris just shook her head. "I really hope you don't regret this."

# 34

# One for Sorrow

Somehow, Suyin helped a disoriented, unsteady Murmur climb to his feet and find his way to her bedroom, where he immediately collapsed. The wounds on his torso and forearms had already started to heal, she noticed. The cuts were closed and already fading.

He really was alive.

He was shivering, so she pulled the blankets over him. He curled up on his side, hair over his face. She reached out and tucked it back, swallowing the lump in her throat. She hadn't forgotten his betrayal, but she couldn't be cold toward him right now. Not when he was like this.

Assuming he was asleep, she was just about to step back from the bed when he mumbled, "Am I dead?" His eyes opened a crack, and it seemed a great effort for him to focus on her face.

"You're alive, Murmur. I brought you back." Against her better judgment, she stroked back another lock of silvery hair.

"I must be dead," he said, closing his eyes again. "That's the only way I could be here with you. That's the only way

you would be comforting me instead of sinking a blade into my chest."

She swallowed. She didn't know how to respond to that.

His eyes opened, and he stared ahead but didn't seem to see her. "But I can't be in Heaven. Not after what I did. So this must be Hell. The Nine Rings. Which level am I in? The ninth, I'm sure. The deepest circle, reserved for the treacherous, the worst of all sinners—"

"Murmur, you're not—"

He sat up with a jerk and lurched away from her. "Don't touch me. Torture me however you will, but don't use her face. I'll survive anything but that—"

"Murmur, just listen to me—"

He closed his eyes again, slumping against the headboard. "But I deserve it, don't I? I suppose I'll have to spend eternity in this room, reliving what I did. I'll be forced to face my worst—"

"You're not in Hell!" she shouted just to get his attention before he fell any farther into his delusion.

His eyes opened once more.

"You're not in Hell, Murmur. You're on Earth. In my bedroom. You're alive, okay? You were dead, but I brought you back to life."

He stared blankly at her, and she wondered if any part of him understood what she was saying.

And then he began to shake, and he grasped his arms as if freezing cold. "The things I've done," he mumbled, dropping his head. "Terrible things. Unforgivable things. I deserve the worst. I must be dead because I can't be here. I can't be free of the voices. I can't—"

"Murmur—" Fuck, her heart hurt, and unshed tears blurred her vision. She could barely stand to witness this. She couldn't imagine how much worse it would feel to experience it firsthand. She shifted forward on the mattress, lifting the blanket and trying to draw it up to his shoulders. "Just lie down and get some rest, okay?"

Gripping his arms, she tried to guide him back down to the pillows. Remarkably, he let her, sliding down the mattress until his head rested beside her lap.

"Stay with me?" He was obviously exhausted. His eyes were closed, and his breathing was already deepening.

"Yes, I'll stay," she whispered through the tightness in her throat. "Just go to sleep. I'll be here, I promise."

"I'll face the pain when I wake. Let me pretend . . . a moment longer . . ."

His voice trailed off, and his muscles relaxed.

She blew out a breath and swiped at her eyes. He was the Necromancer, and evil backstabber or not, she hated seeing such a powerful force reduced to this. She allowed herself one last moment of weakness and stroked a final piece of silver-white hair back from his pale face.

And then she stood and backed away. She would keep her promise, but she also needed to protect herself. She sank to the floor on the opposite side of the room, back against the wall.

Murmur was asleep in her bed. Because he was traumatized after having been brought back to life. Because he had been dead for nearly two days.

What the hell was her life? It was insane. Madness.

She tried to block the sympathy that filled her. She had to harden her heart.

She had cut people from her life for far less than what he'd done to her. She never forgave and she never gave second chances. She'd always been that way, and she wasn't ashamed of it. The world was a cruel and lonely place, and she'd learned to protect herself before anyone else.

Iris had warned her that Murmur was a liar, and she had learned firsthand how true that was. She would never be able to take him at his word again without wondering how many different ways he could twist it. Even if he swore a vow, she could never trust him not to find some minute loophole and exploit it the second it suited him.

When he was awake, they would go their separate ways. While he'd been dead, she'd been heartbroken, and she'd let go of her anger and been willing to forgive him.

But he was alive again, which meant she wasn't forgiving shit.

Belial landed back in the summoning seal in his office on Earth, fighting to get the rage under control. He hadn't willingly surrendered to it in a long time. It was only his shock about what he'd just witnessed that gave him any power over it at all.

But that didn't mean he didn't come back as a flaming tornado, because he did. He punched several holes in the walls and swept all the contents of the desk onto the floor.

He'd just picked up said desk and hefted it overhead, ready to throw it into the punctured drywall, when Ash and Raum came bursting through the door.

He hadn't even realized they were here. His brothers were like stray cats. He fed them once, and they just kept showing up unannounced. Luckily, it appeared Mist and Meph were elsewhere, so he only had to deal with two of them for now.

"What the hell is going on?!" Asmodeus shouted.

There was a whole lot of commotion, which Bel mostly tuned out as he threw the desk into the wall and watched it crumple, the decorative legs snapping off as it crashed back onto the floor.

And then a bucket of ice-cold water hit him in his face.

Always Raum with the goddamn water. Still, it did the trick.

Bel blinked and found himself standing in carnage, his wet hair dripping in his eyes, his brothers staring at him. He slowly regained his normal height and state of mind.

"Fuck," he said.

Asmodeus nodded knowingly.

"What happened?" Raum asked, lowering the bucket like it was a weapon at the end of a battle.

"Murmur called in his first favor."

Asmodeus and Raum exchanged looks. "What was it?" Raum asked.

Murmur's stupid fucking letter hadn't said Bel couldn't tell anyone what he was up to *after* he completed the task, so he went right ahead and told them. "Remember how you used to be afraid of what would happen to demons who evolved after death?" Bel asked Asmodeus.

His brother nodded warily.

"Well, I just learned the answer to that."

"What? How?"

Bel took a breath and started at the beginning, explaining everything—Murmur's letter, the empty library, the portal, the stone door with the broken seal. He told them about the Nine Rings, and the prison he'd opened. He explained how the trapped souls had whooshed past him on their flight to freedom, and as they touched him, he'd seen glimpses of their lives and memories.

"They were all demons. I even knew some of them." He dragged a hand through his sopping hair, pulling it back from his face. He was glad he'd left it long after his last rage. That would have been a waste of a haircut. "Lucifer was keeping them trapped in the Nine Rings, locked behind some kind of seal. I think he must have been using them as a power source, feeding off them."

"Thank fuck we didn't die," Raum said unhelpfully.

Bel shook his head. "Murmur wanted to kick off a war. Why else would he have had me open the door? He knew Lucifer would be able to sense me in his territory and would retaliate."

"Fuck," Ash said.

"But why would Murmur do that?"

"Who the fuck knows what that creep gets up to? But . . ." Bel looked out the window. "I felt them. The demon souls. They were miserable. And Murmur freed them. I could almost respect him for that."

"Maybe that's what he was really trying to achieve."

Bel shook his head. "Guess we'll never know, seeing as he's probably dead now."

"Yeahhh, about that."

They all looked over as Meph's head popped into the doorframe, and the rest of his body followed shortly after.

"I couldn't help but overhear this highly stimulating conversation as I walked in the front door," he said. "And I came because I have some news to deliver."

"What," Bel growled, already sure he wasn't going to like it.

"Murmur isn't dead. Well. He *was* dead. But he isn't anymore."

"What?" Ash, Raum, and Bel said simultaneously.

"Yeah, I just got off the phone with Iris. Suyin enlisted her and Lily's help in a resurrection spell, and they actually pulled it off, those crazy bitches. They necromanced the Necromancer right back from the dead."

"You're kidding me."

"Nope." Meph shook his head. "Wish I was."

Forget respecting Murmur. Bel wasn't free from his goddamn second favor. He wasn't free of the fucking virus of a demon that kept popping up at all the worst times and making everyone's life difficult. Never mind the sense of relief Bel had felt after completing Murmur's final wish.

"I'm gonna kill that zombie freak," Bel snarled. "And this time I'll make sure he stays dead."

Murmur awoke to unfamiliar smells. And quiet. The quiet was so penetrating, it stirred him from rest. It was so quiet, it felt somehow loud.

His body was surrounded by softness and warmth. The air smelled fresh, and there was a subtle scent surrounding him that was both familiar and comforting.

But the *quiet*. There were no screams. No voices. No fingernails scraping against the chalkboard edges of his mind. Those screams had been his constant, undying companion for millennia—as far back as his memory extended. The sudden absence of them now was disconcerting, to say the least.

He opened his eyes, frowning at the white ceiling above him for several seconds until it finally sank in where he was. He turned his head and confirmed it. *Suyin's bedroom.* But how . . . ?

It hit him in a rush. He'd been *dead*. He was dead.

Wait, *was* he dead?

He sat up, blankets falling to his waist, and looked around. No, he couldn't be dead. This was definitely Earth, and he was definitely alive. He lifted his hands and stared at them. He saw the same familiar palms darkening to black fingertips and claws. He held out his arms and studied them too. They were the same. Familiar. Free of scars despite the countless times he had carved into them to draw his blood for magic.

Everything about his body was familiar—the weight of his horns atop his head, the feel of his hair loose against his bare back—and yet something about his body felt decidedly *un*familiar.

But then he realized it was because the mind that occupied his body was different.

His thoughts were quiet. Clear. When he closed his eyes and

concentrated on his breathing, everything else fell away, save for the sensation of his chest rising and falling.

He breathed in deeply, and suddenly, emotion tightened his throat.

The very act of drawing breath felt like a revelation. The silence was liberation.

His eyes popped open. He shifted to the edge of the bed, pulling the blankets off and taking a moment to feel the cool floorboards beneath his feet.

When was the last time he'd felt something like that? The screaming of tormented souls in his mind had blocked out all else, and his body had existed in a perpetually deadened state. He'd never felt much of anything . . . until *she* had come along.

He stroked a hand across the blankets, noticing the softness of the duvet cover and marveling that such a texture even existed. He thought of how the blankets had felt against his skin, the weight of them pressing down, trapping him against the mattress.

But it was a comforting weight. It didn't feel like shackles or confinement. In fact, the memory of shackles felt distant and far away in the face of so much sensation. How could he focus on an ancient memory when he could *feel* so clearly that it was blankets and not manacles?

That was why he'd been able to fight the panic when he was with Suyin, he realized. Because she had brought him to the present moment. She had made him feel. How could he fixate on the distant, dark past when she was right there with him, bringing his body to life?

He stood. His legs shook beneath his weight, but it was a temporary weakness and it quickly passed. He reached back and wound his hair into a long braid, tying it off with a convenient circular band he found on Suyin's nightstand. Then he crossed the room and eased open the door. Stooping under the frame so his horns didn't catch, he stepped into the hallway.

Instinct had him turning right, toward the living room, and he found her there. She was curled up on the couch with a blanket draped over her, fast asleep. She'd left him in her bed and come to sleep out here, by herself. Away from him.

He swallowed.

Crossing the room, he perched somewhat awkwardly on the arm of the couch. He didn't know what he was going to say to her. Everything, he supposed. There was no point holding anything back now.

She awoke gently, her eyes shifting beneath her lids before they blinked open. When she saw him sitting above her, she didn't startle, but he watched a certain hardness come over her features. She was closing herself off from him.

"You're awake," she said.

He nodded. He didn't know what to say. He didn't know how to begin.

"How are you feeling?"

"Better," he said. "The hallucinations have passed."

"Hallucinations?"

He shook his head. There was no need to tell her of the phantom images that had danced at the corners of his sight, making him believe he was trapped in the lowest level of the Nine Rings.

The silence in his head had added to his panic, but sleep had brought clarity. And understanding.

He had died. Which meant that every single soul in his army, bound to his command by an unbreakable bargain, had been set free. His mind was quiet, because for the first time in as long as he could remember, there was no one in his head but himself.

*I'm still here*, his inner voice whispered.

*I'll deal with you later,* he told it.

Suyin shifted backward, away from him, and sat up. She clutched the blankets to her chest like they were a barrier against him.

"Thank you," he said. "When I . . . did what I did, I didn't expect you to—"

"But you left the note. The torn piece of paper."

He lifted a shoulder. "It was a slim chance. The window was so short as the spell had to be performed before Belial carried out my favor, and I specifically stated that he could not hesitate. It's a miracle you were able to complete it in time."

"Belial opened the prison?" she asked.

He nodded and blew out a breath. "My work is complete."

"The souls are free? My father . . . ?"

"He is free to reunite with your mother, just as you wanted. They're all free."

Suyin swallowed thickly and nodded. There was silence as that sank in.

And then he knew it was time for him to face what he had done. "Suyin . . ."

"Don't," she said, stopping him before he could begin. "I can't— I know why you did what you did, and I know you couldn't follow through with it, but it still doesn't change the fact that you betrayed me. And I can't forgive that."

He looked down at his hands. All the relief and gratitude he'd felt at his renewed existence faded away like it had never been. What was the point in a second chance if he lost the one thing he'd found worth living for?

"I understand," he said, because it wasn't fair to burden her with his expectations. He deserved every bit of her distrust.

"You were going to *kill* me, Murmur." To his dismay, her voice shook slightly. "I just can't believe that you would— After everything we went through . . ."

"I know." His own voice felt tight. "I tricked myself into thinking I felt nothing. I'd gotten so good at sealing parts of myself away, I didn't even realize what I was doing anymore. I've never cared about anything before. I suppose I didn't recognize the feeling until it was too late."

And that was the truth, he realized. He straightened and stared at her, and the realization hit him in the most painful, obvious way.

She was the most important thing in his life. She was more important than any spell, any foreseen future. She mattered more than the fate of all Hell. He would give up anything for her, would do anything to have her, to make her happy, to make her want to stay with him. She was the greatest thing to ever happen to him, in all his immeasurably long life.

But the terrible irony was that he hadn't realized any of that until he'd committed the unforgivable. The thought of what he'd almost done made him feel sick now. He was appalled he'd even considered it.

But he hadn't just considered it—he'd *tried* to do it. Some part of his conscience he'd been blocking out had resisted, but that didn't excuse his actions.

He'd once wondered how it was possible that he had evolved a soul when he'd maintained his selfish, apathetic existence, but he understood now. The part of him that excelled at compartmentalizing his own mind had simply taken that newfound conscience and sealed it in a vault. It had been there all along—it was the very reason he'd developed feelings for Suyin in the first place—but he hadn't been aware of it because he'd closed himself off from it.

But now, with his head free of the screams, his mind quiet for the first time, he sensed it there, waiting, existing silently. He couldn't ignore it any longer. He wouldn't be able to ignore it ever again. And that was more than a little troubling when he contemplated the life he had to go back to.

"Suyin, I need you to understand," he began. "I feel everything now. I can't hide from myself, and I know that I lo—"

"It doesn't matter," she cut in. "I get why you did what you did. I'm angry, but I get it. But I don't trust you anymore. I can't ever trust you again. And there's nothing you can say that will change that."

"I'll swear a vow. I'll vow on my blood never to harm you, never to lie or withhold—"

"Stop." She lowered the blanket and held up a hand. "It doesn't matter if you swear a thousand vows because that's not how trust works. You shouldn't need an unbreakable blood contract to trust someone. The very nature of needing one proves you don't. And besides, I don't trust you not to find some hidden loophole and exploit it the moment it conveniences you.

"Maybe, if you'd just lied to me or done something else . . . I could have let it go. But you were going to *kill* me, and I can't—" She shook her head. "That's just not something I can forget."

"Suyin . . ." He understood her perfectly. He didn't blame her in the least. And yet he felt like his entire world was crumbling, and there was nothing he could do to stop it.

"Besides, you and me?" Her lips curved briefly, but her eyes remained sad. "We were never going to work out. You're a demon with a whole-ass kingdom in Hell. And I may be half demon, but my life is on Earth. You hate even thinking about shifting to human form. There's no place for us in each other's worlds."

He wanted to tell her that he would shift to human form and never shift back if it meant she would forgive him, but he didn't. Because pathetic though his understanding of emotion was, even he knew that it wouldn't be enough to regain her trust.

In fact, as someone who'd never trusted another in all his life, he understood very well why she couldn't trust him again. And he understood why she couldn't let him near her.

Before, she had allowed it because of their bargain. She'd believed herself safe from him, she'd trusted in the vow to protect her. Now, that illusion had been shattered, and no matter how much she might have enjoyed his company, she would never believe herself safe with him again.

And that was *his* fault. His burden to bear.

He wished she'd left him dead. Coming back to life, being given a second chance, only to find this reality, was a form of Hell all to its own.

He opened his mouth to tell her he was sorry, that he would spend the rest of his immortal life regretting what he'd done, but a banging on the door snagged both their attentions.

"Are you expecting anyone?" Murmur asked, a tingle of foreboding racing down his spine.

"No," Suyin replied, and another round of furious pounding rattled the door on its hinges.

Murmur rose slowly. His gaze caught on a sharpened dagger, on a table across the room, obviously used in the resurrection spell that was still inscribed on the floor. He grabbed it and approached the door.

He didn't even make it to the entranceway before it exploded inward, revealing a very tall, very furious blond man with hellfire in his eyes.

"Surprise, motherfucker," he said, and then he charged.

# 35

# TRAILBLAZING

MURMUR THREW THE KNIFE IN HIS HAND.

It hit the charging demon right in the center of his chest. His steps faltered and he staggered into the wall. Behind him, Murmur heard Suyin cursing.

Belial only faltered a moment. He reached up and ripped the knife right out of his sternum, and then he chucked it right back at Murmur. Murmur dodged, but he wasn't fast enough. It sank into his shoulder, in the soft tissue between his upper arm and pectoral muscle.

And then Belial charged again.

Murmur called on his powerful defenses . . . only to find he had none. His soul army was gone. He pulled the blade out of his now deadweight arm and got ready to stab his foe.

If Belial wanted him dead, he was going to be dead. Hopefully he'd at least make it difficult for him.

Belial reached him, and the moment he did, he burst into flames. *This is going to hurt.*

Belial's palm curled around Murmur's throat, and fuck, it felt like he was reliving his death vision all over again. Murmur stabbed him in the side, below his ribs, but Belial barely flinched. Murmur stabbed him again, right in the wrist, forcing Belial to release his throat. Belial roared, and Murmur recoiled as more flames licked against his bare torso.

Suyin screamed in the background, and Murmur realized she could be hurt in the crossfire of their fight. That was simply not an option.

He stabbed Belial once more and then threw himself back from the flaming demon. The fire extinguished on his melting skin the second he was away from the source, leaving behind deep welts and bloody burns down his arms and front of his body.

"Stop!" he shouted at Belial when the demon immediately yanked the blade out and stalked toward him again. "Not here!" Murmur held up his hands. "We can't do this here. Think of how many people are around. Think of how many humans could potentially die."

Murmur didn't give a fuck about random humans, and he suspected Belial didn't either. But Heaven tended to get pissed off when demons killed people, so it was best to avoid that.

"It's time to die, Necromancer," Belial growled. "I've had it with you and your fucking schemes."

"You still owe me a favor," Murmur said, backing farther away, leading Belial toward the kitchen and away from Suyin in the living room.

"Not if I fucking kill you."

"I could call it in now. Force you to protect me."

"Again, not if I fucking kill you first." Belial made a terrifying sight as he prowled down the hall toward Murmur. Blood poured all over his body from various stab wounds, and hellfire danced in his eyes and outlined his impressive silhouette. He was nearing eight feet tall, only a few inches below the top of the ceiling.

"Your fucking favor just started a war. A war I didn't want!" Belial roared.

"A war that was coming anyway," Murmur rushed to explain. "I foresaw it long ago. I've always known Lucifer would fall. All I did was arrange things so that you wouldn't fall with him. I'm trying to *help* you."

"Bullshit!"

"Why would I lie about this? I've seen it; I know what's coming. But you don't have to go down too. You can win, you can take him down, and I'm trying to make that happen."

"Why would you want that?"

"Because I, like every other demon in Hell, am sick of Lucifer and his corrupt reign. I'm sick of the constant fighting. I'm sick of defending my territory and living in constant threat of intruders. I want peace. I'm tired, Belial. Sick and tired."

Finally, Belial stopped. They'd made it into the kitchen. Murmur was halfway across the room, and Belial stooped under the doorway. He seemed a little shorter now, like he'd shrunk an inch or so. And the flames around his body seemed to be dying down, though he still threw off heat waves like a desert mirage.

"There's a war coming whether you like it or not," Murmur said. "But thanks to me, Lucifer just lost his greatest source of power. You and I both know you couldn't have defeated him before. But I just leveled the playing field."

"I don't want to fucking fight Lucifer!" Belial's voice boomed around the kitchen. "I don't want any part of this!"

"Too bad!" Murmur shouted back. "You're part of it whether you like it or not. You're *Belial*, the greatest King of Hell in the underworld. You're a fallen fucking angel. You were always destined for this, and you know it."

Belial's nostrils flared like an angry bull.

"I'm willing to help you," Murmur said again. "I want to help you. I want to see Lucifer fall just as much as the next person."

"I don't. Want. To. Fucking. Fight. Lucifer."

Okay, so maybe Murmur needed to stop reminding him of the inevitable. It seemed Belial needed to entertain his denial a little bit longer. Fine by Murmur, as long as he didn't get any more of his flesh seared off.

"Then you need my help to hide from him," he said, switching tactics. "Lucifer would have come for you—for both of us—even if you hadn't been the one to open the door and free the souls. You're his greatest threat, and he wants to take out the competition. You need my help and I'm willing to offer it."

Belial searched his gaze. The flames around his body extinguished, and he gradually returned to his normal height. In human form, he was just as tall as Murmur's demon form. Belial's full demon form was . . . something else. One could only give thanks that he couldn't shift all the way while on Earth.

"How could I ever trust you?" Belial growled. "You've betrayed us more times than I can count."

"Three times," Murmur clarified. "First, when Mist wasn't careful enough in his negotiations. Second, when we bargained, and I forced you to owe me a second favor in exchange for silence, despite the fact that I never had any intention of telling anyone where you were—"

"What!"

"I told you, I'm on your side. I never wanted Lucifer to find you—"

"Then why the fuck did you sell us out to Valefor? You sent him right here! He could have told anyone where we were!"

"Because it was Valefor!" Murmur snapped back. "Have

you ever met a more incompetent halfwit? I knew he wouldn't say anything because he was so desperate to get Mephistopheles back and would break any rule to make it happen. He told me I had to tell Lucifer your location because he'd sworn to Meph he wouldn't in order to get him to shift. I agreed. I told him I would. I *lied*. There was no way I wanted Lucifer to find you."

"Sending Valefor here was a big fucking risk," Bel growled.

"I knew you'd kill him. I knew he'd go too far in his obsession with Mephistopheles, and I was counting on you to take him out to eliminate the threat. I wanted him gone as much as you did."

"And Paimon?" Belial asked. "Why help Mist escape her? Why take her lair for yourself?"

"She and I had a score to settle," Murmur said, eyes narrowing. "I swore vengeance against her a long time ago, and it was overdue. And it doesn't hurt to start the war by taking out Lucifer's most powerful supporter before he was even aware it was coming, does it?"

Belial stared at him. The flames were gone from his eyes, and the fury had been replaced with disbelief. "You were really manipulating this shit from the very beginning?"

"Of course I was," Murmur said haughtily. "I told you I had that vision ages ago. Every single thing I've ever done since that day has been toward this goal. One does not simply overthrow the High King of Hell without centuries of careful planning."

Belial slowly shook his head.

"You should be grateful to me," Murmur continued. "Because of my centuries of prep-work, the war has begun, Lucifer is at a serious disadvantage, and you didn't have to lift a finger. You and your brothers got to go your merry way and enjoy your life. I took care of everything else."

"Jesus fucking Christ," Belial said, and then he dropped

into one of Suyin's kitchen chairs. He hunched forward and dragged his fingers through his hair. "I came here ready to kill you. And now this shit. I can't even . . . My head's spinning."

"I know you think I'm your enemy, but it's not true, and it never has been. And I'm not lying when I say you're going to need my help with what's to come. I'm willing to offer it if we can put the past behind us. You have no idea the things I've done to make it as far as I have. If you're going to survive this, you need me."

Belial straightened, dropping his hands and pinning Murmur with a glare. "And how am I ever supposed to trust a word out of your mouth? And don't tell me you'll swear a vow. I know how good you are at finding loopholes in every single fucking vow you've ever sworn. Your word is shit, Necromancer."

Murmur winced, thinking of the witch in the living room likely listening to the conversation. This was what happened when one spent their life as a liar. When the moment came that they needed to be believed, no one would do so.

But maybe there was a way to prove himself to Belial. He couldn't fix things so easily with Suyin, but at least he had this chance.

"You still owe me one favor," he told Belial, who growled at the reminder. "I could call in that favor right now. You might try to kill me, but I guarantee I could get the words out and tell you to protect me from all harm before you succeed."

"You're not making me any more inclined to trust you," Belial bit out.

"*But*," Murmur continued, "to prove that you can trust me, I now relinquish that favor."

Bel sat up straight. "You what?"

"I free you of your debt to me. There is no second favor owed. The slate is clear."

"What? Why?"

"I told you. To prove that you can trust me."

Bel stared at him. His shock was understandable. Unspecified favors were the most valuable commodity in Hell, and a favor from a demon like Belial was unfathomably valuable. For Murmur to throw it away on a whim was unheard of.

"That's it?" Belial asked. "We're square? Just like that?"

"Yes."

"So I could kill you right now, and there's nothing you can do to stop me."

"Precisely. Especially because I lost my entire soul army when I died. I'm utterly defenseless at the moment."

Belial blinked. Yes, it was shameful for a demon to admit he was defenseless, but this was important, damn it.

"Well, shit," Belial said, slumping back in the chair.

"Indeed," Murmur replied.

"Sorry about your skin," Belial said in a tone that implied he wasn't sorry at all.

Murmur looked at himself. His arms were charred, and his torso hadn't fared much better. It was a good thing he'd braided his hair earlier, or he would have lost most of it.

"Sorry for stabbing you," he replied in a tone that made it clear he wasn't sorry either.

Belial stood. "All right, Necromancer. You've got your alliance. But don't think I don't realize that you need my help as much as I need yours. If Lucifer knows that I opened that door, he also knows that it was your magic that broke the seal and got me there in the first place."

"I'm aware," Murmur said.

"You need to build your own allies or Lucifer's going to finish the job I started of turning you into hamburger meat. And he won't stop when you ask nicely."

"I'm also aware," he said wryly.

"Fuck with me and my brothers again, in *any* way—and that includes twisting our words, lies of omission, manipulating us, withholding important shit to maintain the advantage, whatever—and I will throw this tenuous alliance of yours right out the window and kill you myself. Is that clear?"

"Fine." Murmur rolled his eyes.

"And don't chain my brothers up again, even if they trespass."

He made a face. "Raum tried to steal from me."

"Don't care. We're allies now. What's mine is yours and vice versa."

"Fine," he bit out.

"Good." Belial smiled. He seemed much happier now that he'd regained the upper hand.

Murmur ground his teeth. *This will be a challenge. His ego is so big, I can taste it, and it's bitter.*

"Now," Murmur said, "I do believe Suyin would like it if we got out of her house."

He spoke casually, but it was only to hide the fact that the thought of leaving her hurt worse than Belial melting his skin.

*Funny things, emotions.* Invisible and intangible, they cut deeper than any blade, and they left wounds one might never recover from.

After trying in vain to fix the front door and then offering to pay to replace it, Belial left. Suyin got the impression that he was used to breaking and repairing stuff.

When both Iris and Murmur had told her about Belial, they hadn't mentioned that he turned into a giant flaming rage tornado. She damn well could have used the warning.

While Murmur had talked Belial down from his murderous rage, Suyin had hidden in the living room. It was a perfectly adequate survival response, since there was nothing she could've done against an eight-foot-tall demon with murder on the brain, but she was still annoyed at herself.

Luckily, Murmur had managed to defuse the situation

while revealing some very interesting information that she was still processing. She was still processing a lot of shit, but underneath it all, there was an underlying hurt in her heart that wouldn't go away. And it worsened every time she looked into Murmur's eyes.

The sheer scale of his plans baffled her. He'd been organizing this for centuries, and he hadn't told a soul. She couldn't help but think about how difficult it must have been for him to manage plans of that scale while fighting the instability in his own mind.

She'd never met a more incredible person. From the moment they'd met, his intelligence and determination had amazed her. She'd learned more from him in their short time together than she ever could've imagined, and every instance he'd offered her a peek into his mind had felt like a precious gift.

But it still didn't change what he'd done, and it didn't make it any easier to trust him now. Unfortunately for them, there were no debts he could nullify to prove a point as he'd done for Belial.

The only way for Murmur to regain her trust was if she chose to give him a second chance. And Suyin had never been good at forgiveness.

After Belial departed, she grabbed a mop, and Murmur helped her clean up the remains of the necromancy spell. When that was done, Murmur inscribed a fresh hellgate on the floor, and she stood back and watched him work. He drew the hellgate as easily as she wrote her own name, and, after all those hours in his library, it occurred to Suyin that this would be her last chance to marvel at his skill.

He stood, setting the chalk down among her casting supplies, and then turned to face her. The gate was already activated; she could sense its subtle pulse of magic.

She tried to ignore the sadness and regret in his eyes—eyes that had returned to their normal color after he'd woken up. She tried to harden her heart against him. Trust was everything, and there was none between them. It had to be this way.

"This can't be goodbye," he said.

"It has to be."

He shook his head.

"It is, Murmur."

He looked so fucking miserable, it gutted her. But he'd brought this on himself, she reminded herself for the hundredth time. She had no choice.

Just to prove it to herself, she went over to the desk and scooped up the pile of books he'd given her. "Here. You're not dead anymore, so you can have your books back."

He looked affronted, stepping out of her reach. "Those were a gift to you."

"Yeah, when you were dead. You also gave me your entire library."

"It's still yours."

She blinked. "You can't give me your library, Murmur. You need it."

He shook his head. "Not anymore. My work is complete. Yours is just beginning. I want you to have it."

"I can't— Murmur, I'm not going back there. I can't—" Her voice broke, and she shook her head roughly. Fuck, this was hard. "Keep your library. I'll keep these books." She turned and set them back on the desk. "Deal?"

He just looked sad.

If he didn't leave soon, she was going to break, and there was no way that was happening. So when he took a step toward her, she took one back, keeping space between them.

He flinched. *He brought this on himself*, she repeated over and over. *I can't forgive him. I can't trust him.*

"Goodbye, Murmur," she whispered through the squeezing tightness in her throat.

"This isn't goodbye," he said firmly, and then with one last look, he stepped into the hellgate and disappeared.

She hurried forward and smudged the line before she could think twice and do something stupid like go after him.

Alone, she surveyed her empty living room and decided everything that had happened here was a pretty good metaphor for her life. Her heart, specifically. Only, if her heart had been sacrificed, there was no necromancy to bring it back to life. All she felt in its place was a cold, vacant, *aching* hole.

She tried to chastise herself out of her misery. She was back home, alive and well. There were no more demon stalkers, feelings of foreboding, or haunting, prophetic dreams. She had all the answers she'd sought about herself, and she had a fresh stack of grimoires with plenty more to learn. She was bursting with new knowledge to share with the coven. She had resolved her friendship with Iris, and they were closer than ever.

And most importantly . . . Murmur's spell had succeeded. Her father's soul was freed, reunited with her mother's in the afterlife. She could finally make peace with what had happened to him, knowing he, too, was at peace.

It was everything she'd wanted, and she should have been happy.

Should have . . . but wasn't. Not even remotely.

She sank into the sofa and stared at the wall ahead. Her face was blank. Her chest hurt like a motherfucker. A tear formed in the corner of one eye, so she swiped it away. Another formed in the other eye, so she swiped that away too. All of a sudden, too many tears were forming, and she couldn't wipe them away quickly enough. Her vision blurred until the wall in front of her disappeared altogether.

She let them fall until they dried up. And when she was done, she stood up again, and told herself that was it. That was all she was going to let herself cry over this.

But that didn't mean the pain was gone, no. She didn't think that would ever go away.

# 36

# Hang on Like Grim Death

Murmur surveyed the wreckage of his library. The portal had torn the room apart, ripping pages out of open books and scattering his notes in every direction.

He wandered over to the window and stared out at the plains. There was no sign of the approaching legions. The fires on the mountainsides were gone. Lucifer had retreated to his territory to regroup after losing his souls.

Murmur didn't give a shit.

He didn't give a shit about anything—Belial, Lucifer, his precious fucking spell, and all he'd achieved to get to where he was. He'd never stopped to imagine how he would feel once the spell was complete. He supposed he'd thought he would finally be able to sleep. He would finally rest, take a breath, enjoy his success.

But now that he was here, he felt worse than he had when he'd been so driven to succeed. Because now he had nothing left. He had worse than nothing, because the one thing he wanted more than anything else had forsaken him, and he didn't blame her one bit.

How did someone move on from this? What was he supposed to do now?

A knock at the door pulled him from his heavy thoughts. "Master? Master, are you there?"

He debated ignoring the demon. His servants knew better than to enter the library, and he really wasn't in the mood for company. But that stupid soul-given part of him wanted to make sure the pathetic creatures who served him were at least safe from harm. Now that his mind was clear of the screams and he'd learned what it felt like to have his figurative heart torn from his chest, he sympathized with them more than he would have in the past.

He strode across the room and flung open the door, finding one of his tower guards outside. In the past, Murmur would have threatened to skewer him for daring to come up here and disturb him. Now, however, he was just tired.

"Master!" The demon began a routine of rigorous bowing in which his nose nearly scraped the ground. "Master, Master—"

"Stop." Murmur held up a hand. "What condition is the territory in?"

"The legions are gone, and though the High King was spotted flying toward us, he has also disappeared. Word has spread that His Unholiness is back in his territory with his legions."

*He's regrouping. And this territory will likely be the first place he comes when he's ready again.*

"So all is quiet?"

"It appears so, Master. Thanks to your mistress's excellent instruction, we stayed inside the castle walls, and no one was injured. The legions simply turned and left before they ever made it to the walls."

"My mistress?"

"Yes, she told us you were performing a dangerous spell to increase your power, and that when you returned, you would be stronger than ever. And she commanded us to stay protected within the castle walls and defend them, but not to ride out and fight the legions."

"Of course she did," Murmur muttered.

*She resurrected you even after learning you planned to sacrifice her. And she protected your servants and lair. You don't deserve her. And she deserves far more than you could give her anyway, even if you hadn't betrayed her.*

"So are you better now, Master?" the demon asked. "We were concerned for your wellbeing."

"I'm fine."

"The spell worked, then? You are more powerful than before?"

*More like powerless.* "Something like that," he muttered, already backing into the library to retreat behind closed doors.

"Very good, Master," the demon said, beginning his fervent bowing once more. "We are happy to serve you and eagerly await your orders."

"Just . . . go take a night off." Murmur flicked his fingers dismissively. "There's no need to be hovering around my tower all the time anyway. Go celebrate your victory or something. I don't care, as long as it's not here."

The gargoyle's eyes lit up like Murmur had just popped out of the chimney in a red suit with an armload of wrapped boxes. "Yes, Master! Thank you, Master!"

Murmur slammed the door and leaned his forehead against it, squeezing his eyes shut and wishing he could disappear.

He had a distant memory of feeling the tether of Suyin's resurrection spell drawing him back to Earth. He'd felt such hope then. He'd thought he was on his way to a second chance.

But this felt like more torture. This felt like he'd died again and been damned straight to the Rings.

He straightened and spun around, crossing the room to the hellgate. On a whim, he connected it to the one he'd left in his abandoned former lair in case he needed a quick escape, and he stepped through into an empty study.

He'd occupied this lair for many long years before taking Paimon's territory. It wasn't a castle like his current dwelling, but more of a haunted manor. His ghosts had once stalked the halls, but now his entire territory had been deserted, littered with bones and fading necromancy wards.

He'd lived his solitary life, working toward endless goals, for as far back as his memory extended. Even before he'd set out to overthrow Lucifer, he'd been incessantly striving to amass more power and reach some new pinnacle of achievement in his necromancy practice.

He strode across the room to the cloudy windows, the foul-smelling dust of Hell stinging his nostrils. The lair hadn't fallen into the Abysmal Sea during Lucifer's ground-shaking tantrum as he'd feared it would. But as much as Murmur may have wanted to return to his lonely, lifeless existence here, he couldn't.

He had to look after all the fucking demons who had sworn to serve him the day he'd overthrown their former mistress. No matter how badly he wanted to disappear, even die again, he had to take care of his minions, like a bunch of unwanted children.

He stared at the empty sea, feeling hopeless. In the distance, his resident kraken's enormous tentacles shot out of the water, catching some hapless creature flying overhead, bringing it down to its gaping maw to consume.

How many hours had Murmur spent at this very window, watching the kraken fondly? Sometimes he'd captured flying demons and then released them over the water for the kraken to catch, like the beast was some sort of pet.

The monster's tentacles waved in the air, and he stared at them, desperate for a sign. Anything to give his empty life meaning.

He'd served his purpose. He'd kicked off the war, and he'd positioned Belial to be at the head of it, whether the demon liked it or not. He'd even found a way to make the death sacrifice work without hurting Suyin—though he couldn't undo the emotional hurt he'd caused in the process.

He was done. He had *died*. It would have been the perfect end to his long life. Fulfillment of all his goals and a final sacrifice for the woman he'd learned to love before he'd lost her.

But he had chosen to return to life, and he didn't understand why. Why was he alive if his death would have been a neat little bow tied on top of his life's work? Why was he alive if—

*So you agree with me finally. You love her.*

Murmur stiffened. "It appears so. Not that it makes any difference now."

*Pretty weak love you've got there if you're giving up on her that easily.*

He ground his teeth. Apparently, being resurrected and losing his souls hadn't cured him of the disconnect in his mind that caused him to converse with himself. At the moment, he regretted that immensely.

"I am not— She asked me to leave. I've done enough harm to her. I won't dishonor her by ignoring her wishes. She told me to go, so that's what I did."

*I'm just saying. You wanted a purpose. Well, there it is.*

"What could you possibly—" His eyes widened. "You're saying that just because she doesn't want me in her life doesn't mean I should leave her unprotected."

*Precisely. She's up on Earth, all alone, with no one watching out for her. She might have her witchy friends, but I guarantee no one will protect her the way you can.*

"Yes," he breathed. "That's it."

He would rebuild his soul army— No, he wouldn't build an army. Not yet, anyway. He needed a break from the screaming. He was only now adjusting to the quiet. But he would entrap a few souls, just enough to form a personal guard for Suyin. He would channel all the energy he'd once spent perfecting his spell into protecting her.

And she needed it, too. She was a Cambion, likely the only one in existence. And now that she had that information, she might tell others. And those others might betray her and tell others. Word could get out. She could be in danger.

"I'll protect her," he told himself and the voice in his head and the kraken out in the sea waving its tentacles. Yes, that was the sign it was trying to tell him.

Suyin might never want him again. She might never forgive him. But that didn't matter. Because that wasn't what love was, was it? Love was supposed to be unconditional. And since he was apparently a defective demon, he was going all-in.

If she never wanted to speak to him again, so be it. No matter what, he would make sure she was safe. *That* would be his new objective.

Her park stalker was back.

A week passed, and Suyin cleaned her house, and her landlord begrudgingly fixed her front door. She started shifts again at Le Repaire, assuring everyone she'd had a good trip and enjoyed her time out of the city. She didn't have the energy to tell them where she'd really been.

Every night, she checked out the front window, looking for the unmistakable silhouette of a tall, broad-shouldered man across the street. He wasn't always there, and it became routine for her to scan the park in search of him. Then she would close the curtains, shut him out, and go to bed.

On the seventh day after Murmur left, she was walking home from Le Repaire, texting on her phone while crossing the street—not smart, she knew, but anyone who told her so could fuck right off—and she tripped, the toe of her platform boot catching on the curb when she went to step onto it.

She stumbled, throwing her other foot out to restore her balance. But it came too late. She dropped her phone, hands shooting forward to break her fall, when an invisible weight suddenly pressed against her sternum, catching her before she went down.

It lifted her and set her on her feet, and she was left standing there, looking around for the mysterious person who'd saved her from face-planting. But there was no one there.

Didn't matter. She knew exactly who it was.

On the eighth day, Iris invited her over for drinks at Belial's house. She said it was high time for Suyin to come and properly meet everyone.

She wanted to say no. She wasn't in the mood for socializing right now and would've much preferred to stew alone in her unending misery.

But she forced herself to go anyway. She was half demon, and she figured it would be good for her to meet others of her father's kind. And secretly, she wanted to meet the demons who had recently become Murmur's allies. Knowing them would feel like being close to him again. As close as she could allow herself to be.

She rode her Phantom up the winding streets of Mount Royal until she found the address of the swanky mansion. She rang the buzzer at the gates and announced herself, and they swung open.

Her bike climbed a steep driveway leading to a double-car garage, and she parked in the covered pullout beside a souped-up Land Rover. She followed the path up like Iris had told her to.

At the top, stone gargoyles were perched atop short pillars, their features eroded with time. Steps led to the front door, and she pressed the doorbell, feeling about as welcome as a door-to-door vacuum salesman.

The door swung open, and she found herself face to face with the enormous blue-eyed Belial she'd met under less cordial circumstances a week ago. She briefly wondered how big he was in demon form and then decided she hoped she never found out.

"Come on in." Belial stepped back, and she entered the high-ceilinged hall. Ahead, a dark-stained wooden staircase spiraled up to a mezzanine that led to what were likely the second-floor bedrooms. High above, a chandelier hung beneath a skylight. The floors were white marble.

"Nice house."

"Thanks. Everybody's in the kitchen." He passed the staircase and turned down a hall, so she ditched her boots at the door—the Canadian way—and went after him.

He led her into the nicest kitchen she'd ever seen. Big bay windows overlooked a landscaped backyard with a pool, accessed by glass doors. Across the island, there was a dining room with finely carved chairs. She might have thought it was one of those dining set-ups that no one ever used, except for the fact that the table was covered in dirty dishes.

But everyone was still hanging out in the kitchen.

"Suyin, hey!" Iris announced happily, coming over from beside her extremely tattooed boyfriend to give her a hug.

Suyin hugged her back somewhat awkwardly. She'd never been a hugger, and neither had Iris, but apparently Iris in love was. The demon with red eyes and face tattoos grinned at Suyin over Iris's shoulder.

"You've met Meph," Iris said, pulling back. "Though I guess it was only briefly."

"Yeah, back when you told me he was toxic and you weren't

going anywhere near him," Suyin said before she could stop herself.

Laughter rang out across the room.

"I like her already," a dark-skinned demon with brilliant gold eyes announced.

"That's Raum," Iris said. "He's Meph's partner in crime, so keep an eye on them." Iris then pointed to a stunningly beautiful woman with shiny black hair, dark eyes, and dusky skin. "This is Sunshine."

"Greetings," Sunshine said and then winced. "I mean, hello."

Suyin could only stare. She was looking at a real-life angel—Iris had told her all about Raum's girlfriend and her demon-Earth transition program. There was definitely an otherworldly glow to this woman. Something about her made Suyin feel like she was safe in her presence, and her warm smile was the most inviting she'd ever seen.

"That's Ash and Eva." Iris pointed to another couple leaning against the counter on the far side of the room. "Ash is a demon, Eva's not."

"Can we not be introduced by our species?" Eva said with a laugh. "It feels awkward."

Iris laughed, and then pointed to the other people who Suyin already knew. "Lily, human. Mist, demon. Belial, grump."

Belial shot her a look.

Everyone was looking at Suyin expectantly, so she said, "Suyin, Cambion."

Several sets of eyes widened. Sunshine said, "It's so lovely to meet you," and Suyin was sure she'd never heard a more genuine statement.

"I see it now," Meph said. "She gives off the same don't-fuck-with-me vibe that Murmur does. And the spooky goth look is totally—"

"Meph," Iris hissed, elbowing him in the side. "What did I say about the M word?"

"Don't say it. My bad."

Great. So Iris had evidently told everyone about the catastrophe that was Suyin's relationship with the Necromancer. Had she told them how he'd taken her stupid feelings and crushed them into tiny pieces by trying to kill her? Because that would be the cherry on top.

"So!" Lily announced, apparently sensing the tension. "Who wants a drink?"

There were several murmurs of agreement, and then Belial announced that he was making martinis, and everyone got involved, and that was the last they spoke of Murmur the entire time.

There was also no talk about Lucifer or the coming war Murmur had spoken of, and by the way everyone very carefully dodged around the topic, she figured that was on purpose. Likely Belial didn't want to talk about it any more than Suyin wanted to talk about Murmur.

Unfortunately, not talking about him didn't keep him from her mind. As she sat at the edge of the group, watching them interact, laughing and teasing one another, she thought about him more than ever. No matter what she did, she couldn't get him out of her head.

She declined a second drink so she could safely ride home, watching everyone else get drunk with veiled amusement. Except Belial. He drank the most out of everyone and gave no sign of it affecting him.

When Meph started telling everyone the story of how Belial had chopped his fingers off—showing off his regenerated and freshly tattooed hand—she decided it was time to go. Belial was grinding his teeth, and Suyin had seen firsthand what happened when he got mad and wasn't feeling up for a repeat experience.

She signaled to Iris that she was heading out, figuring she'd slip out without disrupting the party, but of course, that wasn't what happened at all.

"Everyone!" Iris announced. "Suyin's taking off, so say goodbye."

"Bye, Suyin!" several people called out.

"No, wait!" Eva said, running forward. "You can't go until you have a cookie. Bel helped me bake them and they're my pride and joy. Where are they, Bel?"

"On top of the fridge. I hid them from Meph."

"I can reach the top of the fridge, you know," Meph said.

"Yeah, but you're like a dog. Out of sight, out of mind."

Meph laughed, apparently not offended by the comparison.

Suyin happened to be standing right next to the fridge, so she stepped aside when Eva hurried over. Eva rose to her tiptoes, feeling around for the plate. "Jesus, Bel, why do you have a six-foot-tall fridge?"

"Have you seen him?" Ash said.

"Good point."

"Eva, let me help you," Bel said.

"No, I got it— Oop!"

She didn't have it. In fact, in her effort to slide the plate closer so she could grab it, she knocked the entire thing off. Onto Suyin's head.

Suyin flinched, bringing her hands up in preparation for the glass cracking onto her skull. Except it never came.

As if she had an invisible force field around her body, the plate bounced off, flew to the side, and hit the ground a good three feet from her. She looked around to see if anyone else had seen what happened. Judging by the way they stared with open mouths, they had.

"What the hell?" Meph said. "How did that just happen?"

"I'm so sorry," Eva was saying. "Are you okay?"

"I'm fine," Suyin replied distantly, catching the pointed look Iris was giving her across the kitchen.

"Was that a protection spell or something?" Eva asked. "Because that was crazy."

She brushed it off and let everyone assume that was what it was. Conversation resumed, and shortly after, she made excuses to depart, hoping to evade the questions that would follow if anyone guessed what had really happened.

Unfortunately, Iris followed her out the door.

# 37

# To Err Is Human

SUYIN, *WAIT*!" IRIS CALLED AS SUYIN SPEED-WALKED down the path, trying to avoid this very confrontation.

Unfortunately, she wasn't fast enough. Iris caught up just as she reached her bike.

"Jesus, woman! You're fast."

Suyin spun around, tucking her helmet under one arm and cocking a hip.

"I know you're trying to run away from me," Iris said, arching a brow.

"Why would I do that?"

Iris gave her a look that said, *Really?*

Suyin pinned her with a glare. She really wasn't in the mood for psychoanalysis.

"Damn, Su," Iris laughed, "you could turn someone to ice with that look."

She'd take that as a compliment.

"I'm worried about you. I haven't seen you smile in days, and it's like you're carrying a dark cloud around you everywhere you go. I swear even Bel was wary of pissing you off."

She couldn't help it. She was short-tempered and despondent lately, and it was all Murmur's fault. She'd never been the type to get caught up on a partner. In fact, after what happened with Murmur, she'd begun to realize that she'd never experienced true feelings for another person before him.

She supposed it was karma. After years of being a shitty girlfriend and an all-round closed off, emotionally unavailable friend, the first person she really fell for turned around and crushed her in the most brutal way.

She probably deserved it. Her ex-partners would likely find it cathartic to see how miserable she was now. Didn't make it any easier to bear though.

"I never thought I'd say this, but . . ." Iris took a breath. "I think you should give Murmur a second chance."

Suyin's head jerked back. "Are you kidding?"

"You obviously want him. A blind person could see the longing on your face when you even hear his name. You've got it bad, Su. I think you're in love."

The word "love" made her heart leap into her throat. She pinned Iris with a furious look. It wasn't Iris's fault she was such a raging bitch lately, but unfortunately, Iris was her current target. "He betrayed me, remember? Just like you said he would. He carved a sigil into my chest that could have fucking killed me."

Iris shrugged. She actually *shrugged*. "Yeah, he did." She gave Suyin a pointed look. "And then he straight-up sacrificed himself instead. I don't know how else he could've proved that he didn't want to hurt you."

Suyin sputtered. "Are you actually— I can't believe—" She shook herself. "He showed up at my house and fucked me senseless, all the while knowing he was going to kill me after he left. How can you think that's okay?"

"It's not okay. It's messed up. I completely agree. But . . . you have to give him some credit. He's been evil for thousands of years, and this is obviously the first time he's ever not hated someone. He probably had no idea what to do with his feelings. He probably didn't even realize he had feelings. In the past, he wouldn't have hesitated, so I bet he was pretty damn surprised when he went to do his spell and couldn't."

"I can't believe the words coming out of your mouth," Suyin muttered, even though she recognized the truth in them.

"Look, Lily once told me, when I was first getting to know Meph and his brothers, that I shouldn't make the mistake of ascribing too many human attributes to them. It sounds bad, but when you're an immortal being who's survived what they have, shit just takes on a different meaning. I mean, when Belial cut off Meph's fingers, I was screaming, and nobody else even batted an eye. Bel just threw the fingers in the compost."

"That is not the same thing!" Suyin cried.

"Okay, fair enough. But what I'm trying to say is, death and violence mean something different for demons than they do for us. On top of that, you and I were *born* with souls, and we had parents who taught us right and wrong. But guys like Murmur were created to be soulless forces of evil. For longer than we can imagine, they've just been existing as harbingers of darkness, and then suddenly, they start developing a conscience and emotions, and they have no idea what they mean or how they're supposed to act. No one ever showed them what it means to be good.

"So when Murmur realized he needed to sacrifice you for his spell, he probably didn't recognize the bond you guys had because he had no idea what friendship or romantic feelings even felt like. I imagine that it wasn't until he went to do the sacrifice that he realized what it would mean for him to lose you forever, and that was probably when it sank in how he felt about you."

"Shit, Iris." Suyin set her helmet on her bike seat and dragged her hair back from her face. "I can't believe it's you saying this. A year ago, you would have been telling me to practice summoning hellfire so I could kill him."

"I know." Iris smiled sheepishly. "But people change. And that's exactly my point. Think about how big of a jump Murmur had to make between plotting to sacrifice you and deciding to take his own life to save yours. I mean, his spell was so important he was willing to die for it. Not finishing it wasn't an option. So he literally *died* so that you didn't have to. I know he fucked up, and it's good that you made him pay for it, but I don't think there was a better way to prove that he'd changed than the decision he made to sacrifice himself for you. Talk about your grand gestures."

"Shit," Suyin said again. "I've spent the last week trying to convince myself that what he did was unforgivable. And now this? I don't know what to believe anymore."

"I went through something kinda similar with Meph," Iris explained. "I hated demons, but I wanted him. We started messing around, and I thought it was casual. When he told me he had feelings, I wasn't ready to go there, and then Valefor took Meph, and everything went to shit. I guess I sympathize with Murmur in that way. I really hurt Meph, but I felt justified in it. It wasn't till I was faced with losing him that I realized how important he was to me. I hate that I couldn't see it until I thought I'd lost him forever, but that was what it took. And damn if I didn't learn my lesson. I'm never taking him for granted again."

Suyin stared at her friend. Her eyes stung, and her throat felt like it was choking her. "I get it. I just . . . I thought you hated Murmur. You told me to stay away from him and not to trust anything he said."

"Yeah, well, Bel told us everything Murmur said when he confronted him—how he's been plotting this insane thing with Lucifer—and I guess, now that I understand his motives, I can see why he is the way he is. He doesn't trust anybody, and that's smart for someone who lives in Hell. I've been there. It's awful."

"It's not so bad," Suyin said, thinking of Murmur's library, the red-skinned demon who'd called her Mistress, and even the red sky and confusingly long nights.

Iris laughed. "Only you would say that."

Suyin shrugged and suddenly thought about her parents.

Gamigin had been a demon, which meant that no matter how noble or loving he'd eventually become, at one point he'd been just as evil as any soulless being of Hell.

Had her mother struggled to come to terms with that when they'd first gotten together? Had she even known? Surely she wouldn't have welcomed his presence initially if she'd realized what he was. Maybe Gamigin had lied to her and pretended to be human.

If that was the case, how long had it taken her to forgive him when she found out the truth? How had she *known* without a doubt that she could trust his word, that he wouldn't hurt her or lie to her again?

She hadn't, Suyin realized. Because that wasn't how trust worked. Just like she'd told Murmur, there was no vow that could be sworn or contract that could be signed. Trust had to be given freely. It could never be bought.

No matter what had happened with Suyin's parents, at some point Fay would have had to make the choice to trust a demon. She would've had to take a leap of faith, to listen to her intuition and choose to believe in someone with the power to hurt her.

And if she hadn't done that, then Suyin wouldn't exist and neither would *The Book of Gamigin*. And then Murmur's spell wouldn't have come to fruition, which meant that when Lucifer killed Gamigin, there would've been no one else who knew of the prison and had the power to free him.

It was a bit of an oversimplification, but Suyin couldn't help feeling like everything that had occurred all came back to her mother's choice to trust.

And that felt pretty fucking important.

Iris's voice cut through her revelations. "Look, I've been thinking this for days, and now I'm just going to say it, even if it's harsh. You've been miserable since you kicked Murmur out of your life. You're moping around, and no offense, but you're acting like a bitch."

"I know," Suyin grumbled, shuffling a foot.

"I'm sick of seeing you pining for a demon who's equally obsessed with you. I mean, he's been stalking you from the moment he left. That was obviously one of his freaky ghost slaves who kept the plate from hitting your head back there. So hurry up and give him a second chance or just decide to get over him, because you can't keep this up forever."

Suyin stared at the ground. "I don't know if I can get over him. I've been trying, and it's not working."

Iris smiled a little. "You're in love."

Suyin's gaze shot to Iris's. "What? No, I can't— I'm . . ." Shit, she was, wasn't she?

Iris's amusement increased. "You definitely are. Don't look so terrified—it's not a bad thing. Have you even been in love before?"

Suyin thought for a moment and then shook her head mutely. Fifty years old and she'd never been in love—until now. God, in a way she was as bad as Murmur, and she understood his struggle in a way she hadn't before. She hadn't even been able to identify her own feelings until Iris pointed them out to her. How much worse had it been for him?

"This is a good thing," Iris assured her, looking far too pleased with herself. "You love him, he loves you. Everybody's happy."

"I—" She swallowed. "What do I do?

"I think you know."

"Fuck. Shit." She was terrified and exhilarated at the same time.

"As eloquent as ever, Suyin."

She peered into Iris's green gaze. Iris smiled tentatively.

"Thanks for being a good friend," Suyin said, suddenly feeling sentimental. All this love stuff was throwing her for a loop. "I know I've been a shit one, and I'm grateful you're still here for me."

"Oh, we were both shitty—"

"I *said*, thanks for being a good friend." Her eyes narrowed.

"Right. Okay." Iris held up her hands. "You're welcome."

With a nod, Suyin grabbed her helmet and pulled it on, sweeping her hair down her back. Then she threw a leg over her bike and fired it up.

"God, you're hot!" Iris called over the rumbling engine, grinning as wide as her crazy boyfriend. And then she pointed down the driveway. "Now go get your man!"

When Suyin got home, she parked her bike in the garage and ran inside through the back door. Without even turning on a light, she crossed the apartment, threw open the front door, and went out onto the balcony. She squinted into the dark, searching for signs of her stalker.

He wasn't there.

Her heart sank. What if he'd given up on her? She hadn't seen him for two days. Just because his ghosts were still following her didn't mean he was going to wait forever. Now that she'd made the decision, she had to find him *now*. She couldn't waste another second in the tortuous limbo she'd been dragging out between them. It was time to move forward.

A flash of white caught her eye.

There, at the far end of the park, a lone dark figure was striding down the path in the opposite direction. Without a second thought, Suyin sprinted down the staircase after him, across the road, and through the park.

As she got closer, she could see him better. He wore his customary long black coat with the hood up, his head down, hands in his pockets. He was probably on his way back to his hellgate after seeing that she wasn't at home.

He hated his human form. Yet he came here to check on her, day after day. Just to make sure she was okay, not even to talk to her.

"Murmur!" she shouted just as he reached the edge of the park and stepped onto the sidewalk.

He stiffened and turned around. She saw the surprise on his human face when he saw her running toward him.

She kept going until she reached him and skidded to a halt. That confused look never left his face. He genuinely had no clue why she'd chased after him. It only increased her conviction.

"Suyin." His voice was soft, a whisper of disbelief.

Still, when she stood before him, fighting for air and losing her breath all over again at the sight of him, words failed her. He was so beautiful, even in his human form, with his proud cheekbones and pale eyes and glorious white hair. Beautiful and enigmatic, and though she'd never admit it, he intimidated her. He always had.

"I know your ghosts have been following me around," she blurted even though it wasn't what she'd intended to say.

His lips pressed together, like he wanted to speak but was afraid of saying the wrong thing. "I didn't want to leave you unprotected."

*His voice.* God, she'd missed that rough-around-the-edges voice.

"Someone could find out what you are and try to steal your blood," he said.

Another time, she might have protested about needing anyone's protection. But she wasn't mad about the souls. Now that she wasn't fighting herself anymore, she liked the reminder that he hadn't let her go. She liked knowing that a part of him was always with her, even if he wasn't there in person.

"Because you're the only one that can steal my blood, right?" she said.

He visibly flinched. Like the reminder of what he'd done physically hurt.

She inwardly smacked herself. *Way to go, Su.* She hadn't come here to guilt-trip him. Yeah, he'd fucked up, but they'd already been over that. If she was going to do this, she needed to jump in with both feet. All or nothing. There was no such thing as halfway trust. She either gave it to him or she didn't.

She took a breath, unsure how to begin explaining herself. "Murmur—"

"I love you," he said.

She froze, her mouth still open, whatever she'd been about to say forgotten in an instant. "You what?"

Ice-blue eyes pierced into hers. He didn't flinch or hide from her. "I'm not sure I'm even worthy of using that word, but I can't think of another way to describe how I feel about you. Before you, I never cared about anything besides my own ambitions. And now, none of that matters anymore. All the things that once carried so much weight are meaningless without you in my life. You are the best thing that ever happened to me. Your happiness comes before all else, and I would gladly die and stay dead a hundred times over to ensure your safety. You may never forgive me for what I did to you, but that doesn't matter. I probably don't deserve to have you even if you did. But no matter what, I will spend the rest of my eternity protecting you, and I will destroy anyone that so much as lays a finger on—"

She launched herself into his arms, cutting him off midspeech, however moving it had been. Throwing her arms around his neck, she saw a brief look of surprise pass over his beautiful face before she crushed her lips to his.

He went stiff as a board, so she pulled back.

"What's happening?" he asked.

"I'm kissing you."

"I see that, but—"

"Shut up and kiss me back."

He blinked. When his eyes opened again, they fixed on her lips. And then he bent his head and for once, he did exactly what she told him to. Their lips fused back together, and his arms came around her. He pulled her against him so tightly, she could feel the heat pouring off him. It sank into her skin all the way to her bones.

His arms tightened around her until he was practically lifting her off the sidewalk. And then, like this was an old-school cheesy Hollywood flick, one of her knees bent and her foot popped up behind her.

"Suyin," he murmured, pulling back just enough to form the word.

"Say it again," she whispered.

He knew what she wanted. "I love you."

"I love you too," she said, breathing a euphoric laugh. It felt fucking amazing to say it aloud. "I've never felt like this in my life. I'm crazy about you."

"But what about—"

"Are you planning to sacrifice me in a spell again?"

"Never," he said, pulling back to convey the strength of his conviction. "I would rather chop off all my limbs and then decapitate myself than harm a single hair on your head."

She laughed again. "Please don't do any of that. I believe you."

He searched her gaze as if he didn't quite dare to hope that what she said was true. As if he couldn't bear it if it wasn't. "Are you sure?"

"Yes, I'm sure. Now, take me home and show me how much you missed me."

# 38

# No Bones About It

THE FRONT DOOR BANGED OPEN, THE HANDLE LEAVING a dent in the drywall right over the repair from the last time it was thrown open. This time, it was for a much different reason.

Murmur kicked aside a bunch of shoes in his way and pushed his witch up against the wall, kissing her so hard, he could tell she was fighting to draw breath. She didn't seem to mind. When he reached back to slam the door behind them, she grabbed a handful of his hair and yanked him right back to her lips.

He let her grab him. He'd let her do anything she wanted to him. And the dark memories stayed dead, as all ghosts of the past should. They no longer had the power to rise from their graves and haunt him—not now that he'd allowed himself to *feel*.

And especially now that he was with her.

She grabbed his coat and shoved it off his shoulders. He pulled it off and dropped it onto the floor, reaching back to grip the base of her neck and pull her closer. They made it several steps into the hallway before she was trying to tug his shirt over his head. He broke the kiss for a second to tear it off and throw it away, and then he yanked on her jacket until she did the same.

She wore a shirt with thin straps underneath. That was no fun.

Crushing his lips back to hers, he drew the straps over her shoulders and down her arms, trapping them against her sides. While furiously kissing him, she struggled to free herself from the fabric.

Now that was fun.

Still, he allowed her to free herself, and she moved backward, tugging her shirt off and tossing it away. Her breasts were bared to him, small and perky with those little brown nipples. Stooping to kiss her again, he cupped them and stroked all over her skin, feeling the curve of her waist and the arch of her spine.

That was definitely fun.

"Murm—" She couldn't even finish his name before his tongue was back in her mouth, and she moaned as one of his hands closed around her ass and ground her against his hard shaft. "Shift," she groaned.

That got his attention. He pulled back just enough to see her eyes. "What?"

"Shift," she said again, panting. The rise and fall of her bare chest nearly made him forget what they were talking about.

"You don't like me better in this form?"

"Hell no."

"Because I'll stay in human form for the rest of my life if it makes you happy."

"Don't you dare," she told him, hooking her fingers in the waistband of his pants. "I fell in love with a demon, and I'd like him to look like one when we make love."

*"Make love." I like this term.*

He couldn't keep his hands off her long enough to reply, so as he bent to kiss her again, he granted her request and shifted back to demon form. And thank fuck, because while he had meant what he said, if she'd asked him to stay in human form forever, he'd have developed a serious complex. He didn't know how the other demons could stand to be shorter, weaponless, and far less impressive all the time.

But he would've done it for Suyin. He would do anything for Suyin.

Luckily, she required no such sacrifice. In fact, she moaned like he was already stroking between her legs as his skin morphed back to pale gray and he gained a foot of height. He didn't form his horns, knowing he had difficulty fitting them in her tiny house.

Tail wrapping around one of her thighs, he stooped and picked her up. Her legs wrapped around his hips, and she squeezed him like she was clinging on for dear life.

Digging his fingers into her thighs, mindful of his claws, he strode down the hallway. He'd never been more determined to reach a bed in his life, especially as Suyin began rocking her hips against him. Their size difference meant that her core was pressed against his stomach, and he could feel the heat between her legs against his bare skin. It made him crazed.

So crazed, in fact, that he didn't quite make it to his destination before he lost all sense. He turned, pressing her against the wall and kissing her like his life depended on it.

"Take these off," he snarled against her lips, hooking a claw in the waistband of her pants, "before I rip them off."

He let her slide to the ground, and she shoved her pants and underwear down her hips. The scent of her arousal doubled in intensity, and he groaned. He had to taste her, bed be damned.

He picked her up before she'd even finished taking her clothes off and lowered them both to the ground, laying her on her back. Her pants were still at her knees, and he realized she hadn't yet taken off her big boots. It didn't matter; he couldn't wait.

He gripped the bunched fabric and used it to push her legs up. And then he dropped his head and trailed his black tongue through her core, the taste of her desire flooding his senses.

She cried out his name, her spine arching off the floor, and it was the most exquisite sight he'd ever beheld. He licked her again, thrusting his tongue into her opening before sliding it up to her clit and swirling around. Her cries were the sweetest music.

"God, Murmur!" His tongue plunged back inside of her, and there was something so deliciously forbidden about his monochromatic coloring against her warm-toned human flesh. He licked her with increasing intensity until she came apart in his arms, her thighs trembling, her ecstatic sounds filling his head.

"I want you inside me," she moaned as she came down from her peak. "Fuck, please, Murmur. I need it so bad."

*Well, far be it for me to deny such a request.*

He sat back, releasing the grip on her legs and allowing them to fall forward again. He found the zipper on her tall boots and pulled them off, tossing them over his shoulder.

She watched him with a wicked smile, and he smiled right back at her. He couldn't believe how perfect she looked, spread out naked on the floor, her hair a mess, her makeup smudged, her cheeks flushed from her climax.

He pulled her pants off and threw them away.

"That's better," he purred. "That's how you should always look in my presence."

She chuckled and set her perfect little feet on his shoulders, giving him a mouthwatering view of the glistening flesh between her thighs. Her taste was still all over his tongue.

"Come here," she said, her eyes heavy-lidded with pleasure.

"Shall I take you to your bed?" He leaned over her, planting his palms on either side of her head. She reached down and concentrated on pulling his pants down.

She may have answered him, but he didn't hear a thing the second she freed his erection and wrapped her hands around it. Curses spilled from his lips, and he dropped his head, kissing her and then dragging his mouth down her neck. His lips peeled off his teeth and he dug his fangs into her neck, but he wasn't going to bite her without permission. He wasn't doing anything to her without her permission ever again.

But then she said, "Do it," and he lifted his head in question, wanting to be certain of her intent.

"Iris told me you guys like to bite." Her dark eyes were burning. "I want to feel it."

"It hurts," he warned.

"Then you'd better fuck me while you do it so I don't notice."

He groaned and bent his head again to kiss her. Reaching down, he scooped up one of her legs below the knee and spread her up and open to him. She was still stroking his shaft, and she aligned the head with her entrance, lifting her hips and angling them so all he had to do was push forward.

"Suyin," he moaned against her lips.

"Yes," she moaned. "I need it. I need you."

But he stopped. He lifted his head and looked into her eyes. He needed her to understand this first. "I will never hurt you again," he swore. "I will never lie to you again. I will never make you feel betrayed again. From now on, you come first for me. Do you understand?"

"Yes," she said, and her eyes were soft. "I trust you."

There it was—that tender look he'd once chased and fought to understand. This time, it was only for him, and he would guard it like the most powerful, secret knowledge that existed.

And it was powerful. It empowered him to know he had conquered her heart and earned her forgiveness. She had given the gift of herself to him and only him.

He would spend every moment of the rest of their lives proving she'd made the right choice.

He bent to taste her lips again as he sank into her body, her tight core squeezing his shaft. She clutched the skin of his back, her nails biting his flesh hard enough to leave marks. She cried out his name, her chin tipping back and exposing the soft column of her throat.

He dropped his head and fixed his teeth around her neck. She moaned, chanting, "Yes, yes, yes," and he took that as the green light to bite. His fangs broke her skin. Her powerful Cambion blood filled his mouth with a rich flavor that made his head spin. He thrust faster, sinking into her as deep as her body allowed him to go.

She gasped at the pain from his bite, her nails digging deeper into his back. All of a sudden, they were sharp. Sharp enough to pierce his skin and draw blood. Sharp like . . . claws?

He pulled his teeth from her neck, lifted his head, and then blinked in surprise. Her eyes were pure black, sharp fangs framed her mouth, and her skin was faintly tinted with a purplish hue. *Purple.* It was his favorite color.

"You were right," she said with a fanged grin. "I can shift."

He groaned at the sight of her. He'd never seen a more stunning thing.

Needing her even closer, he shoved his hand under her back and picked her up. She tightened her arms around his shoulders as he sat back on his knees, setting her atop his thighs so he could sink even deeper inside her.

She cried out, throwing her head back so her black hair danced across her back, and he bent and licked up the blood trail coming from the puncture wounds in her neck. Her legs spread apart across his thighs, and he held her in place as he moved inside her, her arousal soaking his shaft to the base.

She gripped his shoulders, her claws sharp against his skin, and tilted her head forward to face him. Their gazes met. There was a look of uncertainty, of vulnerability, in her eyes. Her body trembled on the verge of a climax.

He knew what she needed, and he told her with his gaze, *I see you. I see you and I have you. You're mine, and I'll never let you go. Fall and I will catch you.*

And she did. Her body shook, and her cries cut off as she gasped. He felt her clench around him, her inner muscles rippling with waves of release.

The sight of her surrender undid him, and he soared into his own climax. And he experienced his own moment of uncertainty. Because this was about so much more than a physical release.

But she was right there with him, riding the waves of her own pleasure, her beautiful, lithe body spread out and vulnerable before him, her surrender complete. And that was all he needed.

They came down from the high together, clutching each other, their skin slick with sweat and their intermingled releases. He wrapped an arm and his tail around her hips and held her close, his shaft still inside of her, flexing with residual pleasure. He stroked her hair with his other hand, smoothing it off her sweat-slicked neck. Bending, he licked another trickle of blood from her closing wounds.

Her eyes shut, and she sagged against him, resting her head against his shoulder. He kept stroking her hair. She hummed softly, and then she turned her head and pressed the softest kiss against his skin.

And for the first time, Murmur gave thanks for the soul he'd evolved that gave him the capacity to love her.

Hours later, they lay sprawled in Suyin's bed. He'd made love to her a second and third time until they'd both worked out the tension from their time apart and could finally rest.

"Why didn't you use your ghosts to restrain me?" she asked. She lay with her head on his chest, his arm around her, and she traced the line between his pectorals with a light touch. She was back in her human form, her fingertips soft as she stroked him. "I know how much you like that."

"Do you?" he asked, petting her hair.

"You know I do."

"Hm."

"What?" She lifted her head so she could meet his gaze. There was a red mark on her cheek from being pressed against him, and he smiled at the sight.

"I only have three souls at present. I lost my entire army when I died."

Her eyes widened. "All of them?"

He nodded. "Every single one."

"Aren't you upset? You don't seem upset."

He smiled. "I'm not upset. I suppose it was high time I let those souls go. I tortured them long enough."

She rested her head back down. "They knew what they were getting into. They have no one to blame but themselves."

His smile grew. His witch could be a bloodthirsty little thing when she wanted. He approved. "Yes, but some of them had served me for thousands of years. After enough time, that torture is worse than whatever they would've had to face in the Nine Rings. They screamed incessantly in my head, crying for their freedom, and it drove me mad. Now, they're gone, and I find I'm enjoying the peace and quiet."

"But you're still rebuilding the army."

"Yes. I have to keep up appearances after all. And I still have a territory to defend."

"But?" she said, sensing there was more he hadn't said.

"But," he affirmed, "I won't build it to the same size as before. And I won't keep the souls forever. I think I'll let them go after a couple hundred years or so."

She lifted her head and gave him that soft smile that he'd come to cherish. "That sounds an awful lot like empathy, Necromancer."

"Yes, well, this pesky little witch came around and made me feel all these inconvenient emotions, and I can't seem to turn them off anymore."

"She sounds like a handful."

He reached down and pinched her bottom lightly. "You have no idea."

She chuckled and lowered her head again. "I'm glad you have peace and quiet in your head, Murmur."

"So am I."

"Do your new souls bother you?"

"Not really. They still think they're winning, having escaped the Rings, when all they had to do was agree to serve the Necromancer."

She scoffed. "They'll learn eventually, I suppose."

"No doubt."

"You still haven't answered my question though. Why didn't you use them to restrain me?"

"Well, for one, since there are only three, one is currently busy patrolling the newly fortified borders of my territory, the other is moving some furniture, and the third is currently floating somewhere above us, keeping watch over you."

"Moving furniture." She laughed. "Why am I not surprised?"

"And for two," he continued, "I suppose I was reluctant to touch you with them again. I know they frightened you, and I didn't want you to think that I don't care for your comfort. I won't do anything to you without your permission, and there will be no more negotiations or bargains between us. If you need something, you will ask, and I'll give it to you if I'm able."

"Murmur." She lifted her head again and then leaned in and planted a light kiss on his lips. "That's so sweet."

"I live to serve," he said wryly, still not sure he enjoyed being called "sweet."

"I'll admit the ghosts restraining me while we had sex freaked me out at first. But . . . it was a good kind of freaked out." She grinned. "The kinky kind. Like when you used your tail venom on me. I was apprehensive as hell, but damn, I was glad I gave it a try afterward."

His lips curved. "I'll keep that in mind, witchling."

She stuck her tongue out at the use of the nickname, and then she moved down to lay on his chest again. Silence fell for some time, and he contented himself with petting her silky hair and soft skin.

"So what happens now?" she asked after a time.

"What do you mean?"

"I mean, I'm still a human—"

"Half human. I felt those little claws shredding up my back."

"*Half* human," she corrected unapologetically. "And you're a demon. And I live on Earth, and you're a total misanthrope."

"So are you," he shot back. "Let's be honest."

"Fine. Humans suck. I agree. *But* you hate your human form. And you have a territory in Hell and a bunch of demons who call you Master and think the sun shines out of your ass, and you can't just abandon them."

"I know," he grumbled.

"So?"

"So what? So we make it work. There's nothing else to do."

"I guess so."

"But I have to warn you . . . I'm a bit of a wanted man at the moment. Lucifer knows it was my magic that got Belial into his territory to free the souls. He'll want vengeance, and I have every reason to suspect my territory will be the first he attacks when he's ready for vengeance."

"So what are you going to do?"

"If it were just me, I'd cut and run. But I have all these pesky demons looking up to me now, and I suppose I have to take care of them. So I guess I'll have to stay and fight and then figure out an escape plan when that inevitably goes to shit. Also, I told Belial I would help him, and I suppose I'd better keep my word on that so he doesn't kill me and undo all your hard work."

She snorted. "Does that mean you'll be able to visit me on Earth?"

"Of course. I'll be here with you every possible second I can spare. There's nowhere else I'd rather be."

She turned her face into his chest and kissed his skin in response.

"But I'll need to figure out a way to disguise myself while I'm here. It's technically forbidden for me to visit the Earth plane since I have no special dispensation to be here."

"Well, I know how to fix that."

"You do?"

"Sure. All you have to do is talk to Sunshine."

He frowned at the mention of the angel who had once broken into his territory. Playing nice with Belial and his allies was going to be a challenge for his pride.

Suyin looked up at him without lifting her chin and smiled. "I feel the same, by the way. I want you here with me whenever you can be." Her smile turned to a contemplating frown. "Can I visit you in Hell too?"

His brows lifted. "You would want to?"

"Duh. I haven't forgotten about your library. I don't think I'll ever get tired of that room."

"Then it's yours to visit whenever you wish."

She grinned. "I'm loving this new agreeable you."

"I told you, there will be no more negotiations between us. Whatever is mine, is yours."

"Thank you, sweetness," she purred with a teasing glint in her eyes, and he growled. He prodded her ass gently with his tail barb.

She laughed and tried to squirm out of his reach, but he tightened his arm around her.

Rolling to his side, he pinned her beneath his much larger body and bit lightly at her shoulder. "I think someone needs to be reminded which of us is the big, scary demon and which is the soft, delicate little human." He punctuated his words with another nip at her neck.

She giggled in a decidedly *un*-Suyin-like way and reminded him, "*Half* human."

# 39

# Villain of the Peace

WHEN DID YOU REALIZE YOU NO LONGER WANTED TO participate in the battle between Heaven and Hell for dominion over humanity?" the angel across the desk asked, pen hovering above her clipboard. She leaned back in a high-backed office chair, thick braid pulled over one shoulder, wearing a strappy black-lace dress that was decidedly unangelic.

Murmur shifted uncomfortably in his chair. He'd once been hanged upside down until his head exploded, and he swore it was less painful than this interview. He glanced over at Suyin, who sat beside him. Her smile was encouraging with a hint of teasing. She knew how much he hated this, and she found it amusing.

He would spank her for that later. For now, however, he supposed he'd better behave.

"My opinion on that matter has been unchanged for centuries," he replied to Sunshine. "I find humans repulsive, and I have no care for what happens to their souls at all. It doesn't matter to me in the slightest."

"Hmm." The angel ticked a box on her paper.

Suyin shot him a warning look, and he made a face back at her. But he knew she was right. He needed to be good for just this one interview.

If he passed, this angel had the power to grant him free, unrestricted access to the Earth, which meant there was no one who could keep him from Suyin. And that was worth anything—even answering ridiculous, uncomfortable questions.

"Would you say you feel compassion for others' suffering?" Sunshine asked. "When you see someone in pain, do you want to help them?"

"That depends on who it is. Most people, I couldn't care less. In fact, I'd probably enjoy it."

Suyin cleared her throat.

"But only if I especially hated them," Murmur added quickly.

"And if you didn't?" Sunshine asked. "What would you feel if you saw someone you didn't know suffering?"

"Well, then I don't think I would feel much of anything."

Suyin coughed lightly.

"But," he added, "if Suyin told me to help them, then I would."

"Is that so?" Sunshine muttered, marking something down on her clipboard. "So if Suyin explained to you why you should have empathy for another person, what would you do?"

"I would listen to her, of course. I always listen to her."

Sunshine smiled. "Very good. And if Suyin was the one suffering? What would you do?"

Murmur growled darkly. "I would destroy whatever caused her pain. I would annihilate it from Earth or Hell. I would obliterate it."

"Oh, well, I suppose that counts for something." Sunshine marked something else down on her chart. "What is your opinion of humanity as a whole?"

He made a sour face. "I despise—"

He broke off and glanced over at Suyin. She was giving him a pained look, but she still looked amused. And then he really thought about his answer.

"I *used* to despise all humans," he amended, "until I met Suyin. Now I must consider that she is half human and was birthed by a human mother. So I must conclude that I don't hate her mother, or her mother's mother before her. Therefore, there is at least one bloodline of humans that I don't dislike. As for the rest of them, I reserve judgment."

Sunshine beamed at him. "That's great, Murmur. I just have one last question for you. How do you envision your future? When you imagine yourself in five years, where are you and what are you doing?"

"Well . . ." He stroked his chin and thought about that for a moment. And he was surprised to find he didn't really have an answer. "I have achieved all my goals and fulfilled my greatest ambition, and I'm content to be without clear direction for a time. Right now, I don't care what I do as long as I'm with Suyin. Her goals are my goals. She wants to study magic, so I plan to teach her everything I know."

Sunshine smiled and looked between them. "I think that's wonderful." She marked something on her clipboard and then set it down on the desk. "That's all for your interview, Murmur, and I can tell you now, you passed with flying colors."

"I did?" He glanced at Suyin with a frown. She looked equally surprised.

Sunshine had made him promise—without a blood vow—to be completely honest during his interview, so he had deliberately spoken frankly, even if he feared it wasn't what she wanted to hear. He'd expected her to reject him. If she had, he would've just gone on with his illegal Earth trips to be with Suyin.

But he'd passed.

"Your answers weren't always the most . . . empathetic," Sunshine explained, "but they were honest, and that is important. If I feel that I can trust you, then I know we can work together. Also, it's obvious that your bond with Suyin keeps you grounded. I can easily believe that you won't harm humans or upset the balance so long as you have her in your life."

"If she weren't in my life, I would have no desire to remain on the Earth plane."

"Well, that's perfect, then." Sunshine rifled through a stack of papers and then pulled out a folder and slid it across the desk to him. "You'll need to fill out these forms and sign at the bottom of each to indicate you've read and understand the terms."

"Are these magically binding contracts?" he asked, eyeing the papers warily.

"No," Sunshine replied. "That's the whole point of forming this relationship. We start off with a strong foundation of trust and strengthen it with time. There are no unbreakable vows or forced obedience. You check in with me once a month and tell me honestly how your progress is going, and I'll offer guidance and help you with decision-making and communication with humans. We'll trust each other to have the other's best interests at heart."

Murmur cocked a brow. "So you won't be breaking into my lair to steal from me anymore?"

Sunshine grinned unashamedly. "As long as you don't steal Raum from me again."

"Deal," Murmur replied. *I make no promises if I catch him sniffing around my boundary wards*. But he left that unsaid.

"I have to ask you one thing." Sunshine folded her hands atop a stack of papers. "Do you think it would be possible for me to borrow *The Book of Gamigin*? The entire reason I went to Hell was to get that book for my mentor, Adriel.

He's been searching for it for a while and is quite curious to read it."

Murmur opened his mouth to tell her he wasn't giving Suyin's book away to anyone, but Suyin spoke before he could. "I actually have a PDF scan that I can send to you if you want?"

Sunshine blinked. "You can?"

"Yeah. I mean, it's in my email already. I'll just forward it to you. You can print it out if you need a physical copy."

"Oh, wow. Thank you! How very kind of you."

Suyin shifted in her seat. "It's not a big deal. It's just a PDF."

Sunshine smiled brightly. "Adriel will be thrilled. And so will I. I never quite got over how I failed that mission."

Murmur smiled to himself. He was pleased he had foiled the angel's attempt to steal from him.

Sunshine handed him the folder of papers to sign, and they made plans to meet again in a week to finalize his entry into Heaven's transition program, now officially titled DEEMON: the Dark Entity Evolution Management and Oversight Network. How like Heaven to pick the most convoluted and unnecessarily complex name possible.

Shortly after, Murmur and Suyin stepped out of the bungalow situated in the backyard of Belial's mansion. Sunshine lived there with Raum, and her office was tucked away in the second bedroom at the back. Their entire house was packed full of gold that Murmur suspected Raum had stolen from other demons.

The sun was shining as Murmur and Suyin followed the path around the outside of Belial's house toward the driveway. He hadn't seen Belial since the day he'd kicked Suyin's door in, which was fine with him.

Lucifer was amassing his legions and preparing for war. It was only a matter of time before he acted, and Murmur would be drawn back into the conflict whether he liked it or not. He wanted to enjoy every moment he had with Suyin before then.

"So what do you want to do with your newfound Earth freedom?" Suyin asked as they neared where she'd parked her little car. Murmur shifted to human form when they were within sight of the vehicle. His demon form was far too big to fit inside, and there was always a risk of a human with the Sight spotting him on the road.

Suyin had declared that she was going to get him a bike and teach him how to ride because she detested using her car in spring and summer. She'd told him it was a crime to drive a car when one had a bike in the garage. He'd ridden as a passenger on the back of her bike once or twice, and he wasn't sure how he felt about that plan. It was no wonder that she was fearless, if she enjoyed such a vehicle.

He didn't have a clue about automobiles and technology. He was still fascinated by her phone. Despite knowing of the existence of such things for a while, he'd never bothered to use them himself.

"Actually," he said as he opened the rusted passenger door to her cramped vehicle and folded himself nearly in half to fit inside, "I wanted to take you somewhere in Hell. There's something I want to show you."

"Awesome," she replied, hitting the gas and expertly reversing the car down the driveway. "We can draw a hellgate in my living room." The gates opened, and she backed onto the road and then shot forward.

Murmur braced his hands on the dashboard. He wasn't sure he liked cars any more than motorbikes, despite the undeniable convenience of rapid travel. "There's a special kind of hellgate that remains locked to another," he said. "We can draw one to minimize the risk of leaving a gate open in your home while we're gone. It's much safer."

"Double awesome. Teach me when we get home?"

"Whatever you want, witchling."

In response to her favorite nickname, Suyin shot him a challenging grin and then floored it around a corner. Murmur winced as his body was crushed against the side window.

When they returned to Suyin's apartment, he shifted back to his preferred form, and they drew the hellgate, linked it up with his study in Hell, and then stepped through. Suyin wandered about the freshly cleaned library while he readied to draw another gate, since the first would remain permanently linked with her house.

"Whoa, what happened to all the books here?" she asked, pointing to an empty section of shelves that had previously been stuffed full.

Her fingers were tipped with little black claws, and he smiled at the sight. She'd been practicing shifting forms and was already gaining control of it. He encouraged her to take her half-demon form whenever they were in Hell to reduce the risk of anyone discovering what she was.

"You will see," he said from beside the fireplace, where he was inscribing the new gate on the floor. When he finished, he activated it and then straightened and dusted his hands off.

"Ready when you are," he told his witch, holding out a hand.

"I hate surprises," she told him with a smile. Nevertheless, she came to his side and placed her small hand in his big one.

He curled his fingers around her palm and pulled her close, bending down to say in her ear, "You'll like this one." And then he scooped her up and stepped into the gate.

They stumbled out the other side into the study of his former lair. The windows overlooking the sea were freshly cleaned. The bookshelves on either side were filled with grimoires he had transferred from his new lair. He'd brought furniture in as well—a desk sat in the middle of the room facing the window, offering an exquisite view of the tossing waves. Down the hall, he'd had another mattress brought in with fresh bedding.

Suyin rushed forward to stare out the window. "Holy shit. I never pictured there being an ocean in Hell."

"There is, but don't make the mistake of swimming in it. You'll be eaten in seconds."

As if to punctuate his comment, the kraken chose that moment to flail its tentacles out of the water. Murmur lifted a hand and waved back. He was never quite sure if the creature knew he was there, but he liked to think so. And it was always smart to remain on the good side of a kraken.

"Oh my god," Suyin breathed at the waving tentacles.

They descended back into the waves a moment later, and she spun around. "What is this place? These books— Is this your old lair?"

Murmur nodded. "After the souls were released, Lucifer's fury unleashed an earthquake, as I predicted, but my lair survived the tremors. I'm beginning to think it's sturdy enough to withstand the coming tribulations. We'll have to be careful, but if you're going to be visiting me in Hell, I thought you would appreciate a place to come away from . . . everything. My new lair may be heavily fortified, but it's also a target. I always liked this place because no one ever bothered me here. I thought it would be nice for us to have a quiet space to come to where no one can disturb us."

"So you basically set up an oceanside retreat for us . . . in Hell."

He frowned. "I suppose you could say that."

"Murmur . . ." She stepped up to him, and he wrapped his arms around her. "That's the most thoughtful thing anyone's ever done for me."

He made a face. "I hope not. It's not that big of a deal."

"Yes, it is. You've gone to so much effort for me these last few days—sitting through that meeting with Sunshine, letting me drive you around in my tiny car and take you places in human form. You even came to the coven with me and pretended to be human in front of Marie-Thérèse. I know how much you hated that, and you never complained once."

"I can complain if you'd rather," he mumbled, hating the heat he felt rising to his cheeks.

"No, stupid, I'm thanking you for not complaining."

"Well, stop it. I feel uncomfortable."

She snorted a laugh. "Fine. But I hope you know that I see the effort you're making, and I appreciate it. And I love you."

"I love you too."

Their gazes met. She smiled softly. Tenderness filled him at the sight—his fierce little half demon giving him such a gentle look—and he brushed a thumb over her lower lip.

"You're mine, witchling."

*Ours*, his inner voice agreed.

"Always," she replied, and everything in his being practically vibrated with satisfaction.

He stooped to kiss her, and she wrapped her arms around his neck. She held him tightly, but he didn't flinch or feel the need to pull away. If her embrace was a shackle, it was one he never wanted to escape from.

# Bonus Epilogue

Lucifer, the High King of Hell, the Morningstar, his Unholiness—whatever you wanted to call him—stared into the orange glow of the hellfire burning in his hearth. His jaw flexed as he ground his molars, and his fingers drummed a restless rhythm on his thigh.

He could *feel* the diminishment of his strength. He'd had his soul-prison power source for so long, the force he'd gained from it had become part of him. And now he was without.

Crippled. Disadvantaged. Humiliated.

Fury danced under his skin, barely leashed. He wanted retribution. He wanted to strike hard and fast and mercilessly. He wanted to kill, to destroy, to wreak havoc and spill blood. He wanted to remind every ungrateful being in Hell why *he* was High King, why no one had successfully challenged him for the title throughout history, why none dared cross him lest they face his terrible wrath.

Because, evidently, demons like Murmur had forgotten. Demons like Murmur thought they could plot against him and get away with it.

The Necromancer had the gall to continue lurking in Paimon's former lair after what he'd done. He hadn't even bothered to flee in some vain hope of survival. Did he somehow believe himself untouchable? How could a demon reputed to be so skilled at complex magic be so foolish as to think he would not face retribution for his treachery?

Murmur would die. Murmur would die begging for mercy.

But . . . not yet.

Lucifer rose from his perch on the edge of the sofa and began to pace back and forth across the lush, patterned rug before the fireplace. His rage was crawling beneath his skin, begging to be unleashed, yes, but in this instance, he forced himself to contain it. Because he had to be smart about this. He had to be clever and scheming. He had to outwit his foes who believed they now had an advantage over him.

And most importantly, he had to remember who his true enemy was.

Murmur may have created the portal into the heart of his territory, but he was not the one who had stepped into it. He was not the one who had opened the door and liberated the souls. He was not the one who had been trying for millennia to undermine Lucifer's rule and claim Hell for himself.

Belial was.

Murmur was just an underling, another slavering fool who'd been sucked into Belial's false promises of power and greatness. Murmur was a puppet, and Belial was behind the curtain, pulling his strings.

If Lucifer were truly to neutralize this ploy against him, he needed to go straight to its source. He could kill one ally of Belial's after the next, but they would keep cropping up like weeds until he eradicated the source.

So Murmur would die, yes, but not just yet.

First, Lucifer needed a better plan. A more subtle plan. A plan that no one would suspect, which meant it would be a plan that there was no defense against.

His pacing picked up in speed as his mind whirled with sudden inspiration.

There was a certain type of weapon. An exceptionally rare, angelic weapon that he needed to acquire in order to eliminate his nemesis once and for all. He'd known this for a very long time, but normally, such a weapon was impossible to procure, and it was for that reason Lucifer had given up on his plans to destroy Belial many times before.

But right now, it just so happened that he knew the location of one such weapon, because it was in the hands of Belial himself. And he was quite certain that Belial had no idea what it was truly capable of.

When he'd first heard of its location, he had only briefly considered acquiring it before abandoning the idea. The risk was too great, and it would have involved breaking Heaven's rules and angering the Tribunal.

But now, Belial was conspiring against him, and Lucifer could not afford to be complacent. He had to act, rules be damned. He knew how to handle the Tribunal anyway. A bit of careful fearmongering, and the council of out-of-touch, obstinate angels would fall in line. He had manipulated them many times in the past, and this would be no different.

*Yes, that was it.* A plan was beginning to form, the pieces falling rapidly into place.

Lucifer would get possession of the weapon. He would do it subtly, stealthily, so Belial would have no idea what he was planning and thus would make no effort to protect the prize. And then, once Lucifer had it, he would strike, and Belial wouldn't stand a chance.

To retrieve that weapon, he needed an infiltrator.

But who?

His pacing stopped abruptly. He stroked his chin and his brow furrowed as he searched his mind for a solution.

It would need to be someone who Belial trusted, or at least tolerated, whose presence was familiar. Someone who could walk in the front door of Belial's Earth lair and take something from under his nose without him realizing it until too late. It would need to be someone with whom Belial had had close dealings in the past.

He dropped his hand suddenly, and his eyes widened. *Of course.*

He knew the perfect candidate for this role, and he already knew how to assure their cooperation—and thus, his ultimate success.

Belial had become something soft and manipulatable. Every bond he formed with another person was a new way to strike at him. A way to penetrate straight to his weakened core. And that was precisely what Lucifer would do.

He would attack from the inside, cripple him from within the circle of his false sense of security. He would allow him to think he maintained the upper hand, and then, when he least expected it, Lucifer would take him down once and for all.

And so it would be as it was always meant to be.

Belial would finally be destroyed, and the High King would enjoy his rule unimpeded by threats, his greatest enemy vanquished at last. The underworld would crumble beneath his wrath, and any who had dared to plot against him in the past would be wiped from existence.

And when Hell was conquered anew, he would set his sights on Earth. He would remind the humans who had forgotten to fear him what monsters truly looked like.

He, Lucifer, would be at the center of it all, the greatest, most powerful being to ever exist.

The High King stopped in front of the fireplace and looked deeply into the flames. His reflection in the marble tile behind it stared back at him. And when he smiled, the hellfire danced across his wicked features with deadly grace.

# Dear Reader,

PHEW, WE MADE IT. WHAT A RIDE!

Murmur and Suyin's story broke me in half and then put me back together again. In a good way. I loved writing this book, and I'm sad to let Murmy and his witchling go for now. Building their romance from indifference and hatred to passionate, I-would-*die*-for-you love was an epic challenge—but also a fulfilling one.

So, guess whose book is finally next . . .

People have been asking for Bel's story since the beginning, and I forced them to wait until the very end because of my top-secret plans. (Murmur understands.) I always knew Bel's book had to be last, and I think you'll soon see why that is.

Thank you so much for embarking on the journey of the Hell Bent series thus far with me. (And if you just joined in for this book, welcome to Hell!) When I started book one, I never expected to take it quite this far. I just wanted to write about some funny, hot demon brothers bickering with each other. Next thing I know, we're overthrowing the High King.

I want to thank my agent, Brent Taylor, and my editor, Elizabeth May, and everyone on the team at Kensington for seeing my vision for this series and taking it to the next level. It's been such a joy to work with all of you. Also many thanks to my husband, Orion, for his unending support of me in all my endeavors.

Last but not least, thank you, dear reader. And if you share this book with your friends, leave a review, or post on social media, extra big thanks. If you're shy, and you just want to read your romance books in peace, I thank you for that too. I used to be secretive years ago . . . Now, I enjoy telling people I write spicy books just to see if I can make them flinch and I can pounce on their judgments and devour them whole.

All the love and happy reading, and I'll see you soon for Bel's book!

Love,
Aurora

**auroraascher.com**

**Not ready to leave the underworld yet?**

Join Aurora's Underworld Patreon to unlock exclusive art and short stories featuring your favorite characters. You'll get access to illustrations by me (some NSFW!) and cute, funny, and sexy tales to relieve your book hangover.

Join a passionate community of romance lovers, and be part of the adventure!

**patreon.com/auroraascher**

Keep reading for a special excerpt of

# FALLEN DEMON!

Passion ignites between ancient enemies, Belial and Naiamah. But with Lucifer at their backs, can a demon and a succubus lay their pasts to rest?

# PROLOGUE

## 1,200 years ago . . .

BLOOD DRIPPED ONTO THE STONE FLOOR WITH AN OMINOUS echo, the only sound to penetrate the heavy silence. That and the pounding of Naiamah's heart as she gathered her courage and readied to move her arm.

All she had to do was reach up to her chest and she would be free. Safe and free. Just the thought of her rescue sent a rush of reassurance through her fear and despair.

She'd been pinned in place with knives. So many knives. Through her palms, her upper arms, her shoulders, her midsection, thighs, feet. The pain was so intense, she kept blacking out, wavering in and out of consciousness.

Worse, the wooden plank she was skewered to was propped against a stone wall, situated on a tiny platform. That platform was only about six feet across, and it plummeted down to a deep pit. At the bottom were large spikes. As if that weren't enough, hellfire burned around them. If she fell down there . . . well, there was a chance she might never come out again. And the entire chamber had been warded against hellgates. Even if she somehow freed herself from the plank and managed to draw the gate sigil with her own spilled blood, the magic would not activate.

The only possible escape was to fly, but her captor had thought of that too. Her wings were spread and pinned to the wood with still more knives. Even if she somehow managed to pull those free, he had methodically shredded them, tearing into the fine skin like tissue paper. It would take time to heal. Time she didn't have.

A ragged scream tore from her throat at the white-hot pain that shot up her arm as she tried to move her left hand. Her vision wavered in and out as she clung to the edge of consciousness, but there wasn't time to pass out.

Lucifer would be back at any moment. Now that he had discovered the secret to thwarting her powers, there would be no escaping him. In the past, he had feared her because of his attraction to her. The moment a succubus of her caliber sensed even the slightest sexual energy from another being, she could begin to feed, sucking the life force out of her prey until they were nothing but a withered husk.

But Lucifer had learned that if he bled her, beat her, tortured her to a state of debilitating weakness, then her powers were repressed. To begin draining another's energy took a certain measure of strength, and if she did not have that strength to begin with, well, then she was helpless.

Helpless and a fool.

She'd been a fool to believe that she could infiltrate Lucifer's inner sanctum and not get caught. Even with the Necromancer's magic to sneak her past the wards, this was still the lair of the High King of Hell. She had underestimated him—and perhaps overestimated herself—and now she was paying the ultimate price.

Even before she'd done the unthinkable and broken into his territory, Lucifer had always held a certain fixation with her. As the most powerful succubus in Hell, she was a threat to him. One of the few in existence. And it was in the High King's nature to covet what he couldn't possess. Naiamah had been denying him her entire existence, and she would continue to do so until her dying breath.

If she didn't get free quickly, there was a high chance that final respiration would come sooner rather than later. He'd promised her death—permanent, irreversible death, not the temporary death a demon could regenerate from—but only after making her suffer for daring to defy him so blatantly. How long that suffering would last, she couldn't say, but she was sure that before the end, she would be begging him to kill her.

Unless . . . she could get her hand free.

"You can do this," she told herself, swallowing back the despair that threatened to choke her. Yes, she was a powerful force to be reckoned with, but she was also impaled over a pit of spikes and hellfire, facing more torture and certain death, and that was a bit beyond anyone's capacity to endure.

"Just pull it out, and you'll be free. He'll come for you. He'll save you."

Her racing heart calmed at the thought of *him*. Her prize. Her possession. Oh, he would argue that he belonged to no one, but Naiamah knew better. He belonged to *her*. She alone could manipulate and control him. She alone could give him the untold pleasures of a powerful succubus.

And in return, he alone fed her, sated her as no other could. The power of his sexual energy . . . Even now amid the agony, her body throbbed at the mere thought of it. She'd given up fighting the addiction. Now she was enslaved by it. She wanted nothing more than to bask in it, revel in it, be consumed by it.

That heady rush all tied back to *him*, and thus, he had become the object of her obsession.

She was immeasurably glad he'd accepted her gift, and she

could have kissed her past self for her foresight. Wearing the vial required a measure of trust, and until he'd accepted it, she hadn't been entirely certain he would grant her that boon.

Through her contacts at the Blood Market, she had acquired two tiny vials of potion affixed to two chains. Those vials were filled with one of the most powerful spells she'd ever heard of in Hell.

Normally, demons could not summon other demons. They could send a mental summons request. If the other chose to respond, they would be able to arrive through a hellgate, but they could just as easily refuse. The only exception was when a demon owed a favor to another—a common payment for services rendered. Then that demon could be summoned at the other's will.

The vials Naiamah had acquired were an exception to those rules. They had been created long ago by some powerful practitioner of Sheolic arts—whom, she didn't know—and they allowed a demon to summon another, instantaneously, at any time or place, without requiring the use of a hellgate or contracted debt.

But there were two vials; it *was* a contract of sorts. Or rather, an exchange.

Two vials, and two possible summonings, only possible by the wearer of the vials. Each had to agree to wear it for the other to work. If one rejected it or simply refused to wear it, neither vial would have power.

Hence her uncertainty whether her gift be accepted. But it had been. And as such, she could summon her rescuer here and now, and he could summon her too.

When she'd presented the other vial to him and explained its use, his flame-filled eyes had narrowed, and she'd feared he would become enraged. But after some careful coaxing, he'd eventually admitted that he saw the value in it. The moment he'd accepted the vial and donned it, a strange warm sensation had taken root in her chest. The uncomfortable feeling had lingered for days after the interaction.

Regardless, any discomfort would be worth it now, just as soon as she got her hand free. She would force him to come here, convince him to save her, and then reward him until she was positively bursting with power and vitality, and she had drained him to near unconsciousness. She would find a way to convince him that the entire misadventure was his idea so he would not turn his frightening wrath in her direction when Lucifer inevitably retaliated against him.

She imagined he felt a measure of possessiveness over her, the same way she felt for him. She pictured the fury contorting his features when he saw her current condition. Hellfire would ignite around his powerful form, and he would swear to take vengeance upon Lucifer for daring to touch her. That odd warming sensation sparked in her chest again.

Irrelevant. This was a matter of survival.

But strangely, her recollections of him gave her the strength she had been missing to do what needed to be done. Gritting her teeth, she took a long breath. Then, squeezing her eyes shut, she opened her mouth and screamed a feral scream at the same moment as she yanked her hand forward with all her strength.

For a moment, nothing happened besides her impaled palm sliding all the way down the knife to the hilt. She screamed louder, never relenting the force in her arm.

At last, the knife shot out of the board and sailed through the air over the edge of the platform, where it plummeted into the flames and spikes below.

Not that she was aware of it. The pain was all-consuming as it shot up her arm and through her body like a lightning bolt. Her head spun, vision rapidly darkening, until she mercifully passed out.

But she wasn't unconscious for long. Minutes later, she

blinked groggily back to the present, and the moment she was aware enough, her heart began to pound with excitement and relief. Freedom was finally within her grasp. All she had to do was reach . . .

Slowly, painstakingly, she bent her elbow and lifted her arm toward her chest. Every minute movement caused tiny flections in her bicep and shoulder muscles, and the knives stuck through them cut deeper, causing more agony to flood her nerves.

But finally, her fingers touched her sternum.

Gingerly, she stretched her fingers until they hooked on the chain of the vial, and then she carefully tugged it out from within her dress. She was glad she'd tucked it away so securely because Lucifer would surely have taken it if he'd seen it.

Finally, the vial slid against her palm, and she curled her fingers around it. Her pulse accelerated the closer she got to freedom.

She closed her eyes and began the summoning, picturing her rescuer's face in her mind's eye and calling him to her. She visualized his landing beside her on the platform, and the possessiveness she'd imagined before filling his features.

The vial warmed in her hand, to the point where it felt like it was burning. The air gusted around her, lifting her blood-crusted hair off her neck and blowing it around her face.

And then, there he was.

She opened her eyes and found her addiction standing before her.

Belial was in human form, his long, pale hair blowing about from the residual magic of the spell. Even in this form, he was enormous, towering with height, his shoulders broader than most doorways, his hands so large they could easily encircle her entire upper arm.

He was cruel and cold, but his temper burned hotter than the hellfire he could summon at will. Even Asmodeus, the once-great Prince of Lust, who lived with him in his castle and shared his territory, feared him when he was lost to his rages. He was merciless and unbending, and his might on the battlefield was legendary. There were none who dared cross him. It was well known that even Lucifer feared him.

As he should, the miserable cretin.

Belial was possibly the deadliest being in all of Hell, yet he looked like an angel, and that was because he had once been one. Long, long ago, he and Lucifer had fallen from Heaven together and battled for dominion over the underworld.

Or so the stories told. Belial claimed he'd never wanted to rule. Lucifer had never believed him. And thus, their rivalry continued.

At the sight of him, relief filled Naiamah so great, her knees felt weak. She didn't have to fight alone anymore. He would take her away from her and spare her from Lucifer's wrath.

"Belial," she gasped. "Remove the knives. Quickly, there is little time."

He didn't move, instead looking around the dungeon she was held in. "What is this?" he demanded, his voice a deep growl. "Where am I, and why did you call me here?"

She waited for him to rush to her, to demand to know who did this to her, to swear to avenge her. Surely he would. He belonged to her. She had given him what she'd given no other. She alone could control him.

"In Lucifer's lair," she said when he did nothing. "I snuck past his wards and infiltrated his lair, but I was captured. He has sworn to kill me. You must help me escape."

Belial looked around, his face hardening. Why wasn't he coming closer?

"Remove the swords," she urged, more fervently now. Her heart was beginning to pound with something that felt strangely like fear. "He'll return soon. We must go."

"You broke into Lucifer's lair? That is where we are right now?"

"Yes!" she cried, losing patience. Why was he wasting precious time? "I'm certain he has been hoarding some forbidden power source. I was trying to discover what it was so it might be destroyed."

Belial shook his head, his eyes flashing. "You called me straight into the heart of Lucifer's lair."

"I had no choice. He's going to kill—"

"You *know* he's been looking for an excuse to start a war." His voice was a deadly growl. "You *know* that I don't want any part in that, and you brought me right into the middle of this regardless."

"I didn't have a choice," she gasped. How dare he question her? How dare he delay when her very life was on the line? "If there was any other way, I would have—"

"If I take you from here, Lucifer will know it was me. He'll already know I was here. He'll have sensed my presence the second I crossed his wards."

The fear pulsing through her bloodstream with each beat of her heart began to make itself known. Why wasn't he helping her? "I swear," she pleaded, though the tone of her voice disgusted her. She pleaded for no man. She begged for nothing. "I had no choice, no other—"

"I should never have taken this vial." His voice was low. His fury was evident in the hellfire obliterating his eyes. "I should have known you would abuse your access to me."

A knot formed in her chest where her heart should have been. It was hard and firm. Like a stone. Simultaneously, she felt a sinking feeling, like her very organs were drowning in deep, dark water.

"He'll kill me," she said, skin crawling at the beseeching tone of her voice. "He has promised to torture me until I lose my mind, and then he will kill me."

"And I'm supposed to care?" Belial snarled. He was bigger now, falling into a rage. The air sparked around him, heat waves distorted the air around his enormous body. His long pale hair gusted about. His eyes blazed.

Normally, she reveled in his fury. While others fled before the sight of him in all his demonic glory, she savored it. His deadly power awed and aroused her, and she would often do whatever she could to make it unleash itself.

But this time . . . fear made her blood run cold. Blood that was racing and pooling on the floor at her feet, running in rivulets over her skin and soaking into her ruined clothing.

"Summoning me here has given Lucifer a reason to attack my territory." His voice was a thundering boom. Chills raced along her skin. "I've been trying to avoid a war for millennia, and I'm not about to stop now."

"He'll kill me," she repeated in a hoarse whisper. His eyes narrowed. She saw nothing but loathing. No hint of warmth, not a trace of regret.

"That means nothing to me."

Coldness overtook any remaining warmth in her heart.

He truly didn't care that she was impaled and vulnerable, facing horrible torture and death. He was just as cold and unfeeling with her as he was with everyone else. He only played along with her games because of her usefulness to him.

How *dare* he use her that way? How dare he treat her as some possession for his entertainment and then discard her when it no longer suited his fancy?

"Is there nothing I can do to get you to help me?" she whispered. Her pride told her to yell and screech, to make him pay, but right now, she was desperate. Her life was on the line, and he was still her best chance of survival. "I'll do anything."

Her pleading nauseated her. *Later, I will make him pay. Now, I must survive.*

Belial's eyes narrowed as he considered her. She stood before him, her body full of knives, her wings torn to shreds, helpless and weak. Never had she felt so humiliated. The unidentifiable warmth had withered into something cold and cruel. Something that craved retribution.

"One thousand favors," Belial said.

She blinked. It took several seconds for his meaning to sink in, and even then, she didn't believe what she'd heard. "What?"

"If I liberate you now, you will owe me one thousand unspecified favors."

Her eyes widened. Her heart stopped. "One *thousand*? That's absurd!"

It was normal for demons to owe other demons favors, to use them as a currency of sorts. If one got in a tight spot and called in help from another, it wasn't unheard of to agree to owing an open-ended favor.

*One* open-ended favor. Not one *thousand*. To even demand such a price was an insult of the highest order.

"You've lost your sanity if you think I would agree to that!" she shrieked, hatred filling her blood. The chill of her cold fury had turned white-hot, into the kind of heat that made a woman go on a murderous rampage. She had never wanted to behead someone more.

"Then we don't have a deal," Belial replied. His face was flat. His eyes still burned.

"He's going to *kill* me!"

The corner of his lip twisted cruelly. "Then I suppose you'd better agree to my terms."

Forget the pain of a dozen knives impaled through her body. This degradation, this abasement . . . This was worse.

"One hundred," she countered, unable to believe she was even offering such a ridiculously high counteroffer.

But he shook his head. "One thousand, or I leave now."

*One thousand favors*. It could take a millennium for Belial to use that many favors. Or longer. She would have no say in what he asked her to do, no option to refuse the task, no matter how awful. If she agreed, he would be able to summon her at any time or from any place. It would be indentured servitude. A form of enslavement.

It was that or die.

She would not accept death. Not when she had vengeance to exact. Which meant she had only one choice.

"Fine," she bit out.

"One thousand unspecified favors," Belial stated again, hellfire eyes flashing with the light of victory. "At any time or place. Whatever I want."

"Fine!" She ground her teeth and stared into his hateful eyes and disgustingly beautiful face.

"Swear to it now."

"Get me out of here first, and I'll swear to it."

He shook his head. "Swear now, or I leave you here. You're in no place to negotiate."

Her face contorted with rage, but she painstakingly lifted her palm again. The same palm that had reached so hopefully toward her heart mere minutes ago. That heart was cold and dead now, and it would never awaken again.

There was no need to cut her palm to make the blood vow. It already pooled in her hand from the hole pierced through it. She took a breath and then said the words that would alter the course of her life forever.

"On my own blood, I vow it."

Belial's lips curved ever so slightly, and then he finally stepped forward and began extracting the knives from her body. As her limp, broken form crumpled into him against her will, the relief she'd imagined was so far away, she was certain there was no such feeling.

*I will make him pay for this.*

She might owe Belial a thousand favors, but she promised herself then and there that she would make every moment of that debt insufferable.

She would make him feel everything she felt—that was her vow to herself. She would make him hate himself as much as she hated herself for allowing him to humiliate her.

Her heart had returned to the cold stone it had once been. Never again would it soften or warm for anyone. She would dance in the blood of male sacrifices and laugh at the feeble cries of weak men who fell prey to her seduction and then paid for it with their useless mortal lives. She would laugh in their faces as they died before her.

And Belial . . .

He would rue the day he had betrayed her.

**Look for FALLEN DEMON coming soon from Kensington Books!**

# About the Author

© Sergio Veranes

**Aurora Ascher** is a *New York Times* and *USA Today* best-selling fantasy and paranormal romance author. She loves misunderstood monsters, redeemable anti-heroes, and epic happily-ever-afters. A woman of many creative pursuits, Aurora is also a musician and visual artist. She is currently based between Montreal and British Columbia, Canada. Visit her online at auroraascher.com.